Blood Marsh

Ghoulsmen Book 2

A. C. Hughes

Cahill Davis Publishing

Cahill Davis Publishing

First published in Great Britain in 2025 by Cahill Davis Publishing Limited.

First published in paperback in Great Britain in 2025 by Cahill Davis Publishing Limited.

ISBN 978-1-915307-30-9 (eBook)

ISBN 978-1-915307-29-3 (Paperback)

Cahill Davis Publishing Limited

www.cahilldavispublishing.co.uk

Chapter 1

Great golden beams of light broke through the cloud cover to invigorate a few chosen grass patches across the slew of rolling hills below. Rav sat atop a hill, basking under a sunray, hoping to use its warmth to reenergise his failing body, but he still felt tired. Unbearably tired. Tired that had worn his muscles away until only skin sat on his bones. Tired that had sunken his cheeks and blackened his eyes. Tired that had turned him from a vibrant young man into a walking corpse.

The air was windless, his long, greasy hair sticking to his face like strands of tar. Why did he feel so sick? Why was he fighting to keep his stomach from roiling, to keep his jaw from shaking? Why did it feel like it had the first time he'd murdered? All he could smell and taste was bile, something he should've gotten used to by now, but its slick sourness still filled his head as though he were drowning in it. The sunlight did nothing.

Keep going.

He opened his eyes, and dizziness spun the world around him, his vision intermixed with sparkling fog. After steadying himself, he built momentum, then tried to stand. His ankle buckled, but before he fell, Lyra caught him. Two months of travelling had left no mark on her. Clad in polished full-plate armour, with silky black hair and glowing skin, she was a picturesque beauty too precious to touch. Her haunting blue eyes bore down into Rav's.

"You are too weak. Eat."

Her voice still lingered around him like nature's lyre, but Rav had long become numb to its allure. The food wouldn't stay down—it hadn't for weeks. He'd chew until his jaw ached, but then... He broke from her gaze and stared at the ground. Three years to become as strong as a Baron and he couldn't even swallow soup. He dry-heaved and held his mouth, vision darkening.

"This is..." Lyra held him still.

Pathetic. Reckless. ...Nameless. No tears came; his eyes were too dead.

"I do not know what is wrong," Lyra's voice wobbled. "You should be well."

Rav continued dribbling acidic saliva, head hanging, unable to find the answer himself. Why was he so weak? Everything had started fine. They'd eaten mutant meat and talked about the World, making swift progress out of the Stone Steps and into the surrounding hills, nearing the grasslands that led to the Sink. Until.

Shame. Loneliness. Nameless.

The thoughts kept returning no matter how hard he fought them off. Whether he cried or laughed or slept, they were always there. The Sink was ahead, a place said to forge heroes, a place where he would reclaim everything he'd lost, so why...? Why was he so worthless? He'd give anything to feel Cyrn's hand on his shoulder. Kayla's kiss. Wakeman's hug.

Keep going.

He wiped his mouth, used Lyra as support to get up, and managed to stand on his own. "Let's go," he croaked. One hill, then a plain, then the Sink. Just a little further. Rav trudged on, purposeful and powerless.

"You cannot keep wearing that." Lyra indicated Rav's chainmail shirt, the blood that still stained it hidden under dirt and grime. "It is too heavy for you."

He ignored her. Wakeman was dead and only what little he'd possessed remained. It didn't matter how heavy his friend's old armour was; even if he was to die, he'd die with it on.

"At least let me carry your other belongings," Lyra pressed, reaching for the small bag Rav carried, which only contained a small urn with the last of Wakeman's ashes, a scented cloth gifted to him by Kayla, and his journal.

He turned away from her, hugging the bag close to guard it from her grasp. They were his too. No matter the difficulty. One shaking step after another, Rav pressed ahead. Lyra sighed before collecting three bags the size of her torso and following.

Nameless, Nameless, Nameless.

"Tell me... about the grass...lands," Rav wheezed.

Lyra smiled softly. "They are called U'ul Ba'a, or Fool's March." She then furrowed her brow. "You must be careful there; mutants roam the plains."

MUUH. Oil-black eyes and giant horns, Rav saw the mutant goat once more. It never slowed, never rested, never stopped hunting him down. Always with him, a part of him. "...Like the one I fought in Stone's Way?" his voice trembled.

"Some." Lyra nodded.

He sighed. "I'll die." A sliver of desire to live sputtered as he said the word. *No.* How could he die before returning to Pitt? How could he die when his family still needed him? But it faded, as it always did. It was his fault Tibald had found a weakness to control Cyrn with, his fault Pitt was going to be enslaved by Baron Hewett, his fault Wakeman was dead. He didn't have to return. Maybe he shouldn't.

Lyra tried to catch his eye. "I can guard you on the plains, but, Rav... I cannot protect you in the Sink; there are too many dangers for me to face alone. If you do not improve enough to save yourself, you will not survive."

He stared at the ground once more. "And my Calling?"

Lyra gave up trying to meet his gaze. "What you saw is only a possibility, not a certainty."

Looking at his wretched body, Rav tried to laugh, too exhausted to manage more than a quiet wheeze. Wasn't he already close to what he'd seen? Here he walked, more ghoul than man. All he needed was the strength to eat someone. "I think it's coming true," he whispered.

"*Do not talk about it*," Lyra snapped.

"Why can't you know?" Rav huffed. "I don't understand."

Lyra sucked her teeth. "I have told you this many times before. It is for the same reason I should not have hinted that the medicinal paste Tibald gave you was able to heal Finn's injuries. I guided you to change the outcome of his circumstances with a single irresponsible glance. If I know what you have been Called to do, any slight motion of mine could impact the outcome the World desires. That *cannot* happen; the World's plans are not mine to meddle in."

"We saved him."

Lyra hardened her tone. "It was wrong."

They fell silent. Rav thought back to the young man they'd healed. What was Finn doing now? He'd survived a mutant attack only to live under Tibald Sar's tyranny. The Ghoulsmen had all worked so hard just to have every life they'd protected suffer. Everyone's sacrifice was for nothing, all because of him.

"How do you say Sink in your language?" Rav murmured, trying to think of something else before his thoughts dragged him back into the mire. He worked his lips to pronounce the word. "Ga'thew, right?"

Lyra tutted. "It is pronounced *Ga'thew'*. *Ga'ackre* for the broken ground, *thewsh* for the air in the fall, and *silence* for the unknown."

"Silence like 'World'?"

She shook her head. "The World is different. The Sink is silence of the unending fall; the World is silence of eternity, of peace. You can hear the World all around you. If you listen." She tilted her head at him.

"I've tried," Rav mumbled. "Every night, I search for It, but there is no silence. Even when everything else goes still, all I hear is my blood pumping through my ears."

Lyra smiled at him in encouragement. “Keep trying. The World has Called you, Rav, and you are Ah’ ke. A piece of the World already sits in your neck, all you must do is feel it.”

He scowled. Had he really been Called? People were supposed to see their future selves, charismatic and potent as they achieved the impossible. All he’d seen was himself as a ghoul climbing out a stranger and eating them alive. Why couldn’t he just ask her about it? Why was she so adamant about abandoning him if he did? He scratched the back of his neck. As for the Heaven’s Tear, it was no more than a blemish on his skin, a square black stain with a missing corner he couldn’t remove. It did nothing. Where was its supposed power? Or was he just too pathetic to use it?

He stomped step by step to the top of a hill and looked out with a grunt. Finally. Beneath him spanned a plain of straw-coloured grass with a slight purple tint at its tip, reaching all the way to the horizon. Stray breezes sent it shifting in waves, rustling, making it seem as though it were fur on the back of a great beast. Rav clenched his fist. Unnerving. How could so much ground be so flat? It was the opposite of Stone’s Way. How far from home was he? Stomach churning, nausea roiled within him. Lyra was standing at his side, so why did she feel so far away? Is that what being in Heaven did? He was here, alone. Lonely.

“Ga’thew’ has many places more beautiful than this. There is a city called Suelkoff that is built under a river. The riverbed is made of crystal, so sunlight shines through it to glitter over the streets. If you survive the journey through Li’bo Sh’za and reach Ut Sh’za, you can bask in its light too.” She coaxed him forward.

What was the point in beauty when it was empty? And how far away was this Ut Sh’za? How deep did Lyra want to drag him into this place? That’s all she wanted, wasn’t it? That’s why she seemed so far away. Helping him was just to serve her World. Rav eased his way down the hillside, finding the grass blades to be taller than he’d expected, standing a full head above him as he reached the bottom.

“The path is here.” Lyra led him to a narrow gap that split through the grasses, disappearing deep inside the plain. “’Zet Ar attack by ambushing from the sides; keep your guard up until we reach the camp."

'Zet Ar? Rav went hunting through his mind for the term. Where was it? *Ah*. Lesser mutant or descendant from a weak bloodline. The monsters that inhabited the first section of the Sink, Li'bo Sh'za. He nodded at Lyra, uncaring. It wouldn't make a difference if he was cautious or not when he was so weak.

They entered the passage, the thick smell of dust reminding him of abandoned houses and old mineshafts. Rav sneezed. A while later, more unease set in as swaying grass engulfed him, blocking his peripheral vision. This place was so much... tighter, more pressing, suffocating than Stone's Way. Even the mazes within the boulder fields weren't this choking. Lyra marched on, unperturbed. Rav felt his panic rising and let out a wheezing chuckle. He had no energy to spare; how could panic affect him? He shrugged his chainmail up, then continued, the afternoon passing by in a yellow and purple blur.

As the sun set, they came across a large metallic mound, half-buried in the ground next to their path.

"This is our camp," Lyra said, reaching for a handle to open the hatch door.

He stumbled inside the dome and searched for a place to lie down, finding a cloth bed at the far end of the small room, which he collapsed onto before closing his eyes. Freed from labouring, his body melded into the thin mattress, never wanting to move again as he listened to Lyra closing and locking the hatch before rummaging in one of her packs. *Tchi', fwish*, she lit a candle. *Ba, ba, ba*, she walked up to him and shook his shoulder.

"Try and eat." She pressed something mushed to his mouth.

Rav sealed his lips shut and tried to roll away.

"Rav. Eat," she ordered. For her. Even if she was a fanatic.

He opened his mouth and took a bite of some well-mashed roots, finding them sweet and starchy, seasoned with salt. *Chew*. Rav slowly ground the paste and prepared to swallow. Just swallow. *Please*. His throat wouldn't work... it wouldn't let him. Saliva built in his mouth until the roots liquified. It felt as though he would choke if he forced it down. *Force it anyway*. Rav opened his throat, and bile came spewing out, forcing him to spit the food onto the floor next to him.

Lyra kept calm, used to the events. "I will get something for your stomach." She glided across the room to search in her pack, and by the time she returned, Rav had fallen deep asleep.

Rav gasped awake, clammy in his mail shirt. A nightmare. He couldn't piece it together... he didn't want to. It was always his face, dead and smiling. *Wakeman, I'm sorry.* But his apologies did nothing. If only he'd been smarter, stronger, Wakeman wouldn't have duelled Tibald. Wouldn't have died. Wouldn't be no more than ashes to be scattered in the wind. He touched the small urn hanging around his neck. If only he were more like Cyrn, none of this would've happened.

The candle had long been extinguished, leaving him in darkness. It was deep in the night, and now he was stuck. Stuck with his thoughts until morning came and he started walking again.

Nameless, Nameless, Nameless.

Rav's throat went dry. He felt around him and touched the leather of a waterskin. Lyra. His chest constricted as though a boulder sat on him, his cheeks burning with shame. Every kind necessity she did for him was a reminder of the wretch he'd become. How could he be so useless? She fed him, protected him, cared for him. Day after day, she put up with his pathetic state and never complained. And day after day, his gratitude built, growing so heavy it had become crushing. What could he do about it? There was no way to repay her, no service he could perform for her that she needed or wasn't better at. He didn't even know her. Lyra was in Heaven.

The concept had made itself clearer as their journey had progressed. Lyra existed in another world that freed her from the rules of this one, almost gliding as she walked as though she had no weight, everything seeming light to her, no burden too heavy. She had no momentum either, stopping and turning without stumbling. Rav had watched her hunt, failing to comprehend what he was seeing. His mind predicted where she should've been, how she should've leaned slightly forward or taken an extra step to balance, but she never did. Light and carefree, the World let her do as she pleased, unbound by its laws. That's when he'd realised it. Perhaps there was no "Lyra". At his side was Ha'th Bey Riene, a devotee of the World. A stranger. Another fragment of Pitt drifted out of his grasp.

He sipped from the waterskin and washed out his mouth. *Now try.* Little by little, Rav drank, practicing his swallowing. Water went down, so why couldn't food? It wasn't long before the waterskin emptied, and he lay back down in the dark to listen, trying to quiet his thoughts in hope that he'd catch the World. Maybe if he heard It, everything would change. Maybe he'd connect to his Heaven's Tear and gain the power he needed. But there was no silence.

Nameless, Nameless, Nameless. Useless.

Without Cyrn or the Ghoulsmen, Rav understood what he was. All the talk of power. All the plans. All the fights. It was them, not him.

Woooo. He flinched as a mutant's howl rang out across the plains, more following to bring the night to life. But how could those howls compare to the roar of the beast he'd fought? *MUUH.* Echoes of the mutant goat filled his head as he settled back down, never able to hear beyond his memories.

Tchi', fwish, Lyra lit her candle, illuminating the room. "We have to set off early to reach the next camp before dark." She rolled out of her bed and began strapping her armour back on.

Once dressed, she collected Rav's waterskin, shaking it to see how much was left. Empty. Her face remained still, but her eyes betrayed her curiosity. They both knew not to mention it—what if he stopped drinking too once the words were made real? Rav swung his legs out of bed, aching. Lyra pulled out some dried meat and chewed it in front of him, enticing him to try some. Rav looked away and gagged.

Finishing breakfast, they set off into the dawn light, the rising sun heating the damp soil to create a humid environment that had Rav sweating. His hips had begun to give a sharp pain when he strode too far, his left ankle seeming to grate against the bone in the socket. Lunch was over quickly, just more water. Endless swaying grass until the sun was setting.

"We need to hurry; we have been slower today," Lyra urged Rav on.

He strained as hard as he could, but the movements were too tender.

"The camp is close," Lyra kept encouraging him.

Rav hung his head as he lumbered on, fighting to keep himself from collapsing.

"Let me carry you."

No. How could he face the dangers of the Sink if he couldn't even walk there by himself?

"Rav, you will not make i—"

Ssh. From the right.

Lyra dropped her packs and drew her longsword. *Grrrrr*, growls came from all around them as half a dozen ravenous beasts lurked out of view. Rav reached into one of the packs to collect his spear but wasn't strong enough to lift it out the bag. *Pathetic.* He slumped down and laughed at himself as Lyra took a stance next to him, eyeing the grass. *Sh, sh, sh*, the mutants circled around them before—*Arrr*. One of them darted out and took a swipe at Lyra's back. She turned and slashed upwards at its paw, severing it in a gush of blood. Rav smiled in the hot spray, watching the mutant retreat. It was a large wolf with straw-coloured fur and overgrown teeth that jutted out its mouth. Not even as fierce as the normal mutant goats that roamed Stone's Way. He was going to be killed by something that unimposing? He smiled wider, face contorted with shame. The goat 'Zet Ar could've killed a dozen of these things without issue.

Seeing their leader injured, the remaining mutants shot out to protect it, harassing Lyra. One went for her leg, while another barrelled into her. She kicked the first away, then grabbed the other before driving her sword through its belly. It whimpered as it went still. The other two backed away, slinking into the grass while Lyra pulled her sword out of the dead wolf and lunged to stab the kicked one. Paw severed, the leader had hidden behind the grassline, skulking, and with Lyra busy, Rav knew he was vulnerable. He watched the beast sit back on its haunches, ready to pounce at him. A single thrust of his spear would've deterred it, but as he was now, what could he do? This was it. All the scheming, all the running, all the sacrifice, leading to this. Dead in a field. No parents, no brother, no Kayla. *No revenge.*

He'd never butcher Ronin Luke, never see Tibald Sar's dying eyes, never skewer Baron Hewett. Wakeman would be dead, Pitt would be destroyed, and they'd live on. It couldn't happen. He wouldn't let it happen. Being worthless wasn't an excuse; he'd sworn to fight for Pitt until his last breath.

And. He. Was. Still. Breathing.

Rav forced himself to stand as the beast pounced at him, jaw wide, teeth like daggers. *Silence.* Then power surged through him from the back of his neck, flowing out his skin to linger on its surface like rotting smoke. Under its visage, he seemed to rot, flesh falling into hanging scraps, nails hardening into blackened claws, face no more than bone, sinew, and grey teeth. Rav became a Ghoul, swiping at the beast's jaw to tear it out with inhuman strength.

"*AHHHH.*" Again and again, he tore into its body, ripping out chunks of flesh and smashing organs in a storm of viscera until the mutant was no more than scraps of meat scattered across the ground. Covered in blood and stinking bowels, chest heaving as he panted, Rav felt his stomach finally settle as he started to drool. How delicious did all that meat look? Diving into the mess barehanded, he slurped down chunk after chunk until he couldn't stuff any more down his throat. Only then did the power fade. Ghoul receded back into his neck, Rav saw his true self once more, tears dripping off his chin onto his bloodstained hands. He'd tried so hard to help Pitt, but all he'd done was make it worse. He'd fought and bled and schemed and loved. He'd done his part, so why was it all so wrong?

"Rav..." Lyra whispered.

Ah. She was there. He sniffed, wiping away the tears as he took a few shaking breaths. "I, uh... Let's get moving before more come."

Lyra's grin nearly split her face in two.

Chapter 2

Lyra kept glancing back at Rav, eyes alight. He watched the ground, brow furrowed. The way he'd killed that mutant, it was as though he'd been the beast. Disgusting. Barbaric. Inhuman. Intoxicating, enthralling, addicting. What would Cyrn have thought if he'd seen it? Would he have been impressed or frightened? What about Kayla or Wakeman? Did it matter? It was the action that mattered, not the outcome. That was what Wakeman had believed—that was his legacy, the legacy Rav would continue. Killing the mutant was a good action. Eating was a good action. And he'd been the one thing he'd needed to be to help: powerful.

"We are here," Lyra announced, standing next to another metal mound.

Rav came to, realising he'd wandered further down the path than she had. The sun had set, leaving a faint glow in the sky to his back. Turning around, he realised how sticky he was, dried blood on his face and hands. He stretched his skin to break the layer into flakes, then picked at it as he ambled to the mound while Lyra struggled with the hatch, trying to yank it up and open.

Rav blinked. Lyra failing to do something? He lifted his head and focused on what was happening before him. *Wow.* He could see her once more, sweat lining her brow, pink cheeks flushed. How had he forgotten? She was... alluring. Something you strived for, never to achieve. The mound was a work of art too. How much metal had to go into building one of these? How could you transport it through the mutant-infested plains? How had he missed it? An entire room made of metal. Pitt didn't have anything like it. This was the outside world, this was what it had to offer. A world of marvels and opportunities for him to seize. For him to wield against his enemies.

"Can you help?" Lyra stood back and asked.

No... Wait, could he? What if he used his Heaven's Tear again? Perhaps he wasn't so useless. How had it felt? Rav focused on the back of his neck, willing the power to flow out once more. Nothing happened. *Think about the fight, think about being on the brink of death.* Nothing. *Think about the anger.* Nothing. *Think about revenge.* There. A twinge. *Hold it.* Rav squeezed all he had out of his body, desperate not to let the sensation go, and just as the power began to flow... *dong, gung, eee'u.* He lost focus as the hatch opened.

In the dim entrance stood a woman with dark hair. Wrinkles lined her face, her skin well weathered, putting her somewhere between thirty and fifty. Dressed in the same plate armour as Lyra, with black, tight-wound hair that was matted from years of travelling, she appeared to be another Sister. Thin, dry lips, a few freckles, but her eyes... they were like amber in firelight, golden brown with flecks of yellow.

"Ca'ome ' U'ul Ba'a," she called out.

"Ha'th Bey Riene, eh U'ul Ba'a ' Ga'thew' 'ah," Lyra replied.

The woman stepped out to embrace her. "Ar T'ch Shr'." She then looked at Rav, who stood in a daze.

"I don't speak Earth and Thunder," he mumbled.

The woman smiled at him. "Hu v' sh."

Lyra stepped between them, severing the enthralment that held Rav. "That means 'listen in your sleep'. It is a way of saying 'may the World speak to you'."

"I can also speak your tongue." The woman had a high-pitched accent as she changed language, as though if she pronounced the words too harshly, they would break. "You stink of blood. Come in."

The three entered the mound, the older Sister locking the hatch behind them while Lyra lit a candle.

"This is Ar T'ch Shr'. She is also in Heaven," Lyra muttered as she dumped her bags next to a bed, Rav stumbling after her. "Her duty is to keep watch over Fool's March, maintaining the camps."

"Call me Siere." Siere moved to a bed and undid the straps of her armour to get comfortable in the robes beneath, then went over to a pot of rich stew.

Rav touched the smooth metal wall. "You built these things?"

Her laugh was like pearls dropping on crystal. "The God King built these; I only take care of them." She waved her hand to dismiss the matter after catching Lyra's glare. "You are far too weak to concern yourself with him, though. The World will make you who you are meant to be." She served stew into bowls, raising an eyebrow at Lyra.

"I have not explained."

Siere frowned in confusion. "Why? He has been Called."

"We must be patient," Lyra said softly.

Siere snorted. "Fine. He is yours to guide, Sister."

Rav snapped around to face Siere as he caught on to their conversation. "How do you know I've been Called?"

"All those in Heaven will know," Lyra answered. "Just like you will know all those who are in Heaven."

Another of her vague answers. If Lyra didn't want him to know something, there was no point further questioning her about it. He tried another approach. "Why must you be patient, then?"

"You know why."

Rav sucked his teeth. All he wanted was to save Pitt. All she wanted was for him to serve the World. Just as there were things he couldn't say to her, there were things she couldn't say to him, or they'd drive each other away. "It doesn't matter," he spat. "I'll use whatever the Sink can give me."

Siere laughed. "The Sink will not give you anything. You must take it."

"Then I'll take it."

Siere laughed harder. "What will you take? You are weak, skinny, untrained—"

Lyra glared at her as Rav shrivelled back down, and the room followed her gaze, bearing down on Siere. Siere smiled, and the pressure reversed, sending Lyra stumbling back.

"Ee wa, I have been in Heaven far longer than you." Siere picked up a bowl and set it before Rav.

Nameless, worthless, reckless.

He stared at the bowl, bile rising up his throat. Lyra stepped forward again, still locked onto Siere, teeth gritted as she continued fighting against the pressure. Rav glanced at her and grimaced just the same. *Revenge.* He couldn't be weak. Grabbing the bowl, he stuffed a fistful of stew into his mouth, joining Lyra in glaring at Siere. *Swallow.* His throat opened and the bile rose, but Rav stuffed another fistful of stew into his mouth and shoved everything down. One fist after another. Siere laughed again, then froze, eyes wide. As Rav stuffed another fistful in his mouth, his figure shifted, and the flicker of a nightmare surrounded him. Lyra caught it too, turning to Rav as the pressure dropped, but the nightmare was gone.

She faced Siere once more, glowering. "He is mine."

Siere dropped her posture, head low. "Yes, Sister." She brought Lyra a bowl of food, all of them sitting to eat.

"Are you going to Blood Marsh?" Siere asked.

Lyra nodded.

"That is a good place for him to start. Baron Glass is ruler there, acting in Jinkin's name. Give him my token and he will help." She reached into a bag near her bed and pulled out a metal token with a mutant wolf imprint, handing it to Lyra, who tucked it into her own bag.

"Why would an Ah' ke like him be in Li'bo Sh'za?" Lyra asked. "Has Jinkin lost control of their path through the Sink?"

Siere glanced between Rav and Lyra with a slight squint before she answered. "Jinkin remains in control. They claim he has been sent back there to oversee food moving from Blood Marsh to their other cities." She paused. "But there are rumours that he was injured in his last battle and has retreated to the outskirts of the Sink to recover. Despite his presence, the area still has the chaos you are looking for. Another Sister came through a week ago from there saying that three Barons have fallen in the last six months. There are plenty of new teams forming to scavenge."

"I see." Lyra fell into thought.

Rav choked down the last of his meal. It was too much, piling on top of the raw meat from earlier. He lay on his back, clenching his jaw. *It. Will. Stay. Down*. He focused his thoughts on suppressing the gagging. Lyra watched over him, reaching out as though she wanted to stroke his cheek before pulling her arm back.

"I would never have thought him to be Ah' ke," Siere murmured.

Lyra shook her head as she smiled at him. "He is not Ah' ke yet; his Heaven's Tear is incomplete. But he will be. The World must have an important role for him to play."

Rav felt their gazes and worked harder to keep his food down. The Sisters began to speak in Earth and Thunder, leaving him out of the conversation. Fanatics. They were using him, manipulating him towards their own ends, but that was fine. He'd use their help to become powerful enough to do what he wanted, and once he had what he needed, he'd leave it all behind, World and all, running far away with his family just like they'd planned. All the care his guide showed was false, a façade designed to force him deeper into the Sink. She was Ha'th Bey Riene. It hurt, but it was true.

Rav woke in the afternoon, Lyra taking care as she wiped the dust off her bracer with a sweet-scented oiled cloth until it shined once more while she watched over him from her bed.

"Rest for today," she said. "Siere is out patrolling. You must recover from your fight before we walk to the next camp."

He picked more blood off himself, holding his bloated gut, but in the quiet, last night's conversation kept repeating in his head, thrumming in his skull with every pulse of his heart. The only gratitude he could show Lyra was by following her deep into the Sink, but he couldn't do that, not when Pitt needed him. Not when it was obvious that was how she wanted him to feel. An itch started in his bones. His fists kept clenching, his teeth gritting. He hadn't had the energy to be annoyed before, but now... he needed to calm down.

"I'm going out." He marched to the hatch and heaved it open before stomping down the path ahead.

How could Lyra expect more from him than he'd already given? He wasn't born in the Sink or in Heaven, no one had taught him any special techniques like Tibald's movements. He was just himself—a boy from Pitt. Why did he have to be here? Why was she so determined to force him into service for her World? This wasn't where he belonged; Lyra had dragged him along for her own selfish plans, manipulating him like everyone else. He grabbed a fistful of grass and tore it out, ready to scream. But she'd also cared for him, supported him, believed in him. *That was the result, not the action*. Rav stormed ahead until the pain in his hip returned, realising the metal mound had long disappeared behind him.

The sun had almost completed its arc in the sky, leaving little light to get back before dark. An ache also ran down his neck to his back and legs, everything stiff. How had he walked so far? Rav couldn't help breaking into a grin as he realised the answer. He had energy again. The food had stayed down. He'd done it. If he could manage that, then maybe... maybe he'd make it. The Sink, his family, the Ghoulsmen. Tibald Sar. It was doable. Difficult but possible. All he had to do was keep going. Turning around, he managed a limping jog back to camp, soon seeing Siere striding towards him with fierce intent. He rushed to meet her, face falling.

"Has something happened? Is Lyra alright?"

"You cannot walk off on your own," Siere shouted, snatching out to grab him.

Rav tried to dodge her hand, but Siere was too quick, catching his chainmail to drag him back with her. "Let go of me," he growled as he pawed at her arm, too weak to remove it.

"This place is filled with mutants. You are not strong enough to walk it alone," she chided.

"I'm fine," he spat. "And what does it matter to you if I die?"

She pulled him in front of her, lifting him off the ground like a doll. "It matters to the World. You have been Called, Rav. You must answer."

She shifted him onto her shoulder and jogged back to camp, unperturbed by Rav fighting with all his strength to wriggle free. How was she able to treat him like a backpack so easily? How pathetic was all his previous joy? He was still so weak. Rav struggled until exhaustion without achievement. The only way he could break free was with the power in his neck. The Ghoul. Focusing, he tried to summon it before coming to a sputtering stop. Would it even work? No. Even as that monster, Siere was too strong.

"Where's Lyra?" he shouted.

Siere pursed her lips, voice terse. "She went searching back out U'ul Ba'a. She thought you had run away."

Run away? Rav went limp for the remainder of the journey, and back at the camp, Siere opened the hatch, dumped him inside, then shut the door. Rav heard a *thunk* against it, picturing Siere leaning against the hatch to ensure he couldn't get out. Trapped in the dark, it was a long time before he heard anything outside.

"*Let him out*," Lyra shouted. "Rav is mine."

"He is in there for his own safety." Siere's voice was cold. "And he belongs to the World."

"What can he do for the World trapped in there?"

Siere huffed. "You are his guide. That is a duty, not a privilege. Learn quickly, or you will waste him."

Lyra opened the hatch, the light from her torch revealing Rav sitting by a bag, eating strips of dried meat in silence. She rushed to his side.

"Are you safe? I thought you would be back soon; I was worried."

"Worried I ran away," Rav spat. "You thought I was a coward. You thought I'd abandoned everything I set out to do."

She frowned. "No. I was worried you had collapsed."

"That's..." He went silent. How pathetic had he been during the journey here? Wasn't it fair for her to be worried about something like that? Wasn't he still nothing more than luggage to Siere? Maybe Lyra could be forgiven...

Siere entered and lit a candle, shutting the hatch behind her. "See, he is fine. You said he needed to rest this morning anyway."

...But Siere couldn't, not for carrying him when he'd worked so hard to walk on his own. Not for laughing at him or treating him like a possession. Rav didn't look at her, unable to suppress his snarl, listening as Lyra and Siere spoke Ca'ome for a while, eating and washing up until they settled down for sleep in their beds, Lyra to his head, Siere to his feet.

A while later, Rav yawned, rage cooling, finally drifting off. But it wasn't long before he gasped awake in the dark. Nightmares of the mutant goat, of saying goodbye to Kayla, of losing his friends and family. Of Wakeman's dead body rising as a ghoul that tore him apart. Here he was, stuck again until morning... Something felt different this time. Rav looked around him, seeing nothing but black. Hungering black. It wasn't empty as it had been before; something was here with him.

"Rav..." the voice from Ghoul Wood called.

Ghouls were watching over him. He felt it. If he reached out, he'd touch festering skin. It should've been terrifying, but there was a strange comfort in being trapped in the dark, as though it were the dark of his room in Pitt, of waking up before snuggling down and drifting off to sleep again. He wasn't alone when he was surrounded by these horrors, almost as if... he was now one of them. There was something else too. By his feet was a sensation, an inkling of a notion. Fear. Fear of being alone. No, more than that, it was a fear of losing harmony. Being disconnected.

Rav stood and walked to it, the ghouls shifting out of his way. Closer to the fear, he understood: he could make it worse. With his command, the ghouls would dive into the feeling and worsen it, magnifying the fear a thousand times. Siere's fear. A dozen ghouls waited, ravenous. The power of the Ghoul Wood dreams was his to command. Siere's worst nightmare was his to bring to life. A way for his pathetic self to fight back.

"Go," Rav whispered, breaking into a grin.

Ten ghouls tore open her nightmare and dived inside. Rav lay back down, listening as Siere tossed and turned in her sleep.

CHAPTER 3

Rav watched Siere wake shivering, Lyra holding her in place. She was lying on the floor next to the hatch after rolling out of her bed, her clothes ragged. As she unclenched her fists, torn strips of cloth dropped out.

"Are you awake now? What happened?" Lyra soothed her, stroking her hair.

Siere moved her hands frantically, searching for something invisible around her until she found it, relief replacing the frenzied panic that had overtaken her. "I... I... Monsters... rotting corpse monsters dragged me out of Heaven," she stammered, eyes wild.

Lyra looked up at Rav, who remained sitting on his bed, observing Siere and the effects of his nightmare. Siere caught Lyra's look and faced him as well, understanding flickering in her eyes.

She tensed, fists clenching. "You did this?"

Lyra held her still, moving herself between the two.

"Aye." Rav wriggled his skeletal body to life while miasma flowed out of his skin to turn it black with rot, the Ghoul draped over him. "And I can do it again."

Siere was stronger than him. She knew it, he knew it. She held back, unclenching her fists while sinking away from him. Rav towered over her in his Ghoulish visage for a moment longer before stopping the flow of miasma and absorbing the phantom back into himself.

"We've wasted enough of the morning; let's go," he snapped, collecting his bag and walking out the hatch.

Lyra dropped Siere, grabbed her bags, and followed him, eyes gleaming.

Outside, Rav caught his breath, heart thundering. Sunlight shone through the grass tips, tinted purple as it dyed his skin. He held his hand out in front of himself, mesmerised. What else could he do? He strode towards the next camp with a smile, thinking over his Heaven's Tear's power. It produced some strange miasma that hovered on the edge of existence that only he could see. If he wanted it to affect the real world, he had to make it dense. It took effort to push it out of his skin, and the more he squeezed into reality, the more it drained him. Furthermore, the further away he pushed it, the harder he had to concentrate to keep it up and the weaker the wisps became.

Keeping it on his skin made it manageable, though, allowing him to use the energy to give himself a Ghoulish mantle and enhance his strength, as though he was wearing living armour. Anything further was too much for him to make real, but things didn't always have to be real.

Nightmares.

In someone's mind, was the phantom of a ghoul any less real than if they were facing one awake? Phantoms of ghouls that preyed on a person's greatest fear. What was more terrifying to a Sister than losing their connection to the World? With a dozen ghouls, he'd made Siere vulnerable, meek. However, the target had to be asleep; as soon as Siere had woken up, the sensation had disappeared. There was also Lyra. Her fear hadn't appeared, for some reason.

He'd learn more about what he could do later, and besides, his Heaven's Tear wasn't even complete. At least there was a path to grow his own strength now: become better at wielding the Ghoul. Next, he needed soldiers, people who could compete against Baron Hewett's army and protect the citizens of Pitt.

Then, he needed a destination for everyone to flee to, a place far away from the Sink. Most important of all, he needed a Name. The Carvell Name lost to him now. For respect. For a home. For Kayla. He needed a Name.

Three Barons dying in Blood Marsh meant wandering soldiers. What if he found a few more like Thorley and Wakeman? People who understood how dangerous the Sink was and sought to escape it. They could also give him a better understanding of the land around the Sink or maybe even a map to guide him. With enough soldiers loyal to him and the acknowledgement of those in the Sink, Rav could get a Name. He'd return in glory, slay Tibald Sar and Baron Hewett, then leave Pitt behind. Blood Marsh held everything he needed.

Sunlight glinted off Lyra's armour, catching his eye. He also had her. He had to be careful of her. After what he'd done to Siere, maybe she should be careful of him. He tapped into his Heaven's Tear to charge ahead but instead found himself falling.

"*Ah.*" Collapsing to the ground like a carcass, Rav was unable to move his limbs.

What?

Why?

It was as though he were under the effects of a paralytic.

"*Rav.*" Lyra darted forward to roll him over, her gaze filled with worry.

"Why?" Rav struggled to ask.

She inspected his eyes, gums, and nails, finding nothing. Then, she sat him up and pushed his hair aside to see the black mark on the back of his neck. "Ah. You have overworked your Heaven's Tear," she said. "The World's power is not easy to bear; using more than your body can support will exhaust you. It will take time for you to regain feeling. Rest for now." She heaved him onto her shoulder, setting off once more.

Rav didn't protest—*Nameless, reckless, useless*—guts squirming in guilt over his accusation. Every time he thought the worst of her, she only proved herself to care. At what point did her façade become her? Maybe he'd been wrong all along. Maybe it was Lyra who was pretending to be Ha'th Bey Riene. Maybe he wasn't so alone.

Two weeks later, they neared the end of Fool's March. Rav developed his control of the Ghoul, working on drawing it out and dispelling it, testing how long he could last before his body gave out. As he was now, he could become a monster for twenty breaths a day, but after that, he was no better than dead. There were no nightmares for him to practise with. Lyra's fear remained hidden, and even if he'd seen it, he wouldn't have attacked it with ghouls.

For three meals a day, she prepared mashed roots for them to eat, Rav using his brutal eating strategy to finish whatever he was given before showing off the empty bowl to her. She smiled at him with pride each time, as though she was seeing glimpses of the gem buried beneath the rock. She still kept her secrets. He was making progress, and she wouldn't risk changing that. Rav didn't care, though; he'd be gone before they were relevant.

They reached the last camp before the border of the Sink, and as they settled in for another night of paste and lukewarm conversation, they heard banging at the hatch door. Lyra re-equipped her armour, drawing her sword, while Rav grabbed a spear, now able to lift it once more. Lyra pulled the lock down, easing the hatch open.

"Ar T'ch Shr'," Siere called. "I have come to see the Ah' ke before you enter Ga'thew'."

"Sister." Lyra let her in, going to prepare food for her to eat.

Rav lowered his spear but remained standing, watching Siere's every move. The effects of the nightmare had worn off; the Sister was back at her strongest.

Siere nodded his way, solemn and respectful. "You look better. Stronger. It will not be long before you fill that chainmail."

Rav stared into his bowl, his armour suddenly feeling as though Wakeman were still clinging to it.

Lyra shot Siere a warning look.

"You look like you are ready for the Sink," Siere corrected, voice sincere. "There is a place in Ut Sh'za, the second layer, called Varheart. Once you are done with Blood Marsh, head there. It is a place for people to find f'zul, direction, purpose."

Lyra glared at her again.

"I also brought you this." Siere pulled a small piece of curved metal out of her pocket. "It is called a napet. They are fashionable in Ga'thew'. It is a way for people to hide their Heaven's Tears or pretend they have them to deter attackers, like this." She lifted her hair and pressed the metal over the back of her neck, hiding the skin beneath. "Hiding it when you are weak will help you avoid trouble, and if you pass the World's test, it may also be useful in hiding how many Heaven's Tears you have."

Rav looked between the two, lingering on Lyra. His Heaven's Tear made him powerful, but it also made him a target. She'd explained it back in Pitt. Nearly everyone in the Sink would strive to kill him and take it for themselves if they found out. He gulped.

"You said I'd be safe with Sisters, that because they're in Heaven, they're saturated with the World's power already and can't use Heaven's Tears, but what if someone else discovers what I have? Can I—"

"No, you cannot just give it away." Lyra lowered her head. "To take a Heaven's Tear, you must kill the owner and cut it out their head."

Rav sucked in a breath. As if the Sink wasn't dangerous enough. He reached over to receive the accessory from Siere. "Thank you." He placed the metal on his nape, finding it cool as it stuck in place.

"I can guard you in Li'bo Sh'za," Lyra mumbled.

Siere snorted. "You will need to. The first layer usually is not dangerous for Ah' ke, but most Ah' ke are well-trained warriors." She went into her bag and brought out an expensive piece of cloth that seemed to have been spun from clouds. With expert care, she unwrapped it to reveal an ornate flask.

Candlelight flickered over the various illustrations encrusted onto it, displaying mountains, seas, birds, life. It was the World, delicate and savage. Inexplicable, like reading a sound. "There is also a custom to perform for those Called before they enter Ga'thew'. This is King's Blood." Siere held it as though it were her own soul. "Every person to become someone in Ga'thew' has drank from this. Now, it is your turn." She held it out for him.

Rav reached out to collect it, and as his fingers touched the surface, his hand seized up. It didn't "feel" like anything he'd ever touched; it was an emotion that travelled up his arms to his soul. He was holding a piece of history, something archaic, wonderous, infinite. Pulling off the cap, he pressed the liquid to his lips, its scent hitting him first, giving him visions of his parents, Healanor and Senior Carvell, sitting by the fireside. He saw warm nights in the Alley Camp with the Ghoulsmen and hot nights at home with Kayla. The smell of Pitt and Stone's Way in one overwhelming burst.

The first droplet sent his head swirling, drunker than he'd ever been before. His entire body flushed red, burning with heat, making him feel as though he were glowing. It was the taste of every family meal, every victorious return from Stone's Way, every piece of love that Pitt had to offer. A taste of Heaven, intoxicating bliss. Rav gulped a second drop, and the burn became an inferno, searing his nerves. The liquid weighed like a mountain on his tongue, pressing him deep into the ground to be buried for eternity. The love was still there, but now he had to fight off the agony to get to it. How long could he suffer for that love? The love he missed so dearly. Bones creaking, Rav took another drop. His bones cracked, splintering, shards piercing out his skin, each nerve melting into lava. He disintegrated under the weight, incomprehensible.

"*HUUU.*" Rav gasped, pulling the flask away, reeling from the pain, longing for the love.

Siere was next to him, holding him steady as she recovered the flask, sealing and storing it away. Vision blurry, he wiped his eyes, finding them filled with tears, his cheeks wet as he fought to control his wobbling lip.

"Drinking three drops is impressive," Siere murmured. "Most people fall from the smell alone. Most Ah' ke only manage one."

He trembled, eyes wide, yet captivated. "I need, I..."

Siere smiled as though familiar with the look on Rav's face: so desperate for more, yet so terrified. "You only get one drink. One chance. There is only so much to share among all those Called."

Rav slumped on a bed, eyes open but unseeing. He'd experienced it once more—Pitt, Stone's Way, his friends, family, everyone, everything good. He'd been himself and Wakeman had been alive. The pain still lingered, his jaw clenched, but it was worth it. If that was what he had to endure to see Pitt as it had been, a Pitt without Tibald Sar or Barons or the Sink, he'd do it again. If only he could've held on longer. What was his torture compared to Wakeman's death? He would bear it.

Memories fading, Rav regained his senses, wincing at the harsh sounds of Siere and Lyra speaking Earth and Thunder. "What does three drops mean?" he interrupted.

"Drops of King's Blood indicate your affinity with the World," Siere explained. "With a Heaven's Tear, it is expected that you could drink one. Two more drops mean you can handle two more laws of the World, two more Heaven's Tears. That is rare; few manage to bear more."

"You do not need to think about them." Lyra's voice was clipped.

"Tell me," Rav pleaded. "What danger am I getting into?"

"Alright, I will tell you about one of them," Siere cooed. "When the God King drank from the flask, he took a mouthful."

Rav halted his quick response, mouth hanging open. It must've been a lie; three drops had torn apart every fragment of his body, yet someone had drunk a mouthful? It wasn't just a test of willpower; he'd *wanted* to bear the pain to see Pitt, he just couldn't. How had the God King's body not given in? What could have driven him on? How much had he loved his home?

"Ar T'ch Shr', the God King had already reached the fifth layer before he drank from the flask," Lyra interjected, then looked to Rav, face pale. "Rav, the God King is in F'a Sh'za, the eighth layer of Ga'thew'. We will not meet him or anyone like him. We will focus on Blood Marsh. The rest of Ga'thew' can be discussed later."

Siere shrugged. "How deep in the Sink he was does not matter; he still drank a mouthful. Do you understand what that means, Ah' ke? That is what the World can make you."

Rav nodded, slow and determined. *Blood Marsh, Baron Glass, I'll take what I need from you.* His appetite returned in force, driving him to the leftover root paste. This time, no bile rose, allowing him to eat with more poise.

Siere gave Lyra a smug look.

"He is still mine," Lyra warned.

Siere met her gaze with cheek. "He is the World's."

They finished the last of their journey through Fool's March the next morning, Siere accompanying them, coming to a stop at the end. Rav looked up from his feet. The narrow path through the grasslands opened up to a large hill, at the top of which was a metal watchtower four storeys high, a bonfire burning on the highest floor. Silhouetted figures stood around it, watching the surrounding lands.

"That is the guard watching for 'Zet Ar leaving Ga'thew'," Siere informed him.

Rav squeezed his fist and dug his nails into his palm. Were they responsible for the monster arriving in Stone's Way? "Who do they serve?"

She chuckled. "Who do you think?"

Rav glowered. "The God King."

"No." Siere laughed harder as Rav blinked in surprise. "They serve us." She indicated Lyra and herself. "We Sisters guard the instruments of the World, helped by those who love beyond themselves. Perhaps once you have completed your Calling, you will join guards like them and protect other Called Ones."

Rav glared at Lyra, and she winced, dropping her head. "Had they known you were to be Called, they would have helped. Sometimes, mistakes happen."

"And sometimes, mistakes are *made*," Siere murmured.

Rav scoffed to himself as he trembled. Of course. Why would Sisters care for anything beyond their World?

"There is a town on the other side of the hill. We should stay there," Lyra hurried, fidgeting as Siere talked to him.

Suddenly, Rav felt his surroundings go still, stagnant. Sound was dull, as though he were concussed.

"I do not have much time." Siere grabbed him by the shoulders, her eyes fierce. "Ha'th Bey Riene thinks you are too fragile for the Sink, but I see your soul, Rav. Thousands travel these lands, but very few are like you. You are someone who will thrive against the monsters, someone who will give everything they have to overcome the trials the World gives them. You do not need coddling; you need to be thrown into the wild. This is how you will become powerful. It is not an easy path, but when all else seems hopeless, know that the World has Called you to it with the knowledge that you *can* overcome your trials. Whenever you lose faith in yourself, the World will be there to catch you."

Siere broke her seriousness and winked at him. "I will also let you know another of Ha'th Bey Riene's secrets: we Sisters are also called Brides of the World, betrothed from birth. If you want one of us, you will have to become that which we love most." She glanced at Lyra.

Rav's blood roared, his voice breaking out into a shout, "I love Kayla."

Siere laughed as everything returned to normal. Lyra was still focused on continuing the journey, unaware of the words spoken.

"If you wish for a new guide, come find me, Rav." Siere hugged him, drawing Lyra's ire.

Rav shoved her off him and turned his back to her, marching up the hill. Lyra grinned, waving goodbye to Siere before following. Once over the hilltop, he looked across the other side, finding that the hill extended much further down than they had climbed up. The land below was barren and rocky, devoid of grass, with pale clumps of weeds sprouting between cracks. It felt darker. The Sink. Smoke rose in the distance from a small town that had a few carriages travelling to and from it.

"That is Fermuch, named from the Eastern lands," Lyra said.

Rav stretched his neck. "It'll be nice to see people."

"These will not be the ambling people of Pitt," Lyra warned.

"Aye, I know."

They headed down the slope.

CHAPTER 4

They stopped just before they reached the bottom of the hill. This was it, Rav's first steps into the Sink. He took a breath, then strode forward, ready to run at the slightest threat. Nothing happened. He stamped the black, cracked land under him.

"It feels the same as everywhere else," he noted, both with relief and disappointment.

Lyra raised an eyebrow at him. "Why would it be different? This is only the start of the Sink."

Rav huffed before walking on, but as he took his next step, everything melted away, replaced by a vision of an enormous ice castle. It wasn't the structure of the fortress that caught his attention, though, but the bloodthirsty battle taking place beneath the battlements he stood on. Thousands in black and brown armour clashed in the snow below, creating a maelstrom of screams and violence. *Kill.* The thought filled every mind, including his. Limbs were hacked off and guts were split open, dyeing the white landscape red, yet he had no fear. He was used to scenes like this, the veteran of a hundred battles watching with commanding experience.

"Call the charge," he ordered, his voice matured to sound like his Pa's yet heart-wrenchingly sorrowful.

The portcullis heaved open, allowing the cavalry itching inside the castle courtyard to come storming out along the drawbridge to carve a scarlet line through the opposing forces. Thousands died, all under his control, his prowess. The soldiers admired him, loved him. They all fought in his Name. It wasn't long until the brown armoured enemy broke, leaving nothing but pockets of disorganised ragtag units to be hunted down.

"WAAAAH!"

As the castle shook with the cheer, the vision passed, leaving him back on the empty ground. Rav shivered.

Lyra turned back to face him. "Why did you stop?"

He frowned in thought. "I think I had a Calling. This one was as it is supposed to be, yet somehow wrong. Potent and powerful, but also... hollow. The one I had in Ghoul Wood was far more visceral..." He trailed off, holding his tongue before Lyra could reprimand him.

She also frowned. "A Calling? You cannot have another one. Are you sure it was not a hallucination?" She took a guarded stance, scanning the empty landscape around them for any threats.

"I'm sure. It was—"

"Then do not say any more," she snapped.

"How will I know what happened if I don't tell you about it?"

"Telling me would not work anyway; I have not had a Calling, so I do not know what they are like," Lyra said, exasperated.

"But you've heard about them before."

"Rav, ugh." Lyra dropped her shoulders. "When we reach Blood Marsh, I will ask the other Sisters about it."

They continued walking; however, Rav remained tense for the rest of the journey. If he hadn't experienced his Calling in Ghoul Wood, he would've fully believed that vision was a Calling. After all, he'd become who he wanted to be—someone with the power to kill all his enemies. So why did he feel like prey? He growled, shaking off his nerves.

"Do not use your Heaven's Tear unless you are going to die," Lyra warned him. "If others see it, they will attack, and I will not be able to save you from all of them."

He scowled. "I'm not stupid."

It wasn't long before they reached Fermuch. Black stone buildings patched with rope and wood made most of the houses, while those too poor for stone used wood covered in tarp. Two types of people walked its dingy streets: bright-eyed opportunists and crafty nihilists, both dressed in drab cloth armours. They either bartered or lamented by drab stalls, all snatching glances at anyone quiet. If you weren't going somewhere or fleeing something, then you had to have what you wanted and there were no guards to stop anyone from stealing. Between sewage and cheap perfume, it smelled desperate.

Rav followed Lyra through the winding streets, wary of the vicious looks thrown their way. He drew his knife and flicked it between his fingers as Lyra led him through the town. Hidden at the back loomed a stone mansion, its exterior carved with images of different mutants. Plate-armoured guards stood by the single gate leading past the fence surrounding it. Was that where they'd be staying?

Before they left the main town area, a large, unwashed man with unruly brown hair and a scar cutting across his nose emerged from an alleyway to block their path, leering at Lyra with unsavoury eyes.

"I've not seen anyone as ripe as you, heh heh heh." His voice was deep, rumbling. "How'd a sprout like you get such a pretty guard?"

"Ha'th Bey Riene hu v' sh," Lyra replied, staring him down despite being shorter.

The man dropped his gaze to the ground and made to bow, all bravado gone. "Forgive me, Bride. I did not know I was addressing someone in Heaven." He watched Rav from low, all lechery gone as his face fell. "My name is Bo Hart. For you to be in the company of a Bride, does that mean you've been Called?"

Rav looked to Lyra, and upon seeing her nonchalance at the situation, he answered, "Aye."

"Heh heh heh, only someone with such a destiny could receive the aid of the World. If you're looking for helpers in the Sink, I can be of service. What's your Name, Called One?"

Rav's stomach sank. "...Rav," he near whispered.

"Rav...?" Bo Hart urged him on.

Rav hardened his face. "It's just Rav."

"Nameless?" Bo straightened with a snarl. "How wretched was your crime if you're Nameless despite being Called? What a waste." He spat on the ground and stomped away.

"You do not need people like him." Lyra patted Rav on the back, then continued walking to the mansion.

Rav's breath was stifled, the sting of the admission like a hot needle in his soul. That was who he was now, someone to be reviled by common vagrants.

Nameless, Nameless... Revenge.

No. It was a reminder. Of what he'd lost and what he would reclaim. He marched after Lyra with gritted teeth. No one else bothered them until they arrived at the entrance to the mansion grounds, where two guards stood either side of thick, metal gates.

"I am Ha'th Bey Riene," Lyra announced to one. "Send for Baron Hafar." She faced Rav after the guard signalled to a servant within the grounds. "Do not worry; Hafar is only a minor Baron owning little land. He is dependent on us Sisters to protect his territory from mutants."

Soon, a portly man in opulent robes came moseying out of the mansion front doors, surrounded by three people who vied for his attention. Black hair, brown eyes, cheeks wobbling as he shooed his retinue off with a wave. Once he caught sight of Lyra, he smiled so wide his eyes became crescents. "Let them in, let them in," he called, the guards obeying so Rav and Lyra could walk into the mansion grounds to greet the Baron, who bowed to Lyra. "Dear Sister, how may I be of service?"

"We seek food and shelter for a night before we leave for Blood Marsh in the morning," Lyra said.

"Blood Marsh? What a coincidence. I have a caravan delivering ore to Baron Glass leaving tomorrow. You could travel with it if you like. As for staying the night in my home, those of the World are always welcome here." After Lyra nodded, he beamed, but his nose twitched as he faced Rav. "Are you an aide of the World?"

Looking at his smug face, Rav saw every greedy merchant who'd thought they could plunder Pitt. "Aye."

"Your Name?" he followed.

Rav clenched his jaw. "Rav."

"Rav who?" Baron Hafar's voice was tinted with disapproval, as though he knew the answer already and was just waiting to make his remark.

"Just Rav."

"Huh! Nameless!" Baron Hafar put his hand to his mouth, feigning surprise as his eyes glowed with schadenfreude. "I do not allow Nameless to enter my estate; however, for Ha'th Bey Rien, I shall make an exception."

"It is pronounced *Ha'th Bey Riene*," Lyra snapped, turning Baron Hafar's glee into embarrassment. "Prepare food and our rooms."

"My apologies, dear Sister." Baron Hafar bowed. "There will be a room for you in the east wing of the mansion with the best view of the sunrise. Your aide will have suitable accommodation elsewhere. There will also be a banquet tonight." He hurried to lead Lyra into his mansion.

Rav followed, staring at Lyra's back with a twisted expression somewhere between a grimace and a smile. She was a good friend. If only it wasn't all an act to manipulate him.

The mansion doors were huge slabs of stone that had been carved with intricate images of caravans traversing the barren land. Another two guards opened and then closed them as the three entered. Despite the oppressive grittiness outside, the interior was luxurious, consisting of gold chandeliers, thick woven carpets, and varnished wood, all polished until gleaming, with fires burning in every visible room while candles lit every dark corner. Rav looked down at the dirt he'd just trekked in, flakes of dried blood falling from his skin and hair to the floor. Baron Hafar noticed too.

"*Leera*," he shouted.

An older woman in servant's robes rushed down a staircase to the right, then looked to Lyra.

"Sister, allow me to show you to your room. I've had a bath drawn and a platter of fruits readied for you to enjoy. Leera will take care of your companion." He glanced at his servant, and an understanding passed between them.

Lyra looked to Rav, who snorted before going to Leera's side.

"Excellent." Baron Hafar led Lyra to the staircase. "The second floor was completed fifty years ago by my grandfather, Pius Hafar..."

Leera took Rav to the back of the mansion, down the servants' stairs, and into the damp basement, winding between stacked food barrels to reach an empty storeroom. Inside was a small bed, a bucket, and a single candle burning on the bedside table.

"This is our last free room; the others are occupied by those preparing for the caravan to Blood Marsh tomorrow," she explained as though helpless, already stepping away. "Goodnight."

Rav placed his bag on the bed, wrinkling his nose at the sour smell of perishing food as Leera left. He closed the door behind her, breaking his façade to reveal the fury in his eyes. How could they treat him like filth to be hidden away? He had far more honour, loyalty, and filiality than any of those people. Slumping onto his bed, he hit the wall beside him. What could he do about it, though? That was the worst part about all of this; that's what hurt the most. Wasn't this the treatment he deserved? Nameless. Blowing out the candle, he festered in the dark.

Knock knock.

Leera opened the door, flooding the room with light. Rav sat up, knife in hand.

Leera flinched back. "S-Sister Lyra has requested your presence at dinner," she stammered, eyeing his grimy outfit. "I have prepared a bath and fresh clothes for you."

"I'm fine as I am," Rav growled. "Leave."

Leera bolted out the room, shutting the door behind her.

Rav collected his bag and exited soon after, finding the dinner hall by following servants carrying serving platters and cutlery inside, the banquet still being set up. He took his seat on the left of the table, where he could look out the window to the far-off horizon, barehandedly picking at the roasted meats and vegetables being laid out. Maids huffed at his unwelcome presence but said nothing. Rav held back his sneer, ignoring their treatment of him. Besides, why would he care about their opinions anyway? These were greed-ridden people of the Sink. He was here to plunder what he could, then return to kill Tibald Sar.

"Rav," Lyra called as she entered, smelling of the petal-lain waters she'd bathed in. Adorned in light-blue silk clothes, skin still glistening, she took her seat opposite him.

Rav glanced up with a grunt before stuffing more meat in his mouth. Lyra picked at a few fruits herself, the maids' faces falling at the sight of her joining in with Rav instead of reprimanding him. He looked up once everything was ready, noticing five places set. Him, Lyra, and Hafar, but who were the other two for?

"The dining hall is this way. It is one of the oldest parts of my home, built before the Sink was formed," Baron Hafar's gloating voice came from down the corridor.

The Baron led the way into the banquet hall, followed by a young man. Tall, blond, and muscular, with a faint scar across his right ear, he walked, talked, *breathed* like he was a heroic adventurer. Judging by his silver necklace and robes, he was a wealthy Contender too. Rav squinted at him. The young man looked back at Rav and Lyra, showing his disdain and respect in turn.

"I believe you are Ha'th Bey Riene," the young man bowed as he spoke. "Baron Hafar mentioned his delight at hosting you. I am Contender Janson Poole." He turned to Rav. "And you must be the Nameless aide."

Rav grunted, about to turn back to his meal when Lyra frowned. "You have been Called?"

"Yes." Janson brimmed with arrogance.

Called? Rav's eyes narrowed. The final guest entered behind them, a plain brunette with enthralling brown eyes. She looked around the room, catching Rav's eye, and the lulling force he'd felt when first meeting Lyra and Siere started, drawing them towards each other. But this time, he gritted his teeth and tore himself away before he became dazed.

The Sister stumbled back and gasped. "Another Called One?" Her accent was like Siere's.

Lyra stood, fierce as she hissed, "Rav is mine."

Baron Hafar's brow twitched, sweat beading down his face as he looked at Rav. "You're a Called One? I was unaware. I'll have another room prepared for you. If I had known, I'd never have—"

"I'm fine where I am," Rav grunted. "Don't bother."

Baron Hafar flushed red, hands raised in a weak display of apology. The other Sister recovered and stood forward to Janson's side, glancing between Lyra and Rav.

"H'aw E' Sh or Han," she said, leading Janson to their seats, her beside Rav, him beside Lyra.

Baron Hafar signalled to his servants as he sat at the table head, having five steaming mugs served. "I have my own ale, brewed here in Fermuch." He looked to Rav with sincerity. "I hope you enjoy it."

Lyra and Han traded looks while Rav gulped his ale in one swig, wiped his mouth, then picked at more food platters, too aware of how Janson was watching him from across the table.

"Where are you from, Rav?" Janson asked, finger tapping the lip of his mug.

"You won't have heard of it," Rav muttered without looking up, the underlying tone of malice in Janson's voice enough to confirm his suspicions. Hidden behind the Contender's bravado and elitism was something cunning, as though he were a dumber Tibald Sar. Rav acted relaxed while he thought back to the lessons losing to Tibald had taught him.

Janson snorted. "I've travelled far with Han to get here, and I'm also acquainted with many Barons. There are few places I'm unfamiliar with."

It sounded like a boast, but his arrogance was only being used to disguise how much he wanted to know the answer. Rav hesitated as he realised he had to answer if he wanted to trick Janson into thinking he was an easy target. "Stone's Way."

Janson tilted his head back, doing an impressive show of trying to remember the place. Tibald had been better; it was obvious Janson was already familiar with the name.

"Ah. Baron Hewett's territory." Janson pretend-fumbled to the answer. "How interesting. Didn't you mention something about it, Han?"

"A Sister was sent there to oversee an important matter for the World," Han answered, still eyeing Lyra. "I suppose that matter was about finding this Called One. He must have a special role to play."

"Rav must only be himself," Lyra hurried to respond. "That is all the World will ask of him."

Quiet settled like a noose around the room. Rav kept eating. How many secrets was Lyra keeping? Baron Hafar did his best to keep conversation light, talking about his food and family between bouts of Janson questioning Rav, only to receive silence as an answer. Rav kept catching Han glancing his way with slight pouting, face sour. Jealousy. Why? She had Janson. Worse, Lyra was sitting up straighter, shoulders broad and proud after Han's behaviour. Rav shuddered as though his back were covered in itching vomit. It was like they were fighting over a toy. Han didn't even want him; she just wanted to take him from Lyra.

But why was Janson so interested in him? Why did he ask questions he knew the answers to, like he was testing him? Or confirming something. Rav had to stop himself tracing the knife at his belt.

Sipping at his fourth mug of ale, drowsiness sunk him into his seat. Belly bloated with rich flavours, all he wanted to do was sleep. The mood spread to the others, hastening an end to the feast. Beneath his drooping eyelids, Rav watched Janson feign his own fatigue. The man had barely sipped at his first mug of ale, ensuring he'd kept a clear head.

Clutching his belly, Rav stood from his seat, wobbling with the swaying in his head before facing Lyra. "Goodnight."

"I'll also take my leave." Janson yawned, covering his mouth with his hand, but behind it, Rav caught him mouthing something to Han that had her remain at the table, looking to engage Lyra in conversation.

"Sister, we have yet to discuss the caravan leaving tomorrow," Han said. "Baron Hafar tells me you are travelling to Blood Marsh. Do you know of Jinkin's latest movements?"

Lyra glanced at Rav, and he winked at her while wiping his greasy chin. She stayed seated as he left the room alone, stumbling to his quarters. It was evening in the mansion, the windows shuttered. Most of the guards and maids had retired for the night. Rav staggered through empty halls, burping and banging into the doors on his way. Arriving at the narrow stairs leading to the basement, he braced himself for balance.

"Ugh," he groaned, holding his gut once more.

As he took his first step down, Janson lunged out of the shadows behind him with a knife. Twisting to the side, Rav dodged the thrust, miasma already pouring out his skin. The Ghoul enveloped him. Janson froze, face white. Rav punched his chest, ribs cracking around his fist before the Contender flew back and slammed into the corridor wall. The Ghoul receded as Rav approached the dying lump of blood and broken bones slumped in a mangled heap. As if he hadn't noticed Janson palm the knife. As if he hadn't noticed Janson following him out of the dining hall. As if he hadn't known he'd be most vulnerable going down the stairs.

"Why?" Rav barked, standing over the wheezing mess.

"M..y Call...ing." Janson coughed up a spurt of blood, reached towards Rav's neck, then went still.

Rav picked up the fallen knife, kneeled beside Janson's body, and started stabbing into his chest with crazed fury until Han, Lyra, several mansion guards, and Baron Hafar found him.

Chapter 5

"*Janson*," Han shrieked, shoving Rav away to reach the dead man's side.

Lyra caught him as he fell, eyeing the crowd while guarding him behind her.

"He attacked me," Rav spat.

Baron Hafar gazed over the scene from the blood sprays on the carpet, to the wall, to Rav, then looked at the first guard who'd arrived. "What did you see?"

She bowed. "I heard someone banging into things from the corridor and came to investigate. I was at the top of the stairs and saw Rav enter the servants' area, then, as I was leaving, I saw Contender Poole follow in an odd manner."

Rav snarled to hide his grin. With the location of the fight and a witness, the situation was made clear. Besides, Baron Hafar wasn't going to make enemies of a Sister and a Called One over a dead person he didn't know.

Janson's remains still leaked blood onto the floor.

"Take the body," Baron Hafar ordered, and several guards went forward, past a muttering Han, to collect it.

Janson's chest cavity had been mashed to mush by Rav's vicious stabs, hiding all traces of his inhuman punch. Han huffed and threw her hands in the air, no tears or even a frown on her face. It was like she'd just been inconvenienced. Like this had all been a waste of her time. She looked at Rav, then Lyra, sucking her teeth. Jealous.

Rav stood tall next to Lyra. "I'll head to my room," he announced, turning towards the basement.

"Prepare a bed for me in Rav's quarters," Lyra told Baron Hafar, who, after protesting that Rav's quarters weren't suitable, gave the command to a maid.

Once the cramped room was set up and they were alone, Lyra spoke, voice low, "Why did he attack you?"

"He said 'my Calling' as he died."

Lyra frowned. "That cannot be true. Those Called do not come into conflict over their Callings; each is an action for the World."

"Would Han know?"

Lyra shook her head. "If she knew what Janson's Calling was, she would have to abandon him."

"If it wasn't a Calling, how did he know so much about Pitt? He targeted me, Lyra. It wasn't opportunistic; it was deliberate. He confirmed my name and where I'm from, *then* started planning his attack. Who would know about me?"

"Pitt is now under Baron Hewett's control and has Champion Sar in charge," Lyra explained. "People keeping track of Ah' ke would know about it. Perhaps news of the events there have spread. Perhaps Janson received a bounty from Tibald Sar to kill you."

Rav held his knife over the candle flame as he thought. That would make sense, but it still felt like an excuse. Janson's dying words had been clear. The knife was now white hot, distorting the air above it.

"I need you to do something," he said, looking Lyra in the eye while he removed the napet from his neck to reveal his Heaven's Tear. "Janson could've figured out I have a Heaven's Tear. I can't risk people seeing it. You need to brand me." He presented the back of his neck to her.

She flinched. "That will not work, Rav. When Heaven's Tears are complete, they glow. Tattoos and burns are unable to hide them."

"Even if it's temporary, it's worthwhile." He wound a piece of cloth and put it in his mouth to bite down on, ending the discussion.

Lyra calmed herself with a long exhale, then pulled Rav's hair aside and steadied her hand. Rav grunted for her to continue. She pressed the flat of the blade down on the nape of his neck, and Rav's screams filled the basement.

Breakfast was at dawn. Baron Hafar, Han, Lyra, and Rav sat silently around the banquet table, trying to ignore the smell of charred flesh which permeated the air. Rav chewed as little as possible, trying not to move his neck more than absolutely necessary, which was wrapped in a cloth soaked with Lyra's medicine.

"Do you require a healer?" Baron Hafar offered.

"No," Rav mumbled. "Janson cut my back and Lyra has already mended the wound."

Baron Hafar went quiet, head low as he nibbled at his fresh-baked bread.

"Will you still travel with us to Blood Marsh?" Lyra asked Han.

She nodded. "I need to find more information on potential Heaven's Tears and Called Ones."

Rav observed them for a moment, seeing that they no longer clashed with one another, instead smiling and joking in Ca'ome like they were real sisters. Lyra kept her gloating subtle and Han coated her jealousy in respect. It was obvious why: he'd won. Lyra's toy had been better, making her the victor. After last night, he understood the truth about the care Lyra showed him. He was only valuable when he was useful. If he died, he'd be forgotten just as quickly as Janson. That was how Sisters treated those they'd sworn to protect. He munched his bread and winced as pain flared in his neck.

Breakfast over, Baron Hafar refilled their supplies, providing new pieces of flint, clean clothes, and ample provisions. The four stood outside the mansion, watching twelve large carriages being loaded with goods, each with two horses leading them. The beasts were larger than any Rav had seen, with wide backs and dense muscles packed under their thick hides.

"You will have your own carriage." Baron Hafar indicated one being adorned with plump cushions and drapes, then looked at Rav, who wore the same blank expression as before.

"We appreciate it," Han said.

A muscular woman with scalp-short hair in full-plate armour strode over from the carriages. "Baron Hafar, Sisters, Called One." She bowed. "We're almost ready."

"This is Contender Ilin Vene, daughter of my Champion," Baron Hafar announced, patting her shoulder. "She will be leading my convoy. If you need anything during your journey, seek her out."

Han and Lyra nodded, while Rav stood uncaring.

Lyra tutted under her breath before pulling Rav aside in the silence.

"You should accept Baron Hafar's apology before we leave," she whispered. "You are to become someone powerful in the Sink. If Baron Hafar thinks you would be his enemy, he will do everything he can to kill you now. One assassin coming after you was enough. Be his friend."

Rav mulled it over before huffing. "Fine."

As they readied to board their carriage, he faced Baron Hafar. "I appreciate you feeding and housing me for the night."

"If you ever need a place to stay again, you'll always be welcome at my home, Called One," he replied with a small smile. "Your reception here will never be repeated."

Rav waved his hand and stood tall. "We should let such small matters pass; there is no need to dwell on them."

Baron Hafar nodded with relief before bidding them all farewell and signalling for the convoy to set off.

Two days later, Rav lay wincing in the dim, trundling carriage, head rocking back and forth as the carriage bumped over uneven ground. Despite him, Lyra, and Han hanging their bedding on the carriage roof in the sun during the day, the stink of sweat still lingered on everything, the air stagnant as though humid. There was also the sharp scent of medicine coming from his neck, the burned patch of skin still feeling hot. Rav touched where the skin had melted, feeling each scabby bump. At least it didn't hurt as much as drinking King's Blood had. What were a few weeks of pain compared to that?

"Stop picking at it," Lyra chided as she looked up from her book, sitting across from him.

Rav dropped his hand with a sigh, catching Han tut at him from where she was also reading beside Lyra. Once the sun started to set, the carriage convoy stopped for the night. Rav scrambled to his feet and grabbed his spear, hurrying out into fresh air while stretching his aching back. Even if the landscape was still dark, barren, and rocky, it was better than plain wooden walls. He moved away from where the other convoy members were setting up campfires for supper to an empty space and swung his spear around. How long would it take until he was as good as he had been in Pitt? He jabbed, finding the strike much too slow to harm mutant hide. Sky dyed pink, wispy clouds limping lazily across it, Rav swung again. And again. And again.

Exhausted by the time it was dark, he ate as much as he could at supper, then relaxed by the glowing coals of the late-night fire, listening to Lyra and Han speak Ca'ome. The three were alone, everyone else keeping their distance. Sometimes, Rav would spot a labourer walk in their direction, spurred on by their companions, then shy away. The only person who interacted with him and the Sisters was Contender Vene, but even she kept their conversations short, informing them about food or where they'd be camping for the night.

He gazed at a laughing group of boisterous men and clenched his guts. How long had it been since he'd enjoyed himself like that? That's where he should've been, not here, surrounded by haughty Sisters and titles that made people too nervous to approach him. Nameless Called One. That's what he was now. That's all anyone cared about. For a family to take back their Name from someone Called, the dishonour they'd brought had to have been severe. No one would trust someone like that.

He focused on one of the labourers, a broad man with brown hair and a scar across his nose. Bo Hart from Fermuch. His parting words echoed in Rav's mind: '*How wretched was your crime if you're Nameless despite being Called?*' Nothing he did could ever bring Wakeman back to life. Whatever else he achieved, the stain of that mistake would never fade.

Two weeks later, Rav stood outside in the evening once more, throwing his knife at an old tree stump. Winding his arm, a tension gripped him as memories of him throwing his last knife at the 'Zet Ar in the Stone Steps surfaced. Everything fell into place once more, the sensation like the air itself was pushing him into position. Ready, he launched the blade. *Thunk.* The knife hit the exact knot he'd been aiming for. He frowned as he rubbed his arm. That was the third perfect throw in a row. Had he always been this good?

Shoulder aching, he gazed ahead, the sun still above the horizon at his back. Halfway to Blood Marsh. Dense clouds were gathering in the distance, more moisture in the air, the solid rock ground softening to soil that allowed more grasses and bushes to take root. The long spring was ending, bringing signs of an even longer coming summer. Sleep had become more difficult, the lush-lined carriage sweltering even at night. Everything felt slick with sweat. His neck itched so much he'd started to dream about scratching it.

Lyra walked over to him as he collected his knife. "Contender Vene said there is a clear stream over there for those who wish to bathe." She pointed at a patch of grass greener than the rest around it where other labourers were undressing.

Rav raised an eyebrow at her, the corner of his mouth curling upwards. "Are you saying I stink?"

She reached forward and scratched something in Rav's hair, holding her finger up to show black crusted blood on her fingertip. "This is Janson's blood. You smell as bad as he does now. Han suggested we drag you to the water and dump you in."

Rav chuckled. "I thought I'd seen her wrinkling her nose at me." He raised his knife and looked at his reflection in the polished blade. Thin cheeks, hollow eyes, protruding bones. How much worse had he looked before he'd started eating again? At least he had his teeth. Pulling a smile, he tried to capture the charisma he'd had in Pitt. Grotesque. He looked at the porters joking as they led the horses to drink, many washing themselves nearby. "Aye, I'll go later," he mumbled.

Lyra nodded before leaving. Rav watched her go. Still gorgeous. It was another trap he'd fallen into; Lyra didn't change, but he did. She was a reminder of the past, of what he'd been, not what he was.

Once everyone else returned from the stream, he sneaked off on his own, the stream an arm wide and deep enough to reach his knees. After ensuring the area was clear, he set his bag down and pried off his boots. Next came his trousers, peeled from his skin, followed by Wakeman's chainmail. Heavy and crusted with grime, Rav had to fight to lift it over his head. Looking down, he gasped at the sight of his body, able to count every rib. Bruised, beaten, yellowing, and so pale he could see his veins. It wasn't the body that had defended Pitt. This body couldn't defend Pitt. He eased into the cool water, lying down to submerge it from sight.

Sh, olp, bol, the stream bubbled around him, its muddy riverbed soft. Rav took a deep breath and let the water take most of his weight. He would change. Reaching up, he rubbed his hair, and the water around him went murky, then flowed away, clear again. Other dirt had been dried for weeks, staining his skin so he had to scrub himself pink to shift it. But he succeeded. Gone were his scabbed knees and black nails. Rav admired his delicate hands once more. He cleaned Wakeman's chainmail next, dragging it in with him and scrubbing it with his trousers. Beneath the grit coating it, he saw the red tint of Wakeman's blood, unsure if it was really there.

He dressed and returned to camp in the dark with squelching steps, Wakeman's mail now shining. Lyra was waiting for him by their carriage with clean clothes for him to wear. While changing into the new trousers and boots, his hair kept falling in front of his face, some clumps of mud still hanging in it. Returning outside, he showed Lyra. She cut it to his scalp with a sharp knife while he ate by the fire, stuffing himself until he was bloated towards nausea. As he lay in the carriage to sleep, he pulled out Kayla's cloth, took a deep breath of her perfume, and dreamed of his return.

More trees appeared, the ground green with plants, a forest now blocking the horizon ahead, and behind it loomed a rising mountain. The caravan soon entered the treeline. Rav sat on the carriage roof with Lyra as he observed everything. Rather than the gnarled trees that made Ghoul Wood, these had long limbs that shot up before bending under their own weight to droop back down, like they were made of rubber. Most of the branches were bare, save for the tips, which had dense clusters of leaves. Over the relentless squeaking of the carriage wheels came bird calls and buzzing insects. Rav watched one bug with four long legs and eight wings fly up to the leaf clusters in search of food.

"It is a Hot Foot, or S'ah," Lyra said, watching it too. "They have nests all across Blood Marsh."

Rav reached out his hand towards it, extending his finger out for one to land on.

Lyra flicked his arm with a tut. "They are called Hot Foot because they burn skin they land on." She laughed as Rav snatched his hand back. "This is the Sink."

Ree.

Rav shot up in the middle of the night, all drowsiness gone.

Reee. More screeches followed, dozens of them—horses whinnying.

Lyra and Han were gone, along with their armour and swords, leaving him alone in the carriage.

"*Defend yourselves*. The Sisters and I will chase them off," Vene bellowed from the distance.

REEEE. Bang, scratch. Something crashed onto his carriage roof.

Rav scrambled to find his boots, stuffing his feet into them before cracking open the carriage door. Under the starlit sky, beams of orange torchlight swung back and forth as the torchbearer waved the fire around in the darkness, trying to provide visibility for the guards.

Ree.

Rav caught the silhouette of one of the creatures attacking them—a bat-like creature with a long tail that had a needle-like tip. Several more followed after it, shooting through the air to harass the torchbearer. Rav slammed the door shut. A mutant attack. Panic had him feeling each rapid heartbeat, his breath becoming uneven, shallow. This was the Sink.

Coward. He had to help. But what if the tail spikes were venomous? What if this was reckless? He gritted his teeth. What was the point in doing nothing? He lit a candle, then went searching through Lyra's bags for knives, finding five. *Don't get stung.* He pulled a long-sleeved gambeson shirt over his chainmail, already sweating into the thick cloth. Leaning against the carriage door, he steadied his shaking hands. *They are only some bats.* He opened it a sliver to spot a target. The creatures flitted in and out of view in the night sky, the gap too narrow to target any. Rav sucked in a breath as he threw open the door all the way and prepped a knife to throw.

Ree.

There. His knife flew true— *eee*—a mutant crashing to the ground. He readied another. Soon, all five knives had been thrown, and five mutants were dead. *What now?* Hiding back in the carriage, he listened. The mutants seemed to be occupied by the torchbearer at the front of the convoy. Couldn't he dash out to collect his knives, then rush back to throw them again? Aye, he could do it. He *would* do it. He would help and prove he wasn't so useless anymore.

Go. Door thrown open, he sprinted to where his first victim lay and collected the first knife. Hurrying to search the area, he failed to spot another. *Out of time.* Rav charged back for the carriage.

Ree.

He ducked as a mutant swooped over his head, the creature circling around before facing him, hovering in front of the open carriage door to block it. Rav dashed for another carriage, and another mutant shot over his head to block his destination. He whipped his arm up to send his last knife flying and pierced the creature's body. *Eee.* As it fell, he slammed into the carriage door.

"*Open*," he shouted.

No answer.

More mutants arriving.

Rav sprinted for the torchlight and frantic whinnying, ready to become the Ghoul if he had to. Mutants dived at him in waves, their talons tearing out chunks of padding with each strike. Rav struggled to keep his balance under the barrage, working to stay low as he ran. *There.* Vene held the flaming torch, standing on the roof of the front carriage, light gleaming off her helmet. She wielded her halberd one-handed, sweeping it around her in a never-ending cycle to prevent the swarm of creatures from coming closer. Two other figures danced in the light, kicking off the carriage walls to slash their longswords high into the air, claiming wings or tails before descending to the ground as they guarded the horses under attack by their tent. Lyra and Han were acrobats in plate armour. Rav watched as one of them landed, rolled to collect a bolt from the ground, and threw it as she stood, taking out another creature.

There were always more, though. Mutants swarmed a horse, which then charged out the camp and into the night. Rav arrived at the front carriage, drawing the Sisters' attention. One left to help him, piercing a mutant that clawed at his head. Lyra removed her helmet and set it on Rav's head, her black hair stuck to her forehead with sweat, her cheeks glowing in the firelight. The fight worsened, Han unable to protect Vene by herself. A swarm descended, and the torchlight dimmed. Rav froze for an instant at the mess he'd caused before shaking his head and rushing to help. Spotting a glint of metal on the ground, he picked up a knife under Lyra's protection, then threw it. Another mutant plummeted to the ground.

Looking to Lyra, he pointed for her to help Vene instead of guarding him. She shoved him to the carriage, then obeyed, but as she darted around, she flicked more items towards him instead of pausing to throw them herself. Knives, bolts, and stones all seemed to hang in front of him. Rav snatched them out the air and threw them anew, mutants falling from the sky like rain. A pressure descended over him, a thrum that funnelled his mind and body until he could see it all with perfect precision. Catch, aim, throw, and another died. Lyra and Han continued jumping and slashing, melding into his vision as though they too were part of the show. He could *see* them, see the limits of Heaven. It all just made sense.

The swarm thinned. The torchlight was bright once more... no... *brighter* than before. Vene moved back into the convoy, Rav, Lyra, and Han following her from below as she leaped from carriage roof to carriage roof. Wherever the light touched, no mutant survived. The swarm retreated, and with a last *Ree*, the night went still. Vene scoured the skies a moment longer before climbing down, panting. Rav slumped to the ground, chest heaving, arms burning, hands stinging. The clarity was gone, his body wracked with ache, almost as though he'd overused his Heaven's Tear again.

Lyra kneeled next to him and lifted off his helmet to inspect him for wounds. "Have you been stung?" she hissed, voice taut with worry. "Those creatures are called wingtails, and they have a paralytic venom. Too much of it will stop you breathing."

He forced a smile. "I'm in a lot of pain, so I think I'm safe."

Lyra looked up and shook her head, eyes tearing, sending a droplet of blood and a few black hairs onto Rav's face.

He sat up, exhaustion gone, reaching for the small scratch at the back of her head where a stray talon had snagged her. "You're hurt," he whispered. Something pristine was spoiled. "I'll get bandages." Rav shot off running to his carriage, head spinning. Lyra was never injured. She was in Heaven. Something like that shouldn't have been possible. And it was all because she'd given him her helmet. He lost his breath, chest empty, gasping, choking. She couldn't be hurt, not for him, not after everything she'd done to help him. His eyes burned as tears welled. He stuttered in his sprint as he reached his carriage. The door was closed, and in the distance, he caught Bo Hart hurrying away. No time. Rav entered to see everything as he'd left it. After grabbing Lyra's medicine bag, he ran back to her, pulling out bandages that he then wrapped around her head.

"It is just a scratch," she reassured him.

Rav ignored her, tying the cloth as best he could with shaking hands, but as he worked, he noticed that it was his own blood wetting the cloth and Lyra's hair.

"*Your hands.*" Lyra grabbed his wrists to survey the damage. She found a vial in her bag and poured it over his wounds, Rav hissing through his teeth while writhing at the sting.

Han came over with a deadpan expression. "There is another scratch by his neck. And one on his arm."

"Wait..." Rav pleaded.

Lyra was already pouring more liquid on him. Done, she wrapped fresh cloth around his hands. Contender Vene approached them, flustered but smiling.

"Thank you, Sisters." She bowed. "And thank you, Called One." She turned to the rest of the caravan and shouted, "The attack is over."

Cheers resounded across the convoy, people emerging from their rooms with lanterns to celebrate. Rav signalled Lyra to leave with him, and she helped him up as they left. He watched the relieved crowd as he limped by. There, Bo Hart. He was laughing and singing like everyone else. Like he hadn't sneaked out during the attack on their carriage. Why? What did he want that he'd risk his life for? Rav thought back to their previous interaction. *What am I missing?* And then it hit him. No one else in Fermuch had approached Lyra; everyone else had known she was a Sister at first glance. Furthermore, even Baron Hafar hadn't thought him to be Called, but Bo had guessed right away. He glanced at Bo again, holding back a scowl. Bo Hart had only acted the fool. He wanted to appear nonthreatening. It made his joining this convoy ordinary. It made them lower their guard towards him.

Carriage door shut, Rav grimaced at Lyra. "We have an enemy."

Chapter 6

"I saw Bo Hart leaving our carriage while we were fighting the mutants," Rav said, unspooling cloth bandages from Lyra's pack to wrap around his stinging hands. "He must be looking for something, or he's gathering information about us."

Lyra hurried to search her belongings with a frown, looking at Rav with a shrug once done. "Nothing is missing."

"Aye, if I hadn't seen him, I wouldn't have known he'd been in here," he muttered. "What if he's like Janson? More dangerous than Janson? He's sneaked close to two Sisters and neither of you noticed him. That's not something an ordinary opportunist can do."

"I will not let anyone kill you, Rav," she swore. "If Bo Hart attacks, I will protect you with my life."

"I'll not have you die for me," he snarled. "You've done enough already. Since you can't kill people, I'll handle Bo myself. I just need to know how dangerous he is. You've mentioned people who follow Sisters in search of Heaven's Tears. Could Bo be someone like that?"

She paused before nodding.

Rav sighed, his voice lower than a whisper as he spoke, "If he's confident in fighting a Sister, then the Ghoul might not be strong enough to kill him alone. I'll have to catch him in a trap."

Lyra held his shoulder. "You have to be careful, Rav. Until you are strong enough, no one can know. Everyone in this convoy would cut you in two to get in your head. Even Han might snatch you from me if she finds out."

Rav's guts twisted as he grimaced. "Aye, I know. I'll only act if I'm certain no one will see me."

Before Lyra could respond, Han entered the carriage and started stripping out her armour into her robes. Lyra conversed with her in Ca'ome while Rav lay down, mind racing to find a solution for Bo Hart. If only he knew for sure what Bo was after, he could better plan.

Lyra and Han settled down to get some sleep before morning. Rav listened to their breaths until they became long and deep. The celebrations outside also ended, doors thunking shut as they returned to their carriages. He connected to his Heaven's Tear and coaxed out its smoky miasma bit by bit, the wisps easier to conjure than in Fool's March. Making sure to disperse the murky power before it condensed enough to become real, he looked through it. Just like in Fermuch, no one's fear was visible. Had Siere been unique?

But as he toyed with it, a tiny flicker of silver fear bloomed ahead of him. He examined where the fear was, seeing it beyond the carriage walls as though the dream realm had no boundaries. Wasn't that where Bo Hart was sleeping? Tendrils of miasma started drifting towards it. Rav concentrated in that direction, the tendrils lengthening as a piercing headache dug in behind his eyes. At last, the miasma touched the fear, and Bo's nightmare was laid bare.

An enormous worm-like monster with five heads filled with sword-sized teeth arched up out the rocky ground, towering far above a group of soldiers. Corrosive saliva dribbled out each maw to melt the ground beneath it, everything reeking of rotting soil. One of its heads dived down to devour a soldier to his front, its bodily fluids pulsing as it swallowed. One bite and the man was gone.

Ah! Rav broke the tether, the headache too much to bear. He dispersed the tendril, disconnecting from his Heaven's Tear, then shivered, stomach churning.

That was Bo Hart's fear. What kind of monster was that? Not even the 'Zet Ar he'd fought could've stood against it, which meant... Aye, it was a mutant from deep in the Sink. Which meant Bo Hart had travelled deep in the Sink. How had he survived encountering a mutant like that?

Dread pooled in Rav like sludge. Whatever Bo Hart wanted, couldn't he just take it by force? But he'd been secretive. If he wanted to kill him, like Janson, then he could have already, which meant Bo wasn't here for that. And if Bo was looking for a Heaven's Tear, then him not attacking meant he also didn't know that he had one. Rav took a deep breath, a dangerous ploy dancing in his mind.

The caravan moved faster through the forest, keen to leave the wingtails behind. Everyone remained vigilant, watching the skies for any more creatures while Vene conducted extra patrols around the carriages to bolster morale. Rav sat next to Lyra on their carriage roof, his hands and neck wrapped in fresh bandages, itching. They watched as Han left to polish her armour. Rav told her about the mutant he'd seen in Bo's nightmare.

Lyra pursed her lips, voice low. "Mutants like that are called 'Zet Mo and they live in the Mo'za, the middle three layers of Ga'thew'. You do not have to worry about them here; only 'Zet Ar roam the Ar'za."

Rav hardened his expression to keep it blank. How many terrible monsters existed in this place? And Lyra wanted to lead him deeper in this place, right to where they roamed? Never.

"Bo is powerful," she muttered. "You will understand more when you reach Blood Marsh, but for now, know that all those capable of reaching the Mo'za are as strong as ordinary Champions. While Bo might not be in Heaven, he is not someone you can fight no matter what you do. Ambushes will not work either; someone like him will be too cautious." She paused to mumble to herself, "If he has eaten a bezoar...", then hurried to smile at Rav to mask her slip.

He clenched his fist. "I have to do something, Lyra. I'll not sit and wait for Bo to act; I won't repeat my mistakes in Pitt. Whatever he's doing, I'll stop it." He leaned closer to her ear. "If I do to him what I did to Siere, can you keep others away while I strike? I'll only have one chance. If Bo survives, he'll know what I have, but it's my only hope."

Lyra tapped her thigh for a moment, face scrunched as she mulled it over. "Strike at night. I will do what I can."

Han returned. Rav retired into the carriage to rest until they stopped to camp for the night, then spent the evening training with his spear. Still weak. He didn't have to get Bo tonight; he had some time to prepare. But the sooner, the better. Done, he lumbered to the campfire in the dark, shoulders down as he gorged himself on food. Lyra left to bring him more while Han hurried behind a tree while clutching her stomach. As he stared into the fire, a large figure emerged from the darkness and sat next to him. Rav jolted back, but Bo snatched his shoulder and held him firm, breath foul as he leaned in close.

"You've been watching me," Bo murmured. "Heh heh heh, I was caught, right? Too busy watching for the Brides that I forgot about you." He leaned back and sighed, mouth still curled up with malice. "So, what now, Nameless Called One?"

Rav wet his dry mouth, heart in his throat. "Lyra will be back soon."

"*Lyra*?" Bo laughed, releasing Rav while shaking his head. "How was I caught by a pup like you? Do you really believe in whatever great purpose that Bride said you have? I've seen dozens of Called Ones get marched to their deaths for nothing but a disappointed sigh. Learn her real Name—that is who she really is."

Rav scanned around, but Lyra was still gone... Wait. What would happen if she did return? Hadn't she been injured by a wingtail? No, she couldn't fight Bo, not for him. Even if she said she was strong enough to beat him, was she? Hadn't Wakeman seemed so certain he could kill Tibald? All it would take was one mistake. It was too big a risk. He'd be without her. Then what? Rav gulped. What had Bo said? Aye, there was something in that. Maybe there was a way out of this situation.

He cleared his throat and sat taller, forcing a sly grin to mask his fright. "Aye, I know," he whispered. "I've seen it. Han used to have her own Called One."

Bo grinned back, eyes alight with curiosity as he examined Rav once more.

"You want a Heaven's Tear, don't you?" Rav continued.

Bo put his hand around Rav's shoulders, firm and dominant, his face creasing in intimidating delight. "If you had one of those, I would've split you in two and torn it out your head."

Rav gave a dry chuckle. "What if I helped you get one? I can get information from the Sisters for you. That way, you wouldn't have to follow us around all the time."

Bo also laughed. "Why would I trust you to do that for me? Wouldn't you want a Heaven's Tear for yourself?"

Rav widened his grin. "Is that what I want?"

Bo sneered, squeezed Rav's shoulder harder. "You can only say something like that because you haven't seen one. A Heaven's Tear is the difference between a King and a corpse. At first, the God King was just a man like you or me, but now he walks the Sink without contest all because of the powers they granted him."

"I don't care about that," Rav hissed. "I don't want anything to do with them. I'm not here to go exploring; I'm here to win my home back. Before this World nonsense, my family was planning on running far away from the Sink and people like you." His expression twisted to reveal his true hatred. "I'm going to get a Name, slaughter my enemies, and leave this all behind."

Bo examined his expression. "You'd betray the Brides?"

"Why should I die for their machinations?" Rav spat. "I'm tired of the monsters and the fighting. I have a girl I love. I want to be with her. I need to be alive to do that, not have people like you hunting me. Help me and I'll help you. Protect me in Blood Marsh and I'll tell you everything I learn about Heaven's Tears."

"Hmm." Bo waited before shaking his head. "It isn't worth my time to babysit you. Why don't I act as a mercenary? I'll be in Blood Marsh for a while. If you need my help, ask for it, then pay me with information about a Heaven's Tear. But I want details, Called One, the location of a real Heaven's Tear. If you lie to me, I'll break your arms and legs, then carry you around like a pelt as I butcher everyone in Pitt."

Rav shuddered, breath cold. How did Bo know where he was from? "A-aye, it's a deal."

"Good." Bo released him to look ahead as Lyra came running back, one hand holding a bowl of stew, the other on her sword, eyes wide and face pale. "Easy, Bride," he growled, patting Rav on the back. "Your Called One and I are just talking. He's impressive; what were the rumours? Three drops of King's Blood. You'd better find him a Heaven's Tear, or next time he meets someone like me, he'll die."

She squared up to him, nostrils flared. "Step away."

Bo laughed as he stood, leering at her. "What could you do if I didn't? Such a pathetic existence. It's no wonder the other Brides—"

She stepped closer, half-drawing her sword. "If you know them, then know what I am capable of. Leave, Bo Hart."

"Heh." He faced Rav. "Don't die for someone else's ideals, pup. The only person you can rely on in here is yourself." Throwing a last glare at Lyra, he sauntered away to another campfire.

Rav exhaled, breath quick and shallow, tugging at his sweaty collar to cool down. Facing Bo was worse than facing Tibald. Bo was powerful enough to kill him without using his weaknesses. And how did he know about him drinking King's Blood? He'd spoken to Janson about Stone's Way at Baron Hafar's banquet, so any eavesdropping servant or person present there could have shared where he was from, but only he, Lyra, and Siere had known about the three drops he'd swallowed. Had Siere spread that news? Why?

Lyra hurried to his side. "I should not have left you alone for so long. There was a problem with the stew..." Her eyes widened in realisation. "Bo tampered with the pot to distract me. He must also be the one who fed Han rotten meat and made her ill. What did he want?"

"Information on Heaven's Tears," Rav stammered. "If I lead him to one, he'll help me."

"Do not ever help him get one, Rav," she warned, voice fierce. "Heaven's Tears are gifts from the World for its instruments to complete their Callings. To make Bo Ah' ke would be to make him a ruler of Ga'thew'."

Rav nodded, keeping his expression frightened while he thought. Why would he care if Bo Hart claimed land in the Sink? That wouldn't matter once he ran far away with his family. There was another benefit to having Bo as a potential ally: what would happen when he did run from Lyra? Maybe Bo could help him escape.

"I won't give him one," he promised Lyra.

"Good." She nodded with a sigh. "Those Called can only trust us Sisters."

The landscape had changed once more, from forest to wetland that stretched out towards the gargantuan mountain in the distance. Sitting on the back of the carriage roof with Lyra and Han, Rav went dizzy as he stared up at it, the mountain soaring so high that its outline blurred. How could something that big exist? Stone's Way's biggest hills were no more than bumps on its surface. A huge forest covered the mountain's left half, while rocky terrain littered with tors and ridges covered its right, both ending before its snowy peak. At its base sat a large stone city almost ten times the size of Pitt, an outer wall taller than three men ringing the main city area. Donsden, the seat of power in Blood Marsh.

As they neared the city, the dirt road they travelled on changed to stone paving, the convoy winding around flooded ground and passing through several small villages. Rav watched as many blue-feathered, long-legged birds stood in puddles to pick at aquatic insects, while others flitted through the sky. A dozen different birds tweeted while hundreds of insects chirped. Through it all, he picked up a familiar buzz, spotting several rubber trees with clusters of Hot Foots around them. The sounds quietened as they entered an enormous swathe of farmland that surrounded the front of Donsden, replaced by farmers chatting as they tended to the growing crops. Everything was ordered, each citizen dressed in thin robes for the summer, cheeks full. Looking at their demeanour, most of them seemed to be soldiers too. Rav frowned and faced Lyra.

"Is this really Blood Marsh? I thought you said it was filled with warring Barons and vicious mutants."

Lyra pointed to the edge of the mountain. "This side of Mount Don is secure under Baron Glass' control, but the further around the mountain you travel, the wilder the land will get. That is where the other Barons fight."

Closer to Donsden and Mount Don, Rav gazed up and gawped, his next question forgotten as the scale of the city hit him. Backed into the mountainside, it was built up from the plains, watchtowers equidistant along its outer wall, each manned by a unit of soldiers in black-scaled armour. As the city creeped up the mountain slope, it rose, leading towards a smaller second wall. Behind it, at the city's peak, sat a stone keep that had been embedded into Mount Don, its design rough and pointed but practical. An outstretched section jutted out of its front like a beak to tower over everything below.

Dozens of carriages travelled in and out of the front gates, each carrying workers or produce for the farmland, thousands of voices creating a clamour unlike anything Rav had heard before. Thousands of citizens. Pitt barely had a hundred. He found everything fading, sound and sight dulling as a numbness creeped under his skin, Mount Don suddenly seeming as though it were going to crush him. Rav tore his eyes away from it and stared at the carriage roof, fighting to keep himself sitting up. He couldn't be weak, not here. Breaths deep, it took a while before the constricting feeling eased.

Power. An army. A Name. Revenge.

He'd take them all.

"Heh heh heh." Bo jogged up to Rav's carriage and climbed up to him with a grin. "I hope you know a lot about Heaven's Tears." Despite Lyra and Han glaring at him, he sat facing Rav like an old friend, shoulders relaxed as he basked in the hot sun. "It's nice to be back. The first time I came through here, I killed forty people. Baron Glass was just a lackey for Jinkin back then. Lucky brat," Bo spat. "If I'd have caught that girl and taken her neck, I could've made it to the Do'za."

"We do not care for your boasting," Lyra hissed. "If Rav wishes to know about Baron Glass, he can ask me."

"Would you tell him the truth?" Bo sneered. "Or would you hide the details of how Haymitch Glass tore a teenage girl apart to get in her head? That's the kind of man you Brides are supporting to keep hold of this path through the Sink."

Lyra held his stare. "You are worse than a man like Baron Glass."

"That's true. But I don't hide my true self like you do; I don't need a 'World' to justify my actions. When I want something, I take it, no apologies or false platitudes needed." He looked ahead at the city. "Heh, that's why I've been free to travel all the way to the Mo'za while he's stuck here, protecting a place he doesn't care about for people that would discard him the moment someone better came along. You've chained him in politics and favours, while I roam free."

"You are wrong," Lyra snapped. "Baron Glass is helping us Sisters because he has love beyond himself. That is something you cannot understand. We Sisters may want, but what is the point in achieving selfish goals when the World needs serving?

Without It, all riches are no different to ashes. Do not forget that it is the World's power that you are so desperate to acquire."

"A good point," Bo murmured, then faced Han. "You, what would you have done if you had a Called One who'd drank three drops of King's Blood?"

Han gave Rav a skin-crawling smile. "I would have dragged him to the third layer to compete for a Heaven's Tear."

"You'd pit a boy against those monsters? Wouldn't he die, just like the girl Haymitch killed?"

She shrugged. "With the support of the World, he would achieve what he was destined to."

"Ha." He slapped his leg. "Be careful, Rav. The Brides might rule the outer layers of the Sink, but once you enter the Do'za, they die, like everyone else. That's the only reason they help people like you; they hope you'll become strong enough to support them deeper inside. If you survive that long, you'll see just how easily they discard their vows." He threw a vulgar look at Lyra. "The God King has taken a dozen Sisters as wives. He—"

"None of this is important yet," Lyra hurried to interrupt. "We can talk about it after Blood Marsh, Rav. You will understand then how misguided about us Bo Hart is."

"*If* you survive," Bo growled. "Remember, Rav, when you're stuck in Blood Marsh, lost, suffering, destroying everything you care about to survive that little bit longer, it's all for a conversation about how you're a tool for their plans."

Rav sat in silence, Bo's attempt at sowing discord between him and Lyra obvious—as long as he distrusted her, he would keep to their deal and provide information for Bo. All the references to whoever Baron Glass had killed had also only been said to make him fear claiming his own Heaven's Tear. As long as Bo thought him ignorant, he wouldn't think of him as a threat. He wouldn't guess at what was in his neck.

Rav waited for the right moment to fail sneaking a distrusting glance at Lyra, which Bo caught with a glint in his eye. *There*. He wiped the sweat off his face to hide his smile. Who was going to trick who?

Chapter 7

The caravan trundled through the city's main portcullis, the guards manning it watching them from the shade with loaded crossbows, their faces hidden behind smooth, bone helmets. Out the other side, they emerged into a wall of noise—children playing, blacksmiths hammering, merchants haggling. Everything was cramped, as though they'd tried to fit as much as they could between the main wall and, up the soft mountain slope, the secondary wall that protected the Keep. Most buildings were made of wood, those near the gate dour, while deeper into the heart of the city, where the vibrancy from the markets bloomed, stone buildings with hanging banners displaying insignias had been dyed a multitude of colours. Narrow, zigzagging roads ran between them, not allowing anything to travel more than a few hundred steps before you had to turn. Only the numerous alleys allowed people to walk directly between different sectors, crowds of people dressed a bit smarter than those in the villages, their hair long and braided, marching through them.

The caravan bumbled along the wall towards an open space with stables, and as it turned a corner, a smell almost as rancid as Ghoul Wood wafted over them from the sewers. Rav held his nose and gagged, while Bo took a deep breath and laughed. At the stables, their carriage convoy came to a stop. Rav hopped off to collect his belongings with Han and Lyra.

"I've some business to do," Bo told Rav. "I'll find you when I'm done. Don't die before I can save you and you can pay me."

Rav nodded, and Bo left, disappearing in the bustling crowds.

Lyra threw one last glare his way, then faced Han. "Rav and I will go see Baron Glass; there is some business for us to discuss. May the World bless your coming search, Sister. H' hua'."

"H' hua'," Han replied, then looked to Rav. "Hu v' sh."

"Aye, I'll listen."

The three walked to the edge of the market before separating, Rav and Lyra heading up the slope. *So many people*. Rav paused, staring at the market rush. *So many strangers*. He pulled his shoulders in, lowered his head, and crossed his arms, following Lyra as close as he could. She marched into the crowd, her bags stacked above her head, and the packed streets parted as she moved through them, many people giving her respectful nods and even throwing Rav amicable looks. He ensured no one even brushed him, the memory of Janson's ambush lingering on his mind. Breaking out of the market, the winding streets opened up more. Rav remained small, still flinching at any sudden movement near him. This area was wealthier than the lower city, everyone dressed in better materials, and there were no waste wells.

Lyra stopped a few times to check where she was going, the Keep seeming close, but each straight path leading there either shot off to the side or became a dead end. At last, she found the alleyway she was looking for. It led further up before passing between two garrison houses to end at the inner wall gate, where thick, metal bars latticed to block the path forward. Few people were around, gate guards in thicker armour watching them approach.

"We have come to see Baron Glass under the invitation of Ar T'ch Shr'," Lyra announced as they reached the gate.

A guard nodded. "Sister Ee La' Bol will receive you."

They soon heard footsteps as an old woman with dark skin and frizzy silver hair walked across the courtyard towards them in a long, green coat. Rav readied himself as he looked at her eyes.

Warm honey shining in sunlight. The enthralment struck, but he forced it to break. Unlike Han, Ee La' Bol wasn't fazed.

Lyra indicated herself and Rav. "I am Sister Ha'th Bey Riene and this is my Called One, Rav."

"Do you have Ar T'ch Shr's token?" Ee La' Bol asked, her accent more common than the other Sisters', familiar with the language. Once she saw Lyra take it out her bag, she raised her eyebrow at Rav. "How much King's Blood did you drink?"

He looked to Lyra, who nodded, then he answered, "Three drops."

Ee La' Bol nodded in approval. "Come, Baron Glass will see you." She signalled for the guards to let them through, and the heavy gate was heaved open.

Blue banners displaying Baron Glass' insignia, a white hexagonal crystal, were displayed along the Keep walls, maids and porters whizzing about under them to deliver messages or move food from the storehouses into the Keep. Guards were posted at every entrance, armed with pikes.

"Have you travelled far?" Ee La' Bol asked, servants parting around her while giving quick bows.

"From Baron Hewett's territory," Lyra answered.

"Has the Baron recovered?"

Rav frowned. "From what?"

"Baron Hewett lost his central guard in a skirmish entering Ut Sh'za, the second layer," she explained. "A rival Baron from the third layer ambushed him, trying to steal his Heaven's Tear. Only he and his Champion survived, both fleeing the Sink to gather a new army. There were whispers about it for those who listened."

"Tibald Sar," Rav muttered, eyes widening. "What about the Baron who ambushed him?" he hurried to ask. "Will they continue hunting Baron Hewett? Will they chase him to Stone's Way?" *Is Pitt in danger?*

Ee La' Bol gave him a confused look, then turned to Lyra.

"Stone's Way is safe, Rav," Lyra assured him. "Leaving the Sink is not easy—" She caught herself too late, sighing as she saw Rav latch onto her mistake. "Ga'thew' binds all who enter it, and the deeper you go, the harder it is to exit. Think of it like an arrowhead: easy to pierce in, but hard to pull out. It is still possible, though, just... painful. Bo managed it, as has Baron Glass."

Ee La' Bol tutted. "Pain is not the correct way to describe it, Sister. Leaving Ga'thew' is like trying to climb out your own mind. Once you go deep enough, no one even wants to go back."

Sweat dripped down Rav's back, his hands clammy. A Sister like Han would have dragged him straight to the third layer. Even if he'd survived whatever monsters lurked there, would he have managed to get out? He gazed at Lyra. At least she'd spared him that fate. Still, he needed to learn much more if he wanted to avoid falling into traps without even realising it.

Lyra held his hands, lips pursed, voice soft. "You do not need to worry about the binding now. Focus on Blood Marsh."

Rav pulled his hands away, fighting off a grimace as he stared into her eyes.

"Hurry," Ee La' Bol called, having walked ahead of them. "Baron Glass is a busy man."

Inside the Keep, fires and wall-mounted torches shed light in the bare, narrow corridors, the windows all archer slits. There were no chairs or tables, and Rav couldn't even smell ale in the dank stone. Ee La' Bol led them down the winding corridors with efficient precision to a small banquet hall at the back of the Keep, its table already laden with steaming food. Three places had been set, but no one else was inside.

"You can wait in Boar Hall for Baron Glass. I have other matters to attend to." Ee La' Bol shut the doors behind her as she left.

Lyra took a seat to the right of the head while Rav paced around. The weight of the mountain beside them seemed to press on the air, his skin prickling under the pressure. No breeze, no windows, no respite. It was as though he'd been buried alive. Turning around, he caught Lyra's eye and hurried to lose it, staring at the food on the table. The pressure grew heavier as the space around him seemed to become tighter.

"Send a pigeon to Jinkin, for Zera to receive herself," someone ordered as they approached Boar Hall, their voice high-pitched yet masculine, like a singer's. "Tell her I've found another promising unit for Varheart." A tall, thin man with dirty-blond hair and delicate features barged open the doors to the hall, his armour made from green scales. He had no beard and no blemishes, looking like a handsome performer. A silver napet adorned his neck. Baron Glass waved away the guard at his side as he flicked his gaze between Rav and Lyra. "Now, leave. I have guests."

He took his seat at the table head as the guard closed the doors again while leaving, then started eating barehanded. "Siere's friends, yes?" He didn't take his eyes off the food, speaking between mouthfuls. "She saved me from a pack of mutants when I first travelled U'ul Ba'a and has been holding onto that favour ever since. To think she'd use it on you." He waved at Rav, who flinched back. "Sit and state what you want."

Rav remained tensed as he sat opposite Lyra, gaze never leaving Baron Glass, as though he were watching a coiled snake. The wave he'd done had come from nowhere, and even the way he ate was tricksy, everything appearing obvious but hiding some hidden threat.

Baron Glass sneered. "How are you so timid? I thought you'd been Called. Between that and the King's Blood, you must have seen things far more terrifying than Ah' ke already." He sipped from his wine cup. "If you're a coward, then leave and return Siere's token to her. Blood Marsh is not for the weak."

Rav gritted his teeth, fist tightening.

"We have come to find a scavenger unit to join," Lyra hurried to explain with a smile. "One with promise."

"I know a few," Baron Glass muttered, "but the Nameless boy might not be accepted. People won't want to lug a sack of bones around Blood Marsh even if he has been Called. No one will die for him just because of his importance to you Sisters. You should understand that this place is more practical than that."

"I will be accompanying Rav the entire time," Lyra stated. "No one will have to worry for his safety except me."

"Hmm." Baron Glass paused before clicking his tongue. "I know a unit that will accept him, then. Stay here for the night; you can meet them tomorrow."

Lyra nodded. "Thank you."

"Let me tell you something, Nameless." Baron Glass licked his greasy fingers. "I wasn't Called, I didn't drink any King's Blood, but here I am, a Baron with a Heaven's Tear and a Sister at my side. I am what everyone in Blood Marsh dreams of being. Nothing you've been given matters. Only what you take will last because that is all you can protect." He stood, his plate finished. "If we meet again, you will bow to me, or I will cast you out and banish you from my land. Don't bother bracing yourself like we're going to fight either; it wouldn't make any difference if I wanted to kill you anyway." He glanced at Lyra. "Train him better, Sister." Done, he left the hall, joining with his guard again outside to continue their conversation.

"Eat," Lyra snapped, pointing Rav to the remaining banquet food. "Blood Marsh is not your home; the weak have no status here. Learn this lesson now because once you step outside Baron Glass' territory, there are no rules and little order. You *will* be great, Rav, and then you can act as you like, but for now, be polite." She sighed, flicking the table. "It is my fault; I should have told you this when you acted so rude to Baron Hafar."

Rav tore off a chunk of roasted meat with a scowl. Why should he have to bow before men like Baron Glass? They didn't deserve it; if anything, they should've been reviled by all. ...But it was the smart thing to do. It would just be an act to get what he wanted anyway, so what did it matter? To free Pitt... aye, he could stomach it.

Rav woke early in the cot-bed he'd been provided, hands itching. He clenched his fists to stop himself picking at the scabs and listened to Lyra sleeping in the bed next to him. As he lay in the dark, the pressure of Mount Don descended again, and his chest seized, breaths choked. Donsden was huge, Blood Marsh even bigger, and Mount Don was the biggest thing he'd ever seen. People were everywhere. People he didn't understand. People he *couldn't* understand. Why were they here? Why couldn't they be content living safe lives with their families? At the end of it all, wasn't that what they wanted anyway? So why bother fighting mutants and killing each other when they could just go home now?

Greed. Even someone like Baron Glass, who'd gotten everything anyone wanted, couldn't suppress his lust for more. And he'd dared act so haughty in front of him? How could someone be so proud of displaying their corrupted ideals? He could have his stupid mountain; Pitt was worth a thousand Blood Marshes.

Rav connected to his Heaven's Tear and used its inky haze to block out the surrounding world, the stifling feeling dissipating. He practised moulding the smoke, lining his skin and sculpting ghouls. Like this, he wasn't alone. Thinking of the Ghoulsmen, he tried to replicate their faces with the miasma, but the wisps were too vicious, warping the kind features that made his friends into devilish grins. Rav scattered the figments with a sigh.

He rolled onto his side and spotted two nightmares within the Keep. What fears did they hold? Maybe one belonged to Baron Glass. Rav gathered his energy and started building a tendril towards the closest one, headache piercing, focus waning, until finally, he reached it. Ee La' Bol. She too feared being cast out of Heaven, just like Siere. Rav broke the connection and extended the tendril to the next one, thread by thread, more and more miasma squeezing out his body— *Ah*. Sharp pain shot through his brain, the connection to his Heaven's Tear broken. Massaging his temples, he rested until a shaft of light shined through the slit window of their room.

Lyra soon woke and, after a small breakfast alone, led him to meet with Ee La' Bol at the Keep's front entrance.

"Here." Ee La' Bol handed Lyra a note. "The Blood Hounds have a good reputation."

Lyra accepted the paper. "Thank you, Sister. I will visit the outpost before visiting them. H' hua',"

"H' hua'," Ee La' Bol replied.

They walked out of the inner wall area and back into the busy streets until they arrived at a large stone building in the east of the city. A small, empty reception room inside led into a gated area, where another Sister stood guard. Rav kept his gaze down to avoid eye contact with her.

"Sit here while I ask about your second Calling," Lyra commanded before speaking Earth and Thunder to the other Sister and being allowed inside the main room.

Rav sat on the available wooden bench until he went numb, rereading his journal from Pitt to pass the time. When Lyra returned, she signalled for them to leave right away, her brow furrowed and lips pursed.

"What did you find?" Rav whispered.

"Do not tell anyone about what you experienced," she hissed back, covering her mouth as she spoke. "Your first Calling may have come from the Heaven's Tear itself; if others know you had a second, they might guess at what is behind your napet." She continued marching towards the portcullis leading to the east side of Mount Don.

Rav blinked before hurrying to block her way, looking her in the eye. "Is the thing I have alive?"

"It is part of the World." Lyra shrugged. "I thought you understood that already."

Rav made to touch his napet but held his hand back upon seeing the citizens around him. He grimaced. There was more to it, he was sure, but pressing further like this wouldn't get him any answers from Lyra. He tried another angle. "Have other people had this?"

"Yes, but their information is stored deeper in the Sink. Now, come on; we are late."

Rav sighed before chasing after her. If that was true, he'd never find out what this meant. Out of the city, they followed a track around the base of the mountain, leading them to a large town.

"This is Kroom Town," Lyra said. "The unit you are to join is waiting here for their next scavenge." She led the way, heading towards the tavern section.

Rav looked around at the cobbled stone buildings and stoic people, finding it the same as towns he had travelled through on his way to Donsden. They approached The Last Drink tavern and inn, a three-storey building, and entered. Laughter, chairs scraping across the wooden floor, and people banging on tables assaulted him from all sides. The stink of strong ale and bodies unwashed from days of travelling hit him. Everyone wore a napet. The main event was an arm wrestle occurring in the centre of the room.

Two men with arms thicker than Rav's thighs grasped each other's palms, veins pulsing, sweat pouring. One was bald and had a tattooed head, his teeth crooked, his nose set to one side from a poorly healed break. The other one had wild, long hair hanging down either side of his face, brown like his beard. He looked older by a decade or so due to the emerging wrinkles on his forehead. Rav saw the Blood Palm set into his breastplate. A Champion. The man squeezed harder, his eyes bulging.

"*Argh*," the bald man growled, unable to take the surge of strength. He watched as his hand edged closer and closer to the tabletop.

"*Come on*," one of his companions roared in his ear. "*Take him down*."

Just as his hand was about to hit the table, his grip shifted, and he pushed the other man's hand back to the mid-point.

"Is that all you've got, Izen?" He grinned, jaw clenched.

Izen breathed harder, sending spittle spraying over the table. He regained control of the fight, sinking his opponent's hand back down again.

"Too... weak," Izen hissed.

"Too... old," the bald man countered, but his hand continued its descent, no surge of strength coming this time. The back of his hand smacked the table.

Izen stood up, knocking his chair to the floor, arms raised in triumph. He grinned at his scowling opponent. "Too bald."

The crowd swelled with laughter. "Izen, Izen," they chanted, spilling ale in celebration as they patted his back.

"Get Mulk a drink," Izen ordered, and a mug of ale was soon set in front of the bald man, who stared at it for a moment.

"Ah, next time." Mulk slapped the table, joining the revelry.

They each downed a mug, Izen gazing around the audience to show off before choking on his drink as he spotted Lyra watching him. Everyone's gaze turned in her direction.

"Sister." Izen walked over and bowed, leaving the rest to continue their fun. "Baron Glass' messenger informed us about you. I am Champion Izen Delmare, leader of the Blood Hounds. Welcome to our unit." He looked behind her to Rav. "Is this the one you're guiding, the Nameless Called One?"

"This is Rav," Lyra corrected. "He is here to learn."

Rav stepped closer to Izen, chin raised, finding himself half a head shorter. "I'll do my best."

Izen smirked, then turned away. "Come, we're leaving at dawn. I'll introduce you to the others."

The crowd parted as the Champion returned, nodding to Lyra while eyeing Rav.

Izen grabbed Mulk's shoulder, turning him to face the pair. "This is Contender Mulk Garr."

Another man emerged from the crowd, brown-eyed, lithe, with short blond hair.

"Contender Piyo Yaem," Izen said.

Next to Piyo was "Contender Miels Bartov"—a black-haired, stocky man who resembled a walking boulder—and last was "Contender Amine Son", an androgynous person with scalp-short hair and big eyes. Lined up before Lyra, Izen displayed his unit with a puffed chest. Rav examined them all. They looked strong. They *felt* strong.

"I am Ha'th Bey Riene," Lyra muttered after glancing over them. "Rav will be under my care, but I would appreciate you assisting him out on the marsh. He is a quick learner and sure to become a valuable member of your unit if given time."

"A Nameless Called One, eh?" Mulk wrinkled his nose at him. "I'll be watching my back."

"Is that all the armour you have?" Miels sneered at Rav's chainmail.

"How can we keep him alive like that?" Piyo followed.

"He's to be a porter for us," Amine spoke, their voice flat. They glanced at Rav's thin arms. "Our task is to let him accompany us, not to keep him alive."

"*Enough*," Izen huffed. "Baron Glass himself requested for Rav to join us. I'll not disappoint him... will you?" They lowered their heads as he eyed them. "Are you drinking with us?" Izen asked Rav and Lyra. "Since we'll be protecting each other, it'll be good to know who's at your side."

"I have preparations to make, but Rav will stay," Lyra declined, leaning close to whisper in Rav's ear. "Stay here. I will return soon."

Rav watched her pay for a room for them upstairs, then go, wanting to reach out and stop her but holding his arm back. What could be so important that she'd leave him alone? Was it about whatever she'd learned at the outpost? What if another person like Bo Hart approached him?

"Here." Izen stuffed a mug into Rav's hand. "Drink. Put more meat on you."

Rav sipped at it as he glanced around the tavern of leering faces, recalling the last time he'd had ale in detail. Would anyone ambush him this time? He moved to the corner of the room, where he could guard his back.

"Don't you drink where you're from?" Mulk growled. "Men should gulp their ale and stand tall."

"Easy, Mulk," Amine murmured, patting the large man's shoulder. "He's just nervous." They joined Rav by the corner and smiled at him. "How long have you been in the Sink?"

Rav drew a snarl before flattening it. Lyra had told him to be polite, hadn't she? Even if the Blood Hounds went digging for information on him, he had to remain calm. "A month."

Amine nodded. "I knew the Name and face of everyone in my home, a small fishing village at the edge of a lake called SunYuk. You get more used to seeing so many strangers, but I still don't like the crowds here."

Rav examined them again. Was this one of the people he was looking for? Someone like Wakeman? "My home is the same."

"I doubt that." Amine chuckled. "SunYuk is far away from here and has many different customs to what you know. Here, you are 'he' or 'she'; in our language, you are 'zun', meaning 'person'. The closest word you have is 'they'. Being a 'zun' means being an individual. If you want to, you can be your own family with your own Name."

Rav frowned. "What? How can you be your own family? How would your Name be passed down?"

Amine shrugged. "Our Names didn't have to be passed down. Most people chose to have children to continue their families, but if you had a relationship with yourself or another that couldn't result in pregnancy, it didn't matter. Our Names are what they used to be; a way to identify you. There is no legacy behind it; we were all free to be ourselves."

Rav blinked. "I don't understand. Carrying on your family is... My brother's going to have a child, and I've never seen him happier. Having children to give your Name to is essential. It's a duty," Rav stated. "I've not known anyone to not perform it."

"Is that why you have come to the Sink? Are you here to get a Name so you can have a family?"

Rav tilted his head with a half-smile. "I'm here because the World Called me."

Amine covered their mouth, patters of laughter ringing out. "I understand. Do you want to see your brother?"

"I *will* see him." Rav gazed into his ale.

"If you returned home, would you be welcome?" Amine's voice was soft.

"Aye. They didn't want me to leave. They're waiting for me."

"Well, I hope you do see them again, then." Amine sat back, shoulders dropping.

Rav pursed his lips. No mention of how he had to stay in the Sink for the World? It didn't seem like they were a fanatic. "Who does Izen serve?" he asked.

"No one, though many have tried to recruit him. His Baron died years ago, and he hasn't been beaten in a Challenge since."

Rav scratched his head. Another good sign. But something still didn't feel quite right. As he continued staring into his ale, he realised what had been off about Amine's description of SunYuk. "You said were," he mumbled. "You said you *were* free to be yourselves in SunYuk." Had their home been enslaved as well?

"Ah." Amine pulled a sombre smile. "A plague came off the water. There's only me and my Zic, my sibling, left."

Rav flinched like his heart had been pricked by a sliver of glass. If Pitt was gone... No, he wouldn't let that happen.

"I'm in the Sink now, with new friends," Amine finished, indicating the rest of the Blood Hounds.

"Amine." Mulk lumbered over. "Have you asked him what he's good at yet? Don't tell me he can't even fight."

"I can use a spear and throw knives," Rav grumbled.

Mulk waited for more, meeting silence. "That's it? Why d'you get a Sister to guide you through the Sink?" he huffed. "You can't even carry our bags." He trudged away.

"I'll speak to him." Amine stood. "The others are only acting like this because they think you'll worsen their chances of being recruited by Jinkin. Izen and I understand that you'll *help* us join them." They walked over to the other Blood Hounds, leaving Rav alone, sipping the remainder of his ale.

Not long later, he spotted Amine wind through the crowd to exit the tavern. Mulk, Piyo, and Miels continued throwing him grouchy looks, as though he were the source of a bad smell. Rav got up and headed outside as well. It was late afternoon, the sky filled with lazy clouds. He didn't see Amine out the door and wandered further out to see more of Kroom Town. The sound of stone hitting stone caught his attention, a welcome reminder of Pitt. Rav followed it to a group of people building a house at the edge of the town, watching as they coated each of those small stone cubes in some grey paste before stacking them on top of each other.

As time passed, he noticed a woman with a bow watching him from afar, recognising her from the tavern. She was standing further in town, hiding behind a stall. A while later, she left the stall but circled around to the side of a building to continue observing him. Rav drew his knife and pretended to play with it, watching her reflection in the blade. Aye, she was stalking him, and not with curiosity. He gripped his knife tighter as she took a glance at the builders near him. She was waiting until he was alone to strike. The back of Rav's neck went itchy. Another person like Janson. The afternoon sun was dropping, the temperature cooling.

Rav headed back to The Last Drink, but Lyra still hadn't returned. He sucked his teeth before going back out again. The woman needed to be dealt with now; she couldn't be allowed to continue hunting him.

As he walked towards the outskirts of Kroom Town, she began trailing him. Rav searched for a place where he could lead her out of sight and crush her chest, but Kroom Town had many wide streets, its buildings set apart from each other. At last, around the back of a large estate similar to Baron Hafar's home, he spotted an alley, aiming for it. The woman was still following. Rav acted lost, looking around the area before huffing and heading into the alley. Under the cover of its shadows, he readied his knife, listening to her approaching footsteps. *Pa, pa, pa, pa.* They stopped. Did she know he was waiting? No, she was just waiting to avoid suspicion. Or was she? Hadn't it now been too long for her to be acting cautious? He hurried back out the alley, knife raised, ready to— Gone. The woman had vanished.

Chapter 8

Rav hurried to search the wide streets, not seeing any place where she could be hiding. Frowning, he checked the ground for her footprints, a set heading towards the alley before ending in a cluster of others. She'd come close, he'd even heard her, so how had she managed to disappear so quickly? Where had she gone? Standing in the middle of the street, shivers wriggled down his back. He was too exposed; she could hit him from any direction with her bow. Rav raced back to The Last Drink, standing in the corner again, where he could watch the door.

Had she realised he'd spotted her? Then the next time she stalked him, she'd be more careful. What if he didn't notice her again? Where was Lyra? Glancing at the Blood Hounds, he caught Izen's eye before turning away. They wouldn't help him—they'd made that clear. He took a breath. In a crowded room, he only had to be careful of those who came close to him. But Izen kept watching him. Rav caught something in his eye. Concern. But not for him. *From* him. The other members of the Blood Hounds were twitchy, sweaty, breathing quickly, as if they were preparing to fight. Wait, where was Piyo? Both he and Amine were still missing. *Bang*. The tavern door opened, and Amine waltzed inside with easy steps, waving to the others, then joining Rav.

He clenched his fists to stop his hands shaking, tensing his voice to stop its wobble. "Have you seen Lyra?"

Amine shook their head, then smiled at him. "No. Still nervous? There's no need to be; you're a member of our unit now." Amine patted his shoulder. "You have the support of the Blood Hounds. That means something in Blood Marsh."

Rav smiled back, weak, dropping his head as he went quiet. Something red caught his eye. Was that... blood under Amine's sleeve? He smothered his gulp and withdrew his gaze from them, staring out at the tavern instead. The blood was fresh. Had there been a fight? Wouldn't he have noticed if Amine had been ruffled? Aye, their clothes were still tidy, their hands clean. What if they'd hidden signs of them fighting, though? Why? He shifted away from Amine in his chair, pretending to stretch.

"I didn't see you when I went outside," he commented.

"I went to the butchers to get meat for tomorrow," Amine responded as they pulled their sleeve down.

"Oh." Rav readied his knife, too aware of how Amine was watching his every move out the corner of their eye.

The tavern door opened again, and Lyra walked in. He rushed to her, but Amine's leg was out to trip him. *Ak.* Tumbling to the floor, he felt something touch the back of his neck, then, *ting*. His napet came loose and clattered next to him, exposing his burned neck. He snatched it up and scampered to Lyra while others jeered at him.

"Are you alright?" Amine called after him, the other Blood Hounds going back to chatting as though they hadn't been ready to pounce.

Lyra helped Rav stand, then marched forward and grabbed Amine by the throat, pinning them against the tavern wall. Everyone went quiet, the Blood Hounds wide-eyed and frozen in place. Amine wriggled and writhed, pawing at Lyra's arm but powerless to remove it. Lyra stared at them the entire time, blue eyes unblinking. As Amine's hissing became choking, Izen stepped closer with his hands raised but stopped when he saw Lyra touch her sword. Mulk and Miels flinched back. Rav stood at Lyra's back, snarling at anyone else who dared to move. Amine was losing strength, going limp. Lyra squeezed harder.

Rav glanced behind him, seeing every tendon in Amine's neck bulge as the skin got tighter and tighter around their throat as their head swelled red. Was Lyra really going to—

Lyra threw Amine's body at Mulk and Miels, knocking them over before staring down Izen. The Champion lowered his head and kneeled, neither Mulk nor Miels daring to look at her either.

"I'll repay you," Izen whispered as Mulk and Miels hurried to help Amine breathe again.

Lyra sneered at him before grabbing Rav by the collar and leading him up the tavern stairs to the rooms, entering the one she'd rented.

Door shut, Rav hurried to speak. "A woman was following me. She—"

"You need to learn quicker," Lyra hissed, throwing her bags onto a bed. "You need to protect yourself."

Tongue caught in his throat, he looked at the floor. "I know..."

"Stop that," Lyra snapped, eyes fierce. "I will not let you continue acting like this. I will not always be here to save you. Ga'thew' is not a place for you to wallow in self-pity. I have been patient, Rav. I have been lenient. Get stronger. Now."

Useless, reckless, Nameless.

He cowered back. "I..."

"*Weak*," Lyra shouted. "Where is it, Rav? Where is the man who tore apart that wolf? Who slaughtered a Contender? Where is the drive that you started with?" She grabbed his chin and forced him to face her, blue eyes boring into him. "You cannot keep coming and going. You cannot keep sinking into yourself. You need to be thinking, fighting, growing all the time. Disappear for a moment and you will die." She glared at him, nostrils flared.

Revenge.

Rav slapped her hand away, snarling back as the Ghoul flickered over him. "Why should I get stronger? For you? For your stupid World? I don't want to die for your plans; I don't even want to be here. You dragged me into the Sink; you dragged me away from my home. I *loved* Pitt. I *was* loved in Pitt. Can you even understand that? My life was blissful before you people from the Sink tore it apart. You took everything I had, and yet you still want more."

Lyra's rage froze to ice. "You know nothing of the World."

"Don't I?" Rav stared her in the eyes. "I'm supposed to be its instrument, right? I've had two Callings, haven't I? I've had more interaction with the World and its plans than you ever have. Isn't your life and your purpose to serve me? So, take me back to Pitt, kill Baron Hewett and Tibald Sar, then leave me alone."

Lyra slapped him. "Spiteful and ignorant. You will die here," she spat.

"Gladly." Rav grinned, mouth bleeding. "Just to see your plans fail."

Lyra flinched at the sight, ferocity gone. "Who are you, Rav?"

"Who are you, Ha'th Bey Riene?" he snapped back. "You look so similar to a real person, sometimes I believe you are, but you live so far away in Heaven you don't understand the world you're working for. If my Calling means I'll become like you, I'd rather die here so my family never sees me that way." He stomped to the door and opened it. "You're right about one thing, though: I'm tired of being sad." He slammed the door behind him.

Rav wandered the streets of Kroom Town alone, hunting for the mysterious woman in the half-moonlight. Once he found her, once he caught her, the Ghoul would be ready to rip off her limbs and bathe in her blood. But where was she?

"*Ah.*" He punched a wall, then quickly clutched his hand from the pain.

That was stupid. Stupid Rav.

How many stupid mistakes had he made already? If he hadn't cauterised the back of his neck, that would've been it. Dead. The Blood Hounds would've split his head in two for his Heaven's Tear. Lyra had saved him yet again. Or was Ha'th Bey Riene just keeping him alive so she could force him to serve her? Rav spat blood from his busted lip. Once he was strong enough, he'd tear Heaven apart and bring all those haughty Sisters into the real world. He'd make them all just as weak as he was and see how grand their ideals became then.

Someone with long hair darted around the corner ahead, and Rav snapped to throw his knife at them. Izen tilted his head just in time to dodge it, the blade slicing the hair next to his neck.

"*Stop*," Izen shouted, hands raised, sweat beading on his forehead. "I'm not here to fight," he continued as Rav glared at him. "Even if I managed to kill you, I think the Sister would slaughter everyone in Kroom Town in revenge." He gave a dry chuckle.

"What do you want?" Rav growled, Ghoul just beneath his skin.

"To make amends," he stated. "We were greedy, but we're all still alive. Everything can be fixed. Wouldn't you like to know why we attacked you?"

Rav touched his napet. "You thought I had a Heaven's Tear."

Izen nodded. "You're an interesting one, Rav. A Nameless Called One who drank three drops of King's Blood, travelling under the protection of two Sisters, with the token of a third. Then, despite being skin on bones, you killed a strong Contender who'd also been Called. The pieces were all there—you're someone important."

Rav shook his head. "That's not enough to condemn me; otherwise, I'd have been attacked already."

"That's true. If you'd have had a Heaven's Tear, you couldn't have hidden it past Baron Hafar and Baron Glass. So, maybe you just know a special technique. That's what we thought. But then we found an answer to a question I'm sure you're wondering about: why did Contender Janson attack you?"

Rav paused, disconnecting from the Ghoul.

"I doubt you've heard of Contender Suukor Madini, but she seems to know about you," Izen continued. "Piyo and Amine captured her while she was following you. She's still alive if you want to speak to her."

Rav hardened his expression and marched over to him. "Take me to her."

Izen led him to a building in the centre of Kroom Town with Mulk and Miels standing guard outside. As they arrived, Miels opened the door, and they entered a small, empty room lit by a candle. Izen crouched by a spot at the back of the room, pulling up handles to a trapdoor, then lifting a section of the wooden floor up to reveal a ladder down to a basement. Rav followed Izen down into an earthy room with a brazier blazing in the centre. The walls were made of pact dirt that made it humid in the heat. A woman had been tied to a chair next to the brazier, Piyo watching her from the corner. A brunette with freckles and a burn under her chin. Sweating. Distressed. Naked.

"This is Contender Suukor Madini," Izen introduced her.

Suukor looked up at Rav as he studied her. "Please." Her voice was hoarse. "Forgive me. I thought it was my duty," she pleaded. "It was wrong. You'll never see me again."

Rav inspected her torn fingernails and burns. It looked like she had been cut, then had the wounds cauterised. She stank. He avoided the puddle of waste dripping off her chair as he stood before her in silence.

"What duty?" He kept his voice monotone.

"My Calling. I was Called to find you," she stammered. "I had a vision of you, of killing you. In the vision, after I kill you, I cut open your head and find a Heaven's Tear. It was my Calling, I swear."

Rav kept his expression blank, Izen and Piyo watching him. Why would the World tell others about his Heaven's Tear? Hadn't Lyra said those Called didn't come into conflict with each other? "If you're Called, then where's your guide?"

"I haven't met a Sister yet," she whimpered. "I came to Blood Marsh with my Baron, but he died two months ago. The Calling only came last month. Thirty-two days, that's all."

Rav fought harder to keep his face blank. Wasn't that when he'd arrived in the Sink? When he'd received his second Calling.

What was going on? "Tell me about this Heaven's Tear," he ordered.

"It was, it was..." Suukor started rocking back and forth in the chair. "I don't know; I never saw it used. But it has something to do with the woods," she managed. "Yes, it's part of the information on you. The woods, the woods... I can't remember... *Wait*. Ghoul, Ghoul Wood. Rav Carvell from Ghoul Wood has a Heaven's Tear. That's how I knew. I saw you enter the tavern with a Sister and heard your name was Rav. I wasn't going to kill you, I wasn't." She shook her head vigorously. "I needed to confirm you were the right Rav first."

Carvell? Why wouldn't the Calling say that he was just Rav now? It seemed to know everything else about him. Or did it? Neither Janson nor Suukor were certain he was the person from their visions, but he could recall every detail of the Ghoul he'd seen. Even if it was surrounded by a dozen others, he could pick it out. What about the battle in the snow, though? That was blurry. Strange, but he needed to survive first if he wanted to find any answers. Two Contenders had come for him in a month. How many more had had Callings and were out waiting to hear his name? How many strangers would hear the rumours and come for him? Rav paused, then faced Izen.

"Send for Lyra."

Izen called up to Miels, and a short while later, the trapdoor opened, Lyra descending into the basement.

"Has she been Called?" Rav asked.

Lyra looked at Suukor while Rav waited. "Yes, but..." She scrunched her forehead. "It is not the same as you. Her connection to the World is off. It feels lazy, like she has only been asked to perform a small task, unimportant." Lyra faced Rav. "I have never heard of anything like this. Those Called should never come into conflict."

"Was Janson's Calling the same?"

Lyra nodded. "I thought it was because he had chosen Han to be his guide."

"Is that all you know?" Rav asked Suukor.

"Yes, that's everything, everything. Rav Carvell from Ghoul Wood has a Heaven's Tear for me to take. That's what I saw." She looked up, imploring.

Rav pulled a pained smile.

"What should we do with her?" Izen asked, drawing his longsword.

"Kill her." Rav sighed.

Izen lunged forward and pierced her through her eye, then wiped his swordpoint on a piece of cloth as her body slumped down. "It's good to know you can make difficult decisions," he said. "If she spoke to us, she'd speak to others. Should we pursue this further? We know who she's associated with and where she's from."

Rav yawned, exhaustion setting in. "No. Would you tell anyone the location of a Heaven's Tear? All we'd do is tell people that we killed her, then they'd want revenge. Just leave it. The fewer people who know about this, the better."

Izen nodded. "A fair assessment. You may return to The Last Drink if you have no further requests for us tonight. We'll clean this up. If you still want to join the Blood Hounds, meet us at dawn for our scavenge up Mount Don. What happened today will never be repeated even if you do get a Heaven's Tear."

Rav climbed out the basement with Lyra, the pair walking in silence back to the tavern.

"Will you continue in the Sink?" Lyra whispered.

Rav sucked his teeth but nodded.

"You do not believe in your Calling, though." Her tone was softer than a feather.

"No. From what I've seen and what happened here, I don't think there is some great destiny for us all."

"The World is real, Rav. I would not be in Heaven if It was not," Lyra murmured. "I am not dragging you off to die. Those Called receive amazing powers and opportunities."

"I know." Rav made a small smile as his eyes glistened. "I wouldn't be alive if it wasn't for you. Thank you. I am trying… so hard. It all keeps falling apart. I miss Cyrn and Kayla and

Wakeman, all of them... I always knew Wakeman would die for me, but I never thought he'd ever have to." Rav couldn't stop the tears. "I'm sorry. I've been such a burden. I've been stupid, reckless, and useless—everything I wanted to change."

"It is that stupid, reckless Rav that the World has Called. And while you may not have Pitt, you have me," Lyra promised. "Your Calling can wait. It will happen when you are ready. You can do this, Rav. I have seen the brave and cunning man you could be."

"The man I will be."

"Aye," Lyra said, imitating a Pitt accent.

They laughed.

Chapter 9

The Blood Hounds were ready before the sun was up. Izen had his hair tied into a ponytail, standing before the unit, Rav and Lyra included. Amine was absent.

"We'll be entering Blood Marsh. I will be leading; my decisions are final. You will listen, or you will be discarded."

Grim-faced, they all agreed.

"Rav, you're to be a porter. If you can't do something, tell us. No one will die for your mistakes. Amine will show you what to do after they recover." Izen lifted up a thick sheet of paper with some writing on it. "We've received a request to recover Baron Ghourts' body. His armour and hammer will be sold to our benefactor, but anything else is ours."

Mulk, Piyo, and Miels all looked excited at his last words.

"Baron Ghourts' last known battle was at the base of Mount Don, near the Brack."

That erased their energy.

"The goebber nest there is reportedly empty due to infighting, but we need to be cautious. With Lyra's support, this'll be simple. Piyo, we'll need you to track the battle quickly to avoid trouble."

"I've spoken to the survivors and know the land well," he said.

"Good. Questions?"

Everyone seemed content.

"What's a goebber?" Rav asked.

"It's a hairless mutant the length of a man," Izen answered. "They live underground in burrows, move on four legs, and are sensitive to the smell of blood. The battles in Blood Marsh provide food for their colonies. If you get bitten, clean the wound as soon as possible, or you'll die of infection. We'll talk more once we're on our way."

Rav nodded.

A carriage loaded with supplies was waiting for them, pulled by four bulky horses. Miels took the driving seat while Rav entered to see Amine resting inside, their neck mottled with black and red blotches. He sat opposite them with Lyra. No one else joined them on that side. Izen crammed next to Piyo, Mulk, and Amine. Izen, Mulk, and Piyo talked amongst themselves while Rav chewed on dried meat.

"Are we really just climbing up the Brack to find Baron Ghourts' possessions, or is this one of *those* requests?" Mulk asked. "Last I heard, Ghourts was defeated by Baron Tryxwin but fled the battlefield."

"He was injured," Piyo pointed out. "Took a hammer to his chest. Many said he coughed blood. It's been two days since he climbed the mountain; goebbers will have finished him off by now. All we'll find is bones in armour."

Mulk mulled it over before nodding. "Good. I don't like cleaning up messes, especially since this one involves Tryxwin."

"You don't have to worry about her," Izen interjected. "She's not the one who hired us. Niklaus is the one who wants her favour; we're just doing the legwork."

Piyo tilted his head at Izen. "Shouldn't we also be looking to build our relationship with her? Cata Tryxwin's not lost a battle since arriving here. It might help us to become her subordinates. Baron Glass will have one half of Mount Don, and she'll soon have the other."

"Blood Marsh isn't worth ruling." Izen shrugged. "Baron Tryxwin will build her forces, then head to Ut Sh'za just like all the others with any skill. There's no gain unless we go with her, and I'd prefer to join Jinkin."

"Jinkin is better. Tryxwin's support won't last," Mulk grumbled. "No one trusts those who use trickery to win fights." He looked to Rav. "What do you think about that? Is winning worth any sacrifice?"

Rav swallowed his mouthful. "It depends on what 'winning' is. What's the point in destroying everything your Name means in pursuit of providing for your family? You'd only ruin what you sought to protect."

Mulk nodded. "Right. Too many people who come here lie, steal, and murder to get what they want, only to take a dagger in the back. Remember this well: who's going to watch you sleep? Keep good company and you'll survive a lot longer." He paused. "It's good that you understand that. I wasn't really expecting that answer from you—"

Izen elbowed him in the gut while pretending to turn towards the window.

Rav nodded, taking a moment to gather his words. "Because I'm Nameless, right? It's alright. It's what I deserve. There was a Challenge. I interfered, dishonoured my family, and couldn't even stop a close friend from being killed." He lowered his head.

Izen, Mulk, and Piyo looked among themselves before Izen spoke. "It's always hard to lose a friend. Mulk and I arrived at Blood Marsh with an army." He gave a helpless shrug. "We're the only ones left. After our Baron died, we went looking for work, moving between different scavenging units, never finding one that lasted longer than a few months."

"Those were some rough months," Mulk mumbled. "All the good tasks were given to established units, leaving us to do the dangerous stuff. Mutant hunts, vanguard work, that type of thing. I got this face from a boulder-bear charge." He showed off his crooked teeth. "Be glad we're now in a position to just do collections, as it's some of the safest work in the marsh."

"Me and Miels were in the same position," Piyo added. "There were a dozen people in our group when we started. All dead now. But then we found Izen and Mulk, joining them for a scavenge. We've been together ever since."

"That was a crazy scavenge." Mulk chuckled. "Swarmed by wingtails, marsh lizards closing in, you and Miels were the first people who'd risked their lives for us." He grinned at Piyo.

"You did the same for me and Miels." Piyo grinned back, then glanced at Amine. "Amine was also alone, sent to recruit us into a Baron's vanguard for a hopeless battle."

Mulk guffawed. "They didn't want to die either, so they joined our unit. It's been a year now. The best year I've spent in this place."

"We work well as a group," Izen continued, smile small. "We'll achieve our dreams and the dreams of all those who fell behind."

Rav felt himself tearing up and blinked to chase the tears away, looking at the floor to hide his face. "That's what I want too. Wakeman was fierce and clever and honourable and... he was like a brother. He understood what it meant to be a Carvell." Rav's vision blurred with the tears he'd failed to stop. "Always with us, always helping even though Stone's Way wasn't his home. Whenever I needed advice, he knew what to say. He was a leader making decisions a leader should. That's why he fought to fix my mistakes. If he'd been a bit stronger, Tibald Sar would be dead." He lowered his head. "If I'd acted sooner, Wakeman would still be alive."

"Enough," Lyra huffed. "Wakeman made his Challenge on his own. You are not responsible for that or anything else that happened to Stone's Way. You already exceeded what you should have been capable of, so are you not being greedy by wanting to have done more?"

They all went quiet.

Rav wiped his face as he looked at Lyra, her expression unflinching. *Aye, no more self-pity.* There was too much work to do.

Over the rest of the journey, Izen taught Rav about the Brack—a set of rapids that flowed down Mount Don, carving out a small canyon system—and goebbers.

"Goebbers are excellent climbers," he said. "Don't fight them in narrow spaces, or they'll attack from the walls and ceiling."

Rav had his notebook out, jotting down the information.

"They're fast, agile, and they protect their heads well, able to reel back their necks like snakes to dodge blows, so aim for the main body. Sharp blades work best to cut through their skin. Use a shield to guard your legs. They use pack tactics to harass you..."

The lessons continued all afternoon.

That evening, they rested in a shanty town consisting of an inn and Healer's shack. The Blood Hounds camped around the carriage, while the innkeeper offered Lyra and Rav a free room. As Rav settled for sleep, he found a new nightmare close enough for him to reach. Amine's. Was it how much he hated a person that allowed him to see people's fears? How easily had Amine tricked him? Acting his friend just so they could strike at his neck. But now he could make them suffer for it. Rav connected a tendril to their fear.

Lying in a small bed, with a thin blanket pulled up to their chin, was a dead body. There was no fat on the face, nor a nose, leaving them skeletal, forever staring up with shrivelled eyes. It was clear that illness had wasted them away, but it wasn't the corpse that was terrifying. Amine was alone, the only thing in their village not desiccated. If Amine died, their culture, history, legacy all died with them. Amine was the last to remember. Once they were gone, it would be like everyone they'd loved had never existed.

Rav broke the connection, breath stifled. What if he were the last of Pitt? That burden might just crush him. Amine hadn't lied about their home. The reason they'd told him so much... Amine was passing on as much as they could in case they died. Rav swallowed before memorising everything Amine had told him.

The carriage continued travelling throughout the next morning, Rav learning about Jinkin from Izen.

"Organisations are better than armies, often made of several, and help protect you from mutants deeper in the Sink, but you have to be careful in choosing which one you join because of the rivalries between them," he said. "Pick one, and the others will try to kill you to stop you growing. Jinkin's the strongest organisation this side of the Sink, making it much safer than the others, but as the strongest organisation, they only accept the strongest units. Most people looking to join them have to build a solid reputation by completing scavenges." He smirked at Rav. "That's why taking you on is an opportunity for us. News of a Called One travels far, and our achievements will accompany you."

Rav nodded, noting it down.

They stopped for lunch at a far outpost. A few worn soldiers from Donsden were stationed there to keep watch over the marsh. The order of Donsden stopped there; no more roads, no more buildings, no more people ahead.

Amine approached Rav and Lyra after sipping their soup. "So...rry," they croaked, speaking their first word since being strangled.

Lyra nodded, uncaring, while Rav watched her, pensive. The sensation of burden and isolation from their fear surfaced in his chest. He softened. At least Amine had checked for his Heaven's Tear instead of attacking him right away. After he also nodded to accept their apology, Amine signalled to him, requesting him to follow them to a weapons chest. Taking out an oiled cloth, Amine started polishing the equipment, then held out a cloth for Rav. His duties. He took it and got to work. Once the metal was shining, they moved on to straps, shields, braces, breastplates—anything held together by leather was checked, cleaned, then dried. Amine smiled as Rav kept up with them, his experience from supporting the Ghoulsmen showing. He tightened the last string on a scabbard and waited for his next task. The horses were tended to, the carriage checked to be in good condition. Food supplies were plentiful. The Blood Hounds were ready.

"We're leaving the horses here," Izen told Rav. "They're too big and will attract mutants."

Everyone donned their equipment. Mulk, Izen, and Miels were in full-plate armour, while Piyo and Amine wore mutant hides to protect themselves. Mulk wielded a hammer and shield, Izen a longsword and shield, and Miels a two-handed axe. Piyo had two curved swords, while Amine only carried a shield. They all had crossbows slung over their backs. Lyra pulled a set of hide armour out of one of her bags for Rav—something he'd found too heavy to wear before. He strapped it over his chainmail, finding it still a little too big. Next, he looked at the bag filled with bolts, medicinal pastes, and spare items for repairs he'd been tasked with carrying. While strong enough to lift it, it was all he could manage. He looked at his spear, shield, and crossbow.

"I will protect you," Lyra promised, touching his shoulder. "Trust me."

Rav grimaced but nodded.

"We'll also help," Amine wheezed, carrying a bag twice the size of Rav's, containing alternate weapons and camping equipment.

"Everyone ready?" Izen called. "Let's go. I want to be back here in four days."

He led the march towards the Brack. The first stretch of land they walked across was drier and rockier than around Donsden. The water puddles sat in deep pools instead of soaking the ground into wetland. Footing was stable. They walked below the incline of the mountain, where the land was flat. The occasional insect buzzed around them, but there were few birds. They seemed to be the only group in this area.

"Let's practise," Izen said to Rav. "Bolts," he shouted.

Rav rushed to swing his bag down and open the straps, but unable to get one open, he had to pull a quiver out of a small gap. He handed the bolts to Izen, knowing he was too slow. "I tied the straps too tight," he muttered.

"That's why we practise. Fix it."

Rav loosened them.

"Burn," Mulk roared.

Rav hunted through his bag again for the salve, again arriving late.

"Learn where everything is," Mulk said.

"Water," Piyo called.

This time, Rav delivered in an acceptable time. Piyo sipped from the waterskin.

"Better," Izen said.

The afternoon passed quickly. Camp was higher up the mountain, in a dry, narrow cave that was little more than a large crack in the mountainside just big enough to fit them all, plus a fire, in. After Piyo scouted it, Amine lit the fire at the back as Izen and Miels rolled a boulder to block the entrance. Exhausted from the walk, Rav stripped off his hide armour, everything feeling heavy.

"Not bad for a first day." Mulk patted his shoulder.

"I'm... too weak."

"With another month of us feeding you, you'll be strong enough."

Amine handed Rav some more cloth-wrapped meat, and he set about scoffing down the dried slivers. Amine then retrieved a small pot from their bag and nestled it over even coals from the fire, adding broth from a flask along with more dried meat, soon having stew for the unit to slurp.

Piyo took the first watch, sitting against the cave wall as he stared out a thin gap between the boulder and entrance. Rav was exempt so he could rest as much as possible, while Lyra was free to do as she liked. After recovering some energy, Rav went through his bag.

"Which items will you need most?" he asked.

"Cleaning paste," Izen said straight away. "Goebber wounds and other cuts need cleaning to stop rot setting in."

Rav arranged those vials to the top.

"Water," Mulk added.

Always useful. Rav adjusted. "Bolts?"

"It takes too long to reload a crossbow in a dangerous situation," Miels declined.

"Knives," Piyo said.

They were already at the top.

Before he went to sleep, Rav ensured his bag was as efficient as possible.

Dawn arrived in a blink, the Blood Hounds setting off after breakfast.

"We'll soon be entering a dangerous area," Izen announced as he pointed at a rocky outcrop blocking the view ahead. "Form."

Izen took the lead position in an arced line across the dirt path, Miels and Mulk guarding his flanks. Rav and Amine rushed behind them so they were protected, while Piyo covered the back.

"Knife," Miels called.

Rav put it in Miels' hand when he reached back.

"Axe," Izen followed.

Amine used their elbow to hit the bottom of their bag, knocking the top of the axe out for them to grab and hand to Izen.

"*Ah.*" Mulk dropped to the ground, holding his leg.

Piyo covered the gap as Izen and Miels shifted across to guard him. Amine took the rear and Rav tended to him.

"Good." Izen broke position, pleased.

Lyra watched from the side. "I will act around you."

"Right," Izen agreed. "Be ready."

They fell into line, Izen leading the march into Blood Marsh.

Chapter 10

Marching at a quick pace back down the mountain to flat ground, Rav found himself able to keep up with everyone, not out of breath or sore. He smiled, the trek to Fool's March far behind him, stepping in time to the clank of Izen's armour. The short grasses and dirt paths that guided them here started to fade, the grass growing untamed while the treaded paths disappeared. More vegetation appeared, from shrubs to bright flowers. Izen steered clear of anything colourful. Ahead of them was an outcrop of rock from the mountain that formed a barrier separating them from anything beyond it. Once the Blood Hounds moved around it, Rav saw the true Blood Marsh, a wild land filled with waist-high grass and all manner of dense plant life.

Rubber trees grew around stagnant pools of water, each buzzing with dozens of Hot Foots, and moss-covered remains of abandoned structures dotted the landscape. Everything was hot, wet, and sticky. Beneath the cover of some trees, Rav spotted the figures of numerous animals. Too far away to see them in detail, he could only make out scales and tails. They roamed in packs, lounging around as they rested. The occasional bird would swoop down to harass one of them.

Yip. He jumped back, the noise coming from the mountain. A small, furry creature similar to a rodent stood on a rock, watching over the unit.

"Easy." Miels held Rav's arm to steady him. "It's a yipper; they don't attack people."

How had he missed something so close? Too busy staring off into the distance. Rav focused back on what was in front of him as they entered the marshland. *Squelch, squelch, squelch.* He sank into the ground with each step, the energy he'd been so proud of draining into the sodden ground. Looking at the others, he scowled as they danced across the marsh without a splash. Lyra wasn't even trying.

Amine shot ahead of him to whisper in Izen's ear, who then looked forward, searching for something. Amine pointed to a group of trees. Izen nodded, then signalled for the unit to move off their current path.

Once they were a safe distance from whatever had been spotted, Izen spoke. "There's a skirmish past those trees."

The Blood Hounds snapped into combat stances, weapons raised.

"Should we clean up?" Mulk asked.

Izen pondered a moment, looking at Rav. "No. We'll move around them." He turned to Lyra. "Can you cover Rav?"

"Yes."

Izen set off in an arc around the trees. Rav strode forward, but Lyra nudged his foot to the side so that it landed on a more solid patch of ground without a splash. She gave him a glance that said he was making too much noise. Rav tried to be more careful where he stepped and soon fell behind, creating a gap between him and Izen. Lyra shoved him on. As he focused on his footing, he saw a patch of grass move beside him. Rav fell back, Lyra catching him as an emerald-green snake rushed away into the undergrowth. Everyone watched him, tense. Lyra lifted him back up. Izen signalled ahead.

Clang. "Ahh!" *Splash*. "Left!" *Thunk*.

The sounds of the battle became clear as they moved closer. Izen's path led them behind a thick grove to keep the Blood Hounds out of sight of the fighting, while the area in front of them was clear so they could make a quick escape. Izen came to a stop, peering through the leaves to watch the fight. Rav, Mulk, and Miels joined him while Amine and Piyo kept watch, Lyra staring up the mountain. Half the combatants wore green-scaled armour, like Rav had seen on the tailed mutants, wielding curved swords and shields, while the others used basic brown hide and spears. It was a blur of green and brown, water splashing as they fought. The sword swings had their full weight behind them, the blocks shaking under the impact.

"*Ah*," one yelled again as they lunged.

Their opponent blocked the spearpoint with their shield, but as they swung their sword in a counterattack, they slipped, falling into the marsh. With a downward stab, the fight was over. Chaotic scenes like this played out again and again, the battle determined by the environment, not skill. Rav counted a dozen fighters, who were soon whittled down to three. Two green against one brown. The lone figure was exhausted. They saw their death and tried to flee, making it easier for the pair to cut them down from behind.

Izen urged them to run from the carnage. Rav went over the actions. Blood Marsh seemed to favour ambush attacks, relying on positioning and stealth, but his footing was too poor to do that yet. He'd learn.

Amine kept them away from mutants and other units, allowing them to reach the next campsite before dark. It was another cave, much bigger than the last, formed in the side of a small canyon they had to climb down to. Rav teetered on numb feet, the effort required to keep his balance getting here having exhausted his legs. He dropped his bags, slumping down on rough stone before kicking off his sodden boots. Reaching into his bag, he grabbed two old cloths and stuffed them inside to soak up some of the water. Firelight was too risky.

"How do you walk through the marsh?" he asked as he rubbed his soles.

Izen laughed. "Years of practice."

"You need to spread your toes wide and step in the right places," Mulk added.

"You'll get used to it," Piyo said. "Keep low."

"I am," Rav huffed.

"Go lower. Keep your arms out at your sides. Use them to balance and spread your weight over the ground."

"That's how we learned," Miels spoke.

"Low." Rav got up into position, arms out at his waist.

"Lower." Piyo pushed him down so he was almost sitting on his heels.

Rav moved around the cave. "I'll be too slow like this."

"You aren't using your arms enough." Piyo demonstrated, using his arms to pull himself along on all fours. "This keeps you low, helps you hide."

Rav copied him, finding his scrabbling movements much faster this way, though his thighs began to burn from the strain. He stood to rub them. "It'll take time to get used to," he muttered. Giving up moving around, he practised balancing in place on all fours with his bag to save his energy.

Izen looked over to him from where he'd been laying out his belt pouches into a makeshift pillow by the cave entrance. "You're used to running on more solid land."

"Aye, hills." Rav nodded. "How d'you know?"

"You stand tall when you walk. You balance well but put too much weight on each step. You look like you want to run, not crawl. Living in the Sink means adapting. Watch." Izen stood, walking from end to end of the cave in the fading light.

Rav stared until he began to glimpse the changes in Izen's steps. The Champion's pace never changed, but everything else did, like how wide he walked or if he leaned on his heels more. The more he moved, the more Rav envisioned what he was walking on, from rock to grass to marsh to sand, all transitioned between seamlessly.

"This is the foundation of all footwork techniques. They all suit the environment they were designed in, becoming useless in others unless you adapt."

Rav committed the sight to memory, thinking over it as he settled for more rough sleep on hard rock, soon finding Lyra shaking him awake in fresh dawn light.

"Up," Izen called, silhouetted in his plate armour as he tied his pouches back onto his belt. "We're not far from the Brack now. We've a day to find Baron Ghourts, then we leave. Piyo will be leading."

Lyra handed Rav a parcel of dry cheese before beckoning for him to stand with the other already gathered Blood Hounds at the cave entrance with Izen. Rav rubbed his bleary eyes as he lurched to his feet and stumbled over, coming to stand near Mulk's large figure. He stuffed himself as he listened.

Piyo stepped out from the group to stand beside Izen, head high so the strands of blond hair peeking out from under his helmet shined in the bright light. "Information from Tryxwin's Champion says that Ghourts fled up the Brack into the mountain. The survivors from his army claimed the Baron had a place to hide there, a cave system that could be connected to the goebber burrows." He faced Rav. "Do you have any open cuts?"

Rav licked the last cheese crumbs off his hands before checking on his scabs. All closed, leaving no running blood for the goebbers to smell. "No."

"Good. When we're on the mountain, we'll be visible to those in the marsh. Let's look strong to stop anyone thinking they can get anything from us." He tilted his head to Mulk.

Mulk stepped up to Rav and tapped his hide breastplate with a knuckle, his beaten face menacing as he glowered with seriousness. "Puff your chest out." He demonstrated breathing in to swell in size, looking broader.

Rav shuddered as he copied, no longer hunched.

"Carry your bag like this." Mulk grabbed Amine's, pulling it tight over his shoulders so that his arms bulged. "And step like this." He took a long stride, almost kicking off his previous position to power forward.

Rav obeyed again.

Izen nodded. "Good enough. Walk between Mulk and Miels when we're on the slope. We don't need to look like we can win every fight; it's enough to make our opponents think we're too much of a hassle to deal with. Ready? Move."

Scampering forward with his new footwork, Rav felt every muscle in his legs burn with effort but managed to keep pace with everyone while also staying quiet. Lyra still gave him the occasional nudge to stop him slipping, though. Mulk also kept giving him encouraging looks to urge him on at times. The sound of surging water grew louder until it was all Rav could hear, and finally, they reached the Brack. The river stormed down the mountainside, hidden by its steep banks. Piyo took the lead, scanning the ground for traces of battle as they headed upriver. Emerging from the vegetation, Rav sighed with relief as he stood on solid ground once more, puffing his chest out with everyone else to appear as domineering as possible. They strode onwards, *crunch, crunch, crunch,* the hard earth breaking under their heavy steps. Glancing between the broad shoulders of Mulk and Miels either side of him, a ball of fire burned within Rav's gut, feeling like he had when he'd patrolled Stone's Way with Cyrn and Wakeman.

To their right, the ground opened up, revealing the Brack—a river two men wide that thundered down Mount Don in white froth. Its banks dropped straight down, falling onto the rocks that had been eroded into blades. Rav shifted away from the edge, heart racing at the sight, glad to have Mulk between him and the drop. First, the ground started steep, then flattened towards the top of the river, providing a lip to hide the Blood Hounds from anyone watching from beneath them. They slowed, taking extra time to scout the area ahead, and, near the top, Piyo pointed to the ground. Rav recognised what he was indicating: fresh tracks from another unit. They weren't alone here. Weapons ready, they advanced until they reached the lip where the rapids ended and no longer completely drowned out their voices, the sun now at the top of its arc. The fresh tracks were now more obvious and clearly showed five sets of prints ahead of them. Izen grumbled.

"It should be around here," Piyo shouted, pointing at the cracked rocks around them. "Look for a tunnel system."

Izen raised a hand and waggled a finger. The unit split up, Amine acting as watch. Lyra stayed with Rav, the pair marching off over coarse rock to search for holes that could be the tunnel entrance. The fire in his gut still burned. He had a duty to perform. He could be useful. Rav went over to a hole and peered down to see a stream feeding the Brack.

"Help lower me," he said to Lyra as he dropped his bag.

She nodded, grabbing his arm to ease him down into the dark. No tunnels. Lyra lifted him back up. Rav collected his equipment and moved to the next spot, soon having searched a dozen other holes. Despite the Blood Hounds now having covered a large area, they were yet to find anything. *Patience*, Rav reminded himself. He looked at Piyo exploring the larger gaps in the distance, where the tunnel was most likely to be, and observed how he performed the same actions at each potential spot: check for tracks, check the gap, check beneath the rock level. Rav copied him for the next few holes. Still nothing.

Think.

If he could see everyone up here, then this land was exposed. Someone pursuing the Baron would've been able to see him hide. Where could you get out of sight? A few hundred feet from him was a tor. *There*. Rav headed over to it, the outcrop larger than he'd thought. Slowing, he glanced back at Lyra, seeing her remain calm. No danger. He continued. At the back of the rock was a drop leading down to a rock shelf above the water, the stench of rot choking the air around it. A fresh carcass. Down on the shelf, Rav spotted a figure lying on the rock; however, it was too dark to make out any details. *Is that the Baron*? He urged Lyra to help him drop down. She investigated the gap, then nodded. Rav held her arm tight and lowered himself into buzzing flies, then released Lyra's arm to drop to the ground.

The carcass was long, hairless, torn open by talons, and festering with maggots. A dead goebber. Not Ghourts. He spun around, relieved that there were no holes he could be attacked from, but his foot knocked the corpse, causing a swarm of flies to swarm around him as the body fell apart, black liquid oozing. Seeing Lyra's waiting arm, Rav kicked off the wall to grab it and was pulled up to safety.

"What was it?" she asked.

"Goebber carcass." Rav spat a fly out of his mouth.

As they walked back around the outcrop, Amine hurried over while beckoning them to follow with a wave of their hand. Rav and Lyra ran over to the gathered unit, who were standing over a large hole with a chunk of rock lying next to it. Rav peered down into the dark.

"This place was hidden," Piyo hissed. "Someone's already down there."

"I knew we were late," Izen grumbled. "Hurry. Maybe they haven't found Ghourts yet."

Amine handed Piyo a torch, and with two strikes of flint, it was burning. He lit the hole with orange light, moving the flame around the edges to check for any wires, then nodded to Izen.

"I'll lead," he commanded. "Rav, you're not ready to fight goebbers yet; leave them to us," he followed. "Stay at the back. Sister, can you stay with him?" Izen braced himself before facing the tunnel, then climbed down, everyone following.

At the bottom of the drop was a passage that led into the mountain at a downward slope. Izen took the torch, lighting the narrow space. Boot prints and broken spiderwebs provided further evidence of the other unit. Rav squeezed his bag handles tighter, sticking close to Lyra. The Blood Hounds advanced into the earth.

"No droppings," Piyo whispered. "No goebbers."

Rav poured with sweat, having to wipe his face every few moments as they walked until they lost sight of the entrance.

Thin, dank air did little to fill his lungs, the drive to gasp growing ever stronger. But he had to keep quiet. Even as the sense of how much weight was sitting above him sank in. There were no wooden beams to provide comfort like in Pitt's mine. Mulk kicked a stone as he walked, the echo bouncing far into the distance. Rav flinched into Lyra. That could've been it, the mountain falling on top of them. She pushed him forward again but kept a hand on his shoulder.

Rav took a deep breath and carried on until they paused where the tunnel came to a split, one leading straight, the other aiming upwards. Izen held his torch up to both. The flame flickered in the branch tunnel. Wind. The surface. He continued down the original tunnel. Not long later, the tunnel ended, echoes of people shifting coming from a gap at the side. Shadows flickered across the rock wall, but not from their torchlight. The other unit. Rav dropped back, ready to pull out supplies. Everyone else had caught them too, raising their weapons while standing in a tighter formation. They edged closer to the gap. The flashes of light became more frequent, then stopped, everything going silent.

"I guard my home with all I am,

"To honour those who gave me life," Rav sang in his head.

Izen raised his shield, then ran the tip of his sword around the edges of the entrance. No traps. Clear. Everyone was ready. With a nod, he signalled the attack. Advancing through the gap, the Blood Hounds entered a huge cone-shaped cavern with a river running through its centre. Five figures waited in formation to meet them, weapons also raised. Izen halted his charge upon seeing their leader, both units lowering their weapons.

"Izen." She laughed. "Always late."

CHAPTER 11

"Eman." Izen grimaced.

"The mighty Blood Hounds of Blood Marsh." Eman snickered. "upholding their reputation as the second-best scavenger unit."

All five members of her unit wore plate armour, faces covered by their helmets, wielding crossbows, shields, and rapiers. Both Eman and a large man had Blood Palms on their breastplates.

She lifted her visor, showing her snow-white skin and hair along with her pale pink eyes. "Ghourts isn't here, but if you want to waste more of your time, you can stay and look around."

"*Damn*." Mulk kicked the ground. "We're only slow because we've new blood."

Eman looked over Rav and Lyra. "A Called One and a Sister. Isn't that an advantage? Nameless Rav, here as a favour to Baron Glass." Eman walked over to him. "You don't look as scrawny as I was led to believe."

Rav met her gaze.

"What a fierce look." Eman smiled, but though she spoke to Rav, her attention was on Lyra. "We were told you'd be a hindrance to our unit, but maybe you'd fit in."

"I have a unit," Rav stated.

"The second-best unit. If you want to grow in the Sink, you have to be first. Second place is dead." Eman glanced over the Blood Hounds.

"Second best? Ha." Izen laughed. "Who won our last spar? I forget."

"Who arrived here first?" Eman sneered. "Who has the highest chance of joining Jinkin? Who has the stronger unit? You've never beaten us to a scavenge."

"Only because you get extra information from your aunt," Mulk growled. "Without her, you'd still be fighting for good work, not having everything handed to you."

Eman winked at him. "Oh, but I do have my aunt." She faced Rav again. "That's another benefit Champions Guard has. My aunt is Ilina Hagrin, Concubine to Baron Glass, and has a few of his resources at her disposal."

Before Rav could snarl, Lyra's warning to keep polite cut through his disdain. Expression flat, he replied, "Baron Glass requested for me to stay with the Blood Hounds, so I will."

She waved his excuse away as she locked onto him, seeing through his rejection. "My aunt can take care of small matters like that. Don't take too long to change units, Rav; we might be in the second layer when you come asking."

"Enough," Izen huffed. "If you're done searching, then leave."

"It's been a long morning; we'd like to rest a moment before we do."

Izen grinned, eyes gleaming. "Fine. Blood Hounds, let's find that body."

Under Eman's gaze, they stood taller, striding out to explore the cavern. Amine handed torches out to everyone. Rav stuck by Izen.

"That's Champion Eman Hargin, leader of Champions Guard," Izen whispered. "The man staring at me is Champion Maric Trent. Champions Guard had first pick to be your unit but turned it down after learning how weak you were."

Rav glanced back at the second-in-command, who lumbered around with a domineering aura. "How do two Champions work in the same unit?"

"He works for Baron Glass, now under Concubine Hargin's command to protect her niece. It's a good way for someone to get close to Baron Glass."

"I'm not going to join her," Rav hissed. "I'm not someone to be bought or haggled over."

"Don't let her hear you—she's petty," Izen warned. "All of them are, and they can get away with it when they're favoured to join Jinkin."

Rav nodded. That's why they'd rejected him; they thought they could join Jinkin without his help. They thought he'd only be a burden. Only now that he'd worked so hard to have some use did they value him. He gritted his teeth as he looked back to see Eman watching him. *Be polite.* Their eyes met, and Rav held the stare for a moment before dropping back, looking like he was contemplating. Eman seemed pleased. He turned back to continue searching.

The cavern had a wide base, and a torrent of water ran out from a point at the far wall to form a river that then ran under the wall on the other side. Moss grew everywhere, filling the air with spores. Rav itched his nose. Izen saw a tunnel leading out of the cavern and went to search it, Rav following. It went to the side, then came to a dead end. Empty. They looked for tracks. It had been trampled over by the Champions Guard's search. The Blood Hounds reconvened, whispering in a corner.

"I think whatever was here has been hidden," Piyo near mouthed. "There are signs of them stamping the ground to hide marks. Eman must have something significant enough to keep them here. There're signs of a campsite at the riverside they couldn't remove, like black-stained rock from a fire."

"Baron Ghourts camped here?" Izen checked.

"I think so."

"What do we do?" Mulk glanced at Champions Guard.

"We play along," Izen murmured. "If you find anything, keep it secret. We'll speak after we leave."

The Blood Hounds fanned out to search again. Rav headed over to the riverside, the burn marks from the fire easy to see. Where would the Baron have gone? The branch tunnel? That was too simple; the others would have figured that out. Plate armour was heavy, there must've been signs—

"Rav." Champion Trent came over to him. "I was told you were starved, but maybe you're only half-starved." He squared up to him, Rav looking like his skeleton. "I also heard that you killed a Contender. That takes significant skill."

Rav faced him with a lowered head, not meeting his eyes, while Lyra glowered at Trent from the side, causing him to ease up. "How do you know about that?" Rav squeaked, acting shocked, shrinking into his thin features to seem timid. Being unworthy of Champions Guard was the best way to get them to stop bothering him without offending them.

"Everyone who cares knows, the Blood Hounds included. Didn't they mention it?" Trent chuckled.

Despite Trent's helmet, Rav could sense his thick head and haughty expression. He whipped his head around to look at the Blood Hounds. "N-no," he stammered. "People in the Sink are too—"

"It's not a place for the weak," Trent's voice boomed.

Rav stared at his boots and nodded. Trent looked back at Eman, his evaluation apparent; however, Eman indicated for him to continue anyway.

"Why don't I give you a few pointers?" Trent offered. "Some advice for your next fight."

"Aye." Rav nodded with enthusiasm. "I'm always looking to learn." How foolish was he to have revealed his emotions in front of Eman earlier? She'd guessed there was more to him and now he had to prove he was worthless.

Trent moved into position, lacklustre. Rav dropped his supply bag while Lyra pulled out his spear. Holding it, he wobbled under its weight, arms shaking like he was on the brink of dropping it. Izen noticed his performance and signalled for the others to keep searching while Champions Guard was distracted.

Trent raised his rapier. "Let's see what you can do." He lunged forward into an upwards cut.

Rav heaved his weapon across him, the momentum pulling him into a wild swing that missed the sword and sent him stumbling to the side to rebalance. He caught himself, using the spear shaft as a stick for stability. "*Ah.*" He acted frustrated.

"Polearms don't seem to suit you," Trent commented. "You could try a lighter weapon."

"No," Rav growled. "My brother used a spear, so I will too." Stupid and stubborn—more bad qualities.

He launched into another set of attacks, swinging the spear in huge arcs. Trent stepped out the range without raising his shield, waiting for Rav to tire. It wasn't long before Rav failed a swing, the weapon dropping midway to crash to the ground. He leaned on it, catching his breath, open to a counterattack. "You're too fast," he whined. Was that too much? Trent wouldn't see it, but Eman might. Rav peeked at her, relieved that she had already turned away.

"You shouldn't stop like that during a fight." Trent strode inside Rav's guard. "Your opponent won't let you rest." He grabbed Rav's breastplate and shoved him backwards.

Rav let himself stumble far back, leaning backwards to act much weaker than he was. Until his foot missed the ground. *The river*. Falling. *Lyra*. Rav snatched out towards her. He missed, plummeting into the freezing water, sucked straight down by the current. Too deep, his legs hit nothing despite his flailing, then the current rushed into his back, spinning him until he lost all sense of direction. Lashing out his arm, he smacked rock. *Ow*. Blind, dizzy, deaf, he was washed away under the mountain rock and into a tunnel. No rescue. *Breathe*. He tried for the surface again, somehow finding the right direction, but his head struck the ceiling. No air. Full panic. His hand cracked against the riverbed. Rav tucked himself into a ball, rocketing along.

Bang, bang, bang. Water churned around him. He had to slow down. He was going headfirst. *Wait*.

Finding a sense of his position, Rav opened up into a starfish shape, preparing for the pain of smacking into more rocks... there was none. The river had widened. He tensed further. More water had joined it; he had no chance to catch a side now. A stone in a storm, Rav went spinning again.

Breathe. The urge struck again, this time, much stronger. Rav tried swimming to the surface but couldn't kick hard enough. Out of time. His lungs forced themselves open, and he breathed in water. *AHHHH*. Burning, lungs on fire. Heavy, dragging him down. He squeezed his chest, trying to force the water out, but the weight of water around him prevented it from leaving. Agony. More water pressed down his throat. Nothing he did worked. Stuck. A tumbling mess sucked into the abyss as his foot smacked against rock. Again. Again. Again. The bottom.

The bottom. Rav kicked off it with all the strength he could muster, shooting through the water, and finally broke the surface.

Water spurted out his mouth like a geyser, a gasp of air replacing it. Rav breathed deep, sucking in droplets of water from the spray, uncaring. He scratched above himself, feeling the roof over him. It was still black. *Where*? He slammed into a rock, shoulder juddering. *Crack*. Another rock. Rapids. Rav tucked himself into a ball once more, keeping his fingers and face protected. *Slam, slam, slam*. He bounced around, too cold to feel the sting, only the ache, his arms taking the beating for his head. Sucked down into a drop, swirling water spun him while he fought to stay at the surface. He wasn't going under. Never again. Slime and salt streamed down his face, snot and tears. What could he do? Helpless to fight the current, he resigned himself to fate.

...Except, the next expected smack into rock didn't come. It hadn't for a while. Rav opened his eyes, still in the dark. He was floating on the surface, conserving as much energy as he could. Unable to swim, he just focused on keeping his lungs inflated so he would stay afloat. The hide armour Lyra had given him also had some buoyancy, counteracting the chainmail. *Blub, bol, ssh,* the water bubbled. The rush was gone. He could hear the echoes in the tunnel. It was... big. Long. Rav continued to lay there. *Just keep going.*

The course changed, Rav recognising that he was going around another bend. A slower flow meant he could relax more, stretching out his arm in hope of grabbing the side. This time, he scraped against something. Something at his level. Rav snatched out, grabbing a fistful of coarse sand. *Land.* He rolled over, doing his best to kick out of the water, and succeeded in hauling himself onto a riverbank, where he lay, gasping, boots still in the river, face smooshed into the grit. Everything ached or stung, not a single protruding bone that hadn't taken a knock. Rav stayed still, falling into a dreamy state until he could move again.

Where was he? Rav lifted his head. Black. Vision wasn't any good.

Pulling himself out the water, he stood up, clothes hanging heavy. He shrugged them off, keeping on Wakeman's chainmail alone, and twisted the cloth to squeeze out most of the water while checking himself for wounds. No cuts. Or was he just too cold to notice them? Rav traced over his body where he'd taken hits, finding the skin tender but intact. The hide had protected him well. He ran a finger over it to feel it lacerated with grooves, but it hadn't been punctured. Putting it back on, Rav shivered at the cold, then cocked his ear ahead of him.

Judging by the echo from the lapping water, the beach extended in front of him. Rav felt ahead of him, easing forward, finding the beach wall. He listened again, walking alongside it, catching an echo further away. He followed it to a section where the wall disappeared. A tunnel. Holding his hand to it, Rav tried to feel for a breeze, but, hand numb with cold, he couldn't be sure if there was one. Where else was he going to go? Rav entered the tunnel, slow and methodical, flinching at any noise while trying not to think about what mutant could be living inside.

As he walked, shades of black started to differ. Was that light? A sliver of light. Rav hurried to it. Faint, pale, beautiful.

Gazing up through the crack to the surface, he saw just how far underground he was, the light only reaching him by being reflected off wet stones on the way down. Over a hundred feet underground. Everything became suffocating at the sight, vision swirling. Rav looked down again to end his dizziness. How could he be rescued from here? No one would even find him. He had to get out on his own. No Lyra. Taking a breath to steady himself, he looked ahead.

With light, he saw a piece of the tunnels. Moss was growing on the floor under the light in a thick green sponge. There weren't any insects that he could see. No indicator of how to get out. Rav marked this place down as a base, then headed further along the tunnel. Eventually, the passage started to climb. Bit by bit, he moved higher, now certain he could feel fresh air flowing down to him. Cobwebs started to appear, the echoes more varied and the dank smell fading. Closer to the surface. Rav moved faster, almost slipping in something soft, a foul smell wafting up. Excrement. Checking around, he found that the area had been marked exactly as Izen had described. Goebbers.

He connected to his Heaven's Tear, Ghoul just beneath his skin. No new noises. None were around. *Step, step, step,* he now near crawled his way up, the smell of droppings stronger. At least if goebbers stood between him and the surface, the Ghoul might be able to fight through them. The incline levelled, cracks appearing in the roof to provide faint light. Scratch marks from claws covered the walls and ceiling. The passage opened into a cross tunnel. Rav ducked into the shadows. Still no goebbers. He frowned. Maybe they were nocturnal? Shaking his head, he continued, following the fresh air to a tunnel, moving as quickly as he could quietly.

"*Ru.*"

"*Arrr.*" Rav jolted back into the shadows. Goebbers ahead of him, scratching at stone. But a bright patch of sunlight indicated that the surface was just past them. He braced himself—*I guard my home with all I am*—sneaking up the tunnel with careful steps. Nearer, he noticed the noises weren't coming from his path, but from a side room. *Aye*, the path ahead was clear. Rav creeped faster, reaching the side cavern where the noises were coming from, and beyond it was a hole filled with light. The sky. Pressing his back against the opposite wall, Rav shuffled past, now able to see into the room. *Rock, more rock, a space, light from a crack, a tail.* Rav froze. It was the length of his leg, whipping back and forth to rub over the ground, the goebber facing the other way.

"Ru." Something had its attention.

Rav kept moving. Another tail. And another. A dozen of them, all looking away from him. *Almost there...* Rav held his breath. *What is that?* The goebbers were all digging at what looked to be a collapsed section of tunnel, next to which was a shining piece of metal. A hammer. Rav paused, mind racing. What if Ghourts had fallen in the river like him? If he could spot the design on the hammer, he'd be sure, then the Blood Hounds could return and complete the scavenge. But then a goebber turned around.

"RU."

Rav ran, a dozen growls rumbling as they gave pursuit, their hairless bodies crawling over each other to get to him, tails wriggling like worms. Too fast. Going to be caught. One dived to bite his leg. Rav unleashed the Ghoul. The rotting horror. Dead eyes, twitching tendons, cracked nails. The goebbers backed off. Nineteen breaths remaining. Rav swiped at the one near his leg. It reared its head back, dodging the blow. Seventeen breaths. He lunged out again with his other hand. The goebber wanted to retreat further, but the pack behind it hadn't reacted in time. Rav's nails scraped up its belly, disembowelling it as he roared.

Reeling at the sight, the rest of the goebbers fled down the tunnel. Fourteen breaths. Rav chased after them, acting the predator, and they scampered out of sight.

He reached the side room entrance, ducked inside, and stopped the Ghoul. Ten breaths left. They'd return soon. Rav found the hammer lying next to the rock pile, seeing that it was well-crafted, all metal, with carved symbols on the hammerhead and shaft. As described. Blood on the grip. Dried blood. Rav looked around the rock pile. More blood had been spilt in a black-crusted pool. He held his hand to a gap, feeling no breeze. A dead end behind the rubble. From the chop marks, didn't it look like the collapse had been created by someone hammering the ceiling?

Rav grabbed the hammer and slammed it into a stone, shattering it. *Bang*. The rocks shook. He paused as his palms stung. Should he leave to get help? How long would that take? What if he was wrong? It seemed like the noise was keeping the goebbers away for the moment; he had time. Rav glanced at the entrance every few swings, waiting for the moment a pair of beady eyes peered at him and realised he was just a man. A tired man. He grabbed the hammer and swung it again. And again. And again. At last, he took aim at the base rock—the last thing holding the rubble up.

"*Ha*." He threw his weight behind the hammer. *Bang*. The rock burst into pieces and the rock wall crumbled down, leaving an opening at the top. There *was* a space behind it. Rav dropped the hammer, readied his Heaven's Tear, then climbed up to look inside. It was dark. His eyes adjusted as the light from his room filtered in, providing a faint view of a small area, reeking of decay, with Baron Ghourts' figure leaning against the far wall.

Chapter 12

"You found me," he wheezed.

"You're alive." Rav stayed out the room, looking down.

"How observant," Ghourts lolled his words.

"I've come for your armour."

"A scavenger? Where's your unit—" Ghourts went into a coughing fit.

"Nearby," Rav lied. "What's wrong with you?"

Baron Ghourts spat and cleared his throat. "You handled the goebbers alone?"

"I scared them off." Rav squinted, trying to see what condition Ghourts was in, but the light was too dim.

"Then why haven't you left yet, stupid boy?" Ghourts' voice was hollow, like there was a hole in his lung.

"I... I don't know what to do." Save him or *clean up*? No, he couldn't. That wasn't what a Carvell did.

Ghourts tried to laugh but choked. "Seems you're new to Blood Marsh. And you found me? Lucky brat," he wheezed. "I'm about to die; lost too much blood. Which unit?"

"The Blood Hounds." Rav glanced behind himself. No goebbers yet.

"I've heard of them." Ghourts swallowed. "They've a good reputation. Hmm... I'll give you my armour, but I need you to do something for me. Two things, actually. I have a son in the Sink, Ribbick. Help him if you meet him. At least don't be his enemy... He's a good lad. Got a strong heart, but he can't do everything on his own." He grunted. "And the other... revenge. I need Tryxwin to suffer... like I have."

"If I meet your son, I'll do what I can, but as for your other request, I can't do that. I've enough enemies already."

"Right. Asking you to hurt her for me is too much." Ghourts spat again. "At least you didn't just lie and agree. Maybe you've some honour. You need incentive. How about this? I'll pay you. You already have my armour, but I have information... information I died for. Make sure she doesn't win. You can do that; you'll *want* to do that."

Rav could hear his cunning grin.

"Win what?"

"A Heaven's Tear."

The term rolled around the cave.

"You know where one is?" Rav breathed.

"I do."

Rav climbed into the hole.

"Ha. Now you're interested." Ghourts shifted. "I don't care who gets it, just make sure *she* doesn't. Swear on your Name."

"I'm Nameless."

"Maybe that's better than being honourable." Ghourts wet his lips. "There's a place called Harton, where Cive Mort lives..."

Rav listened as Ghourts explained the details.

"I sent two hundred soldiers to die for that information..." he finished. "I would've sent thousands." Ghourts sighed, then grinned at Rav. "Just arrived in the Sink and you've already found traces of a Heaven's Tear, haha. I wish I had your luck. Now... put me down."

"What?" Rav flinched. "I can get help—"

"*Kill me, boy,*" he shouted. "I'm in enough pain." Baron Ghourts tried to stand between coughing fits. "Come on, Nameless, this should be easy for you. I Challenge you—"

Dead. Slumped to the ground without a touch. Rav wrinkled his nose as the smell of blood grew stronger.

Ru.

He darted to the body and pulled a knife off Baron Ghourts' belt, then used it to strip the armour off. *Arrrr.* The armour was too heavy to carry. He dumped everything of value near the rocks, then buried them in the rubble.

Ruu.

Rav fled to the surface, dashing out the room as goebbers bounded in, ignoring him for the fresh corpse. Rav glanced at them scrabbling over each other to get the first bite before scurrying into the light. Late afternoon, clear skies, slight wind. On the mountainside. He could see everything, and everything could see him. The landscape was the same as the top of the Brack. Rav ran to the lip to look down into the marsh.

Where was he? This area was less unruly than before, the stone structures maintained and occupied, the land around them guarded by uniform armies. The ground had turned to mud from constant battles. There would be scouts watching him. Red caught his eye. On his sleeves. Ghourts' blood. *Run.* Guided by the sun, Rav headed south across the mountain, aiming for Donsden.

Caw. A bird swooped down, talons bared. Rav dived into a forward roll, avoiding the attack. The bird flew back up to circle for another go. Too exposed. Rav changed direction, heading down towards a cluster of trees in the marsh. The scent of blood carried in the wind.

Ru. Dozens of goebbers scampered out of cracks to hunt, lithe bodies weaving across the rocks. Different colonies competing for an easy meal. The bird dived to kill one of the smaller goebbers, carrying it away. Rav glanced behind him. They were gaining on him. Giving up running, he jumped into a slide, his hide armour guarding him from the rough surface. It gave him more time, but the sound of claws on rock was still getting closer. Three hairless bodies bounded ahead of the pack. Rav's foot hit a rock, sending him tumbling. Falling faster, he bounced down the hill. The brown blurred into green. *Crack*. He crashed into a bush upside down. Three snarling snouts raced at him.

Rav rolled over, found his footing, and continued fleeing. There was a thick grove ahead of him. Cover. Rav slipped and clawed at the grass to pull himself forward on all fours, using any means to keep moving. Scrabbling into the grove, he saw a clear pond. Empty. *Wash off the blood.* He dived in and smeared mud all over himself, but as he climbed up the bank on the other side, he spotted three goebbers circling around the water, two on his left, one on his right.

Are the trees enough cover? They'd have to be.

Rav unleashed the Ghoul, lunging at the first mutant, blood spraying as he tore it apart. *Eight breaths*. Another darted in, teeth piercing through the Ghoulish miasma to sink into his ankle. Rav growled in pain, kicking back to knock it away. *Seven breaths*. The other goebbers reached the grove and began to surround him. Pack tactics. Rav stood, glaring at them. They circled around him. He had to break out, or he'd be harassed to death. *Five breaths*.

Rav charged at a weak point in the encirclement, arms flailing.

Ru. The goebbers leaped out the way.

Rav swatted through the trees. *Four breaths*. Out the encirclement and out the grove, the Ghoul receded, leaving him to hobble on with just a knife. The goebbers remained cautious as they pursued, nipping at his legs, then dashing away, wearing him down. Rav kept trudging on, glaring at intervals to deter the goebbers from gathering, but the effect was getting weaker. Soon, they'd strike and know the Ghoul was gone. Where was he running to? There was a rubber tree in front of him with giant, green-scaled lizards lounging beneath it. Rav made for it, the chase rousing them from sunning. They gathered to watch, pink tongues flicking. The goebbers backed down. Rav gained a lead. The lizards stomped towards him. More enemies. Rav stopped. Left led to the battlefields. Right led to more marsh.

He eased away from the lizards, wary of how fast they could run, his knife ready to be thrown. A unit of green-scale armoured scouts was watching at the edge of the battlefield. Would they help him? He'd die in the marsh anyway. *Left.* Rav sprinted to fellow humans. A lizard leaped at him, claws slashing. The goebbers also moved in, flanking him. Rav threw his knife at the lizard, the blade bouncing off its scales, but its claws missed, and the lizard landed close to the goebbers, where they backed away from each other. *Run, run, run.* The ground was firmer, rock beneath the mud. His feet slapped as he sprinted. Soon, the lizards gave up, returning to their territory, while most of the goebbers also turned back, only a few keeping going. *So close.* Rav pushed himself as hard as he could, ankle searing. The scouts were moving in his direction.

"*I'm Called*," Rav shouted.

The scouts moved into an attacking formation, shooting their crossbows at the goebbers.

Bolts flew over Rav to splatter in the ground. The goebbers were too nimble, dodging back; however, the barrage worked to slow them down. He was going to make it. He did make it. Rav stopped next to the scouts, panting.

"Come with us," the scout leader commanded as his unit fanned out to protect Rav, chasing the goebbers away. "Return," the scout leader barked.

His unit escorted Rav back to their base, a large fort at the edge of the battlefields, two dropping behind him before they set off. Rav looked around him, seeing the exposed terrain and other scouts staring at him. Not far away, bodies were sinking into the mud. He kept pace with the scouts as best he could, soon reaching the fort.

An attendant greeted the returning scout unit, inviting Rav to follow him. "Baron Tryxwin is waiting for you."

"Baron Tryxwin?" Rav caught his breath.

"Yes. This is her territory."

Rav looked around at the banners displaying her dragonfly as an insignia. He sucked his teeth, too tired to think further. *Be polite.* "Aye, I'd like to thank her." Rav followed the attendant.

The fort was designed in a similar way to Donsden's Keep, winding, empty hallways until a heavy wooden door stood before him.

"Enter," a woman called, voice quick, efficient, dominant.

The doors opened. Rav entered a war room. Baron Tryxwin was seated at the end of a large stone table covered with a map of Blood Marsh. She looked to be in her early thirties, had black shoulder-length hair, and green eyes, her cunning woven into the sharp features of her face. Short and stocky, covered in plate armour, but still alluring, her strong physique also voluptuous. Behind her stood male servants in bound-rope clothing. Two council members were seated at her sides picking at fruits, one grey and old, the other bald, about forty. Baron Tryxwin gazed at Rav. He bowed.

"Nameless Rav." She stood, walking over to inspect him. "Not as useless as Baron Glass would have us believe."

Rav stayed low to hide his pinched brow. *Had someone even this far from Donsden been monitoring him?* "Thank you for saving me."

She waved her hand. "You'll pay me back later." She continued inspecting him, going over his thin arms. "You're supposed to be too scrawny to carry a weapon. How did you escape from the grove?"

Rav's heart pounded. He fought to still his voice before answering. "There was a gap that I ran through."

She raised an eyebrow with a tut. "That's it?"

"Aye. My armour took the blows as I ran. My Sister gave it to me." Rav displayed the scratches with pale hands.

Tryxwin spotted the blood leaking from his ankle. "Bring a cleaning paste," she ordered a servant.

Rav was invited to sit while the servant poured the mixture onto his wound. The sting brought him to focus. "How do you know who I am?"

Tryxwin gazed at him with a half-smile. "Not long ago, Ha'th Bey Riene came running to every Baron this side of Mount Don and requested for them to search for you."

"Lyra?" Rav sat up with a smile. "Is she here?"

"No." Tryxwin shook her head, her half-smile dropping flat. "I've sent a message telling her that I have you."

Rav paused in his fervour as he caught her odd tone. "That you saved me?"

"That you're now mine." She ran her finger down Rav's cheek.

He swatted her hand away, standing up as he scanned the room for escape.

Tryxwin laughed, sauntering away. "How many people in the Sink would love to be mine?" She indicated her servants.

Her councillors maintained their gruff looks.

"I'm not one of them," Rav spat.

"Not yet." She pulled a coy smile. "I'm on the rise, Nameless Rav; I'll be leaving for Ut Sh'za within the year. Friends like me are rare."

Rav caught himself before his disdain grew, flattening his expression until it went blank, voice going monotone. "I'll be here longer than that."

"Will you?" She raised an eyebrow. "You're skinny now, but once you get some muscle, I think Blood Marsh will be too small for you." She stared at him with hungry eyes. "How did you break out of the grove, Rav? There's more to you than you show; you've got some wits. I like people like you. I want them."

"I'm not for you."

Tryxwin paused, then her gaze became toying. "Has the Sister converted you? Are you for the World?" She took her seat.

He stood tall as he stared her down. "I'm for myself."

She grinned wider, eyes shining. "Excellent. So am I. We can use each other to get what we want."

"Our wants are not compatible."

Tryxwin laughed at his posturing. "How can you say that without knowing me? Stay awhile. You may find we're more compatible than you think." Before Rav tensed further, her demeanour changed, playfulness replaced by domineering sternness. "Did you find Baron Ghourts' body?"

Rav flinched at her sudden change, scrambling to find his answer. "No."

She sneered at him. "Where?"

He recovered his blank façade and repeated his answer. "I don't know. I didn't find it."

She tapped on the table as she examined his expression. "But that's a lie, isn't it, Rav? Relax, I'm only making sure he's dead. It's not good to leave enemies alive." She waved her hand as though dismissing the matter. "I can see you're not going to entertain me any further, so I won't pry any deeper. You have a room to rest in."

"Thank you for saving me, Baron Tryxwin." Rav bowed before he left and was escorted to a guest room, which had its own bath, already filled with steaming water. Three medicinal vials lay next to his bed to keep the goebber wound clean. He went through his small bag, everything completely soaked.

No. He hurried to check his journal. Sodden. The pencil markings were streaked across the pages, destroying everything written. Intricate sketches of Stone's Way reduced to grey smears. Rav teared up as he flicked through the pages. Nothing was intact. His home was gone. Even the smell on the pages had washed away.

Smell. Rav snatched up Kayla's cloth. Also soaking wet. He pressed it to his nose and took a deep sniff. Nothing. Her perfume was gone, leaving just a frilled handkerchief.

With shaking hands, he retrieved the last item. Still intact and sealed. He let out a trembling breath. Rav hugged Wakeman's ashes and sobbed.

He bathed in his chainmail and undergarments, too tired and too cautious to change out of them. Hot water worked to relieve his aching muscles. His arms were mottled yellowish black from bruises, and judging by the pain he felt leaning on the right side of his back, he had a large one there too. But the injuries weren't as bad as he'd thought. He was lucky. No, it wasn't just luck. It was the armour Lyra had made for him. Where was she? Without her, he was... vulnerable. Exhaustion lured him to sleep, but each time he closed his eyes, he'd snap his head to look at the door. Still safe. For now. Besides, the sun was setting; Blood Marsh was too dangerous to travel at night. Stuck here with Tryxwin until tomorrow at least. Was this how Cyrn had felt? Tibald had wanted to recruit him, but he didn't care about him. Cyrn was just a tool to him. Cyrn also had to look after the Ghoulsmen. While here, Rav only had to care for himself. How was he struggling so much? Rav slapped the water.

Knock, knock.

Rav was dry and dressed, dealing with the sting from the medicine. "Come in," he called.

A rope-dressed servant entered. "Baron Tryxwin has requested you to join her for supper."

Rav nodded, and the servant left. More work. He dressed in his complete armour before heading out to find the servant waiting at the end of a narrow hallway. The man escorted him to the dining hall in the belly of the castle. It was a private room, had mounted lizard heads along with dragonfly carvings on the walls, and a round table with skewers of meat. Baron Tryxwin sat alone in her armour, waiting for him.

"Come in." She beckoned him to sit next to her.

As Rav pulled out his seat, he moved it further away from her. "Thank you for the room. Have you contacted Lyra?" he asked, sitting down.

"I don't know; I've yet to receive a report." Tryxwin sipped her wine.

Was that a lie? He couldn't tell.

Tryxwin noticed his concern and lolled her head at him. "What use would you be if I didn't ransom you back?"

Rav flattened his expression further, certain he'd kept his face still. What was his tell? He looked at the meal. "I'm a prisoner?"

"A guest," she assured him, pointing to a meaty skewer. "This one was hunted today." Tryxwin nibbled at her own. "The lizards are filled with parasites from the marsh; eating them without special preparation will kill you. When I learned of Blood Marsh, I first thought about how I could feed my army. It took two years to develop this cooking method. I turned a common enemy into a food supply."

"Impressive." Rav held a skewer, taking a bite. Hot and fatty meat. Delicious.

Tryxwin smirked. "You don't care. I've made you nervous."

Rav focused on the food.

"Igor found you interesting. The old man," she said. "He says you're not like most people in the Sink; he says you're not a conqueror."

"Meaning?"

"People come to the Sink to fight for what they want. They're here to conquer land, resources... other people. With the support of three Sisters, King's Blood, and that wild look you have, you should be one of them. You should be desperate to get stronger and dive into the Sink's heart. Conquerors seek to conquer. And if you show intent to own one of them, they push back, wanting to show off their power and conquer you back. What better feeling is there than rising above the figure before you to claim them for your own? I'm a conqueror, Rav. My soldiers are conquerors. They all want to press me down, and I love stomping them into place. That's the feeling of power the Sink holds." She sipped her wine. "But Igor thinks you don't like the Sink; he thinks you want to leave. You're not here to claim the spoils because you already have them."

"Aye, I have all the Sink has to offer," Rav mumbled, voice dripping with sarcasm, hoping she couldn't see the sweat beading on his forehead.

She faced him. "No one has all the Sink has to offer, not even the God King. Maybe you think you can get everything you want from Blood Marsh," she mused. "Maybe that's why you lack the desire to head deeper into the Sink."

"What do I want, then?"

"A Name." Tryxwin smiled, then nibbled at another skewer. "I don't think Igor is quite right, though. While you might not be a conqueror, I can't help but think you want to be one, don't you, Rav?" She gazed at him. "But you've been conquered. Someone's taken control of you, and all you *can* want now is to free yourself. I promise you, once you succeed, you'll be back here. The Sink is too wonderful to ignore."

Rav sat back and met her gaze. "I think you're wrong; I don't think conquerors exist. I think you're all just greedy. You want more and more, never satisfied. You have no goals, no ambitions, it's all just an insatiable desire for power. You don't care for land or resources or people. You care for yourselves. Nothing else matters. That is who you are. No better than beasts who toil for food. There is no end but death."

Tryxwin sat forward. "Then tell me, what do you want?"

"To live."

"You need power to live."

"You need power to survive; you need family to live."

"And the World?"

"I will do my duty."

"Lie." Tryxwin sat back with a satisfied smile. "I want you, Rav. Join my army and receive my Name."

He jolted in his chair. *A Name!* But at what cost? What did 'Tryxwin' mean? What would he have to do to honour its legacy? From what the Blood Hounds had said, betray. From what Tryxwin had said, conquer. That couldn't be him.

Rav firmed his resolve, the words stuck in his throat until he forced them out. "No. My place is not at your side."

Her eyes sparkled. "To whose side do you belong, then?"

"A side you'd never understand."

"Hmm," Tryxwin mused. "Enough. Tell me about your journey here."

Rav settled, taking a breath. Polite conversation was much easier to manage. He recounted the route he'd taken starting from Fool's March, leaving out his lost appetite and other secrets, while Tryxwin told Rav stories of Blood Marsh, how the 'Zet Ar lived and places to avoid. Dinner came to a rather pleasant end.

"Why live in this castle when it's open to attack from all sides?" Rav asked.

"Ah, many make the mistake you have in thinking having Mount Don at your back protects you. Donsden's different to everywhere else," Tryxwin explained. "Their mountainside has been cleared of 'Zet Ar, so they're safe; however, Mount Don is bigger than you think. Goebbers and lizards live at the bottom, while the true mutants live at the top, in the red layer. Don't let the snow confuse you—all that's up there is blood."

MUUH. Rav shuddered at the thought of facing more monsters like that. Tryxwin caught on.

"You have experience with 'Zet Ar?"

"Aye, one attacked my home. It took a lot to kill it."

Tryxwin nodded in acknowledgement. "Mutants like that can slaughter whole towns outside the Sink. The Sisters are supposed to stop them leaving, but a few slip through. How many died?"

"I got it to fight another party," Rav said. "Thirty soldiers were wiped out in one night. After that, I lured it away from my home, alone. I couldn't have anyone else risk fighting it." He grimaced at the memory. "It could only kill itself. I was lucky, managed a perfect throw to blind it, then led it to fall to its death."

Tryxwin tilted her head at his words, her own hardships glinting in her eyes.

"Did you see a 'Zet Ar outside the Sink?" he asked.

She shrugged her eyebrows in acknowledgement. "But my city didn't have someone like you to face it alone. It was an alpha wingtail, much bigger than the common ones you see, with wings as wide as three carriages and claws like swords. It attacked by ambush. The army devised a plan to throw a net over it as it flew beneath the trees, using cattle as bait, but it spotted the trap, picking off the soldiers hiding in the trees. My father dived at its tail, holding on to weigh it down so the pikemen could stab it. He brought it down, but he died."

Rav lowered his head, and Tryxwin smiled at the action. "That information is so cheap it's become gossip."

"It's different for you to share it yourself."

She sipped more wine.

"My friend died, but not from a mutant attack. It was a man that killed him."

"That's what you want from the Sink? The power to kill one man?"

"Two men, actually." Rav gave a dry chuckle. "Aye. That's what I want."

Tryxwin gazed at him with a mischievous glint. "I know what to do now, Nameless Rav. One day, you'll fight for me."

"You want to kill them for me?"

"No." Tryxwin giggled, fluttering her eyelashes at him. "My name is Cata."

Rav tensed up and stood to leave. "It's late, and I'm tired from an eventful day, so I'll say goodnight. Thank you for dinner."

Cata Tryxwin watched him go, her smile as beautiful as it was threatening.

Chapter 13

"*Rav.*" Lyra burst through the door, torchlight flooding the darkness, waking him.

"*Lyra.*" Rav leaped out of bed to hug her.

"Are you hurt?" she asked, voice soft, hugging him back.

"Aye, but there's only one bad one." He stepped back to lift his trouser leg, revealing the bite mark, which she crouched to inspect. "Baron Tryxwin has already given me some medicinal vials to clean it; I'll be fine."

"We've shared dinner now, Rav. Call me Cata." She was standing in the corridor, holding a torch, watching them.

"Aye, Cata." He shifted behind Lyra.

"I will look over it." Lyra grabbed Cata's torch, lit the candles in the room, then returned it to her.

Cata looked between Rav and Lyra before bidding them goodnight and leaving, closing the door behind her.

"What happened?" Lyra asked as she directed Rav to the bed and stepped closer to examine his wounds now that she had better light to work with.

Rav lay down with a wince, facing the high ceiling and its carved arches. "I was sucked under by the current, drifting under the mountain until I found a beach..." He gave her a summary of the events, and as he reached the end, he sat up, leaning in close to whisper, "I found Baron Ghourts in one of the goebber colonies. I can show you where."

Lyra smiled with pride, then hardened her eyes. "We will do that tomorrow. Did you have to fight?"

"Aye, once in the tunnels and then out in a grove. I don't think anyone saw, but Tryxwin's curious about how I escaped an encirclement."

She sighed with relief. "If anyone suspected it enough, there would have been trouble already. Rest. We will leave in the morning when the Blood Hounds arrive here."

"What happened to Champions Guard?"

"When I saw you go under, I left to find where the river flowed to. I do not know what happened after that."

Rav picked at an itching scab on his hand. "When Eman learns I'm not so weak, she'll come back. Another enemy. Trent'll also want to kill me off if he thinks I hate him, but there's no point going after them. There's too much to do already."

"I will be at your side," Lyra promised, "and Eman will make amends. Offending you is a problem for the future; offending me is a problem now."

"You'd take action for me? Han didn't when Janson died."

"My job is to ensure the World's plans come to fruition. If you died, there would be nothing I could do except find another Called One. Until then, I will keep you alive," Lyra swore.

"Without killing anyone."

"I can cause people to die without killing them." She pulled a small smile. "Those with the Sisters' support flourish; if I choose to help Eman's enemies, then they will become strong enough to kill her without my hand. Perhaps in the future she will require the help of me or another Sister. If we ignore her, she will also die then." She caught Rav yawn as he nodded. "We will speak more in the morning." She walked around the room, blowing out the candles as Rav snuggled under his blanket.

Rav woke to late-morning sun. After a few agonising stretches for his seized muscles, he could work them again. The bruises were still tender, though. He walked over to the slit window in his room and watched a unit picking through a few corpses in the distant marsh. Even if he rested, Blood Marsh never did.

He dressed in his armour and headed out. Lyra was waiting in the corridor, wiping away a line of grime from under her breastplate collar with the tip of her finger.

"There is food." She guided him towards the main dining hall.

"How'd you get the oil there?" Izen's voice rumbled down the hallway as Rav approached.

"It was already in place." Cata's voice was low, teasing.

"The scouts would have spotted it."

"Unless they were distracted."

Lyra hooked her slender finger over Rav's collar and dragged him in front of her, pushing him forward to enter the dining hall first. Rav gathered his mind before entering, seeing the Blood Hounds sitting around the table with Baron Tryxwin and Igor, armoured but casual, their helmets set aside so their cleaned faces could shine in the firelight.

"Rav." Mulk got up to hug him, his battered, brutish face lighting up in relieved joy. "You need more food; how'd you go flying back from a light shove like that?"

Rav blinked at his warm reception, stiff as he hugged Mulk back.

Izen also rose to hug him, looking especially dashing with his hair tidied and his stubble shaved smooth to display his strong jawline, ruffling Rav's hair. "It's good that you're alive. Sit, eat."

He guided Rav to a chair at the end of the table with a gentle hand before taking his seat beside Cata once more. Rav picked at the breads and cheeses laid out in front of him, chewing to hide his creeping, wry smile. Lyra came to stand beside him, her hand on top of Rav's chair as though protective. Or possessive.

"Baron Tryxwin was telling us about her battles." Izen gazed at her, captivated by the seductive looks she threw his way. "Baron Brakken had all his supplies burned when he moved into her territory."

"Baron Brakken?" Rav asked.

"He's dead." Cata smiled at him and tapped the table with a nail as if to say, "I don't let my enemies live".

"How did you distract the scouts?" Izen pressed while the Blood Hounds faced her, all appearing as enamoured as the Champion.

"I poured blood into the stream." Cata's attention remained on Rav as she spoke. "It flowed down into the camp to attract goebbers."

Rav ate his food with his head low, watching from beneath his brow as Izen gasped in awe. Cata's teasing smile widened at Izen's response, her big eyes gleaming with the same cunning Tibald's had when he'd felt he was achieving what he sought. Rav flicked his eyes around the table again, this time catching Amine's brief half-squint, then awed stare. An act. Only he, Lyra, and Amine hadn't fallen for Cata's charm.

"Have you found Baron Ghourts' body?" Cata asked Izen.

"We tracked him to a cavern at the top of the Brack, but Champions Guard swept the place clean before we arrived, hiding any further traces of him."

"Champions Guard..." Cata acted as though she were in thought, but Rav saw through her performance. "Led by that white woman... Champion Eman Hargin. They have a good reputation. People say they're favoured to join Jinkin and head into the second layer, but I don't like them. Two Champions in a unit is easy. The Sink is for those who struggle."

Izen nodded, while Mulk, Piyo, and Miels all grumbled in agreement. Cata had won them over. More toys for her to play with. Rav could almost hear her gloating. *Look, Rav. Look what I can do.*

A servant entered and whispered in Cata's ear. After his report, Cata dismissed him. "Business," she announced, causing everyone to sit up. "Saving Rav was requested by Ha'th Bey Riene. It has no cost. However, it has given me the opportunity to meet you all. After you find Baron Ghourts, I have another task for you, another scavenge. This one will be much harder, but your reward will be much higher. You can also think of it as doing me a favour. Make it to Ut Sh'za and I'll repay it. I have the last location of a treasury left by a fallen Baron. I'll give you the location, and in return, I want two items from it. The rest are yours."

"That's very generous," Izen said.

Cata grinned. "Not as much as you might hope. This treasure has been lost for half a decade... and it's in the red layer of Mount Don."

"That's..."

"I'll have an associate provide more information after your current task is done."

"As long as we can do it, we will." Izen gave a grim nod.

"Good. Rav, you have a guest waiting for you. One of the servants will take you to see them." Cata beckoned a servant over.

Rav stuffed a piece of cheese into his mouth before getting up to follow them, Lyra at his side. "Why do I have a guest?" he asked Lyra, fidgeting with his sleeve cuff.

Lyra thrummed the pommel of her sword and stepped ahead of Rav in a protective display, her head turned to catch the torchlight. "Why worry? I will be by your side."

Rav bit his lip in irritation, dropping his head to face plain stone instead. Why even bother asking her anything?

A small square room lay at the end of the hallway, furnished with a brown-furred carpet and two long benches set opposite each other. A second door stood at the far end between the seats, lit by a lantern burning above it. Sat close to it on the left was a familiar figure in dusty plate armour. Helm placed beside her, her white hair and pink eyes were especially catching.

Oh. Rav smoothed his expression as he gathered his thoughts. Why hadn't Eman given up yet? How much worse could he have acted?

Eman stood and bowed as Rav entered after Lyra, first to her, then to him. "Rav, on behalf of Champions Guard, I take responsibility for Champion Trent's actions." Her eyes were sunken from lack of sleep. "I have already reprimanded him, but if you want to enact your own punishment, I'll support you. I've stripped him of his title as second-in-command of my unit and am offering his position to you."

Rav fought to keep his sneer down. As if a show of her callousness would ever win him over. "It's fine." He sighed, standing just inside the room, glancing at Lyra, who kept her hand on her pommel as she faced Eman. "I'm alive. Champion Trent offered to show me some moves and I was foolish in my actions. I'm embarrassed at how weak I was."

"You're forgiving him?" Eman's surprise was freckled with frustration. "You could have died."

"Aye. Accidents happen, and I *didn't* die." Rav watched her squint with a slight frown. She was suspicious now; he was being too easy-going. He hardened his expression. "Besides, we were both playing around. It wasn't Champion Trent's actions alone that led to my fall." There. He was playing along now. This was what she expected. Trent had pushed him into the water, but Rav had tricked her into thinking he was pathetically weak. In Eman's eyes, the offence would be the same. How dare anyone fool her. Rav showed he'd been stung by his own ploy.

"You're more capable than you seem." Eman latched onto the bait. "There are stories of how you escaped a goebber colony alone, then fled through the marsh, even breaking through an encirclement."

Rav smiled. "The World was guiding me."

"A position in Champions Guard is empty," Eman offered again, not even trying to hide her plan to use the "compensation" of second-in-command to bring Rav into her unit.

"I hope you find someone to fill it. My place is with the World."

"The World has led you to the Blood Hounds?" Eman sneered.

Rav nodded, looking pious. "I believe it is where I'm supposed to be. I will be staying in Blood Marsh for some time and don't want to impede your unit from advancing."

"I see." Eman dropped her apologetic façade. "The position will be open to you for as long as we're here."

"Thank you." Rav wobbled on his feet and leaned on Lyra. "I'm still recovering from my excursion. Hu v' sh," he said to Eman as Lyra helped him exit the room.

Rav grinned out of sight. Eman now wanted to recruit him, not kill him. If Trent still wanted him dead, he'd have to act alone.

Safe on their way to the dining hall, Lyra shrugged Rav off her. "Do not do that in front of me again," she warned him.

"Do what?"

"Speak about the World like that. The World is not one of your performances," she seethed.

"I *have* been Called..."

"And I know you do not believe."

"I'm sorry. I didn't think of you. I was just trying to avoid getting another enemy."

"The World is the best support in the Sink," Lyra said. "People go to war against everyone except us. Do not chase us away."

"I'm not chasing you away."

"Me or what I represent?"

"Both."

Lyra clearly didn't believe him but didn't speak further. They returned to the dining hall in silence.

"I'll start planning," Izen finished.

"Good." Cata stood. "Now, I have duties to attend to."

Everyone stood with her.

"Thank you for taking care of Rav." Izen bowed. "We should set off; we still need to find Ghourts."

Cata nodded and left, winking at Rav as she passed. Mulk and Miels glanced at each other as the Blood Hounds got ready to leave.

Once they were out of the castle and following a path back to the marsh, Rav approached Izen, voice low.

"I found Ghourts' body in a goebber burrow up the mountain yesterday."

"So, Ghourts also fell in the river. Excellent. Do we have smoke?" he asked Amine.

"Yes." They pulled a pouch out of their bag.

"Then let's get paid." Izen set off.

The Blood Hounds took a long route into the marsh, then up the side of the mountain, losing any scouts tracking them. Once they were hidden by the lip of the mountain, they marched over to where Rav had been chased.

"This place is filled with goebbers." Rav adjusted his grip on his knife.

"That's why we have these." Izen pulled a powdered ball out of the pouch. "Goebbers have sensitive noses; they hate this smoke." He stopped to put the ball in a clamp device, then sparked it with a flint.

As it burned, acrid smoke poured off the ball to linger around the Blood Hounds. Rav's mouth filled with saliva. He spat and focused his mind, trying not to breathe through his nose. They all walked through the cloud, then continued marching, letting the smoke coil around them. Rav spotted a goebber poke its head out a crack, sniff, then duck back down.

"It's this easy?" he spoke through gritted teeth.

Mulk laughed. "One of those things costs more than my armour."

"Hurry; don't waste the smoke." Piyo pushed Rav forward.

Rav guided them to the right hole. The goebbers stayed deep inside. As he entered the side room, he saw that the rock barrier had fallen further, leaving a large gap at the top to reach the hidden area. The ground and rocks were covered in scratch marks. Amine lit a torch, throwing it into the space. Baron Ghourts' body was gone save for a few bones. Rav climbed down to dig out the untouched armour and hammer as Izen clambered over the rubble after him, the other Blood Hounds and Lyra standing guard outside.

"Good thinking." Izen patted Rav's back, then picked up the hammer and ran his finger over the etchings. "This is it."

"There were also these." Rav showed the belt and pouches.

"Amine, take these. Mulk, take the armour. I've got the hammer," Izen commanded, handing out the items while Rav climbed back out. Once everything had been collected, he stomped over the area until all traces of goebber tracks and Ghourts had been erased, the last of the Baron's bones scattered under the rubble. Amine nodded to him, signalling that everything had been tidied. Izen climbed back into the main room, then led the Blood Hounds in a jog out of the burrow and back towards Donsden.

"You found him dead?" Miels glanced back at Rav after stepping over a large stone.

"Aye," Rav panted, moving around it. "I stripped the body, then ran."

Piyo snorted, speaking over his shoulder, always scanning the marsh ahead. "You're not going to tell us how you avoided the colony or dug through the rocks?"

"There weren't any goebbers when I climbed up from the river, and I used the hammer to break through the rock. I ran when I heard them coming. That's when I went down the mountain," Rav explained with as even a tone as he could manage.

The Blood Hounds shared a look between themselves, but no one said anything.

"We need to prepare for the red layer," Izen grumbled.

"If that's where the stronger mutants live, why risk going there?" Rav asked.

"Because Baron Tryxwin saved your life."

"That's for me to settle."

Izen shook his head. "You're a member of the Blood Hounds now, Rav."

"It's only been a few days."

"It doesn't matter. You get a share of the spoils and we look after you."

Rav shook his head as he scoffed, staring at Izen's back. "You'd risk your lives for me already?"

"Ha, not everything's about you." Mulk laughed as he stepped over a puddle. "Helping the Baron helps us. Next time we're in danger, she might provide some assistance. That's especially important in Ut Sh'za. She might also stay her hand if she catches us in a vulnerable position. You've brought us trouble and opportunity. I think things'll get exciting in Blood Marsh with you around."

Ghourts' armour and hammer were wrapped in cloth to hide them. The return to their first camp was uneventful, and from there, it was a short journey to the carriage. Rav's bruising had faded quickly thanks to Lyra's care. If nothing touched the bad ones, he didn't know they were there. The scabs on his hands had also peeled off, leaving pink marks.

"Get the horses ready," Izen ordered Rav and Amine. "I'll be back soon." He set off towards a small building in the outpost.

"Ghourts' body was fresh," Amine murmured as they checked over the horses. "We know you have a secret. We know you didn't tell us everything that happened." Amine watched his expression. "Will the unit be in danger?"

"I was seen running from the colony," Rav huffed. "Ask any of the watching scouts and they'll say the same."

"No one saw you fight," Amine pointed out. "No weapon, no shield, still alive. We've seen you move in the marsh. Are we in danger, Rav? We all have secrets, but we understand that we're stronger as a unit. The blood and tracks were new; Ghourts died yesterday."

"He was dead when I found him."

"The unit takes care of you," Amine reminded him before dropping the subject.

Rav checked over the stitching in the reins. No one could know he'd spoken to Ghourts; no one could even guess at what he'd been told. He watched Amine. He'd have to be more careful in the future. They'd destroyed the remains in the cave; the Blood Hounds were experienced, preventing anyone else from finding the same traces they had. Was that to protect him? Or did they just know his lies would implicate them? Rav focused on his work, soon sitting in the carriage as they began their return to Kroom Town.

"Champions Guard hasn't left the marsh," Izen said.

"I wish I could see their faces when they realise we've already got the armour." Mulk laughed.

"They've had a bad run," Piyo said, joining him.

"Trent's got the worst of it," Izen noted, looking for Rav's reaction. "Are you gonna do anything?"

Rav continued to stare out the window, watching the strange landscape. "No."

"That's good. Trent's not one to apologise or double down. We'll help mediate. If you change your mind, come speak to me. We'll be smart about it."

Rav nodded. The message was clear. *Don't do anything stupid. You're one of us now.* He watched them out the corner of his eye. A group. He was part of a group. He wanted to be part of a group. He couldn't trust them, though. That was something he refused to fall for again. But maybe the Blood Hounds would be the start of his own unit.

It wasn't long until he spotted familiar terrain as they arrived back near Donsden.

"Kroom Town," Miels bellowed from the driver's seat.

"Let's give Niklaus the good news." Izen jumped out the carriage.

Mulk shoved Rav ahead of him. "You found the body; go be a hero."

"You did the work."

"Rav, go use your status to get our unit a better report." Amine threw him forward again.

"Come." Izen grabbed his shoulder, pulling him towards a square, sturdy building.

Rav looked back. Lyra was with him. Mulk lugged Baron Ghourts' armour and hammer behind them.

Izen burst through the door. "Call Niklaus."

The receptionist hurried from his desk and into the back room before soon returning with a blond, clean-shaven, and rather fat man. Rav squinted at Niklaus, dazzled by the glint coming off the rings and necklace he wore.

"Izen," Niklaus greeted, his round face glowing red. "Sister, welcome."

Lyra gave a polite nod.

"Niklaus." Izen flicked his eyes to where the merchant had just come from. "We need a room."

"Come." He led the Blood Hounds to a small, candlelit, windowless room at the rear of the building with a rectangular table and watched as Mulk set Ghourts' equipment on it with a *thunk*. Niklaus bared his teeth in avarice as he traced a finger over the dried blood staining the breastplate. "I'm surprised you're the ones to complete the scavenge; after your delayed start, Champions Guard were favoured." He lifted his gaze to linger on Rav. "I thought you'd be disappointed."

"We found Rav to be worth the wait." Izen patted Rav's shoulder and threw Niklaus a dashing grin. "He found the body."

"I heard. Birds travel faster than horses." Niklaus smoothed his lips, but the hunger in his eyes remained. "Sucked into an underground river, then chased by dozens of goebbers, yet you look well. You even had time to find Ghourts."

"Ghourts also fell in the river. I found his body on my way out," Rav stated as Izen glanced at him out the corner of his eye. "Goebbers got him."

Niklaus' gaze bored into Rav. "That easy?"

Rav shrugged, his chest growing hot as his skin prickled. "He was hidden behind some rocks."

"I see, I see... Well, I'm not here to pry into your affairs. I move money around, link people together. Here." Niklaus broke his stare and reached into his robe to pull out a small roll of paper used for bird messages. "This is the information I received ten days ago." He handed it to Rav to read.

Nameless Rav: brown hair, plain face, thin. Wears chainmail shirt. Aided by Sister Ha'th Bey Riene, Lyra; H'aw E' Sh, Han; Ar T'ch Shr', Siere. Three drops King's Blood. Novice spearman, throwing knives. Unfavoured to advance.

"And this is what I received two days ago."

Nameless Rav: brown hair, plain face, skinny. Chainmail shirt and hide armour. Aided by Ha'th Bey Riene, Lyra; Blood Hounds. Three drops King's Blood. Novice spearman, throwing knives. Unknown technique used to escape colony of goebbers. Caution advised. Investment required.

"These are from your spies?" Rav asked.

"Informants."

"It seems there are many people watching me."

"My network is only small; Baron Glass will have multiple witness accounts of the events, including from Champions Guard."

Rav looked at Izen.

"We don't report on members of our unit," he swore.

"Thank you for showing me what others think of me," Rav spoke to Niklaus.

"Not at all. I'm happy to provide such gossip." Niklaus smiled. "I'm hosting a dinner tonight and would like to invite you and your companions to attend."

"Champion Delmare is the leader of my unit." Rav looked back to Izen.

"Of course." Niklaus also faced him.

"We'll be there," Izen said.

"Excellent." Niklaus clapped his hands together. "I won't keep you, then. Will you store your payment with me?"

"Yes. We'll collect it when we leave."

Niklaus nodded. "Good work."

The Blood Hounds exited the building.

Back in the carriage, Rav spoke to Lyra. "What did he want?"

"What do you think he wanted?"

"To be friendly?" Rav guessed.

"Because..."

"I'm Called."

"Partly." Lyra looked to Izen.

"He wants to invest in you," Izen answered. "Niklaus keeps what he owns by making powerful friends. He's seen that you have potential and wants to help you grow so that you can support him in the future."

"Is that good?"

"For us, yes. We'll get better tasks, more information, more money. But it's your choice. We're with you for now. If you advance the way Niklaus wants, you'll leave us behind."

"There are other considerations, too," Piyo began. "If you accept, Niklaus' enemies become yours. More resources, more competition. Those Called tend to maintain friendly relations with all parties to avoid being targeted."

Rav shook his head, dumbfounded at the constant emerging conflicts. "For how poorly our first meeting went, you lot don't seem so bad now."

"You weren't one of us then." Mulk laughed. "The other units'll betray each other—they'll fight amongst themselves, use whatever they can for personal gain. We know people like that don't live long. You need friends in the Sink. A good reputation will save you many times more than some extra money or cheap status. Even if you have a Heaven's Tear, if you get surrounded, you die. As I said before, who's going to watch you sleep?"

Chapter 14

Rav mulled Niklaus' offer over before deciding to reject joining him. He wasn't going to stay in the Sink; whatever promises he made to the merchant would be broken when he ran back to Pitt, and once Niklaus learned of his betrayal, he'd hunt him down. There was also Baron Tryxwin to consider. Two people had made offers to recruit him. What if there were more? Shouldn't he look at all the options before picking one? Maybe there was someone who'd give him a Name without hunting him down for leaving.

Izen tapped the carriage floor with his boot, drawing Rav's attention. "This is your share from Ghourts' pouches." He threw a coin pouch at him. "How're you going to celebrate our return?"

Rav jolted as the carriage squeaked over uneven ground, the pouch hitting him in the chest before he caught it. After steadying himself, he looked at the scratch marks on his armour, weighing the coins in his hand. "I need to repair my armour."

"Don't worry about that," Piyo tutted with a flick of his elegant hand. "Money for equipment and carriages comes from the Blood Hounds' coffers. Payment from tasks goes to the unit for the next scavenge. That pouch is for you to enjoy."

"You seem lost; I'll give you some inspiration," Mulk started. "I'm going to drink and feast until I've nothing left. I'll buy you a mug."

"What about the dinner with Niklaus?"

"It's fashionable to arrive drunk," Mulk assured him, Izen and Piyo laughing.

"I'll make sure you don't do anything stupid," Izen added.

Rav pursed his lips as the carriage ride smoothed, the ground flattening, a clamour growing loud enough to carry over the rattling of wooden wheels. Looking out the window, he spotted the familiar streets of Kroom Town as they trundled towards The Last Drink tavern. What else would he do? Rav nodded. "I'll have a drink, then."

Mulk wiped the sweat from his face with the back of his hand, cheer and laughter from dozens of people rumbling from just ahead. "Great. You'll enjoy this."

The carriage soon slowed to a stop, Mulk opening the door wide. The Last Drink was packed with people drinking and jostling. They turned towards the carriage, faces rough and blustered, rising with grins as they seemed to recognise the brute. Mulk stepped out the carriage with his head high and his chest puffed in the same display he'd taught Rav on Mount Don.

"*The Blood Hounds return victorious*," he shouted.

The revellers cheered as they parted out of his way, many patting his back. Mulk marched past them all as though he'd won a Challenge, only stopping at the tavern entrance to wave Rav after him.

Rav glanced at Lyra, who tilted her head for him to follow. Before Rav could hesitate, Amine pushed him out towards the tavern, a smirk curling their plain lips to bring some playful life to their androgenous face. Rav stumbled through the crowd with Amine guarding his back, gathering his decorum as he did.

Mulk grabbed Rav as he caught up and pushed him into The Last Drink first as though presenting him before the crowd. "This here's Nameless Rav. He survived the Brack, he survived the goebbers, he even spent a night with Baron Tryxwin." Mulk grinned as the crowd clamoured. "With him in our unit, we'll fleece Blood Marsh and charge into Ut Sh'za."

"*Waaah*," everyone shouted, mugs banging on the tables.

Rav looked around at all the people cheering at him, memories of returning to Pitt victorious from fighting in Stone's Way surfacing. A lump stuck in his throat. The other Blood Hounds entered and stood around him, also patting his back in triumph. No one was looking at him as someone Nameless. He was a Blood Hound, just as they'd promised. His eyes glistened.

At Mulk's order, the bartender started pouring mug after mug of ale. Amine stuffed one into his hands.

"Drink. You've a reputation to build."

A gulp of warm ale cleared the choke of emotions. Aye, there was always a celebration when he returned. Hadn't he finally succeeded at something? His first victory in the Sink. Rav tipped the rest of the ale down his throat, cheeks reddening, the crowd chanting.

"He'll drink a mug," Piyo sang, riling the tavern to join him.

"He'll drink the sea," they sang.

"And when he's done,

"He'll have to pee."

Rav wiped his mouth with a burp.

"So, you do drink." Mulk laughed, handing Rav another mug of ale. "You said you're good at throwing knives, right? Come, there's a board." He faced the crowd. "Anyone want to wager against us?"

"I'll wager." A woman broke out the crowd to step up to the line. Petite and lithe, she rolled her shoulder to warm up. "I'm here with my unit, Scorpion Point."

Six people from the audience cheered.

"I'll get drinks for the Blood Hounds if you win. If I win, buy us a few."

"Done."

Mulk led Rav to the back of the room, where a painted wooden board was set into the tavern wall. There were different coloured circles across it, each puckered with chips. "Game's easy. Stand behind the line. When a colour is called, throw. First to miss loses," he explained.

Rav nodded, readying a throwing knife, the Blood Hounds and the audience from earlier gathered around. The woman stood next to him with a grin, also ready.

"Red."

"Yellow."

"Green."

"Green."

The rounds flew by, Rav never missing as a sense of clarity locked onto him. Challengers came and lost, the Blood Hounds drinking for free, until there was no one left. The clarity faded. Rav stumbled, thoughts suddenly sloshing around his head along with the ale in his stomach.

"Woah." Izen held his arm to steady him. "You should rest; we've still got Niklaus' banquet to attend."

"*Ha*." Mulk rumbled with laughter. "To think you are this good. You might even be able to rival the Sisters."

Rav frowned. How long had it been? Where was Lyra? He spun around and saw her watching him from the corner of the tavern with a small smile. *Phew*. How had he managed to drink so much without realising it? Why was he only feeling the effects now? He groaned as his stomach churned. He stumbled again, Izen catching him. Amine helped him carry Rav up to a room, and behind a thick, wooden door, they sighed in relief after laying him down on the bed. Lyra followed them in and sat at the bedside, still smiling over him.

"When we going to Niklaush's?" Rav slurred, trying to remember when he'd started lying down.

"You have some time to recover," Izen answered. "You might also be expected to arrive late; I saw some of Niklaus' men downstairs."

"Stupid spies," Rav huffed. "Why's everyone watching me? Just leave me alone."

"Here." Amine handed him a glass of water. "Drink this."

Rav scowled. Lyra looked at him. *Fine*. He grabbed the glass and drank it in one. *Done, now*... He looked around for Kayla—*Oh*. Sadness sunk in. None of his friends or family were here.

Nothing from Pitt was. Surrounded by strangers. Except Lyra. Especially Lyra. His vision blurred with tears, guts twisting as though they were eating themselves. Everything dulled. Where was he? Why was he here? Why wasn't he home? What had he done? *Stupid, reckless, Nameless fool.* He'd ruined everything. One small success wasn't enough to change that. Nothing he did ever could. *Wakeman, I'm sorry.* Rav buried his face in the bedding to hide his tears.

"What changed?" Izen whispered to Lyra.

She gazed down at Rav. "He was reminded of his home. He was loved there."

"Was?"

"Is."

Izen nodded before leaving Rav and Lyra alone.

The sun was setting. Rav still felt warm, but the giddiness of the alcohol had left him. His throat was dry. There was a waterskin next to his bed. He sipped the water down.

"Is it time?" He looked at Lyra, who was wiping down her sword with her sweet-smelling oiled cloth.

"Nearly. What do you plan on doing?"

"I'm staying with the Blood Hounds. I'll be polite but decline his offer."

Lyra gazed down at her sword. "Getting Niklaus' resources would help you..."

Help you stay in the Sink. Make you stay in the Sink. No doubt, she also knew what Niklaus' patronage meant.

Rav pursed his lips. "Baron Tryxwin's a better option. If I'm good enough, I'll join Baron Glass or Jinkin," he said, seeing Lyra nod, seeming to accept his excuse. "I need to get ready." He got up, walking to a basin with a mirror while rubbing his face to clear the last signs of drunkenness.

"I will send for some water." Lyra exited the room.

After cleaning up, his hair neat and armour cleaned, Rav held himself with confidence. A Name would come. People would follow. His Heaven's Tear was powerful. Three years. If people kept helping him, maybe he could return in two.

Niklaus' mansion was smaller than Hafar's, built for defence rather than opulence. Guards, watchtowers, castellations. The building was well-lit with blazing fires guiding tens of guests towards the dining hall. Entering the building, the floors were carpeted with mutant hides, the walls decorated with paintings and weapons. Incense burned in holders along the halls, making the building smell like wildflowers.

The murmur grew louder as they approached the gathering hall before the dining room. People were standing around small tables, sipping from orange-stained glass cups, some wearing polished armour with Blood Palms on their broad chests, others dressed in colourful silk robes. Each one was full-faced. Izen strode into the room, drawing everyone's attention, but they soon looked past him to lock onto Rav. The best-dressed guests approached them while the others continued their conversations, waiting their turn.

"Champion Delmare, the Blood Hounds grow ever stronger," a merchant woman complimented.

"After building years of experience, we're ready to stand proud in Blood Marsh," he replied, catching her glance. "This is Rav, our new member, and Sister Lyra, his guide."

"It's always a pleasure to meet a Sister." The woman bowed. "And I'm sure it'll be a pleasure to meet you too, Rav. I seem to have heard your name a lot in the past few days after your success on Mount Don." She stood and studied his face, wincing. "Your cheeks are thin. I'll have a servant bring some cheeses." She beckoned one over, watching as Rav politely took a bite. "My merchant group has operated in Blood Marsh for six years, so our supplies have contributed to three Barons advancing to the second layer," she told him. "If you need aid, please find one of our members."

Rav smiled as wide and politely as he could manage. She didn't care about him, only what he could do for her. At least Cata and Niklaus had asked him a little about himself. At least they'd interacted with the Blood Hounds. "I'll keep it in mind," he replied, stepping closer to Lyra.

Her turn over, she was shuffled out so that another person could make their pitch. The content was the same. Compliment the Blood Hounds, greet Lyra, give him backhanded praise. It was all about his potential, about what he *could* be. With their help. They always offered help. *"We'll save you, Rav. Then you'll owe us."*

"I've been a Champion since I was twenty-one," the latest spokesman said. "I run a supply line through Blood Marsh. We could always use the help of another unit; the Blood Hounds would be welcome to join us on a run. Our route is safe and well paid. If you have some time, come see how my unit operates, Rav."

"Aye. My duties with the Blood Hounds keep me busy, but if I have time, I'll come over."

The Champion nodded, then left.

"Esteemed guests," a servant announced, "please enter the dining hall."

The others would have to wait. The Blood Hounds seized the escape, heading straight over. An enormous n-shaped table filled the room, a red silk tablecloth covered in empty platters awaiting food adorning it. Niklaus sat at the head seat in the centre, dressed in gold-spun robes.

"Welcome."

As the Blood Hounds entered, servants came to guide them to their places. Rav was seated next to Niklaus, Lyra next to him, then Izen and the rest of the Blood Hounds following.

"Rav, it's good to see you." Niklaus beamed. "Welcome to this humble home. It's a shame I can only use it for business convenience; if the risk of a mutant coming down from the red layer to destroy Kroom Town wasn't so great, I'd have invested far more into it." Niklaus tutted. "When you visit Donsden, you can see where I truly live."

Rav gazed at the lavish tapestries and artworks lining a room half the size of the entire ground floor of the Carvell home. It was almost grotesque. How could anyone want more than this? "Your home in Donsden must be magnificent," he mumbled.

"It is, it is." Niklaus nodded, neck wobbling. "I trust you've spoken to my guests. I suppose they all tried to recruit you?"

Rav forced a smile. "They were all friendly."

"I'm sure they were. See, Rav"—Niklaus directed Rav's gaze to everyone taking their seats—"all these people are part of my network. They all eat at my table. Every piece they've offered you... is mine."

Rav lost his breath.

"You want access to the Blood Marsh supply line? I have it. You want to join another unit? Done. You want your own unit? I'll train you to become the greatest leader Blood Marsh has ever seen." He paused to let Rav comprehend what he was saying. "I have a strong connection to Baron Glass with my cousin, Sarsa Payne, as one of his concubines. That means I also have a connection to Jinkin. I'm sure they'll reach out to you, but with my help, they'll beg you to join them. I know Blood Marsh; I know the Sink. I know what it takes for someone to complete their Calling, and I can give it to you."

Rav gulped. How many Champions were here? How much trade was being conducted? With a network like this, Baron Hewett would be trampled to dust, Champion Sar slaughtered under the rush of Challenges from people keen to receive Niklaus' favour. Wasn't that the power he wanted? He wiped his sweaty hands on his lap, biting his tongue. Pitt was worth more. Everyone here would think like he just had; they all wanted Niklaus' seat. There were no friends. This wasn't a home. No one would sacrifice themselves for Niklaus' mistakes.

Rav smiled. "It's much to think on."

Niklaus nodded. "I understand. You're new to Blood Marsh and the Sink. The scale of things here is much, much bigger than outside. Enjoy the evening, speak to my guests; find what you want from me, then present your terms. No worthwhile friendship is built on deception. We must both be equals, or we'll end up destroying each other."

All guests seated, Niklaus stood to face them. "Friends, we're here to celebrate. I look around this table and I see many new faces, many new opportunities, many new possibilities. Tonight is for you, to thank you for the efforts you've all made. It is for us to ensure our continued prosperity in Blood Marsh."

The audience banged on their tables with cheers. A servant walked up to Niklaus holding something wrapped in silk. Niklaus picked it up.

"Blood Marsh has a new visitor. We're also here to welcome Rav. As a show of our friendship, I'd like to present you with a gift."

Rav stood and held the small item, pulling away the cloth to reveal a clasp made from folded metal that left gorgeous stains across its surface. It wasn't extravagant, though, kept practical so he could wear it on scavenges. As exquisite as it was, an itch prickled the back of Rav's mind, keeping him from admiring the metalwork with anything other than cold suspicion.

"I gift you this napet so that you may better hide your secrets," Niklaus announced. "My blacksmith used a special technique to make the metal flexible, so when you fill out, it will fit just as well." He laughed.

"It's a generous gift." Rav bowed, then plucked his napet off and slotted the new one in place, finding it a little big. "I'm certain it will aid me as I journey through the Sink."

"Excellent." Niklaus clapped. "Now, we feast."

Servants carrying sizzling plates of food streamed out the dining hall wings, setting the food down on the platters. The guests cheered, then loaded up their plates and filled their cups with wine. Rav tried to keep his head low, always catching someone watching him whenever he looked up. He'd smile, nod, or take a bite of food to move them along, too aware of the new napet on his neck. It was a clever gift for Niklaus to give. A reminder that the Blood Hounds had attacked him. A reminder for him to grow. A symbol to others that he was with Niklaus. The perfect gift to cause a rift in his unit and drive him to Niklaus.

Niklaus finished speaking to the person on the other side of him and turned to Rav. "No one seems to know much about you, not even me. You're not a Champion or a Contender or even a soldier. There are no records of you in battles or a clue as to who your Baron is, if they're still alive. It's as though you've appeared out of nowhere. Tell me, do you like the Sink?"

Rav swallowed a mouthful of stew, catching Lyra glance at him, picking an empty answer. "It's different to my home. I'm used to rolling hills and mossy bogs rather than the mountain and marshes."

"Indeed, many who come here stare up at Mount Don in awe." Niklaus chuckled. "Does it intimidate you?"

"It is enormous, but it's not the mountain that's dangerous, is it? I've fought a mutant like the ones in the red layer before. A 'Zet Ar. It trampled thirty men before I managed to lure it into a trap. To build Donsden, how many 'Zet Ar had to be killed? How many venture down the mountain now and have to be culled?"

"If that information interests you, I have a collection of accounts dating back to the first Sink explorers in my library," Niklaus said with a half-smile. "But I'm afraid the paper is fragile and requires special techniques to view. I have a few newer copies that I can send, but they're incomplete."

"Join me to access my information." "I'd like to look at anything you can spare," Rav declined.

"Sure." Niklaus kept his smile. "Where did you live?"

"A town a few months' travel from Fermuch."

"A 'Zet Ar managed to make it that far? People really do have to band together to survive outside now. Good allies are becoming invaluable." He paused. "I'm surprised to hear you fought a 'Zet Ar for your home. Wouldn't a town want to keep such a capable warrior?"

Rav sipped more wine as he thought. Niklaus was searching for why he was Nameless. Rav recounted the events, leaving out important details.

Niklaus looked bemused. "That's it? You interfered in a Challenge? Champions die all the time in Blood Marsh. Banishing a Called One over something so meaningless," Niklaus muttered, "this Baron is a fool."

"He won't be a fool for much longer," Rav sneered. "I'll kill him."

"Well." Niklaus' smile widened. "Perhaps I can help you with that. As a favour."

The feast came to an end, servants clearing away the platters while everyone chatted, the guests looking around for the next event. Rav had to smother his burps, clutching his bulging belly.

Niklaus stood. "There will be music in the adjacent hall."

Returning to the gathering hall, the tables had been removed, and a band was playing an upbeat tune on stringed instruments.

"Do you dance, Rav?" he asked.

He shrugged. "I can tap my foot to the beat."

"Perhaps one of the ladies waiting could teach you." Niklaus directed Rav's gaze around the dining hall to the women looking his way.

Was this another method Niklaus was using to try to bind them together?

"I'll have to disappoint them. I've a girl waiting for me."

"A hopeful romantic." Niklaus clasped his hands together. "I'll scurry the ladies." He whispered to a servant, who went off to spread the word. "Now, I'll leave you to your companions," Niklaus excused himself. "I have some old friends to greet."

Rav bowed, then returned to the others. The Blood Hounds had gathered in the corner of the dining hall beside the servants' entrance, waiting for him. Mulk and Piyo glanced at the women entering the dancing hall.

"I think I'm in love." Piyo was staring at a woman in hide armour, who threw him seductive looks.

"Me too." Mulk was gaping at a woman in a tight dress. Another woman walked in front of him, and his stare followed. "Her, definitely."

Miels patted Mulk's shoulder. "They have to pick you too."

"That's why I'm smart." Mulk pulled a cunning grin. "I don't focus on one like blondie over here; I chase after many. They can't all ignore me."

Miels muffled his chuckle with his hand. "Sure."

"Are you always so... casual?" Rav asked. "Shouldn't romance be about courtship?"

"Life's short in the Sink." Izen shrugged. "Romance has to be quick. It's also a good way to build partnerships."

"If one of these ladies gets pregnant, I'll marry them," Mulk swore, acting a gentleman.

"There are also measures women in the Sink can take to avoid starting families," Amine added. "They drink special tinctures that can prevent pregnancy."

Rav frowned. What was the point in being with a partner if you didn't want a child? Anything else was unfilial. The Sink really had corrupted everyone inside it.

"Go on, then," Izen dismissed the pair.

Piyo glided over to his date, a figure of poise and elegance. Mulk lumbered over to one of the women he liked, muttered something, and was shooed away. Despite Niklaus' message, there were a few brave ladies still eyeing Rav.

"What about you?" Rav looked at the remaining members of the Blood Hounds.

"Married," Miels said. "She's far away from all of this. My children will come join me when they're old enough."

"I've someone as well. She'd outshine all these ladies," Izen followed.

"I've no interest in these people," Amine mumbled, glancing at Rav's new napet, head lowered.

"In honour of having a Sister as a guest, we have prepared a song in Ca'ome," one of the musicians announced. "We present, Ssh Hss r."

Rav winced at their mispronouncing of Earth and Thunder. Still, he went over to see what they'd play, hiding from the coy looks being thrown his way. The band had put down their instruments, replacing them with a basin of water, a box of rocks, sand, and pipes. Lyra stood next to him, also watching. *Ssh*, the sand was scraped. *Tch, blol*, the water splashed. *Tak, clack*, the rocks jumbled. The dancing stopped, everyone listening. Rav cocked his head with a frown. Somewhere in the sounds, somewhere in chaos, there was meaning. Meaning he couldn't grasp. Lyra glowed, delighted.

"What is it?" Rav whispered.

"Come." She held his hand and took him to dance. Leading, she walked forward, then moved into waving motions with her arms, dragging Rav to follow. "This is an ocean beach," she whispered. "Though you have never been to one, through Ca'ome, you will understand it."

Rav fumbled around, flustered, trying his best to match Lyra's fluid movements. Step with a *tak*, wave with a *ssh*. She brought him closer, using her strength to lift him through the motions, stopping, starting, and twisting, all at her whim, pulling Rav along. Rav gasped. It was only a sliver, but as they danced, some of the clarity he felt when throwing knives returned. He lost his breath. Suddenly, Lyra made sense, her every move falling exactly where he expected, somehow melding with the music. Letting Lyra control him, he listened closer. *Tch*, the wave hit the shore; *tak*, a stone beach; *ssh*, sand between the stones shifted. *R, clack*, someone was standing on the shore. It was a story—a walk along the shoreline. Rav leaned into the noise, attempting to follow the words on his own. Free from Lyra's guidance, he couldn't keep up, the changes too quick; just as he was trying to be a wave, it hit the shore, then he had to become a stone, a person, sand.

It was impossible. But Lyra managed it. Rav returned under her control with his new understanding, the clarity building, his dance flowing, the music swelling, all to a great crescendo. And in that instant, for a single, minuscule moment, he breathed salty air.

Rav gasped, the breeze shocking him out his enthralment. How did he know what salty air was? Was that... Heaven? The sound *was* the world. It *was* existing. Lyra noticed the change in Rav, her joy blooming into her dance until its end. With a *tch, ssh*, the last footprint was washed away, the band going quiet. Rav stopped, breathless, his harmony with the World ending without Lyra's guidance. The audience stood still, staring at them.

"Magnificent," Niklaus whispered, breaking the stillness to free everyone from their stupor. "I have seen Sisters dance before, but your movements were exceptional, Ha'th Bey Riene."

"I had a partner." Lyra looked at Rav, everyone following.

He blinked, heart racing. Did that sensation mean the World was real? Did that mean his Calling was real? Everything Lyra was leading him to existed. He had a destiny. What about Pitt?

"Indeed." Niklaus nodded. "The unity between those Called and the Sisters is beyond our understanding."

"It was an honour to perform Ssh hss r for you." The band bowed to Lyra, along with the audience, who then closed in around Rav.

"Do you know Ca'ome?"

"Your dance was perfect; have you danced before?"

"Can you hear the World?"

Swarmed by insatiable curiosity, Rav gritted his teeth, wishing them all away. How could he relive that instant surrounded by all these people? His polite replies became clipped.

"Rav, I didn't know you could dance," Izen called, the crowd huffing but accepting his position as Rav's unit leader as they parted to let him through.

"Lyra carried me through." Rav laughed, moving into the open space created.

Izen patted his shoulder with an understanding wink. "You look tired; come eat some more."

It was a valid excuse. Rav was released back to the Blood Hounds and whispered to Lyra, "What happened?"

She was still smiling. "You listened to Ca'ome."

"There's more to it. I breathed salty air. How is that possible?"

"That is what Ca'ome can do." Lyra indicated the instruments. "You know the stone, you know the water, but salt was in the sand. You know the taste, and when the wind blew, the salt shifted. Your mind remembered them both. We all live in the World. We are all connected by It."

The World. The concept wasn't so hollow anymore.

Rav blinked, too hot, chest stifled. He took a deep breath, finding a slight taste of salt still on his tongue. Too much.

He pushed past the Blood Hounds, towards the mansion's exit, bidding everyone goodnight, declining Niklaus' offer to stay in his guest room. Izen followed with the remaining Blood Hounds, joking about needing rest and having too much to drink as they escorted Rav away. They returned to The Last Drink.

It was late and cold. Rav wrapped himself up in his blanket as he shivered in bed, at the edge of sleep but unable to quiet the last of his spinning thoughts. How could the World be real? Something so great wouldn't need him. Aye, it didn't exist; he was drunk, exhausted, tricked by whatever strange powers lurked in the Sink. But as he finally relaxed, as he succumbed to tiredness, as he embraced the silence, he *listened*. And there, in the nothing... something breathed.

Chapter 15

The World was real. Hu v' sh: It had spoken. Rav lay frozen in bed as the morning sun rose, listening to Lyra dress, tell him she had something to do, then leave. What should he do? It was terrifying. Horrifying. All around him, watching him, pushing him. The World. He'd stand in that ice fortress and conduct the slaughter of a thousand soldiers. He'd become the Ghoul and devour people alive. He had a path, a chosen path, all for some great scheme. All under something else's control. No Pitt, no life with Kayla, no revenge. Bound to the Sink. He'd been Called to face its dangers, to fight against every monstrosity between him and whatever the World wanted.

He gulped. He needed to run. Flee. Disappear. Get his family and go. Being chased by Tibald Sar and Baron Hewett was nothing compared to something that pervaded everything. The Heaven's Tear... Rav traced the back of his neck, feeling the melted skin. It *had* chosen him. Tricked him. Trapped him. He scratched at his neck, trying to grab the incongruent cube and rip it out. *Ah.* He tore some burned skin and winced. Blood. He couldn't get it out. It was part of him now. No...

Breath quickening, trying to match his trembling heart, Rav gasped. Unable to breathe, unable to move, he couldn't fight back. His hands were clenched into fists, nails digging into his palms. He had to move. Rav struggled to roll over, falling out of the bed and landing on his shoulder. The impact loosened him, returning some control.

Dry. Water. He stumbled to the basin and splashed his face. *Better.* Now he could think. He wasn't fighting monsters yet; he was in a room, safe, alone. Rav released a shaking breath.

The World was real. What did that mean? He had a path, but... *that's right.* There was no hand around this throat, no force at his back. If he wanted to, he could sit here and not move. He could do what he wanted. He *would* do what he wanted. His plans still worked. Nothing had changed—

Rav remembered that breath. Something had definitely changed. He didn't know what it would mean, so... ignore it. Face it when it came. He wasn't leaving yet. He'd be stronger, more powerful when it came time to decide. He'd be different too. The new him would deal with it. That was the best he could do for now. Keep everything normal.

After changing, he headed downstairs, finding the Blood Hounds enjoying a light breakfast at a large table. He took his seat and stared at the bread and cheese on his plate. *Ugh*, just the smell made him queasy.

Miels chuckled, nudging him. "That was good food, eh. Get us invited to more of those things. Here. Today's for liquid." He handed Rav a cup of milk, which settled him.

Piyo and Mulk had returned. Mulk was staring at Rav, gloating.

"It went well?"

"I told you my strategy works. It took some time, but anything worthwhile does." He put a hand on Rav's shoulder. "She was robust, flexible, with thick thighs good for holding on. The kind of woman who wrestles for control." He laughed. "Yes, firm muscles capable of pinning me down, techniques that coiled her around my waist..."

Rav endured the odd descriptions as he sipped his milk. At least it was a welcome break from his thoughts.

"We're going to Donsden to prepare for the red layer," Izen announced sometime later to Rav. "I've spoken to Lyra. The red layer isn't somewhere we can protect you. You've seen the 'Zet Ar and what they can do; we'll all be working to stay alive. We'll get your armour repaired and wait until you can carry a shield. We'll also train you."

"Aye." Rav nodded.

"Good. Get ready to leave."

Rav collected his items from his room, wearing a robe with his chainmail, bag, and new napet. Drying out his notebook and Kayla's handkerchief hadn't restored them. He took them with him anyway. Lyra returned as they were about to set off.

The Blood Hounds headed for the city, soon entering the eastern portcullis. Izen led them through the winding streets with practised ease until they reached a three-storey wooden building near the market square. It stood alone, the door painted blood red. Izen unlocked it and entered.

Rav sneezed, light shining through the door showing a month's worth of dust floating in the air. Inside was narrow, unfurnished to keep as much space as possible, with the stairs to the left of the main door, but the wood was all in good condition, oiled without any chips or scrapes. Rav didn't smell any damp or rot. The windows were all shut, leaving it dim everywhere but the front corridor.

"My bed." Miels pushed past Izen towards a side room, entering it before closing the door behind him.

Piyo swatted the dusty air. "Open all the windows."

"I'll show you to your rooms." Izen led Rav and Lyra up the stairs to the top floor, where there were four rooms. "You'll need to clean them; they haven't been used in a long time."

"Is this your house?"

"It belongs to the Blood Hounds," Izen answered, pointing to the first door. "This room is for storage. Choose one from the rest."

Lyra chose the room opposite the first, while Rav picked the one next to hers. Both were small, containing a single bed frame and a table. He walked into his room and dumped his equipment on the floor, stirring up swirls of thick dust from what coated everything. Hurrying to open the window at the end of the room, which looked out into an alley, he propped the latch open, grabbed a cloth, and started cleaning, his eyes itchy. Soon, his room was habitable, complete with some spare bedding and a feather-stuffed mattress that he had found in the storage room.

The stomps of the other Blood Hounds carried through the wooden floors with annoying clarity. *Creak, stomp, stomp, stomp.* He rubbed his eyes, then left to find Lyra, who was polishing armour in her room.

"I'm heading into the market," he said, chest stifled as he faced her. As he faced the World. "There's something I want to do. Alone."

She pursed her lips but nodded. "Be careful."

Izen provided him with a map of the city market, including businesses that were favourable to the Blood Hounds, as well as his insignia to identify himself. He had to be back by supper, or they'd come looking for him.

Rav found Amine kneeling by the door as he made to leave, stuffing frayed thread and scratched armour into a large bag.

They looked over their shoulder at him. "I can show you the arena before I hand these off for repair. It's where we'll be training you."

Rav nodded in thanks before helping them lift the bag, then followed Amine north-east through bustling streets, soon spotting the top of a large, curved stone wall above the rooftops ahead. Closer, he caught the sound of clashing metal over the cries of merchants and porters, seeing a gaping arched entrance manned by two guards at the base of the arena exterior. Sunlight flooded the reception—a plain room with a large desk and numerous doors leading into the building's bowels—but a deep shadow lay just before it. Rav glanced up at the beaked Keep looming overhead, suddenly shivering as though he were being watched.

Amine was recognised at the entrance, able to take him past the guards to the seats that overlooked the arena grounds. A unit was training inside, hacking at each other with blunt weapons.

"This is the main stage," Amine explained. "If you Challenge a Champion, this is where you'll fight, in full view of everyone." They indicated the Keep walls, where Baron Glass and any other officials would have clear sight of the duel. "There are private rooms inside the arena, but they're more expensive to rent." They next led him under the seats to view the other training rooms, some of which were in use. "We'll start training you tomorrow. Basic movements will be done outside, while techniques will be practised in private so no one knows what you're capable of."

After the tour, Amine introduced him as a member of the Blood Hounds to the receptionists and guards so he'd be able to enter on his own, ending the tour back at the arched entrance.

"I have other business to do." Amine folded their arms as they faced him with a raised eyebrow. "Don't get in trouble."

Rav puffed out his chest as he took a defiant stance. "I can handle myself."

"Sure." Amine scoffed at him before walking back out into the crowd.

Rav hunched back over as he checked his map, seeing a bookstore marked down, and headed to it. Without Lyra or Amine, the busy streets closed in, people bumping, shoving, jostling him around in the crowds. Rav fought to stay on his feet, a tight grasp on his coin pouch. After weaving his way into an opening, he pressed ahead to find the shop, seeing it set between two other buildings. The Inkwell was narrow and a little lopsided, stacks of paper towered inside to block most of the view through the windows. Rav had to shove open the door due to it scraping along the wooden floorboards.

"Are you open?" he called.

"Yes, yes," a man replied from within.

It smelled of old books, which lined the surprisingly spacious interior in rows of bookshelves. The roof had windows cut into it, but instead of the shutters he was used to, stained glass filled the gaps, dyeing the room amber. Though every available space was filled with something, it was clean. Rav skimmed over a shelf, reading the titles on the spines, so many words dizzying. So much information. How could anyone read it all? He had to stare at the floor. What would Wakeman have thought of all these pages?

"Can you read?"

Rav looked up to see a middle-aged man with brown hair and a missing left leg. He carried himself around on a crutch.

"Aye, I've never seen this many words, though."

"I offer lessons if you want."

"I have other business." Rav reached into his bag to retrieve his notebook. "Can you restore something like this?" He opened it to show the destroyed pages.

"Come with me." The man led Rav through more winding bookshelves to a wider space separate from the books at the back of the store, where he had a book workshop set up, with a magnifying glass, lantern, and various strong-smelling glues. He took his seat on a high stool behind the desk, pointing to an empty holder under the magnifying glass. "Set it there."

Rav opened the notebook with care, wincing as the paper crinkled, and set it in the holder for the man to inspect.

The bookkeeper pursed his lips as he adjusted his magnifying glass to focus on a grey smudge. "Water damage?"

"Aye."

"How long ago?"

"Five days."

He grunted. "This is difficult work. Is there something specific you want from it? A map or cypher maybe?"

"I'd like all of it," Rav answered. "It's from my home."

"Sentimental value?" He frowned. "You want to spend money on this?"

Rav nodded. "There are drawings of where I lived and the local land."

The man ran his finger down a page, feeling the bumps. "I won't be able to get all of it back. It's good that you use an old pencil, as it leaves grooves in the pages that I can follow, but anywhere the pages are distorted, the surface is lost."

"I'll pay for anything you can recover."

The man nodded. “Where’d you live?”

“Pitt, near Ghoul Wood.” The writing would reveal that.

“Ah.” He got up and went to find a book on a shelf just across from his workshop desk, flicking through the pages until he found what he was looking for. “Baron Hewett’s new territory?” He showed Rav the sketch of a mountain insignia.

“Aye.”

“I’ll pay for the information in your notebook. Any page with a map or details on the local terrain will be free. If you want me to keep it secret, though, it’ll be very expensive.”

Rav hesitated. His notebook contained all the secrets of the Ghoulsmen; it could put Pitt at risk. ...Did the Ghoulsmen even exist now? And, once he returned, they’d leave anyway. Most of all, he wanted to see his home again. “You can have all the information, but I want a delay on its release.” Rav placed the Blood Hounds’ token on the table.

“A member of the Blood Hounds.” The man looked over Rav again. “You must be Nameless Rav,” he realised, standing to bow. “I can delay it,” he hurried.

“Now you know that this contains information on a Called One, it should be more valuable,” he negotiated. “Restore the notebook but keep it secret for one year.”

“A year...” He sucked his teeth but nodded. “I’ll work night and day. Return here in a week.”

With the terms set, Rav looked around the store. “Do you sell information?”

“I do.” The man puffed out his chest. “I’m part of Baron Glass’ network, along with every cartographer in Donsden. What would you like to know? I sell everything except information relating to the red layer, Baron Glass, military matters, and the like.”

“Do you have maps of the tunnels under Mount Don?”

“I do, but those tunnels change all the time due to collapses and mutants.”

“I’ll buy whatever you have.” He’d never be lost underground again.

Chapter 16

After the bookstore, Rav visited several perfume shops; however, the river had washed all traces of Kayla's scent off her handkerchief, so no one could replicate it. He folded and stored it away. Though he could no longer smell her, the cloth was soft and smooth, like her skin, holding it giving him some silly notion that he was holding Kayla's hand.

Next was the leathermakers, where he pulled out Wakeman's urn. "I need a custom pouch to store this inside. I need to keep it safe."

Together with the leatherworker, they built a sling that wrapped over his shoulder under his chainmail and held the ashes at his chest, where he could best protect them. The inside was lined with a single sheet of silk in case the urn broke so he could recover the ashes. Finished, he caressed the bump on his chest. Wakeman was safe now.

Done with what he'd wanted to do, there was still plenty of time until dinner. He visited a weapons shop, finding it packed with people coming and going, ogling, dreaming. These weapons would determine their life and death. Shields and main weapons such as swords, spears, and bows drew most people. Swarms of them gathered around haggling for the items. Rav headed over to the throwing knives section.

There were packs of blades bundled together in pouches, all well-crafted, far better than the knives produced in Pitt, with consistent weight and balance. They were also very expensive. It was a lot of money to spend on something he might lose. Rav shook his head, deciding he was doing fine with what he had, but as he turned to leave, the armour section caught his eye. Arm bracers with slots cut into them where you could keep knives and throw them quickly from lined a shelf. But he quickly realised the slots had been made with the knife bundles in mind. He exited the store.

The next place to visit was an alchemy shop, Rav remembering how effective the smoke Izen had used had been. Situated in the centre of the market was a well-guarded building, three storeys tall, with huge stained-glass windows on the upper floors. The words 'Glass Emporium' had been gilded across the entrance. Two plated guards with red plumed helms and pikes stood tall either side of double doors made of glass save for their hinges. Rav weighed his dwindling coin pouch as he eyed its lavish interior. He'd just look around, he decided as he walked towards the entrance.

"*Halt*," the taller guard called out, voice muffled due to his visored helm. He held his pike out to block Rav's path. "Only those with a sufficient status can enter."

Rav fished his Blood Hounds' token out and held it up for the guard to see.

The guard retracted his pike for Rav to approach, his helmet plume shaking as he lowered his head to examine the token a moment. "I don't recognise this mark; I'll need to check it. Wait here." He stepped across the doorway to mutter to his partner before heading inside. The second guard continued staring at Rav but kept his pike at his side.

A while later, the guard appeared again, beckoning Rav to enter. As he stepped foot inside, he couldn't help but take a deep breath. Varnished wood, sweet oils, steamed clothes—the Glass Emporium smelled incredible. Its carpet was soft but supportive, giving him a spring in each step. It was a grand hall, with walls lined with clear glass cabinets filled with hundreds of vials in every colour and a network of mirrors reflecting sunlight to keep every corner well lit. A sea of colours danced on the nearby surfaces as light shined through the concoctions. People in expensive clothing perused the wares, talking softly amongst themselves. Rav looked dull in comparison, a point where the wonder of the room died. The guard ushered him into a side room, where a plump woman was waiting.

"I am Madam Buschell," she introduced herself. "Under normal circumstances, a scavenger unit like the Blood Hounds wouldn't have access to the interior of the Glass Emporium. You, however, are welcome, Rav. News of Baron Niklaus Sonuk's dinner travelled this morning." She glanced at his neck. "Your new napet suits you."

Rav touched the cold metal. "Thank you."

"What are you looking for?"

"I've seen Lyra work with medicines and the Blood Hounds use smoke balls, so I've grown curious about alchemy."

She raised an eyebrow. "You just want to look around?"

He nodded. "Aye, but if that's not allowed, I'll leave."

Madam Buschell fell into thought, her finger on her chin. "We're not busy this afternoon; I can let you look through our collection. You'll be restricted to the first floor, though."

"That's enough."

"Wait a moment." She left the room and returned with a silver cloak. "Wear this."

Rav put it on, hiding his worn clothing.

"If you see something you like, tell me." She eyed his napet again. "Perhaps we can arrange a gift. A favour among friends."

"Thank you for your generosity." Rav smiled, acknowledging her words before exiting the room and going to look at the many cabinets, where each item had a tag explaining what it was and what it was used for.

Saugim's Vitality: able to enhance the consumer's energy for an indeterminate time. Users feel no cold or weariness while in effect.

Heather's Spark: a powder to sprinkle onto firewood to allow you to start a fire even in the wettest conditions.

Yipper Repellent: a smoke ball that mimics the scent of goebbers to deter yippers.

Liquid Soap: rub it on your skin to remove dirt and smell nice.

This was the cheapest vial Rav had seen. Who would think of something like that?

They were all fantastic, but... he grimaced at the prices. Even his family would struggle to buy these items.

The sunlight dimmed. His time was up. Rav returned the cloak to Madam Buschell and headed back to the Blood Hounds' house, his new pouch for Wakeman's ashes so well fitted he almost forgot he was wearing it.

Stepping through the door, Rav caught the scent of cooking fat. At the far end of the hall, just beyond the kitchen entrance, he glimpsed a boot heel disappearing from view, followed by Izen leaning across the doorway from a chair. He waved Rav over, almost goofy as his loose hair hung around his face, his yellowed shirt baggy. Rav waved back as he walked over, seeing the dining table set with bowls. Amine stood by the cooking pot, stirring it over the hearth in the corner. The other Blood Hounds were all seated in casual clothes, like Izen, seeming to be in deep conversation. Rav adjusted his collar to hide the pouch holding Wakeman's ashes better as he took his seat, allowing his tiredness to mask his expression.

"Rav, welcome back." Piyo leaned back from his bowl as Amine walked over and started serving hot soup. "Did you see anything interesting in the market?"

"I visited a weapons shop and saw an arm bracer, but it was too expensive," Rav answered, monotone.

Izen tapped the table with his spoon, then slurped up a spoonful of freshly served soup, nodding to Amine in thanks. "Well, you won't have to worry about expenses once we complete our next scavenge. We'll start training you tomorrow. Miels is taking your first lesson."

Miels pulled out Amine's chair for them to sit in next to him once they'd finished serving. A warm joy spread across his face, softening his hard features. "I'm going to show you my favourite part of combat: defence. We'll head for the arena after breakfast."

A chance to get stronger? Rav gave a firm nod. "Aye."

"Remember Izen's footwork? I want you to move like that. Here." Miels threw some bandages to Rav from the small bag he'd brought down into the arena bowels with them.

Rav struggled to catch them, on the verge of sneezing as more dust drifted down from the ceiling. How could there be people moving across the stands already? Dawn had barely passed.

"Take your boots off and wrap those around your feet." Once Rav was ready, Miels continued. "I'll look at what you can do first. Head over there"—he pointed to the corner a dozen feet away—"and sprint to me as fast as you can, then you can start jumping and crawling."

Miels spent the morning instructing Rav through various activities that tested his manoeuvrability, tutting at the end. "You're slow. Some of that is malnourishment, most of it is inexperience. There's also a problem with your left leg," he noted. "Did you suffer a bad injury to your ankle?"

Rav touched the healed scabs from the goebber bite. "Aye, when I fought the 'Zet Ar. Lyra fixed it, though; it doesn't hurt."

"Healed is not the same as healthy. We need to build more muscle to support it." Miels fell into thought. "At least you have good reflexes. If you become fast enough to take advantage of that, you'll survive the marsh. Let's start there."

He walked over to Rav, then darted to his flank. Rav twisted, but by the time he'd stabilised, Miels had moved to his side again. Spun into a mess, Rav couldn't keep up. Miels tapped Rav's back, sending him stumbling forward. Rav gritted his teeth, able to see Miels move, just too slow to do anything about it.

"Do you understand your weaknesses now?"

Rav nodded.

"Good."

Miels had Rav lie down and unwrap the bandages, then took him through a series of exercises designed around moving his toes. Rav couldn't perform the exercises at first, relying on working his whole foot to generate any strength, but with Miels' prodding, he grasped what he was looking for.

"Outside." Miels poked the outside of Rav's foot.

Rav squeezed it as hard as he could, lasting a moment before it hurt too much to continue.

"Better. This is what you need to do when you step inside. A stronger push means a faster movement. It also helps on bad terrain, maintaining balance." He tapped Rav's left leg. "Other foot."

The gruelling work continued for the afternoon.

"That's good for today." Miels grabbed Rav's arm to help him up.

Standing burned Rav's feet; he had to fight to stop himself kneeling back down. Sweat lined his brow.

"Small muscles are quick to tire but recover fast. Tomorrow, we'll go again." Miels laughed.

The next morning, Rav felt the improvement right away. When he ran, jumped, and dived, instead of his foot moving in a single block, he could focus his strength into the most important parts for an extra surge of power. His bare feet spread out over the ground to provide better grip.

"We'll train your feet at the end of every day," Miels announced. "Tomorrow, we'll focus on your legs."

Rav spent the next few days in the arena, Miels teaching him how to squat, jump, and land, working his legs until he couldn't feel them. Nights were spent lying in bed, wondering when the aching would stop. Lyra brewed a series of medicines for his recovery, relieving some of the tenderness that accompanied his every step. But it was working. All the food he was eating, combined with the training, was building back his muscles. He still couldn't keep up with Miels. But he would. One day. If he kept progressing at this pace, it wouldn't be long before he'd exceed his old self.

Following a morning of strength training, Miels led him inside the arena to a private room. "Now I can teach you some techniques. You won't be able to do them well yet; this is just for understanding. Copy what I do."

The first thing Rav learned was how to walk across the marshes. Building on Piyo's advice along with the new control he had over his legs, Rav found that he could move much quieter.

"We'll work on combat next," Miels said. "A mutant is very different to a human. They're dumber but bigger and faster. Normal tricks won't be of use. Here's how you survive against them." He held up a finger. "First, hide. Move low, move quietly, then they won't know you're there. That's the best scenario. Second"—another finger went up— "run. Stop whatever you're doing and get away, then wish for it to leave you alone. If it can't fight you, it can't kill you." The last finger rose. "Third, defend. Pick a place where it won't fit or can't outmanoeuvre you, then hunker down. If you're not a threat or an easy kill, it should move on. Mutants in the red layer don't fear us, they fear each other. Energy wasted hunting you is energy they don't have for their next fight. Most of the monsters are intelligent enough to understand that, though there are exceptions, like boulder-bears, which are very aggressive."

"How did Mulk survive against one?"

"Ask him." Miels grinned. "Now, I'm going to teach you how to disengage. This is a basic sequence of events: you get caught, you run, you get chased down in the open. You can't fight here, or you'll die, so we dive. Watch." Miels stepped to Rav, then pushed off his foot to dive into a roll away from him. "This should give you enough space to run further or dodge any attacks."

"Why step towards me?"

"If I just dive, I expose my back, making myself a target. The step in either baits a close attack or keeps your opponent in place." He picked up a wooden staff from the weapons rack. "Here." He threw it to Rav. "Swipe at me."

Rav shifted the staff to match the grip he used for a spear and got ready before charging at Miels, but just as he was about to reach him, Miels stepped towards him, causing Rav to strike early, his short jab hitting air as Miels was already completing his roll.

"You try." Miels took the staff from Rav and walked up to him.

Rav stepped in and dived back. "*Ah.*" The staff struck his back. He tumbled and stood up.

"See, back exposed." Miels laughed.

Rav tried again. And again. And again. *Pah.* The staff was always hitting him.

Another rest day arrived. Rav lay on his bed, whole body aching as he stared at the ceiling, focusing on each knot in the wood and their strange swirling patterns. Each fed into the next, the lines in the wood seeming chaotic but always finding their way to the next point. The next weakness.

Knock, knock. "Rav?" It was Lyra. After he grunted to invite her in, Lyra threw a pair of shorts at him. "Come with me. Leave your armour behind." She headed out to wait downstairs.

Rav pulled himself up, collected the shorts, and followed.

Lyra led him out of Donsden and into the nearby plains, aiming for a river that flowed down Mount Don. She wasn't wearing armour either, instead dressed in a common traveller outfit consisting of a belt-strapped brown shirt and a pair of trousers. Her sword was still at her waist, though. The path they walked down was well trodden, but he didn't see anyone else close by. By the time Lyra led them further up the river, they were alone. She stopped at the river and studied the rushing waters a moment before nodding.

"This will do. Get in."

Rav peered over the bank, seeing that this section of the river was deep enough to submerge him. The current was quick, leading towards rapids further down. His heart pounded, his breath short and ragged. He shook his head and stepped back, suddenly feeling like his throat had constricted. He needed to breathe. Rav gulped down air as tension ran through him.

Lyra came to stand beside him. "You are not a strong swimmer. I will teach you how to fight against a current in case you fall into another river on Mount Don."

Rav clenched and unclenched his fists. "I..." Lyra was right; this was something he needed to do. A shiver ran through him as he remembered hurtling down that river in the dark. He never wanted to feel that powerless again. His voice cracked. "Will you keep hold of me?"

"I do not need to keep hold of you; you can manage this on your own." She faced him. "But I will be here, protecting you. I am your guide."

Rav nodded. He tensed his body further to halt his shivers and approached the bank again. Lyra was here. If he failed to tread water, she'd save him. Like she always did. He wasn't going to get sucked away again.

He kicked off his boots and changed into the shorts Lyra had given him, stripped off everything but them and Wakeman's chainmail. Lyra raised an eyebrow at him continuing to wear it but didn't say anything. Rav held on to the grassy bank and lowered his leg into the water, feeling the current take hold of it right away. Could he really do this?

"Here." Lyra unclasped her belt and dangled it over Rav. "Grab this if you need to."

He shifted to snatch at it but stopped himself. *At least attempt to swim on your own first.*

Rav took a breath and dropped into the water. The current seized him, dragging him down to the rapids. He kicked and flailed, feeling as though he was clawing his way through the water to reach where he'd started. *If I could just touch the riverbed*. But this wasn't one of the shallow, easy-flowing rivers of Stone's

Way; this was more like one of the deadly torrents running under the Stone Steps he'd been warned time and time again not to fall into. Bit by bit, the river dragged him further down.

"Use strong, long kicks, like this," Lyra called to him, demonstrating the movement.

Rav copied her as best he could, finding himself being dragged a little slower.

"Move your arms like this," Lyra followed up.

Rav did the same, keeping his fingers together to push back water rather than scratch at it. He slowed further. Until he felt the weight of Wakeman's chainmail starting to drag him down. Exhausted, he flopped around, but just before he dropped beneath the surface, he spotted Lyra's belt dangling in front of him and latched onto it. Lyra dragged him back up to his original starting position.

"Again," she said.

Rav obeyed, this time swallowing water before getting pulled back into position, coughing.

"Again."

He held on to the riverbank. Lyra stung his hand with her belt, forcing him to let go. He fought but soon started sinking.

"Again."

Rav lay panting on the bank, chest heaving. At least he'd now learned how to hold his breath and keep afloat so swimming wasn't so exhausting.

Lyra stood beside him. "Rest quickly so you can practise once more before we return to Donsden."

Rav flinched at her words. *I have no energy left.* But Lyra wouldn't accept that. He needed to distract her, waste their time until they had to leave. "Why does Baron Glass stay here?" he asked. "Shouldn't someone with a Heaven's Tear be fighting deep in the Sink?"

"I already told you why; he is protecting Jinkin's interests."

"And how can Jinkin get him to protect their interests?"

Lyra tilted her head in thought. "There are many reasons he would listen to them. First, he is paid. People beyond Ut Sh'za, the second layer, can obtain Bezoars from large mutants, but you do not need to worry about that yet. Jinkin gives some of these to Baron Glass so he can be strong without risking fighting. Second, some Heaven's Tears are more powerful than others, or you could say their users have found better ways to use them. Zera leads Jinkin, and she is more powerful than Baron Glass. Better for him to be her ally than her enemy. Third... he might have some personal reason for wanting to stay here, or maybe he cannot advance further for now, similar to Baron Hewett. Perhaps he is recovering before moving again."

Rav nodded. "And why is a Sister with him?"

"Ee La' Bol is here to represent the interests of all Sisters, ensuring..." Lyra locked onto him. "You have not cared about this before. Are you done resting? Get back in the river."

Rav gulped.

Chapter 17

A week after he'd arrived back in Donsden, Rav woke at dawn to visit the Inkwell, finding the middle-aged man already there, opening the store.

"Rav, I have your notebook here." He led him to the workbench. "The restoration was better than I thought. I've pieced together most of the maps, but the merchant banners and some of the goat herd locations have been lost. Some numbers are also missing." He reached behind the desk to retrieve two notebooks. Rav recognised his old beaten one next to the new leather-wrapped one.

"This is the original." The man flicked through it, showing Rav pages washed in a blueish solution that revealed the lines drawn on them. "As you can see, it's hard to read with lines from other pages mixed in, so I've copied your notes into this book."

He opened the other one, and there it was, written in ink to match his own handwriting: Stone's Way. Rav grabbed the book, scouring through it. There was the Alley Camp, Bear Camp, the locations of the supply caches.

"This book has been coated in a water-resistant solution to protect the pages. Raindrops should roll off, but submerging it in water will ruin it. The ink I used is made with oils. This one will be much sturdier."

The ledger was missing along with a few merchants' insignias; however, the most important one was still there.

Rav grimaced at the sketch of a mountain. Baron Hewett. "Thank you."

He re-entered the city streets to return to the Blood Hounds' house, holding his journals close to his chest, the sharp scent of whatever blueish fluid coated his old one filling his nose. The warm scent of familiar paper was gone along with its comfortable texture. Too weak to last. Was that Pitt?

He returned to his room and worked at prying up a piece of floorboard under his bed, which soon came up, revealing a small space. He traced a finger over his notebooks, then laid them in the gap, where they'd be safe. Rav touched his chest, feeling the urn. *No, not that.* The last of Wakeman couldn't be left here in the dark; he needed his friend by his side. He'd carry Wakeman's legacy and show him as much of the world as he could.

Rav pushed open a creaky door to a small windowless room beside the kitchen, wrinkling his nose at the stuffy air. Three fur-covered benches, with the Blood Hounds filling them, faced a large board set against the room's back wall, which was lit by candlelight from candelabras placed beside the board. Smoky air shifted as he entered and shut the door behind himself.

Izen stood from his bench and unfurled a mix of parchment, hide, and cheap paper maps from where they'd been rolled under his arm, using pins to hold them open on the board for everyone to see. Rav examined them again, seeing the side of Mount Don they'd be climbing in detail. Mutant dens, potential caves to camp in, streams, and viewpoints to scout from had all been marked. Through it all, two paths towards the red layer had formed, each separated by a rocky ridge.

"Hiking straight up takes us too close to the boulder-bear," Mulk warned, pointing to a pencil sketch depicting a forested area to the right of the ridge.

"It's the fastest route; there's nowhere else that has a direct path to the red layer." Piyo tapped his thigh.

"This path is safer." Mulk stood and ran his finger along the left side of the ridge, showing a longer route that ran through two mutant dens.

"There's two 'Zet Ar on that route."

"Yeah, but rabbers don't hunt outside their territories."

Rav looked at the papers to find sketches of the mutants. The boulder-bear was like bears he'd heard of but had a calloused hide instead of fur that made it impregnable to most sharp weapons. Rabbers were mutant hares but bigger and with longer claws. They ruled warrens consisting of hundreds of members.

Piyo squinted his eyes with a shake of his head. "The warrens have too many scouts for us to avoid. We'll be spotted."

"Then we run. I'd rather be chased by two of them than a boulder-bear—I only survived my last encounter with one by luck. The thing came charging down the mountain, chasing some dumb yippers that annoyed it, when it spotted me. Izen stayed hiding while I ran. I didn't watch where I was going and fell down a hole, hitting my head on the way down. I lay there for a full day listening to it try and dig down to me. Those things are crazed. If Izen hadn't captured a goebber and used it to lure the beast away, it would have gotten to me." Mulk shook his head. "I can't explain it; you have to see one yourself. Izen, you know we can't fight one of them."

Everyone's attention turned to Izen as he looked from path to path. "We go through the rabbers," he announced.

Piyo nodded. "I'll see if I can get some more smoke balls so the scouts ignore us."

Rav followed everyone as they shuffled out the room once Izen had rolled the maps back up, then climbed the stairs to his room. Door shut, he reached under his bed to retrieve the set of maps he'd bought and brought them to the window, sitting on the floor to make use of as much daylight as he could to read them again.

The maps only covered the tunnel systems at Mount Don's base towards the marsh area, all information regarding Donsden privileged, but that was enough. He wouldn't be scavenging near the city anyway; knowing where to escape in the marsh was all he needed to memorise. *Though…* Rav smirked as he followed sets of tunnels running from the marsh towards the city. Even if the maps stopped, judging by the other tunnel systems, those ones could be predicted. *There, by the Brack*. An underground passage ran straight towards Donsden.

Chapter 18

"Keep your arm up," Miels instructed.

"I've used a shield before," Rav muttered as he took his practised stance.

"Against people. Mutants are bigger; your shield is too low to protect you."

Rav raised it over his shoulder and head. "Aren't my legs and torso exposed?"

"You're worried a mutant will do a leg sweep, eh?" Miels laughed. "Neither boulder-bears nor rabbers have long tails. This position is to stop a boulder-bear from smashing your head to pieces."

"Will it even work?"

"I don't know, but it's better than nothing."

"I thought we were avoiding the bear anyway," Rav panted, his strength fading fast from holding his shield up so high.

"What if it leaves its territory? What if another one comes hunting?" Miels raised a staff above his head and slammed it down on Rav's shield.

Rav braced for the pain. *Crack.* His arm juddered, pushed back to smack into his head, but the shield stayed in place.

"Good. This time, move to absorb the impact." Miels readied another strike—"*Ha*"—and put more strength into this blow.

Rav shifted to the side, deflecting the strike away, then dived, rolling on the shield.

"Excellent." Miels grinned. "That's a good sequence of moves. Again."

"Again."

"Again."

That night, Rav couldn't pick up his cutlery.

As Rav held his shield high to endure another barrage of attacks from Miels the following morning, the door opened. He snapped into a defensive stance, facing Amine as they shut the door again. They had a large bag slung over their shoulder and a shield. They walked over to Miels. He stood with stoic pride beside Rav, his staff resting against his side, nudging his square head in Rav's direction to show off his student.

"Not bad." Amine raised their shield as they approached Miels. "Miels said you were getting better at defending yourself. Now, I'll show you how to support others while you do so."

Miels nodded, taking his attacking stance once more, then darted at Amine with low jabs, mimicking the attacks of a rabber. Amine blocked with their shield while reaching over their shoulder and into the bag with their free arm to retrieve a vial. Vial retrieved, Amine lowered their arm again and used it to hold the bag against their side as they leaned in different directions. Rav watched mesmerised as Amine used the weight of their bag to provide extra momentum in dodging to the side. Miels used a feint to get past Amine's shield, but they swung their bag around to block the strike. Rav awed at the control Amine had over their muscles.

"You won't be as good as me," Amine said once Miels stopped his attacks. "So practise until you are. Here." They took off the bag and hung it over Rav's shoulder, sagging him down.

Miels moved in without warning as Amine stepped aside. Rav rushed to raise his shield, and as he did, the bag slipped down his shoulder, pulling him down as he fought to catch it.

Miels paused, and Amine stepped close, tapping Rav's leg with their foot to push it further under him to better support his shoulder. "Your feet are too slow. If you need to block up, move your foot when you lift the shield."

Rav shrugged the bag back up as Miels moved in again, practising balancing with the new weight over and over, enduring hit after hit. Then it went right. Foot under him, shield high, the weight of the bag bolstered his body, helping absorb some of the impact. The attack didn't feel so heavy. He wasn't as fast as before; however, if he could take blows like this, he didn't need to be.

"You felt it?" Amine asked.

"Aye." He nodded with a grin.

Amine smiled back. "Try this." They strapped a throwing knife to the side of the bag. "This time, when you block, draw the knife and throw it."

Rav tried for the rest of the afternoon, failing every time.

As Rav thumped down the stairs the next day for his lesson, he saw Piyo waiting at the bottom in his armour, leaning against the wall beside the door with two swords wrapped in cloth in his arms. His brown eyes gleamed as he spotted Rav, bringing a wolfishness to his lithe face.

"Miels is busy today. You can train with me if you want. I'm heading out to work on my swordplay; want to throw some stones at me? You can practise hitting a moving target."

Rav paused, feeling a frown forming as he noticed something taut in Piyo's expression, but he smoothed it and shrugged, not sensing any malice. "Aye."

"Let's go, then." Piyo led him out of the city, along the main, winding road, past swaying crop fields, to a clear pond shimmering green from the long grasses growing along its bank. Blue long-legged birds standing in its shallows scattered at their presence, taking flight in a frenzy of chirping.

"I like the outdoors." Piyo breathed in the early morning fresh air. "It's nice to see some real colour."

"Aye." Rav stretched as he gazed around the open land, admiring the same small villages and wide pools of water he had seen when first arriving in Blood Marsh, the sun warm on his skin. "It's nice to be out that stuffy arena room."

"There's still work to do. Get some pebbles." Piyo held out his swords to point at the stones embedded in the soil while he stepped closer to the water. Once Rav had dug a few small ones out, Piyo flourished his swords, spinning them, then bouncing the blades off each other. "When I was a child, I used to play a game like this. Someone would throw a ball made of leather and you had to hit it as far as you could with a stick." He went through the striking motion. "I never had the strength to launch it far, but I always hit it." He signalled Rav to start throwing.

Rav took care to weaken the power in his throw, remembering the damage he'd done to the wingtails.

Piyo swatted. *Ting.* The stone flew far into the distance. "If you're going to throw like that, there's no point in you being here," he muttered. "Miels taught you how to move, right? Circle around so you're not so easy to predict."

Rav obeyed, dashing to the side before flinging a stone underhanded at Piyo's belly. Piyo twisted his body before the stone left Rav's hand, putting his swords between him and the projectile. Arm outstretched, he flicked his wrist, sending the stone away with the flat of the blade. *Ting. Plop.* Deflected into the water. They trained until the sun rose to its highest point, then Rav lay in the grass, sweating, chest heaving.

Piyo stood next to him, unwrapping his swords. "You lasted longer than I expected. You also move much better than before, but your left leg is still slow."

"I... know," Rav wheezed. "I'm working on it."

"Good lad." He gazed back at Donsden and squinted. "Let's head back and get some food." He reached out to help lift Rav up but stopped halfway through with a chuckle. "You're a little heavy."

Rav got up by himself with a smile. "With the amount you're feeding me, I'd have to be."

They set off back to Donsden, soon stepping from soft grasses to hard, stone road. Rav gazed up at the Keep and all that lay under it, from buildings to the outer wall to the fields. A great city that he now lived in. But Pitt was better.

Piyo twirled his swords, catching Rav's attention. "Can you still see your ribs?"

"At the sides."

"How're your hips?"

"No bone sticks out."

Piyo nodded. "Keep it up." He patted Rav's back, squeezing the growing muscle. "It's hard to see how much weight you've gained through that shirt. Some might think you've not made any progress."

Rav caressed his chainmail. "That's good, right? I might catch some people off guard."

"Is it worth tricking your friends just to trick your enemies? Weakness also invites attack. Maybe you should take it off once in a while to show off your hard work. Maybe you'll attract a few more potential patrons like Baron Tryxwin. Help like that is essential; you don't know how scarce resources get further in the Sink."

Rav held his chainmail tighter, pace slowing at Piyo's odd tone. "I don't need her help."

"Sure you do," Piyo tutted. "You need as much help as you can get. Where would you be without us? And more help is always good. We all have ways to be useful to each other, which makes us stronger together. That's part of being a unit."

Rav glared at him. "What, you think we're all just swords to be wielded when needed? What about loyalty? Honour? Filiality?

You'd have me be used by people who don't care about who I am?"

"What's wrong with that? You'd use us too. That's what you're doing anyway, right? Using us to train." Piyo looked ahead. "Ah. Play your part."

"Rav." A well-dressed man approached him as he entered a Donsden portcullis. "It's good to meet you. I'm Philius Rexim, son of Baron Albert Rexim. We've heard that you're preparing to venture forth on a very dangerous scavenge and wish to offer our support."

"Champion Delmare is leading my unit. You can speak to him about the scavenge."

Philius looked at Piyo with a questioning eyebrow, then turned back to Rav. "We wish to support you specifically. We're aware that you have Baron Niklaus Sonuk's backing and want to offer you ours."

Rav caught the look, also noticing Piyo's subtle nod to encourage Philius further. Disgust burned in his chest, his expression about to ripple into rage. *Be polite.*

"I'd be grateful for any help," Rav replied, pulling an easy smile.

Philius beckoned over a servant carrying a pair of leather boots that had been polished until Rav could see his reflection in them. "These are made from goebber hide and have been sealed to prevent water from the marshes seeping in. We have a cobbler if you want to make any adjustments."

Rav accepted them, feeling the thick wool that lined the insides.

"We understand that you're busy. After you complete your scavenge, we'd like to invite you and the Blood Hounds to a banquet at our home. If you require any further assistance, please reach out. The Rexims have always supported those Called."

Rav nodded. "Thank you. I shall speak to Champion Delmare."

"I'll leave you, then." Philius gave a small bow before he entered back into the Donsden crowds.

"That wasn't difficult, right?" Piyo mused. "You're welcome. And think, maintaining your relationship with Niklaus will worsen your relationship with everyone else; show that you're friendly with everyone so none of Niklaus' enemies start thinking about how to get rid of you."

Rav snorted. "You just want to attend another banquet."

"The Blood Hounds build their reputation and connections, you get gifts." He laughed. "You weren't planning on accepting Niklaus' help, were you? And since you don't like Baron Tryxwin either, you're open to offers."

Rav revealed his snarl, but Piyo met his gaze firmly.

"You're part of the Blood Hounds now, Rav. We'll laugh and joke and have your back, but everyone has their purpose. Mulk's strong, Miels guards us, I'm good at killing, while Amine's good support. Izen leads, and you... you're our image. You can't fight or scout or defend, so you're doing your part to contribute: helping us gain allies so we can leave this place and enter the second layer."

Rav looked around, seeing people watching him from the crowd with gratuitous smiles. "You made this all public. You used me as bait without telling me. Did you listen to me earlier? Have you listened to *anything* I've said?"

"We all have sad stories, Rav, most of them even true." He beckoned Rav onwards. "Come, I'll make it up to you. I know this place that does roast waterbird. It's—"

Rav stormed away, soon reaching the Blood Hounds' house and stomping up the stairs to his room, flinging the door open and—

Rav jolted back, hands bared, the Ghoul a thought away from erupting over him. At the end of his bed sat an amused Bo Hart.

Bo looked up from flicking through Rav's maps, the grimy scar across his nose twitching as he grinned. "Close the door," he mouthed, oozing threat.

Rav obeyed, heart pulsing, sealing them inside, the Ghoul still ready to pounce. "How did you get in?" he whispered, skin clammy. "Does anyone know you're here?"

"You left the window open," Bo replied, unperturbed, "and the Bride is out. She's doing normal Bride things, like scheming and skulking. No one else can find me, and if they do, heh heh, they won't talk."

Rav looked at the open window leading to the alleyway beside the Blood Hounds' house, sure he'd closed the shutters before he'd left. Bo shrugged, as though he didn't know how it was open either.

"I hear you're going on a dangerous scavenge," he murmured with a half-smile. "After hearing about what happened on your last outing, I thought I'd better act before you get yourself killed."

"I shouldn't need saving," Rav hissed. "I survived on my own last time."

"But I could've gotten information on a Heaven's Tear." He stood and looked over Rav. "What? Why hesitate to accept? You think it's too expensive? Look at you now; I can't see your skull anymore. Your cheeks almost look full. It won't be long before you're strong enough to start competing for them... Well, until the Brides think you'll compete for them, heh heh. You never know what might happen up that mountain. Better to have some extra help."

"There's still—"

"Shhh." Bo's hand covered Rav's mouth and looked to the door, eyes unfocused as he listened. "They're talking about you..." he whispered. "What did Piyo do to annoy you?"

Rav pushed him away. "Made it clear that I'm being used to receive gifts from patrons."

"Not making any friends, then." Bo grinned. "Smart. If you get too comfortable here, we move to the second part of our deal."

Rav grimaced. "I know, broken limbs, family dead. My plans haven't changed."

Bo nodded, leering down at him. "Good. Perhaps I've not been clear. I'm *going* to follow you up Mount Don, and I'm *going* to help you. Then, you're *going* to pay me. That's our deal. Be glad I'm helping at all; there are easier ways to squeeze information out of you."

Rav gulped, remembering the giant mutant from Bo's nightmare. "Aye, fine. Keep us all alive, but stay hidden. Lyra can't know I'm accepting our deal."

"Heh, she won't see me. Dome and I will act before you even know there's danger to smash." Bo caught Rav's questioning gaze. "That's my hammer. Nothing on Mount Don will survive against it." He walked to the window. "I'll see you when you get back. Enjoy your scavenge. I've had some especially brutal ones, heh, heh, heh." Bo jumped out into the alleyway.

Rav dashed over to see Bo land on the ground three storeys below, then saunter off into the market. Once he closed the shutters again, he moved back to his bed to reveal the loose floorboard under it, prying it open. Everything was still there. He sighed in relief.

Stomp, stomp, stomp.

He turned his head to the door. Someone was coming. After hurrying to return his bed back to its usual position, he caught sight of dirt from Bo's boots.

Knock, knock.

Rav rushed to smudge the dirt with his foot before smoothing his hair and gathering his breath. "Come in."

Izen entered, gazing at Rav with suppressed concern, as though unsure whether his presence would end up causing the worry he sought to soothe. "Are you alright? Piyo said you were in a rush to get back."

"Aye." Rav wore his usual blank expression.

"What Piyo said, the Blood Hounds do care for each other, Rav. You've seen that. You're one of us."

Rav revealed a dejected huff, waving his hand. "It's fine; I understand what I'm supposed to do. Everyone contributes. I'll do what I can. It was just... surprising."

"I see." Izen gazed at him a moment longer. "If you're sure you're alright, we'll let you rest," he continued, looking every part the caring leader. "If there's something you don't want to do, come speak to me. As I said, you're one of us."

He left the room, shutting the door behind him.

Rav scoffed as he flopped down on his bed, glaring at the wooden ceiling, a full sneer consuming him. The training, the shared meals, everything, it had all seemed so much like the actions of people who cared. And they did care. About their investment. If he left, their precious dinners and gifts would leave with him. These weren't the Ghoulsmen.

Loud thumping rumbled from the stairs. "*Rav,*" Amine shouted. "*You've a visitor.*"

He swung his legs out of bed and stood, slapping his cheeks to regain control of his expression, replastering it smooth before heading down. Amine was standing by the door, talking to a man dressed in red silks, a black feather in his cap. He held a pair of varnished hide bracers.

"Ah." The man's shaved, babyish face lit up as he saw Rav, stepping away from Amine to nod at Rav in greeting. "It is my honour to greet Blood Marsh's great Called One." He presented the bracers to Rav. "Baron Easle would like to offer a token of friendship. I am also offering an invitation to you, your Sister, and your unit for a banquet my Baron will soon be hosting."

"How wonderful." Rav beamed as he collected the bracers. Amine frowned in bemusement at his overacting from behind the messenger. "When can we expect such a glorious event?"

The man coughed into his fist. "*Ahem*, well, the date isn't yet set. It is our understanding that you have an upcoming scavenge, and we would not wish to cause any disruption to your plans. Perhaps when you return from Mount Don, you will have more time to attend such events."

Rav clasped his hands together. "Fantastic. I agree; better to wait. What good would it be if we died and your good food was wasted? Contact my leader, Champion Izen Delmare, when we return, and we'd be glad to attend."

The man's smile twitched. "Indeed. We'd be honoured to host you. I'll leave you to prepare, then, in hope of your success. And should you require any assistance, please reach out."

"Of course." Rav moved to usher him out as Amine opened the door. "I'll not forget your kindness." He shut the door.

Amine folded their arms at Rav. "Was that wise?"

"I have my gift, and you have your invitation." Rav spun around to head back upstairs. "Everyone is happy."

Just as he reached the top floor, Amine called him down again, the same conversation repeating with a different messenger representing a different Baron. Then another arrived. And another. And another. Of course, all their invitations had been set for *after* the Blood Hounds returned from their scavenge. Rav's disgust burned hotter and hotter behind his bright smile until, hidden in his room, it collapsed in on itself, going pallid and mushy. How obvious could it be that this scavenge was just another test? That he was only worth recruiting if he completed it. Only worth *using* if he proved himself capable.

That night, room laden with new cloaks, boots, shirts, and armour pieces, Rav pushed them all aside to pry open the floorboard beneath his bed. Reaching in, he pulled out Kayla's handkerchief and held it tight as he read through his journal by candlelight, memories of home only making everything hurt more.

Chapter 19

Training continued for another three weeks, going over the same sequences until Rav could retrieve items from his bag as he blocked. His legs were thicker, his back had got used to the weight of his bag, and Wakeman's chainmail didn't hang so loose. He participated in the Blood Hounds' discussions and jokes, acting his amicable self, but he avoided being alone with Piyo. The others were at least tolerable, knowing to hide their selfishness. He'd used the last of his money to purchase some things from a herb shop.

Sitting in the meeting room, the Blood Hounds scanned over the plans once more, everything from the route, to escape methods, to potential plants they could collect written down.

"I think we're ready," Izen announced. "Sleep well tonight; you won't get much rest for the next few days."

The Blood Hounds exited the planning room and headed to their rooms. Rav stared at the repaired hide armour lying on his bed. The leather had a new varnish over it to fill in the scratches from the goebbers and now looked new. Next to it was his shield, which was large enough to cover his torso and thighs. Amine would prepare the supplies he'd carry, but he was already familiar with how much everything would weigh. He even knew how much he would be eating and drinking.

The red layer—a place supposed to be filled with 'Zet Ar. Could those other mutants really compare to the one he'd fought? Even if they did, he wouldn't be as hopeless as before with Lyra and Bo Hart protecting him. He looked at his new pouch and tube, its smell stinging his nose. There were also his own preparations. He took a breath to calm his shaking hands. This was just one scavenge of many until he could return home. He'd complete them all. He had to.

The next few days were spent travelling, following their previous route to the Brack before climbing the mountain until they were over by the lip. That's when they doubled back, hidden from the sight of curious scouts in case rival units wanted to follow them.

"It's here." Piyo checked the map a few times in the early morning light, making sure the landmarks were the same.

A cave next to a stream. There weren't any other streams in the area; this had to be it. Rav looked up the mountain, following the dirt, rock, and then snow. That's where the treasure was, just inside the white, at the bottom of the red layer.

"Look there." Amine pointed to a spot far ahead of them where there was a dark green patch just below the snow. "That's where the boulder-bear den is."

"It's a good thing we're not heading in that direction, then." Mulk said as he kicked his boot against a rock to adjust it.

Staring up, dizziness struck Rav; how could there be so much above him? How could you climb for days and days, yet still not reach the peak? Rav dropped his head and clenched his guts as Lyra patted his back, the swaying ground steadying.

The real hike started, the Blood Hounds taking a diagonal route across the mountainside, no paths leading them through the bumpy and uneven terrain. Rav drove his legs into the ground, surging forward in large strides. Most of his strength was recovered, and upon feeling the muscles in his feet tense to push off some stones, he realised he might have even improved. He didn't stumble, now able to keep up with the rest of the Blood Hounds without help.

"Sticks," Izen called.

Rav and Amine already had them out, prepared for the steepening gradient from the planning. With a pair each to help pull them up the slope, the Blood Hounds trekked up a rocky outcrop, aiming for a large tree peeking over a flatter stretch of ground above them. Rav trudged until his shirt was soaked with sweat, the grip on his walking sticks slick and slipping. Why did the tree never seem to get closer? Movement caught his eye—a yipper jumping to their right, but it kept quiet. Birds with wide wings and wicked talons circled above, but they too stayed away. Step by step, Rav lurched on, eyes stinging and vision blurred by droplets of sweat, finally seeing the tree right in front of him.

"Rest," Izen announced.

Rav blinked, wiping his face on his sleeve before slumping down against the tree, breath ragged. A moment later, his vision cleared, the last of his breath gone with his gasp. *Wow.* Beneath him lay the edge of Blood Marsh, a chaotic swirl of green and blue with the occasional block of fortified stone. It was all so small, every tree cluster and pond they'd passed looking as though they could be crossed with a single step. As he watched, the land breathed with the breeze, tiny dots flitting along the ground. That had been them.

Out beyond the green deluge lay a huge grass plane, dozens of animal herds drifting over it in the afternoon sunrays while floating clouds cast fluffy shadows over them. After the plane, the terrain split into two distinct features: a forest and a... Rav squinted, the far end of the water lost in the horizon. *Is it a river?* How could there be one that big? But the flow was unmistakable. It *was* a river, just... huge. And were those ships? If he could see them from here, how big were they up close? At the river's left was an endless bright and vibrant canopy forming a forest that put Ghoul Wood to shame. It covered everything the river didn't, hiding everything beneath it. Enough wood to build ten thousand Pitts, maybe more. A pang of nausea twisted his stomach, nothing quite seeming real anymore. How could landscapes like this exist?

Lyra sat beside him and pointed beyond the horizon. "Ut Sh'za begins on the other side of the River Tuul. You too can take a ship across it and see wonders even greater than this."

Rav gulped. Why did he keep staring? The way his heart was racing wasn't fear. Why wasn't he afraid? Aye, it did look spectacular from a distance, but every single one of those black dots would be a mutant that wanted to kill him. A mutant that would attack Pitt. So why did he want to see more? To experience more? What was it like to stand on a ship? To sleep under the Afil Forest canopy? What could possibly be greater than what he was seeing now? Wasn't Pitt barren and lifeless compared to this? Rav flinched out of his daze, the faces of Cyrn, Kayla, his parents, and the Ghoulsmen surfacing in his mind. Not lifeless. He already had all the wonder he needed.

Izen stepped forward with a grin. "We'll get there. Beyond there. The Blood Hounds will experience all the Sink has to offer."

The other Blood Hounds cheered, thumping the ground with their boots. Rav tore his gaze away and stared back at the dull mountainside.

Break over, they continued, *crunch, crunch, crunch*, stomping ever upwards. Birds screeched, insects clicked, everyone panted. Rav sang under his breath, using the thrum to keep going, careful not to be too loud in case something dangerous heard him. As he swigged from his waterskin, Lyra grabbed his shoulder and pressed him low. Up ahead, Izen had his hand raised. All the Blood Hounds had crouched, watching him. Rav looked ahead. The landscape was the same as before, clumps of dirt with the rare tree or shrub. Izen pointed to their right, where there was a trench in the ground, signalling to move. The Blood Hounds hurried into it, hiding from view, only Amine and Izen poking their heads up to keep watch. Rav tensed as Izen drew his crossbow, taking aim in the distance. *Twang. Uuuu,* the weak whimper faded.

Izen waited for a while longer. “Keep your guard up,” he whispered, then led them back up to their path.

Clear. They carried on, Izen kneeling to pull his crossbow bolt from the corpse of a goebber as he passed by. Piyo inspected its tracks before whispering to Izen, who grimaced. A goebber? Rav frowned. There wasn’t supposed to be a colony near here. Did that mean their information was wrong?

“Move quickly,” Izen commanded.

The Blood Hounds grunted as they forced themselves to move faster, Lyra pushing Rav on. Evening came and went, the sun almost set. It sat just above the horizon to cast long shadows across the mountainside, Rav squinting at the ground as the last of its bright light blinded him. Walking out of the rays, he entered the dark of a deep shadow behind an outcrop of rock where the others were waiting.

“This is it,” Piyo said, pointing ahead.

Behind a cluster of trees was a cave, and judging by the greenery, there was a stream close by for them to refill their waterskins from.

Rav caught a scent on the wind. Something familiar. Old soil maybe? No, it was a smell from the tunnels beneath Mount Don. Faeces. Piyo examined the ground for a moment, Amine joining him.

“I count twenty,” Piyo said, Amine nodding in agreement. “Should we find somewhere else to camp?”

“It’ll be dark soon. This cave’s the best we’ve got,” Mulk grumbled.

“We’ll fight. Form up,” Izen hissed.

The Blood Hounds took their positions, Izen at the front, Mulk and Miels flanking him, everyone else behind.

Helmets on, weapons ready, they moved between the trees to reach the cave entrance. The *scratch, scratch, scratch* of claws scrabbling on rock echoed out of the cave. They’d been found. *Ru.* Rav readied to reach into his bag, copying Amine, Piyo waiting for an opportunity to charge out. Lyra watched over them with vigilance. More noises echoed out of the dark cave, dimming light making it ever harder to see. Rav reached for torches when Amine grabbed his hand, shaking their head. *Torchlight will attract every mutant around.* Rav sucked his teeth as he obeyed, the goebbers reaching the front of the cave, where they stopped, hiding at the edge of the darkness, watching with glinting, black eyes.

"*Bolt*," Izen barked.

Amine slung their crossbow up and shot wild over Izen's shoulder into the gaping mouth of the cave. *Tchik.* It hit stone. The goebbers growled but continued to wait, the sun now set.

"Rav." Amine nudged him, the last pale light fading fast. "Draw them out."

Rav dropped his shield and bag as he grabbed a knife, Mulk stepping aside. After winding up, he threw, the blade flying like a bolt as it vanished into the cave. *Tu. Uuu.* A hit. *Ar.* Goebbers poured out of the cave.

Mulk strode forward and closed the gap to Rav, Miels surging ahead with a big swing of his axe. The goebbers' charge halted as they dodged back, their torsos lurching up. Izen darted out and pierced one of the front runners through the eye, Mulk right behind him, hammer swinging upwards to crush the ribs of another creature, sending it flying back.

Then the next group of goebbers pounced. Exposed from his wide swing, one targeted Miels, its long body extending like a flesh spring as it struck at his head—*bang*—straight into Amine's shield as they covered Miels. Izen and Mulk retreated as more goebbers snapped at them, some aiming for their throats, others biting at their ankles. They slammed their shields down to deter the attacks while Miels jabbed with the butt of his axe to clear one away, but two more aimed at him and got through his guard. Izen slashed the neck of one in time, while Amine came to Miels' aid once more, this time punching the goebber with their shield. Rav stumbled back as two dozen mutants wriggled over each other to continue the fight.

"*Rav, my right,*" Mulk roared, his hammer and shield occupied with a goebber that had leaped up at him, leaving his legs open for another to bite at.

Teeth gritted, Rav grabbed his shield and dived forward—*crack*—his arm shuddering as he blocked just in time. The goebber's claws scratched against the wooden disc as though it were trying to burrow through it, then it heaved against him, and Rav slipped, falling onto his back. It pounced on top of him, snarling, snapping, one of its rear claws digging into his leg armour. He fumbled with his free hand to find a knife. There wasn't one; he'd thrown it. With a groan, he used both hands to push the shield and tip the goebber off him. But then the weight vanished, the goebber's broken carcass slumping beside him after a shattering blow from Mulk. Rav clambered to his feet and darted back behind the big man, Lyra stepping forward to help guard him.

Mulk, Izen, Miels, and Amine fought on, Mulk delivering heavy, bone-cracking blows, while Izen moved his sword arm like a snake, his wrist twisting into different positions to find the optimal angle to bypass each goebber's guard. A dozen mutants soon lay dead around them, the rest seeking to escape back into the cave.

"*Piyo,*" Izen roared.

Twin swords drawn, Piyo dived into the disorganised mess the goebbers had become with efficient strikes—cut, slash, draw, cut—and the goebbers were reduced to dying lumps of meat, none able to make it back inside. Izen called everyone forward to support Piyo, the front line finishing off anything still twitching, Rav and Amine pouring some vials onto the bodies to help hide the smell of blood. With a final slash of Piyo's sword, the last goebber lost its head. Everything went quiet, the soft rumbling of distant thunder now audible.

"Clean up," Izen hissed. "Throw the bodies down the mountain, or we'll attract more mutants."

Ga Gome. More thunder rumbled, now close enough to sound just like how the Sisters pronounced it. The Blood

Hounds worked quickly to heave up the carcasses and then throw them down the path they'd climbed up. The air went cold. Rav's skin bristled, rain about to pour. He dragged the last carcass over to Mulk, who then slung it into the dark. Done, Izen stood at the cave entrance and patted each member of his unit as they walked past. Everyone accounted for, he followed. Deep inside was a turning, and once everyone was hidden around the corner, Amine sparked some flint to start a fire. As the orange glow bloomed into flame, the rain began, swelling into a storm that suppressed all other noise behind the wall of water. *Flash.* The cave lit up as a bolt of lightning burned across the sky. More thunder rumbled. Huddled around the fire, the Blood Hounds checked themselves over, voices soft.

"Any injuries?" Izen went over to each person, seeing that they were all alright.

Rav wrinkled his nose, breathing shallowly so he didn't taste too much of the fetid goebber stink choking the air. No one else complained. He covered his mouth with the sweat-soaked lip of his shirt and breathed through it.

"Supply check." Amine dragged him over to them to go through both of their packs. One lost bolt. One broken knife. Acceptable losses. "Good," Amine muttered, next having Rav hand out dried meat and fruit for supper.

"I'll take first watch," Izen announced once everyone had finished eating. "Rest. Once we refill our waterskins at the stream, we'll be moving again. We might have to fight again."

The Blood Hounds nodded, solemn.

"Is this normal?" Rav whispered to Amine.

"Mistakes in information happen often. Everyone's just worried because this mistake happened near the start of the mountain, where we're supposed to know the most."

"This is worth learning," Mulk whispered as he joined them. "Why were there goebbers here?"

"This cave is a good shelter and there's water close by," Rav answered.

"Right, but do goebbers just appear?" He pulled a half-smile. "These goebbers must have come from somewhere."

"So, they're from another territory. Their old colony got too big, or they've been chased out." Rav's eyes widened. "The territories we're going into have changed."

"Yeah," Mulk grumbled. "We don't know what we're walking into. What if the route we've chosen no longer avoids everything? We don't have the resources to keep fighting up here; we'll tire quick, then die."

"It won't go wrong," Izen spoke up. "There were only twenty goebbers and no young; that's not enough for a full colony. Things won't be too different from what we know. Now, get some sleep."

Izen kicked the fire out, leaving just the hot coals for warmth. Rav lay still, focusing on the crackling remains of the fire and the others breathing around him. Anything to avoid that breath in the silence.

Chapter 20

Morning arrived. The rain stopped, the sky lightening. The Blood Hounds all woke to another meal of dried meat and fruit. As they refilled their waterskins by the stream, they all watched the flock of birds circling a short distance away from them, where the goebber bodies had been dumped. Izen hurried everyone on before they attracted anything bigger. Hard ground had turned to slick mud after the storm. Progress was slower but still quick enough to reach their next camp before night. Worms, beetles, snails, all sorts of creatures had been flushed into the open for Piyo to pick up as emergency food.

Rav covered his mouth and nose before sneezing again, the stink of goebbers lingering around him like a cloud of flies. He rubbed his face, puffy from lack of sleep, eyes bleary as he spotted a now rare yipper. Likewise, the birds flying overhead had also reduced in number, only the largest remaining. One flew high in the air, circled, then folded its wings in to fall like an arrow towards the ground, reaching its target before Rav saw that there was one. Talons bared, it plucked a smaller bird out the air, then rose back up, heading to the top of a distant tree.

Higher and higher they climbed, what was once a clear and beautiful view of Blood Marsh now just a hazy blur of blended colours. Up ahead, snow gleamed in the sunlight, the wind starting to cut clean through Rav's clothes. He wrapped up tighter, using his shoulder to take the brunt of the cold. They ate as they walked, reaching their next camp by late afternoon. Beyond it, the ground became much steeper, then levelled out, hundreds of tiny holes pocking the flat land. Rabber warrens. At the camp's right lay a rocky ridge that sectioned off the dark green forest. Mulk glanced at it with a grimace, Izen following him. The boulder-bear den.

Piyo raised his hand, drawing the unit's attention, then pointing to the side. He guided the group to the ridge, where a crevice in the rock led down to a shelf hidden from the top. After searching the area for any signs of unexpected guests and finding it clear, Izen braced against the top to help lower everyone onto it, then jumped down onto the cramped shelf.

"No talking," he mouthed. "No fire. We run before sunrise."

He pointed to Piyo and Amine, then to the map. Everyone gathered around. Piyo circled where the map suggested the rabber warrens were, then handed the map to Amine. They circled a wider area towards the left of the ridge. Rav sighed with relief. Although the warren was larger than expected, it hadn't moved into their planned route. Izen indicated the extra zone, then drew everyone's attention to the top of the map, where the second rabber warren was. Amine and Piyo made some adjustments to where they thought the top warren could have moved but shrugged to make it clear they were guessing. At least they still seemed to keep away from the ridge, which protected them from the boulder-bear den. The boulder-bear would still be in its known place. The plan would still work. *Hooo*, cold wind blew up the crevice. The Blood Hounds huddled together for a night of dry food and restless sleep.

Rav woke with freezing hands, toes numb. Still night, still dark. Tucking his hands under his armour just froze his chest, no hot coals to warm him this time. More and more of his body heat sank into the cold rock beneath him. He curled up in violent shivers, unable to feel his ears, teeth chattering. A large hand coated in dried blood and grime covered his mouth. Rav leaned into it, desperate for any warmth. The ache in his jaw eased, and he regained control of his jaw to quieten his chattering. The hand released him, but everyone had been broken from their slumber, starting to stir. They all got ready in the pre-dawn light.

Amine patted Rav, then his bag. Rav retrieved the breakfast rations he had and distributed them. The Blood Hounds checked their equipment through touch while they ate, then all went still. Rav sensed that everyone was staring up at the sky, watching for the first sign of light. It wasn't long before he noticed the black edge of the crevice against the bruised black of the sky. Light enough to see. Izen grabbed everyone, and one by one, he boosted them back up to the surface.

The ridge was a barrier of darkness along the land. Miels pulled Rav into the group, then lay down at the edge to lift Izen out. Leader at the helm, the Blood Hounds set out into the ridge, using a similar system to the Ghoulsmen, where they touched each other's backs to keep in a line. Rav was towards the back, Miels in front and Lyra behind. The unit moved slowly and low, shuffling over the uneven ground. Rav used everything he'd learned to maintain his balance, keeping his steps as soft as possible. Seven people sounded like a light breeze as they entered the rabber warren territory. Rav drew a knife, the other Blood Hounds getting their crossbows out, ready to kill any rabber scouts as quickly as possible. They reached the steepest part of the terrain, climbing the ridge becoming more difficult, everyone now moving on all fours to cling to the rockface. *Sch, cla*. Rocks clattered. Everyone froze. No other noises. *Phew*. Izen guided Mulk to avoid the part where the ground had crumbled, then Mulk showed the same to Amine, the message passed along until they were all safely across.

Sky now dark blue with a growing glow of creeping orange behind them, faint rabber tracks could be picked out on the flat ground beside them. A third of the way through, Rav reached forward for the next handhold— *Ah.* Sharp rock cut his hand. Teeth gritted, he just about managed to keep himself from crying out. Through hissing breaths, Rav reached back to grab a spool of bandage cloth from the side pocket of his bag, taking a moment to wrap his stinging hand before continuing, crawling ever closer to the halfway point. Sweating, arms aching, toes crushed from digging for purchase in the rock, his bag felt ever heavier. Rav covered his mouth with more cloth from his bag to dampen his gasped panting. *Clatter.* Dust glittered over him. He blinked until he couldn't feel grit in his eyes anymore. Three-quarters of the way past, he wasn't the only one breathing loudly. Sky now orange as bright rays began to shine over the horizon, the Blood Hounds clung closer to the rocky ridge to avoid sticking out from its silhouette, the path forward easier to see. Birds chirped, insects buzzed, rabbers started scurrying beneath the ground, the mountain coming back to life. Rav looked up to where the ridge flattened out at the end of the warren. Almost there. Driving on, he reached it, grabbing hold of the last bit of steep outcrop to pull himself over the top, ready to collapse and stretch.

Miels pushed him low to the ground, holding him still. Wiping his eyes, Rav saw the others in the same position. Brightening light revealed more burrow holes beside them. The warren hadn't ended like they'd expected. Down on the flatter section of mountain to their left, a small rabber poked its sleek head out of a hole to scan the land around it, then bounded out, more following it out to graze. Some were as large as dogs, their long ears pinned back, small, pointed tusks jutting out their mouth, and curled claws at the end of their paws. Lyra and Piyo made their way to the top, joining the crouching figures. Izen nodded to them before scampering on. Rav rubbed his thighs as he followed, clearing gaps and dodging teetering rocks to advance quicker, but more rabbers emerged, soon dotting the area to their left. Worse, large birds took to the skies and circled above the rabbers, watching everything below. Rav hid beneath his bag, hoping the Blood Hounds appeared too difficult to attack. If one swooped down at them, the rabbers would notice, hundreds of the mutants rushing out to defend their territory.

The sun broke the lip of the world, casting golden light over Mount Don, exposing the holes that continued all the way alongside the ridge. More rabbers came out to graze. More birds circled above. More sweat poured down Rav's face. At last, they neared the end of the warren, the rabbers here larger and more aggressive. Having grazed until full, the smaller rabbers found sections of the ground where the soil was softer to begin digging new burrows. A smaller rabber bounded too far from the group, a bird diving straight at it, but as the bird opened its talons, one of the guarding rabbers leaped at it, gliding through the air with its front claws bared. The bird spotted the threat and swerved aside, dodging the strike by a finger before flying back up.

Izen's pace never slowed, never paused, never faltered. Rav pushed himself further, aiming for Izen's back, exhaustion muddling his thoughts and vision. Izen's back distorted, growing wider, his armour looking like furs. *Aye, if I just turn my head, I'll see Cyrn's face...* Rav blinked and came to. *Stupid*. He shook his head to clear his fatigue; this wasn't a place for dreams. They passed the end of the warren extension and entered an open area where the ground was at an angle but not as steep as earlier, finally finding a safe space to rest. Beneath the morning sun, the Blood Hounds slumped down and guzzled their waterskins dry.

"The warren ahead will be growing too," Izen whispered. "It's going to take us longer to pass it. We don't have much time to rest."

Everyone nodded, grim.

"Water?" Izen asked.

"Enough," Amine replied, refilling everyone's waterskins from a larger skin in their bag.

Lyra shuffled over to Rav and reached for his bandaged hand. Rav held his hand out, Lyra rewrapping his bloodied bandage in fresh cloth from his bag, tight and fitting. Rav nodded in thanks before she slunk away, silent.

Lying on his back as he rested, he stared up at a circling bird. It folded its wings, plunging towards Amine's bag. Piyo snapped his crossbow into position and clicked the trigger, the bolt striking the bird in the abdomen to send it falling into the dark side of the ridge.

"Bolt," he hissed.

Rav whipped one out his bag, presenting it to him. Piyo watched the skies as he reloaded. In the distance, another bird spotted its comrade fall and shot over to get the easy meal. Izen signalled for them to move again, three more birds coming to fight over the corpse.

Hidden under the shadow of a chunk of rock, the Blood Hounds watched the rabbers of the next colony graze and burrow, each looking like a fluffy dot. Another one hopped too far from the group, another bird dived down. This time, the guard didn't react in time. *Eep, eep eep.* It was carried into the air, where another bird flew in to contest the prey. The two had their talons hooked deep into the rabber, and they tore the creature in two, ending the fight. Other birds swooped to the ground to catch any stray pieces of rabber organ that had fallen out in the struggle, then just as suddenly, they all shot back into the sky. A rabber far larger than the others bounded out of the ground and leaped high into the air, its great paw swatting a bird out the sky.

"That's the alpha," Izen hissed.

The birds all fled from the area, the rabbers continuing to dig.

The Blood Hounds shifted further up Mount Don over the course of the afternoon, arriving at the second warren. This time, they were entering past the guards. Rav gulped. If the warren was as wide as the previous one, they had to start crossing it early, or they'd run out of light, but that meant crossing the most dangerous section in daylight.

"We need the dark to hide," Izen whispered. "Wait until evening."

Minds honed, sun lingering at the bottom of its arc behind the mountain, wind icy cold, the Blood Hounds set off crawling along the rocky surface to hide. Rav pushed his bag ahead of him, copying Amine so it wouldn't stick up, head down, no idea where the rabbers were or how many of them were out. Only Izen stole the occasional glance between the rocks to make sure they stayed on track. *Eep. Eep.* The noises got louder as they moved. *Cha cha cha*, they dug.

He held his breath, squeezing his bag, wishing nothing rattled as they passed the warren border. *Eee. Eep. Pah.* But something happened. Something close. Miels maintained his calm movements. Rav followed his lead. Then his eyes widened as something hot dripped on his neck. Unaware, vulnerable. He pinched himself. Lyra was behind him. Lyra would surely slaughter anything hungering over him. *Ignore it.* He was safe. For now.

Sometime later, the thundering of his heart faded. The rabbers' squeaking dampened. Past the border, but they still had a long way to go until they left the warren.

A crevice had formed in the rock ahead they had to cross. Izen lowered himself down, then stretched across to grab the other side. From there, he pulled himself over and back up, silent. He lay down and reached out for Mulk, who, with Izen's assistance, made it over. One by one, they each followed Mulk's method across. Rav tensed his body to stop it moving as Miels lifted him along, followed by Lyra pouncing across the gap, the World assisting her with an almost impossible movement.

Red light glowed as the sun touched the horizon, and while the Blood Hounds continued onwards, it slipped down until it vanished. Biting cold returned, Rav's hands going stiff. The rough surface started to sting. Almost there.

"*Run*," Izen shouted, jumping up to sprint forward.

Rav clambered up to follow, snatching glances either side of him. *Eep.* Rabbers bounded over in a swarm from the left, eyes crazed, tusks jutting. Izen shot his crossbow into them, then slung it over his shoulder, drawing his sword and shield. Rav stumbled on the uneven surface, his foot smacking into a dead guarding rabber with a bolt sticking out its eye. Lyra pushed him on. The warren's end was just ahead, the pocked grasses turning to barren dirt. Amine, Mulk, Piyo, and Miels also shot their bolts into the approaching mutants to little effect. *Eep. Eep. Eep.* Silhouetted in the dimming light, hundreds of bodies lunged towards them. Rav scowled, flicking a knife into the pack to slay one of the front-runners. Where was Bo?

"Up there." Izen pointed to a cluster of trees beyond the barren dirt.

The unit jumped off the ridge and onto more even ground, dashing for the treeline. The rabbers surged forward, but it wasn't enough to catch them before they left their territory. Scrabbling at the ground, the Blood Hounds crossed the open land and vanished into the thicket, rushing through it before breaking out the other end, where Izen took a sharp left towards a boulder, then turned right after running behind it, using its large size to hide their route up the mountain. The *eeps* faded, quiet settling once more. Izen ran further before stopping, squinting back down the mountain in the darkening light. Everyone panted as they caught up to him.

"Where?" he hissed at Piyo.

Piyo pulled the map out and took a moment to recognise their position. "Right. There's an opening over there." He led the way across the mountain and into a dry riverbed.

Adrenaline pumping, they scoured the area for any other living thing. Clear.

"What happened?" Amine whispered.

"One of them was guarding the ridge," Izen muttered, turning to Piyo. "How far away's the treasure?"

"Very close. We can get it at first light."

"Isn't the treasure in a tunnel? Wouldn't it be better to sleep there?" Mulk asked.

Izen shook his head. "It's too hard to search in the dark. Besides, there could be mutants with it. Rest until morning. I'll keep watch until Amine takes over."

Ga Gome. Hooo. Another storm brewed. Another bad night. Rav tucked himself further under the lip of the dry riverbank, hoping that water didn't still flow where he was lying. Worse, it was hail.

Three nights of poor sleep had Rav peeling his eyelids open upon waking. Body numb, he lay still and waited, hail pattering the riverbank lip above him. When would the sun rise?

"It should be near dawn," Amine whispered beside him. "The clouds are covering the sunrise."

"Let's get moving, then," Mulk growled. "Lying in the cold's not gonna help us."

"I-I've m-memorised the map in relation to the campsite. I'll be sl-slow, but I can lead us into the general area in the d-dark," Piyo stammered, teeth chattering. "By the time we arrive, it sh-should be light enough to search the area."

"Good. Up," Izen ordered.

Piyo at the head, the Blood Hounds moved by touch up the riverbed, shields pelted by hail as they covered their heads. The cloud cover broke far in the distance behind them, pale light starting to shine.

"Up here," Piyo said as he climbed out of the dry riverbed, going left towards some shrubs. "Tryxwin's report said the Baron hid the tunnel entrance under a flat rock between the empty river and a fist-shaped boulder."

The Blood Hounds moved into a line, then started to sweep the area, soon spotting the outline of a large fist-shaped boulder ahead of them.

Miels broke formation to check something. "There's a tunnel here," he called back.

The others hurried over, seeing a hole as wide as two people heading into the ground at an angle.

"What about the rock supposed to be covering it?" Piyo asked.

"Terrain changes," Izen grumbled. "Let's get down and search it, even if just to get out of the hail." He readied his weapons before taking the lead as they headed into the tunnel. "Careful; the ground's smooth."

Rav braced himself before descending, holding his hand out to steady himself against the worn tunnel walls. Deep enough down that sunlight no longer reached them, Izen called for a torch to be lit. Amine handed him one that flared to life. A short stretch below them, the ground levelled at the bottom into a cave. Izen threw his torch to the bottom and retrieved another from Amine. Nothing stirred. Rav gazed around the tunnel for any other signs of inhabitants, seeing nothing but smoothed-out rock. Izen entered the cave first—a small, cramped, earthy hovel that soon filled with the warmth of the burning torch. The others rushed down to join him. Another tunnel led off to the cave's side, and at the back sat four dusty chests.

Mulk grinned, patting everyone's back except Lyra. "We found it."

"Check that the chest Baron Tryxwin wants is here before we celebrate," Izen ordered, but all could see his smile.

Piyo wiped a layer of grime off each of them, pulling out his map to match the drawings to the etchings adorning each chest. "They match." He laughed. "This one's for the Baron, and the rest are ours." He shifted Baron Tryxwin's out the way, then used the pommel of his sword to break the lock on one of the remaining three. "Who wants to open it?"

The Blood Hounds pushed Izen to the front, who grabbed either side of the lid and lifted, firelight glinting off the polished metal inside. Izen picked up a bracer out the sawdust, and after laying out a few more pieces, the Blood Hounds saw a full suit of plate armour with a Blood Palm set in the centre. This metal wasn't the dull grey found in Pitt; it was near silver, decorated, strapped together with mutant tendon and lined with hide. Looking at the pauldrons, the stitching, the menacing slits cut in the helmet, the immense skill required to forge it was obvious. Izen ran a finger over the slight distortions in the silver colour where the metal had been tempered. From the even finish, the polish, the etchings, it was an expensive set comparable to Lyra's.

Izen picked out the last two items, a hammer and shield, both matching the armour's quality. Mulk lifted the hammer up, a short shaft with a rounded head, while Miels tested the shield, which covered his torso and thighs, swinging it with ease.

Mulk smashed the lock off the next chest with the hammer, then opened it. Wrapped in cloth and buried under more sawdust were several weapons: a bow and quiver, three swords of different designs, an axe, two shields, and a sheath of throwing knives. Though not as high quality as the previous equipment, they were close. Mulk flourished the axe, its blade cutting through the air.

Amine's eyes gleamed. "Weapons like these would draw Champions."

Mulk threw them the bow, then Izen a longsword, Miels the axe, and Rav the sheath, leaving himself with a shield and hammer. Izen drew the blade out its scabbard, inspecting it for damage, then grabbed a cloth and bottle from Amine's bag to oil it, the others copying him to preserve the blades. Rav balanced one of the nine knives on his finger. Light as a feather. The sheath could be strapped to his waist. He looked to Izen, who nodded. Rav tied it on, practising moving with it. Piyo glanced at one of the swords with a curved blade but tore his gaze away to focus on his armour.

"I want it," he said, lifting the breastplate up, which was a little too big for him. "Me and Amine are the only ones without plate armour and this suit's light enough for me to use," he argued. "You can have the other stuff; I just want this."

Izen grimaced. "It's worth more than anything else; you'll have to pay us our share of it."

He nodded. "Done."

"Do you want anything?" Rav asked Lyra.

She tapped her sword against her armour. "I already have everything I need."

Izen dragged the last one forward, the clinking of coins catching everyone's ear. As they cheered, the cave shuddered like something was wriggling in it, and Rav stumbled, putting his hand on the cold tunnel wall to steady himself. *Hissss.* All heads turned to the side tunnel. A forked tongue flickered, an enormous pair of slit emerald eyes behind it glimmering in the torchlight, both set on a head that filled the entire width of the passage. Copper scales shimmered as it slithered towards the Blood Hounds.

"*Formation*," Izen roared, dropping his new weapon in favour of his familiar one. "*Piyo*."

Piyo snapped into action, pulling a pouch off his belt and lighting it. He threw the smoking bag down the tunnel at the approaching mutant, a burning grey cloud soon filling the tunnel.

Izen led Miels and Amine to the left of the opening, signalling for Mulk to lead Piyo and Rav to the other side, where they waited in ambush.

Hisssss. The serpent writhed in the smoke, the cave shaking as it slammed into the tunnel walls.

"Snakes see heat; throw the torches to the back of the cave," Izen ordered. "*Hammer*."

Amine retrieved one from their bag for him. Izen grabbed it and began slamming it into the tunnel walls. Mulk followed his lead, hacking away at the lower section of the tunnel. Combined with the shaking tunnel, dirt and stones rained from the ceiling, filling the room with dust. The tunnel entrance gave way, collapsing down to block off the snake.

"Get the chests and run." Izen raced over to the discarded weapons, throwing them into a chest, then dragged it towards the exit.

Piyo came to help him while Mulk and Miels grabbed another two with Rav and Amine's help. Lyra picked up the last one. *Bang.* The collapsed entrance blew apart as the tip of the snake's nose poked into the cave. The Blood Hounds fled as fast as they could up the exit tunnel.

"*Ah*." Miels slipped, crashing to the ground, letting go of the chest. Amine buckled under the unexpected full weight of it.

Rav reached back to help Miels back up as Amine righted themselves and their grip.

Bang, crash. The blockage was broken through, light from the torches engulfed in a great cloud of dirt. The cave vanished from sight as everything rumbled. Izen dodged a falling stone from the breaking roof, urging everyone to move faster. Rav glanced back. Giant green eyes emerged out of the dust cloud and locked onto Lyra. She slashed her sword into the roof as she ran, causing another collapse that buried the serpent's massive head. Rav held his breath. Had that done it? The tunnel rumbled once more as the snake burst through, unscathed.

Surface within reach, Izen lugged Piyo behind him and scrabbled out into the ongoing storm, hail shattering against the ground. He made for the riverbed they'd followed up, hail bouncing off his armour. Amine and Miels climbed out and chased after him, then Rav and Mulk. Rav turned to check on Lyra, but by the time she reached the surface, the snake had caught up. He screamed, heart in his throat as their eyes met, the fear in his never reaching hers. She turned and stood tall at the entrance, then lunged down, driving the tip of her longsword into the serpent's nose. It flinched, its scales absorbing the blow, then struck as she dodged back.

Rav dropped the chest and dashed back. Pulling his pouch and tube off his belt, he stuffed a handful of powder from the pouch into the end of the tube, then blew a cloud of red dust into the tunnel.

HISS. The snake lurched back under the sting of the burning powder, smacking into the roof of the tunnel. Ground too thin to take its strength, the monster burst out the rubble and into the light, shaking its head from side to side as its tongue flickered. Rav choked for air, lips on fire as though he'd kissed a hot coal. Lyra yanked him away as the serpent writhed. He tore his waterskin off his belt to pour over his swollen lips, all water emptied before he could breathe again. Mulk continued dragging the chest across the ground on his own. Rav rushed to catch up to him and picked up his side. The others had already jumped down into the riverbed and were peering back over the lip. Rav raced towards them in the pelting hail as the two-storey monstrosity writhed in the air to his back.

The snake blinked again and again as its tongue flickered. Its huge maw opened, fangs springing forward out of its black gums, and hissed. From the tips of its fangs, black venom shot out in an arc to strike the fist-shaped boulder, then it surged at its target, fully emerging from the tunnel to slam its head into the rock and shatter it to pieces. *Hisss.*

Mulk, Rav, and Lyra slid down into the riverbed. Rav grabbed a pile of ice and pressed it to his swelling lips. Together again, the Blood Hounds hurried down the mountain as fast as they could. But not fast enough.

Ssssshhh, scales grinded against the ground, rocks cracking under immense weight, growing louder. Rav glanced behind them. The snake reached the riverbed, paused to flicker its tongue, then turned in their direction. *Hisss.* It slid into the riverbed, filling it, slithering after them like a flood, hail pinging off its scales. Rav faced ahead, pushing himself with all his might.

"*Dodge right*," Lyra shouted.

The group darted just in time to see a spurt of black venom shoot past them and spurt across the ground.

"Do we dump the chests?" Mulk shouted.

"Not yet," Izen roared.

The section of the riverbed they'd slept in was within reach.

"*Shield*," Lyra called.

Rav threw her his. Lyra caught it by the edge, then flung it towards the snake's open mouth to intercept another spray of venom, the wood splintering from the pressure. *Where are you, Bo?* Rav whipped his head from side to side, but there was no sign of the brute.

Arriving where they'd exit, the Blood Hounds threw the chests out the riverbed and climbed up the side after them, nails digging into the ice for purchase. Izen led them straight down the mountain towards the rabber warrens. *EEEP! EEEP!* The guarding rabbers screeched, hundreds of them gathering but not attacking.

"*Ridge*," Izen roared.

He didn't stop to follow it down as they had on the way up, instead jumping over the rocks to slide down the other side. Mulk gritted his teeth as he followed. Out the corner of his eye, Rav saw the snake break through the riverbank in pursuit, then flick its tongue once more before turning to the gathered rabbers, the alpha bounding over. *Hisss.* Its tail wagged from side to side as it dove into them, a constant screech of piercing squeaks following.

CHAPTER 21

EEEEEP! Hissss. The Blood Hounds never stopped running as the noises faded behind them. Across the ridge now, Rav paused, eyeing the lush flora beneath the dark forest canopy. Was the boulder-bear near? None of the long, yellow grass had been flattened, blowing in the howling wind. They dropped beneath the trees to escape the hail.

"Rest," Izen whispered, doing his best to ease his panting as he eyed their surroundings. "We're going to run straight down from here."

Mulk stood in a guarded stance, hammer and shield drawn, head cocked to catch any noise. Amine opened their bag and tossed out anything not essential, nodding at Rav to do the same. Next, Amine opened the weapons chest and emptied it, loading as many items as they could into their bag. Rav did the same, the pair managing to fit everything except a shield, which Rav carried to replace the one Lyra had thrown. Piyo strapped the suit of armour over his hide set, looking bulky, as Mulk and Miels tied everything else over their backs. Izen opened the last chest, hundreds of coins, jewels, and a few ingots packed into more sawdust. As it all glittered, smiles creeped up everyone's faces. Izen filled his pouches to the brim, then Mulk, Piyo, and Miels followed, anything that didn't fit tucked under their breastplates.

Izen took Baron Tryxwin's chest off Lyra. "Thank you for carrying this, Sister. Without your help, we might not have all survived."

She nodded, sucking her teeth at her damaged sword, its tip rolled, its edge chipped.

"We'll make it back tomorrow," Izen decreed. "Sleep once we're out the boulder-bear territory."

He moved as close to the ridge as he could while staying under the protection of the tree canopy, leading his unit down Mount Don. Bag heavier, Rav teetered as he hurried down, Lyra helping steady him whenever he tipped too far over. The hail softened until it stopped, the sun halfway across the sky, and the roar of a rushing river thundered from deeper in the forest. Mulk kept snapping his head towards any odd sound, the others doing the same, but there was no sign of a boulder-bear. Had they hidden away from the storm?

Arriving at the forest's edge, tension eased, the mountain opening up before them. Being high up provided a clear view of the terrain they were heading into, no mutants in sight. Mulk sighed with relief, wiping his face and rubbing his bloodshot eyes.

Clouds cleared, and Rav took a moment to adjust his bag under the bright light of the sky, feeling the sting from lack of sleep. The ground steepened, and the Blood Hounds jingled with coins as they slid down from one rock to another, covering the distance they'd climbed the past two days in one. The cave they'd stayed in the first night was just below, but Izen stopped, hand raised. Mulk snapped into a guarded position, everyone copying him, all facing the large, hairless, unmoving body at the bottom of the slope. A cloud of flies buzzed around it.

Izen looked over the carcass and whispered, "A dead boulder-bear."

Mulk covered his mouth. "Where's its head?"

Saliva built in Rav's mouth at the rancid stench. Izen slid down to the body and kicked it over, swatting at the flies that buzzed around. Half the body flopped over, the rest smashed to paste. Rav gagged at the sight of a thousand squirming maggots. Calloused hide, bulging muscles, giant paws. A monster. How had it died?

The others slid down to inspect it.

Piyo examined the rot. "It's been dead for a few days. It looks like it's been hit by something, but I can't tell for sure."

"Whatever happened here isn't for us to get involved in," Izen muttered. "Move."

He led on, Lyra taking a few more moments looking over the wounds before re-joining the group. Rav hurried on as the sun set. Hadn't Bo mentioned using a hammer? Who else would be strong enough to crush a beast like that? He *had* been here, watching. He *had* helped. Rav glanced at Lyra, but she was watching their surroundings, not him. She didn't know. After shaking his head, he smoothed his expression and pressed on.

A cautious inspection of the cave revealed no sign of more goebbers, the corpses thrown before no more than gnawed bone. Waking at dawn again, Mulk, Piyo, and Miels rubbed their new equipment in mud to scuff it up. Next, Rav and Amine repositioned the weapons in their bags so their shape didn't stand out. Last, everyone ensured every coin pouch was tied tightly to stop them clinking. Anyone looking at them would think they'd returned from a gruelling journey with little to show except for a single grimy chest.

Carriage waiting for them beyond the Brack, they travelled straight through Kroom Town to Donsden, only speaking in hushed whispers until they entered the Blood Hound house and dumped their spoils on the floor of a side room. Seeing the glittering gems, Mulk's shoulders started to shake, followed by Miels', soon having everyone laughing, even Lyra.

Rav slumped on the floor next to the treasure, running his hand over the pile to make sure it was real as tears blurred his vision. "That was cold," he said, laughing.

The Blood Hounds guffawed, pulling their clothes tighter as they shivered at the memory.

Mulk kneeled to pat Rav's shoulder. "When I touched your face on that rock shelf, I thought you'd been turned to ice."

"I nearly fell down the start of the ridge," Izen snorted. "One of the handholds gave way and smacked Mulk's hand."

"That stung." Mulk grinned, showing a bloomed black bruise on the back of his hand.

"I sat on Rav's head at one point." Miels chortled, looking at Rav in apology. "Good thing I put you through so much strength training; otherwise, you might've crumpled."

"That bird got torn out the sky right over us." Amine shook their head with a smile. "If there'd been goebbers, that blood would've attracted them all."

"It was hot blood," Piyo said. "Nice and warm." He grabbed Mulk's shoulder. "I told you the boulder-bear way was quicker."

"We got away with it," Mulk grumbled. "But I've a new fear now: snakes."

"I'd rather face a hundred goebbers than that thing," Piyo grunted.

"I'd take two hundred." Miels shuddered. "It didn't even flinch under the Sister's lunge."

"It *was* very heavy." Lyra tutted, drawing a burst of laughter.

"What was that powder you used?" Miels asked Rav.

"Fire leaf."

"Ha. Who'd dare put that stuff near their mouth?" Mulk nudged him with his elbow, but Rav stayed tall. "You're joking, right?" Mulk flinched away from him. "Rav, if you'd breathed that powder in, you would've died screaming."

Rav's shoulders dropped, grin twitching. "It worked though, didn't it?" He gazed at Lyra, who held his jaw and examined his mouth.

"I thought it was flash powder," she muttered. "It does not look like you have breathed any in, but if you feel your lungs burning, find me right away." She picked up Rav's powder pouch and threw it out of the room.

Miels snorted. "You're an idiot."

"No wonder it had such a big effect." Amine laughed.

Mulk grimaced. "That monster took a full cloud of that stuff and still didn't go blind."

"Try not to use it when I'm nearby." Piyo winked at Rav as he made a show of stepping away from him, towards the doorway. "I like my skin unblistered."

Izen patted Rav's back. "It was a big risk, but you're right. It worked. Now, don't ever do that again."

More laughter followed, Rav's jaw aching from grinning so much, but as he tried to listen to another joke, a yawn struck him, so big that his body shook with it. Sound dulled, grogginess latched onto his every limb to drag them down into slumber. Bidding the Blood Hounds goodnight, he lumbered up the stairs to his room step by tender step.

At last, he pushed open the door—*bzzz*.

"What the—"

Flies, rotten stench, blackened blood. Rav covered his mouth as it filled with saliva, staring at the large, calloused head sitting at the end of his bed. The decapitated head of the boulder-bear. Rav spun towards the corner of his room by the wide-open window, fists raised.

Bo was leaning against the wall, wrapped in a brown cloak, picking the dried blood off the head of the massive hammer he carried with his filthy nails as he eyed Rav. "I kept to my part of our deal," his voice rumbled. "Now it's time for you to honour yours."

Rav rushed to shut the door behind him, then threw his bedding over the head, hoping to smother the stench, heart pounding to drive away his weariness as he breathed through his teeth. "What happened?"

Bo lifted his war hammer and stood, stepping face to face with Rav. "You should know since you stood where I killed the bear." His muscles rippled.

"It spotted us coming up the mountain from its den and came down to kill us?"

Bo nodded.

Rav clenched his fist, staring straight back at Bo. "But you didn't help with the other mutant; that snake almost killed us all."

Bo shrugged. "You look fine to me. I'm sure it was nothing the Bride couldn't handle."

Eyeing the hammer, Rav took a breath, unclenching his hand. "Fine, I'll honour our deal." He paused to gather his thoughts. "First, I'm not the only one who's received this information. Others will be after this Heaven's Tear, but not for some time. They need to wait for the season to change."

Bo stayed standing as Rav explained what Baron Ghourts had told him, going over Harton and the sea caves beneath the town that filled with water during spring, then emptied in autumn. A man had spotted something shining gold in a new chamber after he fell in and was sucked into a new cave system last winter. He escaped and sold his knowledge at a secret auction to Baron Ghourts; however, he got greedy, also selling the location to Baron Tryxwin. Ghourts caught and killed him for the betrayal but was then pursued by Tryxwin.

"A sea Heaven's Tear..." Bo mused, "or is it rock?"

"You can tell what Heaven's Tears can do from where they're found?"

"Does it matter to you?"

"I guess not."

Bo paused and tapped his hammer. "That traitor set a good example. Are you going to follow his poor decisions?"

Rav raised an eyebrow. "And risk dying for nothing?"

Bo grinned. "You're strange, Rav. Get home safe."

"I've got a while to go." He sighed. "I've got a good start, though."

"That trash downstairs?" Bo laughed. "Everything you found isn't even enough for one bezoar."

"Is that something from deeper in the Sink?"

"Yeah."

"Then don't waste my time talking about it."

Bo laughed again. "Do you know any more locations? If my journey to these sea caves doesn't work out, I think we can get on quite well."

Rav pursed his lips. "Aye, one more. But I won't need your help for a long time."

"Knowledge of two Heaven's Tears already? Lucky boy," Bo spat. "Don't I feel a fool, having lived here a third of my life without finding one."

"I hope you succeed, Bo Hart." Rav cracked a smile. "That way, you won't break into my room anymore."

Bo smirked. "Yeah, no more cryptic chats—"

Bang.

Rav jolted back as Lyra burst through the door, sword drawn. Behind her stood Izen and the rest of the Blood Hounds, also equipped for a fight. His mouth dropped, unable to produce words. Would they fight? For him? To honour the camaraderie they'd shown on Mount Don, or to protect their investment? Rav glanced at Bo's war hammer. Either way, they'd lose.

"I guess we were a bit loud," Bo sneered, eyeing them all as though he could decimate the group whenever he wanted... except for Lyra. He'd tensed a little when he saw her.

"Who is that?" Izen seized up as he faced Bo.

"This is Bo," Rav hurried. "He helped us on Mount Don." He unwrapped his bedding to reveal the boulder-bear head sitting at the foot of his bed.

The Blood Hounds gasped, holding their noses.

"You are still in contact?" Lyra scowled. "What did you offer for his help?"

"Our deal is between us," Bo growled, Rav glancing at the Blood Hounds behind Lyra.

Izen's eyes went wide as he stepped further across to block the doorway. "He's here for the money?"

"No." Rav shook his head while Bo laughed. "This deal has nothing to do with you."

Flies buzzed in the silence that followed, everyone bristling.

"As amusing as your little group is, I've a journey to prepare for. I won't be here for the next few months." He faced Lyra. "He's a good candidate, Bride. Give him all the help you can get." Bo vaulted out the window. Rav watched him fall three floors to land on the ground as though he'd hopped out a carriage. He rushed to shut and lock the window behind him, not that either of those seemed to make any difference when it came to Bo.

Izen lowered his sword, jaw tense. "Where's he from?"

Rav smoothed his expression to press down any nervous twitches, keeping his voice steady. "Bo? He said he's from Mo'za."

The Blood Hounds sucked in a sharp breath.

"'Zet Mo," Mulk whispered.

"Y-you know someone from there?" Amine stammered.

"No wonder you didn't accept anyone else's offer of support." Piyo looked down in thought. "One person from Mo'za could kill them all."

"Aye, Bo offered to save me if I got in danger."

They gulped, tensing further, a tremble now in their grips.

"I need to speak with Rav," Lyra snapped.

Izen nodded. "Of course."

The Blood Hounds backed off to whisper among themselves. Lyra closed the door, leaving her and Rav alone.

"What did you offer?" she asked again.

"You know what I offered." Rav hardened his face. "I already told you during the journey here."

Lyra shook her head. "No, you said you *promised* Bo a Heaven's Tear, but people like him do not act like this unless they have direct benefits."

Lip starting to twitch, Rav wiped his face. "You said he'd follow me for a Heaven's Tear, and he did."

Lyra pinched between her eyes. "Helping out when he is nearby and going up Mount Don to kill a boulder-bear are two different things. There is no Heaven's Tear to be found up there." She looked him in the eye. "Rav. What did you offer him?"

His expression cracked, his eyes narrowing as he clicked his teeth. "I can't tell you."

Lyra sucked in a breath, her eyes glistening with worry. "You know very little about the Sink and how things work further in. If you have made a deal for the future or to join some organisation... There are some things you cannot undo no matter how hard you try. If you ally with the Unaffiliated, you will become enemies with the God King, and no one survives that."

Rav hurried to dispel her fear with a nonchalant wave of his hand. "You think Bo would trust me that far? He wanted something I have, and in exchange, he killed the boulder-bear for me."

She frowned, picking up its head, then throwing it up and down. "I could have killed it. Things like boulder-bears are weak; even that snake 'Zet Ar would die at my hand."

Rav shook his head. "Just because you can fight monsters like them, should you? It's still a risk; you'd still be risking your life for me. Again." He sighed. "I know what he did didn't really count as saving me, but he acted on my behalf, and I'd rather keep him as an ally than an enemy."

"Bo is dangerous, Rav."

"So is everything," he huffed. "Not just to me either. I won't have you bleed again."

Lyra flared her nostrils. "I am here to bleed for you, Rav. To bleed for the World. That is my duty. It is my honour to see my blood shed in place of yours so that you can complete your Calling. You are here to learn about the Sink and how it operates under my protection. For you to get used to the chaos. Bo is someone you cannot understand yet."

"Which is why I made a deal with him."

"Rav..."

He hesitated. What kind of deal did she fear so much? He relented, dropping his head to whisper, "I'm not supposed to know what I know. If anyone found out, I'd be hunted down and killed. I'd also break the deal I made with Bo. I can't do that."

"No one is going to kill you," Lyra growled.

"For this, they would. You couldn't save me."

She held her retort, stopping to think. Her brow furrowed deeper and deeper before her eyes widened and she gasped. "How?"

"Baron Ghourts," he mouthed.

Her face swelled red, veins bulging as she snarled, "How could you give up an opportunity like that?"

Rav fought to remain quiet. "Baron Tryxwin also knows. Even if I did go find it, how could I fight her and her army? Everyone else who found out about it is dead."

Lyra turned away, tendons in her neck writhing. After a long breath, she turned back. "I must report this to the Sisters," she hissed.

Rav stood firm. "No."

She glared at him. "Rav."

"If I tell you, Bo Hart will kill me. I don't want to die."

"You would get protection."

"I don't want to need protecting."

"How could you do something so stupid?" Lyra seethed. "Do you know what it means? Do you think that because you found your Heaven's Tear so easily, others are also easy to get? Do you know what it means to be Ah' ke? How much control people who wield the World's power have in Ga'thew'? Can you imagine how much worse a place like Blood Marsh would be if a man like Bo Hart ruled it?"

"Bo wouldn't care about a place like this," Rav spat. "He just wants to advance deeper into the Sink."

Lyra flinched, mulling his words over. "And why would that not be a problem for you? This was careless, but you are not careless, are you, Rav?" She locked onto him. "I have seen you be clever; I have watched you work to avoid risks. You would never make a dangerous man more powerful. You would take that power for yourself so you could become stronger, so you could survive the greater dangers that are yet to come. Unless you do not think you will have to face that danger or the consequences of making Bo Ah' ke. You are planning on running away. Why else would you give up on this chance? A chance I would fight to the death to help you obtain."

"A chance to have more people try to kill me," Rav grunted.

"A chance for you to become powerful enough to save your home. After our argument, I thought it was the World you did not trust. I did not worry then, as the World will make itself known to you in time, but this..." She went quiet. "Even if you heard the World, would you listen? Even if you knew your Calling to be true, you would turn away. Turn back to an insignificant village to live a life of nothing."

"That's all we are to you people, isn't it?" Rav snapped. "That's all you think of my family. Insignificant distractions that meddle in your great plans. Tools to be used and discarded."

"All people have value in the World; anyone can be Called."

"That's your doctrine, but do you believe it?" Rav jabbed his finger at her. "Would you have cared about me if I was just another Nameless vagrant?"

Her voice went cold. "You *were* Called."

"Why doesn't my family matter? Why doesn't Pitt matter? We exist as a resource to you, nothing more. Take our stone and our blood, then abandon us."

"There are more important things than living a dreary life in a far-off village."

"Not to me."

"You have not heard the World; you do not know what it means—"

"*I have heard it*," Rav roared. "I lay down to listen, and as I did, I heard Its breath... and it terrified me." He stared at her, daring her to continue.

Lyra froze, aghast. "How?" she asked, her voice trembling. "How could you hear the World and not believe?"

"Believe in what?" Rav threw his hands to the ceiling, stomping across the room. "Some great plan? That I'm being led to fight for someone else's future? That I'll be pitted against monster after monster for something I don't even care about?"

"You have been Called; you know the destiny awaiting you—"

"You *haven't* been Called, Ha'th Bey Riene. You don't know what I saw or what it means. You don't know what I'd have to do. There is no greatness in my supposed future, just war and death."

She gasped, covering his mouth. "I have been patient, Rav. I have fed you, washed you, tended to you. I have eased you towards your Calling, taking it slow so you could adjust. I have been kind." Her eyes filled with tears.

He pushed her hand away. "I know, and I'm gratef—"

"But if I must, I will drag you to your destiny. I will force you into place for the World." She glared at him, eyes going bloodshot.

Wisps of Ghoulish smoke rose from Rav's skin. "Then I'll fight you every step of the way."

"Why? You know how great of an honour it is to be Called. To be a part of the World."

"You don't know what it's like to have a family that loves and cares for you. You don't know what it's like to *be* in love." He stared her down. "You're a product of the Sink."

She shook her head, then took a combat stance. "I know more than you can imagine."

"You know what it means if you do this, right?" Rav's skin rotted, on the verge of becoming the Ghoul.

Lyra's stance faltered, her hands trembling, tears falling. "I hate you, Rav."

"I pity you, Ha'th Bey Riene." The Ghoul receded as Rav turned away. "I wish you were a real person."

Lyra stared him in the eyes, conveying every emotion she felt—all the sadness, all the anger, all the real emotions of a real person. She dared him with her stare to hurt her again, then with a wipe of the back of her hand across her tear-streaked cheeks, she stormed out of the room.

CHAPTER 22

Rav lay in bed as the morning sun rose, pinned down by the black rock of guilt sitting in his gut. Was Lyra gone? Would he have to face the Sink without her? He smacked the wall beside him with his fist. How could he have said all that? How could he have hurt her when all she'd done was help? He dropped his fist. But he hadn't been wrong. He was still leaving. He still hated the Sink. He was still terrified of that breathing.

After rolling over, Rav rolled back, never finding the right position. With a huff, he forced himself to sit up, the growing pang in his guts too much to bear. How could he fix it? ...He couldn't. At least he hadn't told her too much about his Calling, but everything else was ruined beyond repair.

Getting up, he paced between the door and window, brow furrowed, scratching his head. If only he hadn't spoken to Bo Hart... He shook his head. No. If only he hadn't gotten *caught* speaking to Bo Hart. Rav stopped, his hand on the windowsill as he looked down through a gap in the shutters to where Bo had landed. How had he gotten caught speaking to Bo? It was one thing for Lyra to have heard them, but the rest of the Blood Hounds? Why had Bo come when Lyra was in the house anyway? Why make such a show of dropping off the boulder-bear's head? It didn't make sense. Unless... who benefitted from him and Lyra fighting? Who benefitted from them splitting apart? Who benefitted from him fleeing the Sink? He'd made them fight. Bo Hart. The rock in his gut began to smoulder.

Rav waited until he no longer heard the other Blood Hounds moving around below before creeping downstairs for breakfast, wincing at each creak from his steps, as though any sound would draw them out. What did they think of the fight? Would they still want him as a member if he didn't have Lyra? Rav pressed his hands over his face, breathing heavy, thinking back to the time they'd attacked him and his conversation with Piyo... Better to avoid them. Better to delay losing everything he'd worked for. He drooped down as though wilted. Maybe starting again would be easier this time now that he knew what he could do. What he *would* do.

Rav eased open the door to the kitchen and startled back. Izen, Amine, and Mulk were sitting around the table with big grins, their oats untouched in their bowls as they stared at a sheet of paper set in the table's centre. Izen slowly turned to face him. Rav's heart pounded, sweat cooling his back, his cheeks warming with shame.

"Morning, Rav," Izen greeted him as usual.

Amine looked Rav's way, pointing to the paper, eyes shining. "We've gone over the treasure already."

Mulk slapped the table with a big palm as his joy spilled into laughter. "We're rich." He shook his head in disbelief. "Rich like merchants."

Rav kept his posture in check as he searched their expressions for any signs of discomfort. Behind their joy and avarice lay caution—a slight narrowing of the eyes, a tension in their postures. And a little respect? A willingness to meet his eyes, to shuffle in their seats as though welcoming him in to share the table with them. Whatever it was, it wasn't bad. He matched their wide grins, standing taller as he strode into the room, heading to the kitchen counter to fill a bowl with milk-cooked oats from the main pot hanging over the extinguished fire.

"Great. I can finally afford a few things I want."

"You'll get a lot more than that." Mulk snatched up the piece of paper and held it up to the morning light pouring in through the small window. "It was all worth it."

"That's only an estimated price from a few jewels," Izen tutted to Mulk while beckoning Rav to sit. "Eat, then I'll give you your share."

Mulk read through the numbers again. "Even if we only get half of this, we'll never want for food or shelter again."

Rav dragged his chair out with a scrape before sitting, glancing around the table again as he did, but nothing changed. It was as though they hadn't heard the argument. All they knew was that he'd met Bo. Had Lyra done something like whatever Siere had done at the end of Fool's March to ensure only the two of them had heard their conversation? Delayed the Blood Hounds finding out? Was that yet another kindness she'd done even though he'd rejected everything she loved? Rav faced his food as he munched to hide his burning cheeks.

Once finished, Izen directed him to the treasure room, where more than one-sixth of the pile from yesterday was left, tidied into neat piles to separate the coins from the jewels from the ingots.

"Why is there so much?" Rav asked, gormless as he realised he could now buy all his family's land in Pitt.

"Ah, some of it's from Piyo as compensation for his new armour," Izen said. "We've also gifted the weapons out to everyone. The knives are yours, the hammer Mulk's, the shield Miels'. I've got a sword along with Piyo, and Amine has the bow. The other axe, sword, and shields are being used as our equipment. You can keep using the shield you borrowed and can buy it from the unit if you want."

"How much?"

"An ingot and a sapphire."

"Aye." Rav pulled them out of his pile and handed them to Izen, the dozen other glittering jewels remaining catching his eye.

"We're meeting Baron Tryxwin in secret outside Kroom Town tonight. We need you there."

Izen left, leaving Rav to carry everything pouch by pouch up to his room, the space under the floorboard filled, the rest hidden in a blanket under his bed. Grabbing a plank of wood, nails, and a hammer from the storage room, he nailed his window shutters closed, hearing the front door open as he finished.

"Sister," Izen called in greeting.

Rav gulped, hands clammy, staring at the door.

Step, step, step, she climbed the stairs.

What should he say? What should he do? Was she coming to say goodbye? Would she drag him off into the Sink? Would he have to fight her? Rav rubbed his face. He would. For Pitt, he'd do it.

Knock, knock, knock.

Rav stood frozen by his bed, eyes glistening, as Lyra walked in. She looked gorgeous: clean skin, flowing hair, no sign of the teary fury that had warped her last night. But a bag hung over her shoulder. *No...* Rav couldn't stop his lip wobbling.

"Are you leaving?"

Lyra snorted. "Do you think I'd give up so easily?" She threw the bag at Rav, hitting him on the chest. "These are herbalist books. There are three local plants with a similar effect to fire leaf that won't kill you."

"Lyra, I—"

"We're not going to talk about it," she snapped. "I connected to the World so the others didn't hear. It happened. We made our points clear. Now we have to work through it. I'm never going to give up on you, Rav."

No matter how much it hurts me. Rav nodded, wiping his tears.

"Have you eaten?"

"Aye."

"Then come." She beckoned him out the room. "I've got something for you to do."

Rav collected his cloak and a coin pouch before following her out the house. Lyra led him away from the markets and taverns; instead, going out of the city to enter the farming fields.

"Sister." The farmers paused their work to greet her with bows.

Many were on their knees at the bases of the crops, pouring milky snot-like liquid on the plants from glass vials. Lyra led Rav past them to a hide canopy a dozen feet wide that looked to have once been brown, its colour now faded to a pale yellow. Under its shade lay a chipped wooden desk covered with disorganised paper slips, and hunched over it was a wiry older man, his hair short and grey, his stubble peppered, dressed in a loose shirt and muddy trousers. At his feet were five large chests, one open to show glass vials twinkling inside.

He looked up from his desk as Lyra approached. He bowed, "Sister," then stood to eye up Rav, his well-tanned face suiting his dark eyes. "Is this him?"

Lyra nodded as she came to stand in front of the desk, stepping aside for Rav to come beside her.

"I'm Paulo Sousa, manager of the eastern fields." Paulo reached over to grasp Rav's forearm in greeting. Rav squeezed his forearm back. "Not bad. The stories are true."

Rav frowned. "What stories?"

"Tales of a scrawny Called One too weak to lift a shield. But you see, it was all an act, a deception. When mutants in the marsh came for his life, he revealed his true strength and cut them down, leading his unit to victory."

"Ran for his life," Rav corrected.

"Managed to survive." Paulo smiled. "Ha'th Bey Riene says that you're looking to get stronger through labour."

Rav looked at Lyra, who indicated for him to agree. "Aye, but I've not farmed before."

"It's not really farming this season anyway." Paulo picked up a vial from the open box and showed it to Rav. "There's a fungus that grows on the crops during the summer. We pour this over the plant bases to stop it." He threw it to Rav. "We always welcome volunteers."

Rav caught the vial and examined the milky liquid inside.

"Hard labour's good for your growth," Lyra added.

Rav glanced at her. There was something different in her words, her demeanour. "I fight and train all the time."

"Now you also farm. Your shift ends after lunch." Lyra walked away.

"When's lunch?" Rav asked Paulo, who simply laughed.

There was no lunch for the farmers. Rav breathed heavily under the hot sun, his cloak long discarded, the sickly-sweet scent of the milky vial fluid stuck in his nose. Back aching, joints creaking, his only thought was of snuggling down in his bed. That and stinging remnants of the argument. Lyra had helped him so much... Ha'th Bey Riene was using him. He threw himself into his work, soon three-quarters of the way done with his crop row. Still about a hundred to go, though. Rav sighed, standing up from where he'd been pouring fluid over a plant stem.

"Not long now," someone called from behind him.

In the next row, a young man with straw-coloured hair and a freckled, goofy expression, dressed in loose clothing, smiled at him while leaning backwards to stretch his back.

"I'll get it done," Rav muttered, kneeling to pour another vial onto a crop.

The young man straightened, then stretched forward to arch his back. "Take your time. Learn to do it right once to save time for the next hundred."

Rav emptied the vial and stood up, wiping the sweat off his forehead. "What am I doing wrong?"

"You're not dressed well for the sun."

"I know that," Rav huffed, his chainmail burning his skin. Wasn't it what he deserved? For Wakeman, for Lyra, for everything.

"You're also leaning down with your back, not squatting with your legs. Maybe that will work for today or a week, but in a month, you'll be hunched over like an old man." He straightened again, twisting from side to side with his arms tucked in. "Taking breaks to move like this also helps. No one wants to sleep with a stiff back."

Rav squatted, the strain on his back vanishing. "Any other tips?"

"Wear gloves. Your hands are going to be cracked and dry for a few days; no amount of washing can clean this stuff off. Believe me. I've suffered it."

After retrieving another vial from his pocket, Rav took extra care with his next pour to ensure no liquid splashed on him, still moving a little faster than before. "Have you worked here long?"

"Every summer since I was eight. That's nine years of practice," the youth answered, going still. "My parents are both soldiers under Baron Glass, you see. I'm Pierre Joude. You must be from outside. How long have you been in the Sink?"

Rav nodded. "Rav. Aye, I arrived a few months ago from a small town two months' travel from Fermuch."

"Here to find wealth and glory?" he asked with cheek.

Rav winced but pushed the words out, ready to endure what he deserved. "I need a Name."

Pierre chuckled. "I haven't heard that one before. The few Nameless I've seen over the years are always chasing what everyone else is."

Rav stopped his work to look over at him with a quizzical frown. "You're not bothered that I'm Nameless?"

"I know it's supposed to be bad, but it's not really a thing that happens here. Those made Nameless in Jinkin territory never return, and the few that wander in from elsewhere are often forced out when they fail to find good work. I've not met enough of them to make a judgement on everyone exiled."

"I could be a thief or a murderer."

"Are you?"

"No."

"Good."

Rav blinked, dumbfounded. "That's it?"

"This is the Sink; who isn't a thief or murderer?" Pierre lolled his head at Rav, his sandy hair flopping over his forehead. "Just because you got caught doing something bad doesn't mean everyone else is good."

Rav rocked to his feet with a frown, looking at the man's belt and boots, failing to spot any weapons. Judging from his light-brown eyes, he didn't appear to have even a glint of cunning or desperation. But how could he be sure? "Are you a murderer?"

"No..." Pierre winked. "I have stolen, though."

Rav found his smile creeping up. "Anything interesting?"

"A pie from a shop window."

Rav snorted. "Did it taste nice?"

"Ah." He grinned from ear to ear as he gazed down the crop row he'd almost finished working on. "There's nothing better than a meal hard earned."

"Aye, that's true." Rav wiped the sweat off his face and flicked it onto the soil. "There'd be feasts for us whenever we returned home from defending Stone's Way. No meal could ever compare to that, even when everything had been burned."

"Did you also serve your Baron?"

Rav shook his head. "We had to guard against Barons. After our original Baron marched off and died in here, the others came to steal our wealth and our people."

"No Baron?" Pierre raised an eyebrow. "Then, shouldn't your land have deferred to another? Wouldn't fighting against that make you a bandit?" He tutted. "That's dangerous work. Every bandit group that's come here has been slaughtered. They don't even send the army to deal with them; village militias hunt them down by themselves."

"This was outside the Sink," Rav reiterated. "What we did was filial."

Pierre shrugged with an amused smirk. "I'm sure it was. So, other than land, what else did you steal, Nameless bandit?"

"We were protecting our people," Rav corrected.

"Sounds like a thief's excuses."

Rav stared at him but saw no malice in his goofy face, Pierre's eyes shining with curiosity and delight. "Equipment from invading soldiers." Rav sighed.

"Robbing armies? That gets people tortured here. Anything that disrupts supplies will bring everyone's fury."

"They shouldn't have attacked us."

"Sure, sure." He pulled a cheeky grin. "So, not a thief who steals. Who've you murdered?"

Rav raised his hands in protest. "All self-defence."

Pierre shook his head at Rav as though disappointed in a naughty child. "You stole someone's land, then murdered the people who came to take it back? My, my. You're quite the rapscallion."

Rav bit his tongue as he turned back to his crop and uncorked his vial. Was that what had happened? Hadn't it all started with him murdering a man? Pitt had almost rebelled to defend a murderer. He gritted his teeth. It wasn't murder; he'd saved his Ma. Cyrn wouldn't have defended a murderer.

"I'm joking, I'm joking," Pierre called upon seeing Rav go sullen. "I've been rude." He stepped across the crop line to reach Rav and held out his forearm. "How about I treat you to a drink after work? I know where all the best ale in Donsden is brewed. You can tell me about being a hero bandit."

Rav pursed his lips, squinting as he faced Pierre. The offer appeared genuine. Had it been made in Pitt, everything would seem normal. But this wasn't Pitt. The only way to uncover if something else was going on was to agree. Besides, maybe it would be fun? Rav grasped Pierre's forearm. "Fine. I need to actually finish working first, though..."

Pierre darted back to his row with a laugh. "I'll finish up my row, then help with yours. But you have to pay for the first round."

Rav squatted back down and continued shifting from plant to plant, coating their stem bases in fluid. As he worked, the small blot of shadow under him started stretching east, growing longer and thinner as the afternoon waned, the heat cooling as a breeze rolled in. A new shadow fell over him. Rav glanced up to see Pierre beside him, already dropping down to work on his next plant. Looking at Pierre's row, he saw sunlight glimmering off every crop's wet stem. How had he managed to get them all done so fast?

Pierre had already moved on to the next crop. And the next, and the next. Rav finished his and rushed ahead, but by the time he'd coated that one, Pierre had done another three. As the sun entered the final quarter of its descent, Pierre stood at the row's end and stretched his neck.

"Done."

Rav pushed himself to his feet off his dry, cracked hands, dusting his knees where soil had stuck to his trousers. "Aye. What now?"

"Now we get to enjoy a hard-earned drink and meal." Pierre pointed to the adjacent crop rows, where other farmers had finished their work and were gathering as they walked from the fields back into the city. "Come. I know the best tavern."

He set off marching, Rav just behind him, soon joining the growing throng of farmers walking under the portcullis. Winding down several alleys, Pierre led him past reeking waste wells to a quieter area on the outskirts of Donsden's right half, away from the upper markets, yet clean. *Scythe's Rest* tavern had a hanging scythe-shaped sign outside its open door, the building made of stone but reinforced with wooden beams, the scent of ale wafting from it.

"This one." Pierre made for the entrance. "A couple dozen of us usually get tables together. I'll introduce you."

Rav watched Pierre step inside and hesitated, gazing in to see an ordinary main room with six long, wooden tables lined with chairs, an empty fireplace at the back wall, and a bar counter that had eight large ale barrels placed in racks above it. Wide windows with open shutters gave him plenty of light to see the dozen or so people already inside, greeting Pierre. Rav gathered his breath, then walked after him, guts clenched.

"This is Rav," Pierre introduced him to the dusty group seated at the rearmost table. "He used to be a bandit, so he must be rich."

Huh? Rav sucked a fleck of spit down his windpipe in surprise, coughing into his fist. He looked at Pierre with watery eyes. "I've"—*cough*—"never been introduced like that before."

"What? Are you poor?"

Rav drew a raspy breath to protest but ended up just sighing in acceptance.

"See, I told you." Pierre laughed.

"Rav?"

Rav spun around to Paulo's voice, seeing him enter the tavern behind him.

"I wondered where Pierre was dragging you." He walked up to Rav and patted his arm with a strong nod. "You worked hard today."

"I was far behind everyone else," Rav mumbled, watching the other farmers out the corner of his eye.

"It's your first day. And it's volunteering that counts. Most people who visit Donsden just scavenge and fight in Blood Marsh; very few help the city out."

I didn't volunteer; Lyra brought me here. The words sat on the tip of his tongue, too heavy to say.

"All that matters is that you're helping. Want a drink?" He pointed towards the bar.

"Aye, uh, I'm buying." Rav scratched the back of his head. Maybe buying a round could make up for his lack of integrity. "I had a deal with Pierre." He pulled his coin pouch out his pocket. "A mug of ale for everyone."

As Rav headed for the bar, whispers about him being Nameless caught his ear for a moment before going silent. He turned to work out what had caused the silence and noticed Paulo's heavy glare. The farmers hid their scowls to cheer in thanks. After receiving a handful of coins, the barkeep lifted a small ale barrel from behind the counter and handed it to Rav along with a tray of mugs. Rav held the barrel over his shoulder and balanced the tray with his other hand, carrying it all back to the table, too aware of every gaze boring into him.

"You're a bandit?" someone asked while Rav set everything down with a clatter.

"I used to be—"

"He defended a territory," Pierre interjected, reaching across the table to pour out a mug of ale for himself.

"That's hard work," the person commented, also reaching for a mug. The other farmers nodded with respect. "Without soldiers, none of this would be possible." He gestured towards the crop fields. "People who risk their lives against mutants and invaders to protect people like us are honourable."

Paulo pointed for Rav to sit beside him and Pierre as Rav spoke, "Without food, how could people fight?"

"Ha, we all do our part." He chuckled.

Rav leaned over to serve his own ale and took a sip, soothing his dry throat with cool, bitter liquid. "Are you all volunteers?"

"Some, like Pierre here. Most of us are growing old or are injured, so we farm all year."

"What's this boring drivel?" Paulo clamoured. "We've done our work for the day and we'll do more work tomorrow. Got any interesting stories, Rav? Something funny or weird, but no battles. We hear enough about them already."

"All I've done since arriving in the Sink is train or fight."

"Do you at least sing?" Paulo grinned. "I haven't heard a new song in... ha. Near three summers now."

"I, uh... I know one," Rav mumbled. "It's the song of my town, sang for celebration, for battle, or for new life." He cleared his throat.

"I guard my home with all I am,
"To honour those who gave me life,
"We march far to conquer our foes,
"A Bloodline to keep out all strife.
"Go forth and fight 'til your last light,
"Gifting land and lineage to our flesh made young,
"We'll love and marry for our blood to carry,
"Into the future bright."

"Mmm." Paulo nodded once Rav finished. "It's powerful; I like it."

"It sounds best when a group sings it."

"Don't they all?" someone joked, the crowd laughing. "Here, I've got a marching song that's quick to learn. It goes like this:

"*Stamp your feet and break the earth,*

"*Use your strength to show your worth.*

"And then you sing whatever you feel like singing."

"Right, more ale"—Paulo looked around the tavern as he finished his mug—"and then we're singing."

"I dig the ground; I plant the seed."

"STAMP YOUR FEET AND BREAK THE EARTH,"USE YOUR STRENGTH TO SHOW YOUR WORTH."

"I broke my back; I broke my spade."

"STAMP YOUR FEET AND BREAK THE EARTH,"USE YOUR STRENGTH TO SHOW YOUR WORTH."

"I found a girl; I made her smile."

"STAMP YOUR FEET AND BREAK THE EARTH,"USE YOUR STRENGTH TO SHOW YOUR WORTH."

"Gave her my Name, now she's my wife."

"STAMP YOUR FEET AND BREAK THE EARTH,"USE YOUR STRENGTH TO SHOW YOUR WORTH."

The tavern rumbled with song.

"What d'you do the rest of the year?" Rav asked Pierre.

"I'm training to be a soldier." He sipped his ale. "I'll be good enough to serve Baron Glass, just like my parents." He lowered his voice. "With their training, they say I could even become a Contender, and from there, heh heh."

Rav smirked. "You want to be a Champion?"

"Shh," Pierre hissed. "Champions are vicious. If they think I'll Challenge them, they'll kill me early."

Rav frowned in amused confusion. "Why tell me, then?"

Pierre lolled his head at him. "Are you going to tell anyone?"

"No."

"Then what's wrong with telling you?"

Rav shook his head with a snort. "I wish I had your view of the world."

"I'll tell you another secret: I'm actually a genius manipulator," Pierre slurred.

Rav laughed harder.

"Why laugh? It's true. See, if you act simple, people'll treat you as simple. That way, there's no need to involve me in some cunning plan."

"What if people still want you to do something, though?"

"Then I'll just do it." Pierre nodded at his own foresight. "Good workers are always welcome."

"Your genius plan to avoid betrayals and conniving Barons is to give in?"

"Exactly. Seems dumb, but it's the best way to survive. People work too hard to look smart just for others to assassinate them. Eat your food, follow your orders, and things'll go well."

"And what if you have to do something you don't want to?"

Pierre held up a swaying finger. "First, pick someone you trust not to do that to you. Second, people view those problems backwards. They try and solve the act—'*How can I avoid doing it?*' '*How can I do the least harm?*'—all that nonsense. The trick is to work on you, not the action."

Rav gave him a gormless gaze. "What?"

"Instead of being like, '*How can I not do this?*', think, '*How can I make myself want to do this?*'"

"That seems..."

Pierre patted Rav's back as though consoling him. "It's a different way of thinking; that's why you have to be a genius, like me, to understand it."

"I hope it goes well for you."

"It does." He took a serious expression. "Do you think I like working in the fields? I didn't at first, but I changed how I viewed the labour and now I do extra work to help out new guys, like you."

"I appreciate it." Rav stood, foot tapping to the thrum of another song starting. "Another mug?" As he turned, the tavern door opened. Izen walked in and signalled for him to leave. Rav fell from his revelry.

Baron Tryxwin. Kroom Town.

"Aye, I'm coming."

He said goodbye to Pierre, Paulo, and the other farmers before following Izen out.

CHAPTER 23

The Blood Hounds were waiting outside, all armed and armoured, Mulk carrying the small chest with Miels. Piyo and Amine guarded their backs, Lyra at their side.

"Here." Amine came forward and handed Rav a cloak to cover his grubby outfit along with a waterskin.

"You're in front with me," Izen informed him, everyone taking position like they were out in the marsh.

Rav sipped his water as Izen lit a torch and led the Blood Hounds out the gates, head already clear from his cautious drinking. Instead of heading into Kroom Town, the unit walked around it, and off in the dark, a lantern fluttered to life, illuminating a dozen people standing under a tree. Most were soldiers wearing unmarked armour, the rest in heavy cloaks. One flashed the insignia of a dragonfly. Izen approached them, and once close, he signalled for Mulk and Miels to present the chest.

"Is this it?"

Rav locked onto the hooded figure who'd spoken, recognising Cata by her husky voice. She stepped out from behind her guards to inspect the chest, her face half-hidden under her cloak's hood so only one green eye and a stray curl of her black hair could be seen.

"It was as you described," Izen answered.

She rattled the lock, smiling as it remained shut. At her glance, two soldiers came forward to take it. "I trust whatever else you found was enough for your journey to have been worthwhile?"

Izen nodded. "Just about."

Cata leered at him, then faced Rav. "Come find me. I'll be waiting." She turned away before he could respond as though she already knew his answer. "Let's go," she called to her guards, who got in formation with her and the chest in the centre, then set off towards the marsh.

Mulk patted Rav's back. "She likes you."

"I still want to know what's in that chest," Piyo muttered.

"It's a good thing you don't," Miels said. "I reckon you'd be dead if you did."

"Are you going to visit her?" Amine asked Rav, their tone indicating that they'd also picked up on the mysticism within Cata's parting words.

Rav stayed staring as he watched Cata leave. *No.* Cata was about to go after the Heaven's Tear. The Heaven's Tear he'd sent Bo after. Maybe she could hurt the brute. The corner of his lip creeped up at the thought, then flattened again. Maybe she was marching to her death. Did it matter? Even if Cata had been polite now, she'd tear into his neck if she knew what was in it. She was a conqueror. A greedy Baron. She and Bo were as bad as each other.

"Maybe," Rav murmured.

Rav tugged at his new leather gloves and linen trousers, each inflexible, as he arrived at Paulo's canopy the next morning. The only way to make them comfortable was to work and sweat in them.

"I need a message delivered," Paulo said, breaking Rav from his daze. "Don't worry; it's easy to find. You'll get used to running the city's alleyways soon enough. Here." He handed Rav a closed note. "You're looking for Giant's Fist, a metalwork shop in the west of the city. Oh, and you've got half a row to do, so come back quick."

Rav set off jogging, hugging the note close to his chest as he entered the ever-jostling crowd in search of the street Giant's Fist was on, finding people giving him little room to move in while nodding his way. He cocked his ear to catch hushed muttering about the Mo'za and being Called under their breaths. News about him meeting Bo Hart had spread. Rav clenched his jaw. Who was it? Bo? Was he trying to further push him and Lyra apart? Piyo? Did he want to raise the Blood Hounds' status by association? Someone else seeking some hidden benefit?

Rushing through alley after alley, he found the shop and handed over his note as quickly as he could before running out of the city to the fields, finding his steps slowing as he got closer to the swaying crops. Would they think differently of him too?

"*Hurry up*," Paulo shouted at Rav from behind his desk as Rav emerged out the portcullis' shadow and hurried to the fields, other farmers glancing at him with playful snickering. "You've taken too long."

Rav released a shaking exhale, turning it into a chuckle as he continued running to the row of swaying crops beside the one Pierre was currently coating.

"I see your new clothes fit. And I see you've already soaked them." He pointed to the sweat stains on his trousers.

"Aye, I had an errand to run," Rav muttered. "Have you heard anything? About me?"

"What?" Pierre smirked. "Do you have another great tale of ambushing soldiers or something? Or is it about you being some special Called One? Can those words be eaten? Can they take care of crops? No? Then hurry, as I spotted some fungus."

Rav broke into a smile as he got to work.

The dreaded call to continue training with Miels had come to drag Rav back into the world of mutants and scheming after a morning of tending to crop rows. In their usual arena room, a halberd and common spear were leaning against a weapon rack.

"You're strong enough to practise with a real weapon now, not one of those twig spears." Miels picked up the spear, jammed its butt into the dirt, then snapped it in half with a powerful kick. "See? They're too light; you need the weight of a halberd to damage 'Zet Ar and people in heavy armour. We'll start with basic grips."

Within the arena bowels, he held a halberd out at full reach, arms shuddering until they dropped, this time unable to rise again. Following Miels' dismissal, he trudged to his room and slumped on his bed, then flicked through the herbalist books Lyra had gifted him. What was different about her? Words blurred before his eyes as he thought. With work and spending time with Pierre, he hadn't seen her so often. Was it a relief not to have her always nearby? *Aye*. So why did it always feel as though something was now missing? With a sigh, he shook his head and refocused on the page in front of him.

Ground fire leaf wasn't safe to use and blowing powder was a terrible way to attack. How far could he blow it? What if the wind changed direction? What if he needed to charge into where he'd spread it? He squinted as he read, still finding no good answers. While many different substances could cause extreme irritation and pain, beyond coating a blade, there weren't any effective ways of wielding them, and how would he have had any hope of cutting through 'Zet Ar scales that not even Lyra could pierce?

Dressing in his most expensive clothes and cloak, Rav headed off to the Glass Emporium as the sun set, the guards allowing him inside after recognising him. He looked over the wonderous items again, now lit by candlelight. First, he examined the various smoke balls. Each had a substance that was quick to light but burned slowly to produce as much smoke as possible, but he'd already tried mixing tree sap with Ant's Itch, one of the tamer stinging powders, seeing that as the powder burned, its irritating qualities were lost. All it did was smell bad.

Next, Rav looked at the soap solutions, one of which was a capsule that dissolved in water to release the liquid inside so you could carry and store it as a solid. Was there some way you could make transporting and handling the powder safe, then change its state when you needed to attack something? Rav sucked his teeth. Maybe, but he didn't know it. Another idea was discarded. *Wait*. Hadn't an alchemist introduced himself at Niklaus' banquet? And wasn't he now rich enough to pay for lessons? Where had the alchemist said it was? Rav hurried out of the Glass Emporium, soon finding the small alchemy store mentioned squeezed between a bakery and a tavern at the edge of the city market just as it was closing for the day.

"Rav," the alchemist called from behind the counter as he wiped it down with a wet cloth, recognising him as he entered the bitter-smelling shop. "What are you looking for?"

"I want to learn more about alchemy," Rav said, pulling out his coin pouch and setting it on the counter. "I'm paying."

The man accepted the pouch with a smarmy grin. "What does a Called One wish to know?"

Two weeks later, Izen called for a meeting. The Blood Hounds gathered in the planning room, and he announced the news. "I've got another scavenge for us. A special one."

The room rumbled to life, Mulk sitting forward. "Where?"

"The other side of Mount Don. Some scouts have gone missing, and we need to recover their possessions. They were mapping the area. We need those drawings. Anything else is ours."

"Is this one of *those* scavenges?" Piyo asked, breathless. "The kind given as tests to units before they leave for the second layer? Do well and we progress with Jinkin?"

Izen nodded, and the Blood Hounds cheered, Miels patting Rav's back.

"Good work, Rav. See how our reputation has grown?"

Izen started writing on a sheet of paper pinned to the planning board. "A landslide has shaken up the mutants on the far mountainside, causing them to change positions. Baron Glass sent a unit to track the new positions; however, they haven't returned. It's low pay and high risk but connects us to Jinkin."

"When?" Rav followed.

"We need two weeks to prepare, as new mutant territories are dangerous. We'll start here." He pointed to the base of Mount Don. "Climbing up along this path."

Izen guided them through an initial plan, the Blood Hounds asking questions and providing solutions to problems. Rav walked out the meeting with three new maps to memorise and headed for Scythe's Rest tavern.

Rav sighed as he rubbed his eyes, tired from staring at the three sheets of parchment displaying the western side of Mount Don over and over again.

"You're leaving in two weeks?" Pierre asked from the seat next to him, leaning forward on the wooden table.

"Aye. I've got a scavenge." Rav took a swig from his mug.

"When're you back?" Paulo followed.

Rav shrugged. "A week, maybe?"

"You'll be longer," John, an older farmer with wispy grey hair and tanned, almost leathery skin, said. "I heard that the landslide took out the main path up. You'll be treading new ground."

Rav nodded. "Aye, I've seen a sketch of the damage."

John tapped the map with a long, grimy nail. "What the sketch won't show is how soft the topsoil is. Stuff's full of good minerals for crop growth, but it's like sludge when it gets wet. Bring a spade; you might have to dig a path up."

"Thanks, I'll tell my unit."

Pierre downed his ale. "You'd better buy us another round."

"I got the last," Rav protested.

"Yeah, but we have to make use of your money while you're here." He laughed.

Paulo swatted the back of his head.

Rav squinted, eyes alight. "Aye, I'll buy them now, but you have to buy them when I get back."

"Done." Pierre grinned.

Rav sat back in his chair. "You won't be smiling when I bring my unit with me."

"You better return and drink the barrels dry, Rav. Wipe that smug look off his face."

"Don't worry." Rav patted Paulo's shoulder. "I won't die."

A week of gruelling work and preparation later, Rav wandered the Inkwell for alchemy books, walking down crooked aisle after crooked aisle, running his finger over dozens of tattered book spines. He sucked his teeth upon reading the same titles he already owned over and over, others known to him through his alchemy lessons. With a sigh, he arrived at the end of the shelves before turning and searching the next ones, stopping just in as he touched a well-kept tome with a black-leather hardcover. Pulling it out of a stack of frayed paper, he saw no title. Nameless. Inside, beautiful, intricate illustrations covered the first page to detail plants so well he could see every vein, and beside them was clear methodology for producing some salve.

"Ah." The owner hobbled up to him as he flicked through its smooth pages. "That's a debunked book regarding all sorts of theories. It won't have the answers you're looking for, but maybe it can give you some inspiration. Or just look nice on your shelf."

"Why was it debunked?" Rav frowned, not finding the author's name.

The old man shrugged. "The alchemist who wrote it never came forward to claim the work or defend and prove some of their theories. Others have tried to replicate its claims; however, the methodology is flawed, resulting in different results. The drawings are delightful, though." He shook his head. "Ah, truly, some of the claims written inside are quite wild, haha. Ensure you use gloves and a face covering in a well-ventilated area before attempting any experiments from it."

"Aye, I'll be careful."

Rav bought it, then hurried back to his room in the evening light to read by candle as he listened to the Blood Hounds readying for sleep below. Running his finger over the detailed drawings of material combinations that couldn't possibly work, he sighed. Combining iron filings and crushed Hot Foot blackened the metal and produced no smoke, yet the book claimed that you could produce a liquid that healed scars. It was nonsense. Beautifully illustrated nonsense. Who would put so much time and effort into something so easily disproven? Wouldn't they be a better artist than an alchemist?

He gazed at another fantastic sketch of a flower that supposedly caused you to grow excessive hair. In a meadow of a thousand different plants, you could use this drawing to find the exact one modelled, detailing every splotch, every pocked mark, every hair on its leaves. Wasn't his notebook laughable compared to this? Perhaps it had been worth buying just for the artwork.

He yawned, ready to rest before another long day of working through crop fields and being beaten with a staff. Then... *what is that?* Rav turned back a page to a sketch of some medicine that you took by swallowing a capsule, the cross section showing a powder sealed inside a hollow ball. The methodology didn't even seem too whimsical. Sure, the medicine was impossible to make, but the capsule... Rav's eyes went bloodshot as he stayed awake, drinking in the words.

CHAPTER 24

"*Twenty breaths under a candle, then tip into a separate pot containing the sap of a north-pond lily root.*"

Rav followed the words exactly in the spare room opposite his that had become his alchemy research room, but the substance created still crumbled apart. Was the candle too hot, or were his breaths too long? Adjusting over and over, a hot but malleable substance was formed, which he rolled into a ball. He then used a hollow needle to blow into it, filling the centre with a pocket of air. At last, the powder ball he wanted took shape.

After leaving it to cool, Rav picked up the ball, its surface brittle, leaving traces of powder on his fingers. He aimed at a board on the other side of the room and threw it as hard as he could. As the bead struck the wood, *pah*, it shattered in a burst of powder that coated a circle as large as his head. Staring at the grey remains drifting through the air, Rav nodded. Now he needed to fill it with Ant's Itch.

Lighting a new candle after the old one had melted to the base, Rav moulded more powder balls, but instead of creating them whole, he left them in two halves. Mask and gloves guarding his skin, he tapped his vial of Ant's Itch to sprinkle red powder in the two sides, then smeared the edges with Trap Wax—a sticky, yellow sap. Hand as steady as he could manage, he pressed the two halves together, creating a makeshift pellet. The wax held. Nothing crumbled.

Rav stood back and wiped his forehead, catching sunlight seeping through the window shutters. Another morning of delivering messages and cleaning fungus, followed by an afternoon of training with Miels, awaited.

"Good. That's the most important training done for today." Miels placed his staff back in the weapons rack in the arena room corner. "I've got extra time this afternoon, though, if you want to ask about anything else. Maybe check before you do something like blowing fire leaf." He eyed the two prongs and length of elastic that Rav had nailed onto the top of his bracer, looking like a slingshot. "What's that?"

"It's to give me more range," Rav panted, pulling the elastic back with his arm raised.

"That rubber's no good. It'll stretch too long in the heat and snap in the cold."

"What should I use, then?"

"What're you slinging?"

Rav reached into his pocket for one of the thin gloves he wore while coating crops and slipped it on before pulling out a lopsided pellet from a pouch. "It's filled with Ant's Itch."

Miels stood back. "Then it's good you're checking now; I don't want those pellets bursting near us. Show me how it works."

Rav held the bead with a tender grip where it was strongest by the wax line and loaded it into the slingshot, aiming at a target board at the back of the room. He stretched the elastic as far back as he could, then released it. The ball whizzed through the air, struck the centre of the board, and burst into a cloud of red powder that coated a torso-sized section of the wood.

"Not bad," Miels murmured, keeping far away from the glittering powder. "Hmm, have you tried using a sling? You'll be able to fling the bead quite far without putting too much stress on it. Here." He passed one of the training ones to Rav. "Put a stone in it first," he instructed, guiding him through using the weapon until night.

The day had come. The Blood Hounds donned their armour and loaded their bags, the weight of Rav's equipment almost comfortable as it sat on him. He ensured the added shovels had been tied tightly in place.

"Ready?" Izen checked, looking over his unit one last time.

They all nodded.

"Let's go."

The carriage journey out of Donsden lasted a day, ending with them sleeping in a small garrison village for the first night. Once morning arrived, Rav found himself standing at the start of the remaining dirt path they'd use before entering the fallen soil, which lay like a gaping wound through the lush vegetation this side of the mountain. Only the thickest trees still stood along the path. Izen signalled them onwards, and Rav started moving again, boots crunching over the compact dirt, soon slipping as they entered the landslide. Ahead was a choke point between two rock formations, providing a narrow passage that would separate them from civilisation. The soil became thicker and thicker, mud sapping everyone's strength as they pried their feet from it over and over again. Rav gave out the shovels, everyone throwing mud out their path to keep moving. Only birds and light-footed yippers lingered around, picking off anything still trapped in the mud or anything that wanted to set up in it, ignoring the Blood Hounds.

Piyo stopped to check the ground, then shook his head. Signs of the scouts were long gone. They could only rely on the information provided about their planned route and areas they were tasked with mapping. Witness reports suggested the unit had made it into a forest before traces of them were lost. Izen had multiple smoke balls hanging at his waist, ready to escape whatever monster had made its new home there. True to the

Skywatchers' predictions, the skies remained clear. Breathing heavily, legs burning, they made it through the rock passage by night and climbed a lone tree to sleep. Rav and Lyra took the first watch, eyes glued to the starlit sky. Watch over, they woke Piyo and Mulk, falling straight to sleep.

Caw.

Rav's sleep shattered as he almost fell off his branch, holding on white-knuckled, heart pounding. A clump of feathers spiralled down around him, the culprit bird already hurrying away in the predawn dark.

Piyo drew back his sword from the space above Rav, sighing. "It got close."

"Are there more?" Mulk grumbled, searching the dark.

"Just that one." Piyo shrugged at him. "Sorry, Rav. Thing fell straight out the sky."

Rav snuggled back down on the tarp platform they'd stretched between branches, hand on a knife, unable to drift off before dawn arrived to light the sky pastel pink.

The Blood Hounds packed up and continued, the end of the landslide in sight. Beyond it stretched the dark green canopy of the forest they'd enter, a short area similar to the marsh with thickets and rubber trees, but dotted with caves and fewer ponds, between it and the mud. More birds flitted overhead, cawing as they circled over whatever was below. More mutants. More danger. Rav touched his Ant's Itch pellet pouch.

"The scouts were tasked with tracking a colony of goebbers, right?" Mulk checked.

Izen grunted in affirmation.

"What else could be here?"

"Snakes, badgers, birds," Piyo answered. "Things we can deal with. The main concern is that the rabber warren at the top of the landslide was ruined. Which could have forced them to travel further down to dig a new one."

"This is a quick scavenge, silent and uneventful," Izen murmured. "Find the scouts, get back. Nothing else will find us." He marched forward, lowering his stance.

The unit copied him, exiting the mud and entering the grasses, aiming for a cave within a thicket that would keep them out of sight. Rav caught the familiar buzz of Hot Foots, clouds of them whizzing at the tops of the rubber trees, and felt where the soothing creams sat in his bag, ready to be applied. Watching them a moment longer, they held still by their nests, indicating no mutants around. The Blood Hounds sprang forward on more stable ground, entering the thicket and passing the cave with silent steps in case anything was living inside. Climbing further up the slope, they reached a cluster of bushes beside a stream and cleared a small space inside for their camp. Rav peeked out the leaves as he ate his salted meat, not seeing anything below. Next, he looked out at the forest, which stood only a day away now. As the sun set, the treetops started to shake, then the skyline went dark, hundreds of wingtails taking flight into the night.

"They're off," he informed his group.

"Salves," Izen commanded.

Rav and Amine brought out yellow vials and poured the musty fluid onto a cloth to then smear on everyone's clothing, masking their scents. Done, Rav settled down and slept through the night, waking at dawn to ready breakfast. In the hazy light, Mulk and Miels grumbled as they got up too, pushing out the surrounding bushes with crunching steps as they headed to a nearby stream with a bundle of waterskins. Rav listened to the pair stomp around while unwrapping cheese and meat from their leaf-wraps, catching the soft glug of water entering the skins once they'd reached the gurgling stream—

Bzzz.

"*Ah,*" Miels hissed.

Rav stood with Izen, Amine, and Piyo to see Miels' stocky figure dashing back to camp, a hand clutched over the side of his neck.

Snapping into action, he lifted a vial of cream from his bag, but Amine was quicker and had already reached Miels with their own vial and was slathering the thick cream onto the blistering patch of skin across Miels' neck. Miels grimaced, breaths hissing through his teeth as he clenched his jaw, then eased, Amine finishing. Lyra stood from where she'd been wiping her armour with her oiled cloth and leaned over to check the blisters, nodding to indicate that he'd be fine. Mulk hurried back from the stream too, hugging six full waterskins in his arms, muttering about how a swarm of Hot Foots had descended to the stream for their morning drink. Izen shook his head, looking to the forest. *No more filling up. Let's head off.* Everyone ensured their helmets were strapped on tight, filling any gaps with spare cloth.

Miels twitched and grumbled as they moved from tree cover to tree cover, holding his neck. During a break, Rav tied his waterskin around Miels' neck to keep the area cool under his helmet, Miels nodding in thanks. Closer to the forest, they passed a lone badger lying desiccated on the ground with a small puncture mark in its back, courtesy of the wingtails. A startled snake spat venom from a tree as Piyo stepped near it, but a rapid dodge followed by a swing of his sword ended the threat. Everyone sighed with relief. At least with so many smaller, more manageable creatures, the birds left the unit alone. Rav spotted a small lizard race down from a tree carrying an egg and smiled.

Further along, Piyo pointed out a colony of yippers living in a cave, each rodent keeping far away from the forest as they roamed the grasses. What was in there? Rav's gut sank as he thought. Would goebbers be able to live beneath wingtails? No. Whatever was in there had to be bigger. Worse, Piyo failed to find any tracks relating to the scouts or whatever occupied the forest. Nearing the forest, Izen raised his fist, then pointed to a circle with a cross-carved mark on a tree. The scout unit had come this way, but there were no other indications of them.

Away from the Hot Foots, they climbed trees for the night. As Rav closed his eyes, all he could hear was the fluttering of wingtails.

Piyo took the lead into the forest in the morning, the Blood Hounds stepping out of bright sunlight and into the green-tinted, murky depths beneath the trees. Each conifer was thick, tall, and spaced apart, with a multitude of flora growing between them. Wide canopies covered everything, trapping the smell of damp earth and sap in the humid air. And excrement. The wingtails well-fertilised the forest floor. Rav held his breath as he waded across the squelching ground after Piyo.

Piyo paused to inspect the ground, still reporting no signs of the scout unit. Any prints had been buried beneath dung and any path they'd trodden had grown over. They waded further in, starting to spot sleeping wingtails hanging upside down from branches like bats. Between the canopy and excrement, most sounds were dampened, the Blood Hounds' careful steps quiet enough to not wake the ever-growing number of wingtails above them. No sign of anything all day, they sneaked back out to their tree camp and slathered themselves in wingtail deterrent again.

"How much of the forest have we covered?" Izen whispered to Piyo.

"Not enough. We only have enough deterrent to last a week; if we don't find any signs soon, we'll run out of time."

"We can't keep looking for tracks." Izen pinched between his eyes. "We'll just have to guess where they went and hope we're right. If that doesn't work..." He shook his head. "We'll try *that.*"

Piyo picked a path scouts would take to move straight into the depths of the forest. The Blood Hounds creeped under so many sleeping wingtails sunlight no longer reached the forest floor. Rav kept his head cocked for the slightest sounds, but there weren't any. No birds, no yippers, nothing. Only wingtails. Goebbers would've dug tunnels all over this area, rabbers would've too, and there should've been snakes slithering in the trees, hoping to constrict sleeping wingtails or lone goebbers. Why was nothing living on the ground?

Ree.

The Blood Hounds dived beneath the flora as a wingtail woke up, all the others nearby soon taking flight with it. A moment later, the area was clear, the milky liquid still sticky on Rav's skin. As wingtails fluttered around above the canopy, the Blood Hounds crawled back out to the forest edge.

Ree. Reee.

"The scouts couldn't have come through here," Piyo whispered. "No one can. There are too many of them."

"Yeah," Izen grumbled. "I think the only way we're getting through is with these." He held out one of his smoke-ball pouches. "We're going to smoke them out."

A wave of grim nods went around, the Blood Hounds returning to their tree camp for the night to prepare. Rav ensured his bag straps were secure, packing everything to keep it from rattling when he started running, Amine doing the same. A tense night of preparation bled into a pale, cold morning, sky overcast with rolling white clouds. The Blood Hounds ate well until midday.

"It's time." Izen patted Piyo's back and gazed at the forest. "The wingtails will be in their deepest sleep now."

Piyo stood and lit five pouches of smoke balls before the pair raced off into the forest with them, smoke already starting to billow. Mulk led Amine, Miels, Rav, and Lyra to a trench hidden by bushes, crossbows out, Rav with his sling, where they had clear sight of the forest. Would Izen and Piyo make it back, or would they need rescuing? As Rav scanned the trees for whatever great mutant lived within them, he noticed the faint haze of smoke rising above the canopy in a line, moving deeper and deeper into the forest with Izen and Piyo.

"It's started," Amine whispered.

REEEE. A screech like metal being torn rang out, hundreds of wingtails taking to the air to escape the pouring smoke. Rav readied a pellet in his sling. Izen and Piyo would now either find the missing scouts or whatever had gotten the unit would find them. Time crawled by. More smoke wafted into the sky. The wingtails flitted in a frenzy, piercing the area with their horrible screeches. Staring hard at the forest, Rav still couldn't see anything new. *REEE. Ugh.* He tied his helmet tighter, failing to hide from the noise.

Crash. Deep in the forest, one of the trees shook.

REEEE. The wingtails fled, dozens of them scattering in all directions.

ROOOOAAAR.

"There." Amine pointed at two sprinting figures, each desperate to escape the forest.

Piyo was ahead, eyes locked forward as he sprinted. Izen charged through the trees behind him, breaking thin branches and twigs, uncaring for the noise. At their backs was a cloud of wingtails, the creatures closing in. Unable to outrun them, Izen was soon engulfed in the cloud, but Piyo burst out the treeline in time, heading towards them. Amine jumped up to rush to their aid, Rav, Miels, and Mulk right behind.

"RUN!" Piyo screamed.

The wingtail swarm arrived at the end of the forest and flew straight up into the sky, joining their fleeing brethren to reveal Izen still sprinting unharmed. He ignored everything else, straining to be that little bit quicker.

HU, GR HU, something panted. *Snap. Crash. ROOOAAAR.* Out of the trees behind him, with a pale, calloused hide, came a charging boulder-bear.

Chapter 25

Frothing mouth, surging muscles, crazed eyes, Rav froze. A 'Zet Ar. The trench wouldn't save them. Mulk bolted, vanishing around a boulder. Rav stood and gawped, jaw trembling. Izen was far ahead of the boulder-bear, but the beast was faster, catching up with every bound. *Crunch.* The 'Zet Ar grazed a tree, bark splintering around it. Rav blinked out his daze. *Think.* How had he defeated the giant goat in Pitt? But there were no holes nearby. He focused back on Amine, Miels, and Lyra. Amine and Miels were already following Mulk's retreat path, while Lyra was waiting on his decision. *Rule one: hide.* Rav fled, arriving around the other side of the boulder, where Mulk was waiting.

"Did it see you?" he hissed.

"No."

Mulk touched his chest with a long exhale before puffing it back out in confidence. "Izen knows what to do. We need to find something to distract it with," he whispered.

"The yipper den," Amine urged.

Mulk shook his head. "You'd have to run out in the open to catch one of them, and most will have hidden after the wingtails' screeching."

Ba ba ba. Footsteps getting closer.

"That idiot." Mulk ducked around the boulder, returning a moment later. "We need to run from Piyo; if he joins us, the bear will know we're here." He started running in line with the boulder so he couldn't be seen from the forest, and the others followed in single file.

ROOAAAR. Rav heard the boulder-bear burst out the forest and into the open—*do doh, do doh, do doh*—its great paws slamming into the earth. Piyo's footsteps were catching up with them.

Mulk dashed inside another thicket, Amine, Rav, Lyra, and Miels crashing inside after him a moment later. Peeking out, they spotted Piyo arriving around the boulder to see it empty. Wide-eyed, thin face swollen with red behind his half-visor, he searched around, finding nothing in his frantic state, then looked back at Izen. *Do doh.* He turned and sprinted back in the direction of the landslide. Mulk licked his lips and gulped, everyone turning to spy Izen running across the grasses further down the mountain, heading into a dense grove of bushes. *GRR.* Ten breaths later, the fortress of a mutant came barrelling after him.

"We've got some time," Mulk said. "Izen'll keep going for a while, but he's too clear a target for the beast to switch to another now. We need somewhere for him to hide, then once it gets bored, we can lure it away."

"We can use a cave," Rav panted. "We dig a hole in the top, then Izen runs in, climbs up where the bear can't follow, and we collapse the entrance."

Miels shook his head. "We don't have time for that."

"Lyra, you're strong enough, right?" Rav pleaded.

"If you're going to involve me, then we should just kill it."

He flinched at the fierce glint in her eye.

"That th-thing's an armoured set of claws and teeth," Mulk stammered.

"I'm in Heaven." Lyra shrugged. "If you don't want to fight it, think of something else."

"There's no time for planning," Amine snapped. "Mulk, you've faced one of these before. Choose."

Mulk paused. "We search the caves for bait. If we see any easy gaps, then we can try Rav's idea."

Everyone nodded.

Mulk led the way out the thicket, keeping track of the boulder-bear by its destructive path. He pressed everyone down as it roared into the open once more, Izen dashing into a new, undestroyed thicket. Boulder-bear gone again, he pointed to a low cave. He and Miels moved up front, while Rav, Amine, and Lyra guarded their backs. Amine sparked a torch and threw it inside. It was empty. They darted in, weapons ready, huffing at the sealed roof. Boulder-bear still busy, they dashed out and into the next cave. And the next. And the next. Rav gazed out once more. Izen's fleeing figure had slowed, the bear gaining ground despite having to barrel through narrow terrain.

"What about this?" Miels pointed to a head-sized gap in the latest cave roof where sunlight beamed down.

Mulk nodded. "It'll do."

Climbing on top of the small cave, they used shovels to dig up the ground until, *tchik,* metal hit rock. Mulk drew his hammer and smacked away at the hole. *Tang.* The loud sound carried far, and soon, Piyo emerged from the shrubbery in their direction. *Tang, crack, crumble.* Rock shattered as the hole widened enough for a person to climb through. Mulk was breathing heavily, sweat pouring. Amine dropped a rope down the gap while Mulk moved back to the cave entrance, starting to whack away at the supporting rock. *Crack.* A little more and it would break.

"You stay out of sight up here with me," he ordered Rav, Amine, Miels, and Lyra, Piyo joining them. Then he faced out towards where Izen was running. "*Here,*" he bellowed.

The 'Zet Ar looked over. Izen darted behind a rock. The mutant turned back, slammed its paws down, and went searching for him, saliva dribbling from its maw. Izen doubled back behind some trees, gaining enough of a head start to head up to Mulk. Piyo lay panting next to Mulk as Mulk explained the plan to him.

"Do... you... have any bait?" Piyo wheezed.

Rav and Amine kept scouring the area, failing to spot anything to use.

"Trapping it'll be good enough."

Do doh, do doh, the boulder-bear powered up the hill after Izen. Rav squinted. With a clearer look, it seemed to be limping. *Aye, it is*. Its back left leg was twisting inwards as it ran, its whole left side seeming tender. It had taken some damage.

Izen spotted the rope hanging inside the cave as the beast lurched after him. Mulk and Piyo grabbed hold of it at the top. Miels, Rav, and Amine waited around the back with two hammers and a shield. Izen dived forward to grab the rope. Piyo and Mulk heaved. Izen flew up. The boulder-bear barged into the cave, its back scraping along the ceiling. Miels, Amine, and Rav dashed out from hiding, hammer and shield in full swing. *Crack.* The weakened rock broke, collapsing the entrance while Izen was heaved out the hole. The boulder-bear swiped at air. Rav cheered—

The boulder-bear swiped again, paw gouging a chunk out of the roof. Dirt fell. The hole widened. It leaned back on its hind legs and surged into the gap, snout breaking through to snarl at Izen with wicked teeth. Izen, Mulk, and Piyo fell backwards, rolling down the cave top as the ground shook. The bear pressed its paws to the ceiling, tearing the rock apart. Rav gasped. Too powerful. The 'Zet Ar flexed again. This time, its snout and neck breached the surface, where it wriggled and writhed, frothing saliva spraying in the air.

"What do we do?" Mulk shouted, looking at Izen.

Face pale, Izen wiped the coat of sweat off his face. "*Run.*"

Slam. One of the boulder-bear's shoulders broke out.

Rav dashed up the hill, sling ready, Lyra at his side. "I'll get us time." He released the sling as the bear's snout stuck out, the bead bursting over its hard hide.

ROOOOAAAAAR. The beast ducked back down, swatting at its face to clear the burning powder, but it couldn't escape the cloud. Eyes bloodshot, tongue and gums speckled red, it rubbed its head on the cave floor with pained grunts. Rav grabbed the bead pouch, crushed everything in it, then poured it down the gap. Bright red particles melded with the dust, floating down out the sunlight and into the raging dark. Rav coughed, guzzling water just from the smell, the cave now a pit of fire. The whole cave shuddered as the boulder-bear rampaged, the ground breaking under Rav's feet. Lyra caught him, flinging him back down the hill, where Amine helped him to his feet.

"It should be blind. We can make it," he wheezed.

"I don't think the Sister wants to do that," Amine whispered.

They all looked to the top of the crumbling hill where Lyra was standing tall, longsword drawn. She looked down at Rav, smirking. Gloating. Arrogant. *Watch me, Rav.* Though the ground kept falling apart, it remained firm where Lyra stood.

ROOOOAAAAR. The back of the cave roof collapsed into a slope, and the boulder-bear came charging out, shaking its head, sneezing, dribbling red-tinted spit. Out the dark and fiery cloud, it growled. *GRRRR.* The boulder-bear jumped at Lyra, maw wide, teeth bared. She stepped to the side, slinking away from the bite and arriving at its flank. Her sword was already in position. Repaired and polished, it drew an artful line across the bear's hide, then she stepped back, waiting. Biting into air, the mutant turned in Lyra's direction, bringing its paw down in a big overhead slam. Lyra glided around it, heading to its open shoulder, where another delicate slice cut across its hide. The paw thumped the dirt, its other paw coming across its body in a punching motion at her.

Rav screamed, "*Lyr—*"

The beast winced. The expert thin cut down its left flank tore open at its reckless movements, blood spraying from the gash. Lyra moved to its hind, dodging a bite to deliver her next carving. A moment later, the slice on its shoulder opened. Round and round the beast spun, trying to smash her, and scarlet line by scarlet line, it was whittled down, blood pooling at its feet. Rav stared, jaw hanging. Was that really a 'Zet Ar? Hadn't the goat endured a dozen strikes without injury? Hadn't it taken him everything he had just to take its eye? Yet another precise slice opened a cut across the bear's neck, blood pumping out in powerful bursts. The calloused giant stumbled, roaring, still trying to kill Lyra, now too woozy to have any hope as the cuts she delivered over and over again opened one by one. Roars weakening, it slumped to the ground, at its last breath. Lyra stood at its head, took a heavy stance with her sword, and swept down to behead it in one clean motion. She kicked the head down to Rav's feet. Bloodless. Gorgeous.

"You don't need anyone but me, Rav. I'm better than a thousand Bo Harts."

Rav found his hands shaking, a croak stuck in his throat. Dozens of wonderous cuts delivered in what felt like just a moment. A moment of art, of beauty. A sliver of Heaven. Untouchable. Unreachable. Indiscernible. The Blood Hounds also gawked, but Rav caught Izen flinch back, trembling, returning him to focus. He hurried to her with his bag, ready with bandages she didn't need.

Izen coughed. "Rest, then we'll track it back to its den to find the scouts."

As the unit settled, Mulk wiped a tear from his eye.

Rested, fed, and watered, the Blood Hounds rose in the afternoon to head into the forest. The wingtails had yet to return, leaving the place empty and somehow sorrowful. Rav stumbled down the boulder-bear's path of destruction, everything blurring around him. Looking at the giant paw prints and shattered trees, the danger they'd been in was obvious. That thing had been a true monster, a predator, the ruler of this territory. Reduced to a bleeding mess under Lyra's sword. It had fought so hard for itself and its land. Now the forest was vacant, open for anything to enter. He rubbed his face.

Beneath the canopy, they soon found the main cave the boulder-bear had charged out of, at the heart of the forest. Surrounded by bones of yippers, goebbers, badgers, Rav shivered in the gloom. *Grr.* Two cubs barely up to his waist cowered inside. Being so young, their hide wasn't as thick, their bite not so ferocious. Miels' and Piyo's eyes gleamed.

"We can bring these back and sell them to the arena for a fortune," Piyo said.

"We could keep one as a battle mutant," Miels followed.

"I'm not dealing with any more of them," Mulk stated.

"Think of the money," Piyo persuaded.

"I don't care."

"We should kill them." Amine stood with Mulk.

The unit looked at Izen.

"They're not ours to claim." He turned to Lyra, who gave the decision to Rav.

He sighed. "We should kill them. Mutants like them don't belong down here, not when they'll cause so much harm once grown."

Izen and Mulk nodded, stepping into the cave. Rav watched the cubs growl and nip at them, powerless to stop Mulk's hammer from cracking their heads. A potential future where they grew to trample Blood Marsh residents had been averted. Rav bit the inside of his cheek, never cowering as he watched. If the intention was to save, then this was the right choice, no matter the outcome, right? Wouldn't Wakeman have said so?

"Here," Amine called.

Torchlight illuminated the torn hide armour belonging to Baron Glass' scouts. Amine picked a satchel out the bones, handing it to Izen. He inspected it, paper rustling.

"We've got the maps we're looking for. Let's go."

Rav stared at a patch of black blood at the back of the cave, then the cubs' corpses, remembering the boulder-bear's injuries. A pregnant boulder-bear had been swept up in the landslide, fell here, then entered the forest to birth her litter. A mother had fought for the survival of her offspring, her Bloodline. What difference was there between men and beasts?

Rav dropped his head as a sharp thought pricked his mind. Lyra spoke of the future. Spoke of his potential. The assassination attempts on his life. ...Was he a boulder-bear cub to something?

He followed the unit out the forest, never easing. They stayed the night in a cave. After skinning the boulder-bear for its pelt and meat in the morning, they set off for Donsden.

"Those powder balls were great." Mulk patted Rav's shoulder to break him from his thoughts as they marched back through thick grasses to the landslide. "You're an alchemist?"

Rav stepped out the way of a short shrub. "I'm learning."

"It's an expensive hobby," Amine commented.

"We've got more than enough money. And if we run out, we'll make more." Miels grinned.

"After this task, we'll be able to access more shops, more sponsors, more everything." Piyo beamed.

"We still have to get back," Izen warned. "Rav, it was brave of you to attack it like that."

"And to come up with the plan." Mulk nudged Rav's arm.

"I was following Miels' rules."

"Yeah, I'm a good teacher," Miels agreed.

"You just beat him with a stick," Amine tutted.

He grinned. "Teach what you know."

Two days of travel later, they arrived back in Donsden. Rav trudged through chaotic crowds from the western gate, grateful for the fierce faces of Mulk and Miels ahead of him as people parted around them. They plodded up the familiar path towards the Blood Hounds' house, Rav's head hanging, eyes watery from exhaustion. After stepping inside the gloomy hallway, about to head upstairs, Izen snagged his bag with a finger.

"Drop off your equipment, wash your face, and clean up your armour," he said as Rav turned to him. "Then come back down. There's still work to do."

More work? Rav rubbed his cheek—he snapped his head up, eyes wide as realisation struck. "We're heading to the Keep?"

"We're announcing that we've completed our scavenge. With you, we might draw Baron Glass' attention as we do, so look smart."

Rav dumped his bag aside before scampering upstairs. After unclasping his armour, he kneeled in the centre of the room and set about wiping it with a cloth. Amine arrived in the doorway with a water-filled bucket and more clean cloths.

Rav stood to receive them, careful not to spill any water as he did. "Thanks."

"Hurry." Amine dashed back downstairs.

Once his armour gleamed wet and clean, Rav held his chainmail taut and scrubbed the sweat and grime from its front, using a fresh cloth when done to wipe his neck and face.

"*Rav*," Izen shouted up to him.

"*Coming*," Rav called back, strapping his armour back on, then thumping down three steps at a time. If they met Baron Glass, this time... This time, he wouldn't embarrass himself. This time, he'd make Lyra proud. Not to display his potential. To prove how far he'd come. No longer was Nameless Rav pathetic.

The Blood Hounds were already waiting by the door, Izen leading them, Lyra looking bored as she leaned against the wall. As she spotted Rav, she pursed her lips, looking like she wanted to smile but was holding it in check. Not wanting to appear proud. At least attempting to treat him as his own person rather than her ward.

Izen pointed to an open space at his right flank, Mulk at the left. "Stand here, Rav. Head high. Let's show our strength."

Rav nodded as he took his position, and the Blood Hounds marched out for the Keep, Lyra at the rear. Winding through narrow streets, it wasn't long until Rav gazed up at the looming Keep, picking at his sleeve as he followed Izen. Would his reception be the same as it had been two months ago? With a shake of his head, he pushed on. He wouldn't be rude this time.

Izen was expected, the guards opening the gate for them to enter the courtyard, and from there, they headed to a side entrance for servants rather than the main doors, leading them into the building's bowels. Inside, a guard guided them down a cramped, dark corridor lined with shut doors to a small office, where a pale woman with a missing nose sat behind a desk.

"You have the maps?" She raised an eyebrow.

Izen placed the satchel on the desk with both hands. "This is what we recovered from a boulder-bear den."

She showed no expression, opening the bag to get out and flick through the notebook and pages inside, then tutting upon seeing one of the pages wet, the sketch on it smeared. "Who killed the 'Zet Ar?"

"The Sister, Lyra," Izen said with a bow. "With the help of Rav, the Called One."

Piyo pushed Rav forward for her to examine.

"Keep making progress," she stated, then dismissed them with a wave of her hand.

The unit, except for Rav and Lyra, bowed, then were escorted away. Back out in the sunlit courtyard, the Blood Hounds cheered as Rav deflated. Was that it?

"Those are the first words she's spoken *to* us." Miels laughed.

"We must be close to earning a place in Jinkin," Piyo added. "Keep working and we'll get there."

Izen ruffled Rav's hair as they reached the gates. "This is your influence. I'm sure to you, this might not seem like much, but it is. Know that." He paused at the sound of the Keep doors opening.

"Is that the Blood Hounds?"

Izen scowled. Eman Hagrin.

"Have you just returned from Mount Don? I thought following the scouts would've only taken a few days; did something delay you?" She walked over with feigned concern, Maric stoic at her side.

Izen sneered at her with a half-smile. "We ran into a boulder-bear."

"A boulder-bear?" Eman gave an exaggerated gasp. "No wonder you took so long. Maric and I ran into one on our last scavenge. Fearsome thing took a bit of effort to kill. Who delivered the final blow?" She flicked her gaze through them, ending up staring at Rav and Lyra.

"It was Sister Lyra who slayed the 'Zet Ar," Izen answered, tilting his head in Rav's direction. "With Rav's help."

"You fought a boulder-bear?" Eman examined Rav with narrowed eyes.

"He's the one who trapped and blinded it." Mulk put his hand on Rav's shoulder.

Eman broke into a smile. "Why don't you have dinner with me, Rav? I'd be interested to hear about your scavenge."

Rav examined her back, catching the twitch in her brow, the tension in her jaw. Uncertainty. How could a unit like Champions Guard have killed a boulder-bear? If any of them were as strong as Lyra, they'd be deeper in the Sink by now. Whatever they'd managed to do, it wasn't the achievement they presented it as. Rav feigned a yawn. "As you said, we've just returned from a scavenge, and I'm keen to get some rest."

Eman stepped forward. "Then after you've rested—"

"Our unit needs to reflect on our battles," Izen snapped.

"Aye, I have other duties in the coming days," Rav followed. "Perhaps I'll see you some other time."

She glared at him and Izen. "I'm sure you will."

Chapter 26

"*You're back*," Pierre shouted, wrapping Rav up in a hug.

"Aye, and I've brought my unit." Rav leaned to the side, revealing the Blood Hounds behind him, except for Lyra, who was visiting the outpost.

Pierre stumbled back as Mulk, Miels, and Izen lumbered towards him.

"You're Pierre, right?" Mulk patted his shoulder as he passed him to the bar. "Thanks for the ale, haha."

"Good lad." Izen and Miels also patted his shoulder, joining Mulk.

"I'm thirsty; how many barrels d'you have back there?" Mulk's voice rumbled.

"Rav..." Pierre latched onto his friend with pleading eyes, thinking of all the ale this group could consume.

Rav laughed as Pierre's meagre coin pouch was converted to ale at rapid pace, song and revelry sweeping the tavern. Paulo soon also arrived with a group of farmers, joining the building throng. After drinking an entire barrel, the Blood Hounds let Pierre's coin pouch go, buying their own ale until the tavern had been drunk dry. They moved to the next. And the next. And the next.

"He faced the monster alone." In the latest tavern, Rav directed the crowd's attention to Izen. "Champion Delmare against a boulder-bear."

"I ran," Izen grumbled.

"Aye, all over the plain after fighting off a hundred wingtails. He had the beast going in circles." Rav laughed.

"Is this that Champion who took you through the rabber warrens?" another farmer asked.

Rav nodded, chest puffed. "He is. He and Amine. Amine has eyes like a hawk, spotting creatures so far away they don't even know how they die. And this is Mulk." Rav picked him out the crowd. "He shattered a cave with his hammer. Where's Miels? He taught me how to survive on the mountain. Without him, I wouldn't be here to buy you drinks."

The crowd cheered for them, Miels getting the loudest clamour.

"And me?" Piyo asked.

"This is Piyo, the fastest man I've ever seen. He's got the legs of a horse."

Piyo embraced his lukewarm reception.

"Who killed the boulder-bear?"

"My guide, Sister Lyra. She carved it to pieces, one cut at a time." Eye's gleaming, Rav recounted the battle, and while he did, he noticed the door swing open as a group of well-dressed men in expensive silks walked in. They ushered farmers out their way with irritated waves of their hands as they approached Rav, plastering fawning smiles on their faces. They reached Rav just as he finished speaking.

"Called One," their leader shouted over the farmers cheering for Lyra's valour, "we've a private room at Silk Slippers, the most expensive tavern in Donsden. You're welcome to join us. We heard that it was you who first trapped the 'Zet Ar for your Sister to slay. Is that true?"

"Ah, I didn't do much," Rav mumbled, his energy waning as they stared at him. "I'm staying here awhile. Maybe I'll join you later."

"Are you sure? We have excellent wine."

Rav met his gaze. "I'm sure."

They looked amongst themselves, going sheepish at the rejection. "Of course." They nodded, then retreated.

Rav looked around the tavern and nodded at the familiar farmers. Better. Maybe some of them were schemers only seeking to use him, but at least they kept it well hidden among those who wanted his friendship for ordinary reasons. At least he didn't have to dance with his words all the time.

"What's that song from before?" John asked him. "The one from your home. This is a time for celebration, right?"

"Aye, it is." Rav gathered his breath. "*I guard my home with all I am*," he bellowed. John, Paulo, Pierre, and the farmers joined him. "*To honour those who gave me life.*"

The night blurred by, and soon, dawn's light shone. Rav stumbled back to his room with swaying steps and slumped onto his bed, not waking until evening, pulse thrumming in his head. After guzzling water to the point of nausea, he wandered downstairs, stomach grumbling, finding the Blood Hounds lounging around the dining hall with bowls of broth and bread.

"We need a new bucket on the bottom floor," Mulk grumbled.

"What did you do?" Miels sipped a spoonful of broth.

"Too much ale."

Amine threw a bread roll at him.

"You also must've suffered." Mulk picked up the roll from the floor and dipped it into his heaving bowl.

Piyo gagged. "I thought there was a problem with the sewers."

Mulk grinned. "There will be."

Everyone groaned.

"They're a good crowd," Izen commented. "I've not been drinking like that in years."

"It was nice to let loose," Mulk followed.

"I was invited to Silk Slippers," Piyo spoke up. "*Silk Slippers*. They wouldn't let me near the door before."

"I quite like the outskirts taverns," Miels stated. "They remind me of The Last Drink."

"We'll do it again," Izen said. "If Paulo forgives us for ruining his workforce."

"Ugh." Rav stood from his latest crop and massaged his temples, his eyes closed to shut away the bright morning sun. "I've still not recovered."

"I don't think I ever will," Pierre murmured, voice small. "How could one man drink so much?"

Rav peeked out from under his eyelids to see Pierre crouched at his own row, seven crops behind instead of his usual three ahead.

"Come on. I'll buy the rounds until you've recovered. Being listless doesn't suit you."

Pierre looked up, a spark of energy returning. "Really?"

"Aye."

A bright glint caught Rav's attention, coming from the portcullis. A buckle on hide armour. Amine's armour. Rav opened his eyes too wide for his current liking as Amine came running straight towards him, their expression sombre, stressed, scared. Rav dropped his vials and ran to meet them at the field's edge, stomach churning with nerves.

"What is it?"

"We have a meeting. Now."

Amine led the way back to the Blood Hounds' house, and Rav followed, always running. Entering the building, he found everyone gathered in the planning room, looking as though they were about to embark on another scavenge to the red layer.

Izen stood before everyone at their arrival. "I've received a Challenge," he growled. "It's set for the day after tomorrow."

Mulk slammed his fist on the table. "You've just come back from a scavenge."

Izen glowered. "The officiator has set the date. Since I was well enough to go drinking that evening, I've been deemed well enough to fight."

"We'll appeal," Amine stated. "We'll get you more time to rest."

"We need to know who's Challenged you, how they fight, what they want," Piyo huffed. "You can't be forced to fight blind."

"I can and I have."

"What else d'you know?" Miels asked.

"The timing and the way this was delivered... someone's planned this out. Someone with influence."

"Eman Hagrin." Amine gasped. "Why now?"

"Either the Blood Hounds have become a competitor to reach the second layer or she's making a play for Rav. Or both. Getting rid of me does both."

"I'm not going to join Champions Guard," Rav spat.

"If the Blood Hounds get dismantled, where will you go?"

He scoffed. "Why would I have to go anywhere? I'll make my own unit."

Izen smiled. "Well said."

"Can I do anything?" Rav asked.

Izen shook his head. "If this has been planned, then I don't think so. My Challenger will have support that you can't be hostile to. Support related to Baron Glass himself."

"I've made enemies for less. Besides, they've now become enemies with me." Rav glowered. "I'm not some toy for people to fight over."

"I like that look of rage"—Izen grinned—"but I don't need it. I'm a Champion, and I've been Challenged. I'll fight and I'll win. I'll make my opponent suffer in that arena. Give me what I need to make that happen."

The unit nodded. "We'll start gathering information."

Amine spread out the stack of paper they had returned with after a day of visiting every information broker in the city with the others on the central table. "His name's Contender Karac

Tulmic. He's one of Baron Glass' men, sponsored by Concubine Ilina Hagrin."

Piyo tutted. "No wonder they're certain Rav won't interfere. The gossip is that since Champion Trent has joined Champions Guard, Ilina is looking to have a new Champion as a bodyguard. Fighting you is just for the title."

"He's been trained as a potential bodyguard for Baron Glass, so there's little public information about him," Amine continued. "I've tried to loosen up a few Keep servants, but they won't speak. He's around thirty and will be very well trained. Everything else is about Keep bodyguards in general; we have no other specifics."

Izen sat to listen. "Let's hear it."

"They're all trained in a variety of weapons, from spears to swords to bows. The speciality of the bodyguard training is improvised weaponry designed for close combat in narrow spaces. He'll know how to grapple, how to close gaps quickly, how to use his gauntlet to kill you.

"I also got this." Amine brought out another stack of papers. "This is all the information they have on you. I'm sure the Keep has more detailed reports, but this could give you an idea of what Karac's expecting."

"Good, thank you." Izen received the stack. "I'll go over them tonight. Tomorrow, I'll be training with Miels to prepare. Take care of everything else."

The Blood Hounds nodded.

"The blacksmiths haven't adjusted my plate armour yet," Piyo spoke. "You can wear it."

"I'll use my own, as it's more comfortable." Izen chuckled. "Now, I need rest." He headed to his room with the information gathered so far.

The others sat in silence, broken by Mulk smiling at everyone. "You haven't seen him duel before."

"I know he's good enough, but he'll be tired," Amine said.

“Good enough?” Mulk laughed. “Izen was born for single combat, man on man. This is serious, but he wasn’t lying when he said he’ll win. When he fights, you’ll see.”

“I hate this,” Rav grumbled. “It feels like Pitt all over again.”

“We’re growing, Rav. When you’re big enough, you’re always in someone’s way,” Miels said.

He clenched his fist. “I want to be big enough to crush them.”

“You will be,” Amine comforted.

“I’m not leaving it like this.” Rav got up and headed out.

Where should I go? What should I do? How can I make Eman Hagrin regret her actions? The Keep was untouchable—that was clear. Bold moves would lead to conflict. He needed something more subtle. How had Tibald swayed Pitt to his favour? What could a Called One get away with? Rav went scouting to find where Champions Guard slept.

CHAPTER 27

Rav yawned as he pushed his small wooden cart through the empty city streets up to the market by torchlight, the air chilled, sun still below the horizon. Seeing a few other merchants also setting up their stalls, he waved, and they waved back. Arriving at the spot in front of a large mansion he'd picked yesterday, he stopped, opened his cart into a stall, and lit a fire underneath the central pan. *Tsss*. Rav placed thin slices of meat onto the now-spitting oil, then diced vegetables before throwing them into the frying pan. It wasn't long before the early-morning workers started to make their way through the streets.

"Morning, Samson," he shouted to a greying farmer on his way for the dawn shift.

"Rav? What's this?" Samson wandered over.

"I used to cook in my town and missed it. Come try some." He flicked a slice of meat and some bronzed vegetables into the centre of a bun, then seared the opening closed. "It's a meal from my home."

Samson sniffed the tantalising aroma, spice bringing out the rich flavour of the meat, while a hint of sweetness came from the vegetables. "I'll get one." He reached into his pouch for some coins.

Rav waved his hand. "No need for that. This is a hobby; all my food's free."

Samson raised an eyebrow. "You're giving away free food?"

"I like cooking." Rav shrugged. *Tsss.* He stirred the pan. "Here." He handed the bun to Samson. "Careful; it's hot."

Samson blew on the top, clearing some of the steam, then took a bite, breaking into a wide smile. "This is delicious." He took another bite. "Wait here, I'll get the others; they have to try this." Samson ran off.

"You there," Rav called to a woman on her way to set up a market stall. "Are you hungry? My food's free."

Samson returned a short while later, joining the growing crowd with a group of farmers. There was a shout from the window behind Rav's stall.

"What's that noise?" He sealed another bun and handed it out, the hundred portions he'd readied already dwindling.

"Are you sure this is free?" A young man with gaunt features stared at the bun in his hand.

Rav nodded. "Aye. All my food's free."

"Thank you." He bit deep into the bun.

"You there, at the back." Rav pointed to a young girl stuck at the edge of the crowd. "Come through."

The crowd parted to let her reach the stall.

"Here." He handed her a bun. "Come back tomorrow for another."

"You'll be here again?" someone asked.

"Aye, every day that I can."

"It's all free?"

"Aye."

"*Clear off*," Maric roared, bursting out the door of the house behind the stall. "Who let you set up a stall here? I'll break your jaw."

"I set up this stall." Rav stepped out to face him.

He raised his fist. "*You?*" Then he dropped it. "You?"

Rav folded his arms. "Aye, me."

His snarl dropped flat as he glared at Rav a moment longer, then returned inside.

"Anyone else want a bun?" Rav turned back to the ever-growing crowd, many wealthier citizens now among them, each trying to chat with him, then talking with each other about their businesses.

"*Move.*" Champion Trent exited the Champions Guard house, followed by members of his unit, and made to leave through the surging crowd. He looked to Rav to restore order.

Rav stayed facing his stall.

Maric pushed his way through the jostling crowd, many people parting as they eyed his Blood Palm, but the Champions Guard members behind him didn't receive the same effect, and as the crowd closed again, they were knocked about. Not long after Champion Trent left, Champions Guard returned with Champion Hagrin leading them, the crowd parting again as she approached Rav.

"Rav, it's good to see you so early in the morning." She sniffed the air. "I'd like to try one of your buns."

Rav shrugged at her with a smile and shook his head. "I seem to have run out." He prepared another bun from the frying pan and handed it into the crowd. "All this has already been ordered."

Eman faced the crowd. "Would anyone here like to gift me their bun?"

Eight buns were immediately presented. Eman picked the best-looking one and took a bite. "Mmm. This is good." She smirked. "I know you want my attention, but there is no need to do something as petty as this; there are easier ways for us to share each other's company. Join Champions Guard as my second-in-command."

Rav laughed. "Aye, this is petty. But I don't have to be. Using a Challenge to try to remove Izen is clever, yet I can't help thinking that you've overlooked something."

Eman glared at him. "And what's that?"

"You're also a Champion." Rav leaned closer. "Perhaps one day I'll Challenge you."

Eman flinched before sneering. "That would be a stupid way for you to die. What would the World do without Its Called Ones?"

"You know Izen is exhausted after our scavenge," Rav hissed. "If you want something from me, deal with me alone."

"I tried, but you kept saying no." Eman's eyes gleamed. "Don't you understand? We're heading to the second layer, Rav. The Blood Hounds don't matter."

"Fine, since you insist on hiding behind Baron Glass, I'll just have to continue being petty. I wonder who has more influence in Blood Marsh—the leader of Champions Guard or a Called One?" Rav turned back to his cooking. "Hope that Izen wins, Eman, because if he doesn't, I *will* kill you."

"Good, make your threats." Eman grinned. "We'll see what they're worth when you have nowhere to go but to my side." She signalled her unit and marched back into the mansion.

Izen was absent for dinner that night, spending his time alone meditating. Rav woke before dawn and headed out to his stall, this time with rabbit meat and roots. Deciding on a flavour combination, he lit a fire under a giant pot and began preparing rabbit stew. He didn't have to wait long before a steady stream of chatting customers arrived at his stall. *Bang.* Rav smirked at the sound of someone breaking things coming from the house behind him.

"*Share the bowls,*" he yelled as loud as he could, dipping another into the stew for a worker.

Grumblings about the workday ahead filled the air, along with raucous jokes. Samson brought a larger group of farmers with him today, and many new unwashed and uncared-for faces stood among the crowd—people with boils, old injuries, or crippled limbs.

"There's a Challenge on at the arena," someone mentioned. "I heard one of the Baron's Contenders is looking to become a Champion."

"Aye, the Champion being Challenged is my friend and unit leader, Champion Izen Delmare," Rav said, then sighed. "I'm a bit worried about it. The Challenge is official, but the timing is rushed. We only returned from a scavenge up Mount Don three nights ago, where Champion Delmare had to fight a boulder-bear."

"He has to face a Challenge a few days after something like that?" Samson frowned.

"Aye, an officiator set the day and time." Rav wiped away his worry and took on a proud and admiring expression. "But Izen's a Champion; facing Challenges is part of his title. I'm looking forward to watching him defeat Concubine Hagrin's bodyguard."

"I'll come watch," Samson promised.

Eman emerged from her house during the premarket rush when the crowd was busiest, puffing her chest out in front of Rav as she looked out to the crowd. "Will anyone gift their bowl to me?"

This time, everyone glanced between the two before shrinking back. One of the merchants mulled over the dilemma, staring at the bowl in his hands. Head low, he walked to her under the gazes of those around him, hand shaking as he held out the stew. Eman scowled before re-entering her home. The merchant handed his bowl to someone else, then left the crowd, face swollen red with embarrassment.

Morning work over, Rav headed back to the Blood Hounds' house. Izen was preparing alone in his room. Rav sat with the others in the planning room, everyone sitting taut.

"You're still cooking outside their house?" Amine asked him.

"Aye. I'm going to make every morning in Donsden as horrid as possible for them. I'll take away their sleep, their reputation, their unity, everything. They're going to be chased out of Donsden. Besides," Rav continued, changing his tone upon seeing everyone shift away from him, "I like cooking and talking to people. Have you received any more news about the Challenge?"

"We'll have the best seats in the stands," Mulk spoke. "Right next to the podium."

"Not on the wall?" Rav asked with a frown.

"No."

"What's with that look, Rav?" Amine tutted. "We're not Barons."

"Things like where we sit don't matter," Mulk added.

"They do," Rav grumbled. "It's a sign of respect, of influence. Having us sit beneath them shows we have no say in the management of this Challenge."

"We don't."

"Which is a problem."

"We still need to act calm," Amine warned.

"I know," Rav huffed. "I will be."

"Izen will win," Mulk stated. "Everything else comes later."

Chapter 28

The sun climbed higher, the time for the Challenge arriving. Champion Izen Delmare emerged gallant from his room to begin the march to the arena in shining plate armour. Hair brushed, face washed, he wore a steadfast smile, the ruby set into the Blood Palm seeming to shimmer with his pulse. He held his shield, while his sword was strapped to his waist in its sheath. Steady steps, straight back, head high, he moved like a Champion. The Blood Hounds stood armoured and waiting, also dressed pristine, Mulk holding Izen's helmet. Izen nodded to them, opened the door, and led his unit to the arena.

Sunbeams scorching, Mulk strode to Izen's right, Rav to his left, Miles and Amine taking centre position, with Piyo and Lyra at the rear.

"Move out the way," people called, pulling others out the Blood Hounds' path. "Make way for Champion Delmare, leader of the Blood Hounds. Leader of Rav the Called One."

Citizens stood either side of the streets, watching Izen lead the Blood Hounds through with excited grins or respectful nods. Even the market crowd divided in two for them to pass. Rav kept focused, always facing forward despite the many recognisable faces that waved or bowed towards him. The roar from the arena could already be heard rumbling through Donsden, hundreds of chanting voices clamouring for Izen's victory. Izen puffed out his chest, sneaking a knowing glance at Rav behind him. As they reached the arena, the Blood Hounds split up, Mulk leading the others up to the arena stands while Izen donned his helmet before striding through the entrance to the arena grounds.

"Citizens of Donsden, Champion Izen Delmare," a deep voice echoed down from the Keep wall.

"IZEN! IZEN! IZEN!"

Izen took the field, and the frenzy only grew, the crowd pumping their fists and beating their chests in support. He approached the podium—a wooden block setup under a cloth canopy hanging from the Keep wall above it—and handed his weapons up to the robed Overseers for inspection. Mulk led the Blood Hounds to their seats next to it. Rav glanced around the heaving stands. Every seat was taken by roaring farmers, urchins, merchants, even minor Barons. Was this what a real Challenge was like? Not whatever ramshackle event Pitt had managed to cobble together. Blood pumping, he hardened his expression and marched onwards, never even glancing up towards the Keep. His stance would be clear.

"*Rav*," people called from the stands. He nodded in their direction, and noting his serious temperament, the callers left him alone.

Tension filtered into the audience. As the Blood Hounds reached their seats, Izen's weapon inspection was completed, the Overseers handing back his sword, shield, and various knives. The Blood Hounds took their places, backs straight, eyes forward, the audience copying their lead. The uproar took on a deeper throb as Izen walked the arena and tapped various places with his boots, ensuring he was familiar with its terrain, when the main Overseer, an old man with short, grey hair, stood above the podium once more.

"Citizens of Donsden, the Challenger, Contender Karac Tulmic."

The echo bounced for a moment before chants for Izen drowned them out. A young man with a black beard and shaved head, dressed in plate armour and wielding a halberd, marched over to the podium. His brow was scrunched, lips pursed. Once his halberd and knives were deemed fit for the Challenge, he pulled on his helmet and waited for Izen to finish checking the grounds, then conducted his own inspection. Izen opened his visor as he watched, his arrogant smirk visible to all. Tulmic maintained his determined demeanour until he finished. The main Overseer stood again, the crowd quieting.

"Champion Izen Delmare, you have been Challenged by Contender Karac Tulmic and will fight to the death to defend your title, do you understand?"

Izen nodded. "I do."

"Contender Karac Tulmic, today, you will either die a Contender or live on as a Champion. Do you understand?"

Tulmic hit his gauntleted fist to his breastplate. "I do."

"Take your positions."

They both moved to opposite ends of the arena, Izen throwing Karac one last smirk before shutting his visor. Karac moved his halberd into a defensive stance. Izen drew his sword with a flourish before resting it on his shoulder.

"FIGHT."

The crowd erupted.

Karac started closing the gap, slow and defensive, keeping his halberd raised in front of him to keep Izen far back. Izen stood still, waiting, sword still out of form. Karac kept calm, steady, *crunch, crunch, crunch,* moving in step by step, no waver in his stance. Seeing him coming within range, Izen flourished his sword once more, then raised his shield high, setting his sword at its side. He crouched and shifted his feet into position for an attack. Karac paused just outside of engagement distance, then started stepping left. Izen turned with him, abandoning his attack.

Karac started moving right. Izen followed. Karac darted in before feigning a jab and retreating. Izen didn't budge, seeing through the bluff. Karac backed further away, leaving a threatening range. Izen relaxed, resting his arms by lowering his weapons. They waited a moment. Izen raised his sword back up and moved in while Karac remained defensive. This time, Izen probed, motioning left. Karac moved the point of his halberd to block him. Izen motioned right. The halberd guarded again.

Rav was still unable to find any weaknesses in Karac's technique. Would Izen be able to find a way to beat a weapon with a longer reach? Maybe his shield could help. And Karac's halberd was heavier than Izen's sword; he'd tire quicker as they maintained their guards. Another exchange followed, this time their weapons clanging off each other as Izen tried a quick thrust at Karac's throat and the Contender blocked. Rav sat forward, mid-gasp, as he spotted the way Izen had twitched his leg before moving to make Karac think he was going the other way. Everything only looked simple.

Izen attacked again, going right, no, left. Karac fell for it, his halberd a moment too slow to stop Izen darting past the point and stabbing at his hands. Karac twisted his body to bring the halberd into a sweep at Izen's head, forcing him to duck under it, aborting the stab. Karac strained to halt the sweep, then pushed with his entire body to drive the butt forward at Izen's chest, arms shuddering as they struggled to control so much force. Izen scampered backwards, still mid-duck, escaping the blow, and as the halberd butt completed its motion, the air seemed to shift around it, compressing under the pressure. Dust blew. Izen hurried away. Karac took his stance again as the crowd roared.

Miels gritted his teeth.

"What was that?" Rav asked.

"It's a technique called a Squeeze," he muttered. "It activates as many muscles as you can to increase your strength for a moment. When I taught you to move, I showed you how to use one muscle. Squeezing has you use your entire body. When you attack with it, you gain immense strength."

Izen moved back in, this time stepping in a strange pattern that made it much more difficult to predict what he was going to do. Karac was slow to guard a few times, but the threat of that blow held Izen in place.

"Doesn't that use too much energy?" Rav asked.

"Mm, that's why using it so early is bad. It means Karac has the stamina to do a few of them... or it could be a bluff." He grimaced. "Izen needs to figure out which one it is."

Izen made another dash inside Karac's guard but retreated straight after. Karac didn't Squeeze again, using a basic slash at Izen, who dodged to the side. Izen continued retreating after each failed attack, soon finding the arena wall at his back. Karac seized his chance and stepped forward in a thrust, his body shaking with effort as he Squeezed again. Izen shifted his stance as Karac wound up, then he glided sideways, looking as though he were sliding on ice. *Crack.* Karac's halberd struck the arena wall, shattering the stone, but Izen was at his flank, sword slashing at the gap between Karac's helmet and his breastplate. Karac threw a punch at the sword, gauntlet meeting the blade. *Clang.* Izen's sword was smacked away, wobbling.

Karac punched again. Izen raised his shield to block it. *Bang.* Rav gasped at the sound; how heavy were Karac's gauntlets? Izen had to fight to keep his shield arm strong after the impact, finally regaining control of his sword to bring it around to stab at Karac's shoulder. Karac shifted his arm to close the gap in his armour, the sword glancing off the plate, and managed to regain control of his halberd, tearing it out the wall to jab the butt at Izen. Izen retreated again, back to the wide-open arena, giving him all the room he needed to manoeuvre in. Rav clenched his fists. Heavy weapon, heavy gauntlets, Karac had to be tiring quickly.

Izen dug the tip of his boot into the ground, then kicked up a cloud of dirt at Karac, which the Contender backed away from. Izen kicked up more dust. Karac stood back and used the opportunity to rest, chest heaving. Izen kept kicking, stomping, dragging his boots to gouge out chunks of the earth until everything was rough. Karac's posture changed, taking on a more serious tone as he stamped forward, halberd moving in small arcs to sweep the area. Izen moved away, continuing to rough up the ground. Karac pressed his boots into the loose dirt, compacting it with his heavy weight, but while some of the topsoil was restored, it wasn't much.

Seeing more dust gather in the air, he started his own strange footwork, seeming intent on stopping Izen from ruining the ground any further. He raised his rear elbow high so his halberd was pointing from a higher position, then stomped forward, one step at a time, momentum building until he was charging. Broken earth cracked under the power of his movements, dust stirring behind him, but he had to catch Izen, who made full use of the space behind him to retreat as Karac built up his pace like a boulder rolling down a hill.

Izen dashed to the side. Karac set his foot down and drove off it, following him, jabbing out with his halberd. Izen used his shield to block the jab. *Dang.* He used the force in the blow to move sideways again, shield arm shaking. Karac turned the jab into a swing, halberd blade chopping horizontally at Izen's chest. Izen braced his shield with his sword arm to take the blow. *Bang.* He went reeling backwards, struggling to regain his balance, pointing the tip of his sword at Karac to keep him from closing in. Karac continued the flurry of heavy movements, knocking Izen around with glancing blows. Rav clenched his jaw. Was it happening again? Just like in Pitt, just like with Wakeman. *Stomp, whoosh*, Karac whipped his halberd through the air. Izen stumbled back in a near-impossible position, guard broken. Karac strode out for another attack... and slipped.

Just a small slide forward ruined his momentum, bringing his assault to an end. Karac hesitated, allowing Izen to glide out of reach. Rav looked around. Karac's rampage had done more to break up the surface than Izen's previous efforts. Izen swiped his sword just above the ground, stirring the dust into a cloud and stepped into it, his feet vanishing from view, then shifted to his right, whipping more dust into the air. Karac hunkered down. He swept out in another wide attack, clearing some of the encroaching dust, while Izen changed his footwork again. This time, he dragged his feet around, still moving quickly.

Everywhere he stepped, dust followed, some starting to rise to his knees. As Rav stared, all his twitches and sly actions disappeared.

Closing in on Karac, Izen became a phantom, movements ethereal, unreadable. Every time Rav thought he'd go right, he went left. When he was attacking, he'd retreat. When he slashed, he'd thrust. With flexible wrists and ankles, each motion could turn into any other. He began getting past Karac's halberd more and more often but still held back. Spinning Karac around until dizzy. Dodge, thrust, *ting*. Karac lurched back as his gauntlet was struck. He abandoned his passive defence, coming out in wild attacks, and as he missed a blow, Izen struck his elbow, a sliver away from the gap. Rav held back his cheer. If Izen made one mistake, he'd die.

Karac began making more reckless swings, opening larger gaps for Izen to take advantage of. Izen focused his attacks on Karac's hands, aiming to pry his halberd out his fingers. Karac made an upwards slash, falling for another of Izen's feints, and missed. Izen lunged up from his low position, and with his arm up, Karac's gauntlet had a tiny gap where it met his bracer. The tip of Izen's sword pierced through it.

"*Ahhh.*"

Blood dripped from his gauntlet. With a one-handed grip, Karac chased after Izen's shadow. Miss, miss, miss. Squeeze. Still a miss. He thrust out, but his foot slipped again. Dust particles swirled around them, glittering grains shining in the sunlight. Izen cut at Karac's other hand, slicing between the gap at the gauntlet fingers, and his halberd fell from his grasp. *Clang*. Izen slammed his shield towards Karac, driving him away from the weapon.

"IZEN! IZEN! IZEN!"

The Blood Hounds stood as the crowd cheered.

"Too young," Izen said, taking a new stance. "Too slow, too weak, too... bad."

Karac just stared at him, his panting audible from the podium.

"You fight like a Contender," Izen continued, "you fight like someone who isn't good enough to be a Champion. But you knew that. You knew you weren't good enough. Were you hoping I'd be tired or injured? Both? Has it shocked you that I'm not?" Izen chuckled. "I must admit, I was worried about the techniques of the Keep bodyguards, but the more I fight you, the more I see who taught you. And I already beat Eman Hagrin."

Karac picked up a clump of dirt and threw it, roaring as he charged. "*Ahhh.*"

Izen wriggled his sword, and Rav lost sight of it within the dust cloud. Karac barrelled through it, stumbling past Izen into an open area before spinning around, blood now pouring down the side of his armour from his neck. Izen lowered his sword. Karac pressed his hands to the cut, but the blood wouldn't stop spurting out. He tore off his helmet and dropped to his knees, packing dirt into the wound, then tore a piece of sweaty cloth off his undershirt to soak up the blood, using both hands to try to keep the cut closed. *Pump, pump.* Soaked in his own blood, Rav recognised the last look on his face. He didn't care about Izen or the Challenge or becoming Ilina Hagrin's Champion, he just didn't want to die. He felt... weak. Cold. Dizzy. Rav watched the young man slump unconscious, never to wake.

"Citizens of Donsden, the victor: Champion Izen Delmare."

Izen turned around from the corpse at his feet, took off his helmet, and smiled at the roaring crowd, showing them his unblemished figure.

"*Delmare, Delmare, Delmare,*" The Blood Hounds led the chant.

Rav fought to stop tears emerging, hands shaking. Mulk grabbed his shoulder, bellowing with cheers, and Rav joined him, screaming until he lost his breath. Servants came out to collect Karac's body while Izen sauntered back to the podium. He looked up at the Keep wall, and Rav followed his gaze to see white hair blowing in the wind. Rav laughed at Eman's sour grimace. At Eman's side sat an older blonde woman, looking sullen at the body being carried away. Rav laughed at her too.

Ah. Bright light shined in his eye from a window at the top of the Keep. Was that... Baron Glass? He'd been watching. Then why hadn't he intervened in the Hagrins' machinations? Rav flinched. He couldn't be part of this, right?

Izen signalled for the Blood Hounds to leave, the unit rushing out the raucous arena and out into city streets swelling with people coming out to see the Challenge winner.

"I feel like I didn't see anything," Rav commented as they acted as Izen's guards, guiding him back to the house to rest.

"I've watched Izen duel nine times and I still don't know what he does." Mulk laughed. "I think the only way to understand would be to face him yourself."

"*Champion Delmare*," people shouted, eager for him to look at them.

Izen acted the part, waving to the crowds as they marched until he bid them farewell outside the Blood Hounds' house. Once inside, he entered the planning room and collapsed in a chair, wiping the sweat from his face with a cloth. Amine helped take off his armour while Rav brought in waterskins and food. After wetting their dry throats and filling empty stomachs, everyone slumped down.

"I told you he'd win." Mulk laughed.

Miels grinned. "We never doubted it."

"That last moment, why did he run right past you?" Rav asked.

"The dirt he threw." Izen winked. "I hid behind it and used one of my techniques."

"I want to know about your sword grip," Piyo spoke. "How are you so flexible? You moved from a front grip to a reverse grip and back in an instant. I'd tear every tendon in my wrist if I did that."

"That's easy. I'm not. I never changed," Izen said with a grin. "Karac was a decent fighter. And I crushed him." His face glowed with pride. "Now, are we going to lounge around asking questions, or are we going to celebrate? I want every corner of Donsden to remind Eman Hagrin of her failure."

Dressed in lavish robes, the Blood Hounds headed out for the night, chants of "Champion Delmare!" rumbling through the city all the way to the Keep.

Chapter 29

Rav woke before dawn with a thundering headache and bloodshot eyes to start cooking, bringing the streets outside Champions Guard's mansion to life with congratulations for Izen.

Beyond the known faces of farmers, he recognised the delicate frame of a small urchin girl, a brush of freckles across her button nose and cheeks, shoulder-length strands of straw hair bobbing as she nodded in thanks while Rav handed her a fresh bun. "Have some more." Rav readied another bun for the urchin girl he'd invited to eat on his first day at the stall.

Her cheeks reddened as she received her meal.

"Cooking all this every morning's tiring. Want to help me? I can pay you."

She hurried to nod.

"What's your name?"

"Vip."

Rav showed Vip how to heat the pan and how to mould the buns, letting her take care of getting ingredients prepared while he chatted, the morning sun already starting to burn. From there, he returned to the crop rows, everyone ending early as the relentless heat wore them down. Miels gave a short halberd lesson, clutching his guts the entire time as he grumbled about ale. Rav fell asleep before reading through the first page of a new alchemy book.

Easy days passed by one by one, Lyra spending more and more time at the outpost as Rav fell back into his routine. The Keep was quiet. Until, three weeks after the Challenge, a servant bearing Baron Glass' white, hexagonal crystal on his surcoat arrived at the Blood Hounds' house in the evening. Rav listened as Izen invited the man inside to speak in a side room, then scampered downstairs from reading, joining Mulk, Miels, Amine, and Piyo in eavesdropping by the door. Their voices were quiet, muffled. Rav glanced at the others, everyone's eyes alight, each creeping closer and closer... Izen's boots thumped as he strode to the door, the Blood Hounds scattering down the corridor. Rav peeked out the kitchen doorway as Izen saw the messenger out.

Door shut, Izen faced the hallway with a knowing smile. "Gather in the planning room. I've got a scavenge for us."

"*Piyo*," Izen bellowed as the Blood Hounds fled up a decrepit tunnel beneath an abandoned castle, dozens of snapping goebbers at their heels.

"*Ahhh*." Piyo dropped to the rear, swords whirring to slay creature after creature.

Rav took a moment to recover, rubbing the falling dust from the tunnel roof from his eyes. Vision clear again, he looked up, the swaying firelight from Mulk's torch revealing dozens of hairless bodies wriggling above them. Izen grabbed his collar and dragged him along the exit tunnel as Piyo covered them, everyone setting up at a point where the tunnel narrowed.

Miels readied his shield, axe strapped to his back. "*Piyo*," he roared.

Piyo dashed away from the colony, armour dripping scarlet, running past Miels, who then blocked the gap with a grunt. Izen dumped Rav beside Lyra, strode back to Miels with two already smoking powder balls in his hand, and threw them down the tunnel.

Ruuuu. Goebbers howled in pain, their assault ending as they fled beyond the grey cloud.

Amine and Rav grabbed Mulk, helping lift him up, the Blood Hounds racing back up into the daylight. Following the path they'd taken across the marshes, they soon reached the small outpost where their carriage was waiting. Safe inside, Mulk grumbled while Amine tended to a bite wound on his leg.

"Who'd have thought they'd know how to bury themselves in the ground to ambush us?" Mulk shook his head and winced. "Why'd we have to fail a scavenge from the Keep?"

"We didn't know those tunnels were filled with goebbers," Amine said.

"And we're alive," Izen stated. "We didn't fail."

"Whatever was supposed to be left behind under that castle is now in the centre of a goebber nest," Miels said.

"That information is still useful; there are other Barons near it," Izen added. "We'll head back to make a report."

"I hate this." Mulk looked up from the wide swathe of flowered mountainside the Blood Hounds had spread out on, then stared down at the marshland far below them with a huff. "What's the point? Let us fight mutants and find treasure, not pick stupid roots."

"Is this one?" Miels held up a pale, white plant root with rounded ridges at the top that made it look like a clenched fist. His meaty hand struggled to hold it with the necessary dexterity.

"What leaves does it have?" Rav asked, coming over to check.

Miels plucked an obovate green leaf from the main plant stem and showed it to Rav.

Rav held it up to the sun. The midrib was the same pale as the roots, but... "See the lines inside it?" He showed Miels. "We're looking for ones that are a faint yellow colour."

"How are they not the same?" Miels tore the rest of the plant out the ground and flung it down the mountainside.

The Blood Hounds spent four days on Mount Don gathering two hundred Knuckle Roots.

"Are they set?" Izen asked Piyo as he gazed down at the six large burrow holes at the bottom of a deep crevice, the stink of goebber wafting up.

"Yes."

He thumbed the smoke balls in his hand. "Then let's hope we get all fifty pelts in one catch."

Rav gave a long exhale as he touched his crossbow's trigger. What would Baron Glass do with fifty goebber pelts? Was only a week of preparation enough for this scavenge? Would the trap they'd set up be enough to handle an entire goebber colony? He released another long exhale, glancing either side of the crevice lip at the other Blood Hounds holding a large net, their crossbows, then to Lyra as she stood off to the side, watching them all with bright eyes. Izen opened a large bag to reveal the bleeding carcass of a giant lizard, its stench filling the air. He dropped it into the crevice with a wet smack.

Ru. Ar. The barks echoed out of the tunnels.

Mulk, Miels, and Izen each grabbed their section of rope holding the net, with Rav, Piyo, and Amine supporting them. Goebbers poked their heads out the tunnel, seeing an easy meal. Once the first group started tearing away at the carcass, others came out to fight for a piece. The Blood Hounds lifted the net above the group. Only about twenty had gathered below, but if they waited any longer, the shadow of the net would be noticed. Izen nodded. They dropped the net down. *Ruu.* The goebbers were entangled. The Blood Hounds aimed their crossbows and shot a volley into the targets.

Hssss. Rav spun around to see a giant lizard dart out the dense marsh and onto their rock platform, quick as a blink. He tensed, heartbeat quickening as he gulped, staring at the scraps of rotten flesh in its exposed gums. The other Blood Hounds turned too, watching as it stopped to prepare another sprint, its tongue flickering. Three more mutants scampered out the marsh behind it.

"*Form up*," Izen called.

They dropped their crossbows and drew their close-combat weapons as they strode into formation, Izen at the head to face two alone while Mulk and Miels inched closer to one each. Izen snarled as he lunged at the frontmost lizard with his sword, the mutant hopping to the side, but Izen turned the lunge into a slash and struck the scales around its throat. His sword bounced off, only a few glimmering scales coming with it, the skin beneath unharmed.

Rav threw a knife as the other lizard bit at Izen, the blade cutting into its softer mouth. Izen barged it away with his shield, his sword clashing against the other one's claws. Piyo sprinted out from behind the group to flank the lizards from Mulk's side. Disregarding his defence with his new armour, he charged in, slashing at the lizard's scales. *Scrape.* The blade couldn't find a gap in its scales. *Hssss.* The mutant smacked a claw into Piyo's gut. *Dong.* The breastplate took most of the impact, but Piyo fell backwards, scrambling to get back to his feet.

Mulk used the distraction to bring his hammer around in a heavy arc. "*Ha.*" The hammer slammed into the lizard's head. *Crack.*

The lizard tried to rush away, but dizzy from the blow, it teetered about before slipping and falling, then trying to get back up. Piyo lunged forward and pierced his sword through its eye.

Mulk charged at one of the lizards occupying Izen, forcing it to face him. Freed up, Izen focused on slaying his only opponent. He used weird footwork to draw out a swiping strike from it, then blocked with his shield and stabbed it in its bleeding mouth.

Miels was keeping his lizard at bay with fearsome swings of his axe. Amine moved behind the creature. It jumped back in a dodge from Miels, crashing into Amine's shield. Amine held firm. *Whoosh.* Miels' next swing connected, burying the head of his axe deep in the lizard's midriff. It twitched, hissing in agony.

Miels used another burst of strength to push the axe towards the ground, where, trapped between the hard surface and sharp axe head, the lizard was cut in two.

Rav returned his attention to the goebbers. Some had managed to wriggle free of the net and were escaping back into the tunnels. He dived over to another rope and pulled. The top of the crevice over the tunnel entrance crumbled, rocks plummeting to block them from escaping and stop reinforcements from arriving in time. He threw out two quivers of bolts from his bag to Izen and Mulk, then started flinging knives down into the crevice. After a few more rounds with the crossbows, the goebbers were all dead or dying. Rav and Amine were lowered down on ropes to grab the ends of the net and pull it into a bag shape for everyone to heave up to the top.

Twenty-two goebbers killed, with nineteen usable pelts. They covered the corpses in a powder to stop the smell carrying, then retreated to a cave they were using as a base. Rav set about skinning them as Izen discussed their next target colony. Lyra smiled in approval.

"That was long." Mulk shook his head as they carried the pelts up to the Keep.

"That smell makes me sick." Miels held his half of the pelt bag as far away from himself as he could.

"Think of Rav and Amine," Piyo said.

Rav scratched his cracked hands, stained from being soaked in so much goebber blood, while Amine picked their blackened nails.

"I didn't mind it," Rav commented. "My mother worked with pelts all her life; I'm used to them."

"Goebber meat makes good stew," Amine added.

"I'll be eating bread and mashed roots for a while." Miels shuddered.

The noseless commissioner indicated for them to dump the pelts in another room, then handed Izen another scavenge, due in a week. He stopped Mulk's protest and accepted with a polite smile. Once they were back in their house, Mulk looked over the pages.

"The other side of Mount Don? When do we rest?"

"We don't. Clean up," Izen ordered.

"I'll get a carriage." Amine headed out.

"We have no preparation or information," Mulk protested.

"That's the point." Piyo grinned. "We're being readied for Ut Sh'za."

"We'll have to be tireless in there," Miels said as he inspected his equipment.

"Fine," Mulk grumbled. "As long as we get there."

"When are we leaving?" Rav asked.

"Half a day," Izen answered.

Rav dashed upstairs to start making more Ant's Itch pellets.

Chapter 30

"I want to sleeeep," Mulk whined, slumping through the door to the Blood Hounds' house.

The other members of the unit groaned in agreement, eyes sunken, limping, wincing, hair unruly, and skin weather-beaten.

"You need to clean the wound on your arm," Amine reminded him, handing over a vial from their bag.

"I stink of that stuff," he muttered as leaned back to accept it.

"Is it healing well?" Lyra asked, the only one still picturesque.

Mulk dumped his bracer on the floor and pulled up his sleeve to reveal three scratches on the inside of his elbow.

Lyra checked them for pus. "Keep applying the medicine for another week and cover the scabs."

He groaned.

"Your leg?" she asked Izen.

He hinged his knee to prove it was working. "It doesn't hurt anymore."

"And your ankle?"

"Swollen."

"You need to eat berries."

She looked at Miels.

"My shoulder's bad," he muttered. "I'll eat my berries and not lift anything."

Next was Piyo and his wrists, then Amine's back. The only person uninjured was Rav, skin bronzed from a deep tan. He yawned and stretched as he entered the house, dumping his bag in a storage room as he scratched his head. How long had it been since he'd seen Pierre or Paulo? A month? And how was Vip doing? Pulling off his armour, he left it with the spare weapons for repairs, the once-fine outer layer of the hide scratched off, while teeth and claw marks pocked its once-smooth surface.

Rav caught sight of the faint scars on his hands as he undid his boots and paused in thought. The carriage ride here felt so long ago. But things had gone too well too fast. The relentless scavenges meant the Blood Hounds would be leaving Blood Marsh soon. The time for his decision was getting closer. He couldn't look at Lyra. He was going to stay. His guts churned at the thought. What if the Blood Hounds lost their place at Jinkin because he left? He couldn't do that to them. He'd be dead without them. Was it fair of him to make them wait? Make them wait so he could abandon them anyway? Everything was going to become a mess. *None of this matters*. He was going to leave the Sink and all its problems behind. That was the plan.

"What're *you* frowning for?" Mulk joked. "You look better than before." He patted Rav's muscled back.

Rav sniffed. "Stay back. Ugh, that stuff's like sweaty feet." He swatted the air and escaped Mulk's stench.

"We're a unit." Mulk laughed as he gave chase. "We have to share our troubles."

Rav ducked under his hug, kicked off the wall to land on the stairs, then raced up to his room. Mulk stood at the bottom of the stairs, mouth agape.

"When did he get so fast?"

"I'm a good teacher." Miels smiled.

Amine hit his shoulder. "Like you could teach that."

Rav ambled down to Scythe's Rest for the evening. Sitting in his room had started to feel like sitting in a coffin as the relentless swirl of thoughts about him leaving had drowned him. As soon as he stepped through the door, he spotted Paulo and Pierre seated at the rear table, but before he could smile at them, Paulo turned in his direction and came rushing over.

"Hello, is—"

Paulo shook his head, cutting Rav off. The older farmer ushered Rav to sit with him and Pierre, his eyes darting around at the other tables filled with scavengers. Rav glanced around too, noting the unfamiliar faces, and lowered his head along with dropping his posture as he sat close to the pair.

"Have you heard about Baron Tryxwin?" Paulo whispered, covering his mouth. "Apparently, she went to war with Jinkin in some town called Harton. People are saying it was a massacre, like sending soldiers to the butchers. Her army's gone, dead, but she came out with a Heaven's Tear. *A Heaven's Tear, Rav.* Supposedly, she can create mist. There's a bounty on her from Jinkin; any unit that can track her down will be taken straight to the third layer."

Rav flinched. There was a knot in his gut that tightened the longer he thought until it compressed like an anchor of dread inside him. She'd got it? How? What about Bo Hart?

"Rumour is, she's already in the second layer with the survivors from her army," Pierre added. "Don't think the Blood Hounds can catch her."

"You can use Heaven's Tears, right, Rav?" Paulo pressed. "Get your Sister and go hunting for her. Having one of those things will guarantee you completing your Calling."

Rav blinked, leaning back in his chair, hands clammy, heart pounding.

"It's too much for him to just go running off into the second layer," Pierre said to Paulo, his voice rising.

"But the longer he waits—"

"It's been over a week and Jinkin is already after her."

"Baron Tryxwin—"

"She's not a Baron anymore," a gruff man in matted fur armour interrupted them, standing from the next table to leer at Paulo.

"Sorry, habit."

"Who are you?" Rav stood up to the man, finding himself half a head shorter.

He sneered. "I'm the leader of Hawk's Claw, little man."

"Never heard of them." Rav looked at Paulo, who shrugged.

"You will. We'll catch that—"

Rav crouched and slammed his palm into the man's knee. *Pop.* His leg buckled. The man flailed to grab something, aiming for Rav's back. Rav dodged to the side and rose, watching him fall to the floor. The man tried to protect his head with his other arm. Rav drove his elbow past the slow defence and into his temple. *Crack.* Dazed, he crawled away, trying to keep his arm raised to block a follow-up attack. Rav grabbed his shirt and delivered a jaw-rattling punch to ensure he couldn't fight back, then dragged him past the tables and out the door of the tavern, dumping him in the street. The man's companions had stood up, watching Rav, snarling—

One of the group's eyes widened as she recognised him. "Wait," she warned her unit. "Rav, I apologise for my companion's rude behaviour." She raised her hands. "We're new to Donsden, passing through before going after Cata Tryxwin."

"When me and my friends are talking, you wait until we're finished before speaking to us," Rav growled.

"We will, we will," she hurried.

Rav returned to sit with Pierre and Paulo, who sat waiting, expressions strained.

"Who's he?" members of Hawk's Claw whispered.

"Nameless Rav of the Blood Hounds," the woman answered.

They all drew sharp breaths.

Paulo raised an eyebrow at Rav. "You didn't need to do that."

"I know. Tell me what happened in Harton," Rav snapped, tapping the table.

Paulo pursed his lips. "Tryxwin moved her army out of Blood Marsh, claiming to be going on a training exercise. People knew that was a lie, but the other Barons were glad she was gone, so they just let her go. Whatever happened in Harton must've been genius for her to beat Jinkin. I've only heard this part once, but someone said Tryxwin had some war-beast that she used to harass Jinkin's lead unit."

Bo. Rav sat back and sucked his teeth before standing to leave. "I need to go."

He hurried out as Paulo and Pierre frowned in confusion at one another, then sprinted back up the road, breaths heavy with foreboding. As he reached the Blood Hounds' house, he checked the alley outside his room, seeing that his window was now open, with a candle lit inside. Maybe Bo could help him face Lyra? Or would he just make everything worse, like he had before? And he had no information on Heaven's Tears left. Aye, Bo wasn't a friend. He couldn't be forgiven. Rav itched the back of his neck with a gulp before heading up to his room.

"You're back," Rav muttered as he entered and closed the door behind him.

"Yeah," Bo Hart grumbled, going through Rav's papers on the edge of his bed. "You like alchemy?"

"I'm learning." He took a breath. "I didn't know Jinkin was involved."

Bo smirked. "I know. When's your next adventure up the mountain?"

Rav gritted his teeth and clenched his fists to stop his shaking. "I don't need you to save my life anymore."

Bo stood, the bed frame creaking, glaring down at him. "Every moment I stand here is a moment I'm saving your life."

Rav stared at him, paling as his heart palpitated, fighting to keep himself steady.

"Is it?" Lyra slammed open the door and marched in with her longsword drawn, snarling at Bo.

Bo smirked but stepped back. "Is the Bride participating in our chats now?"

Rav dropped back to her side, heart in his throat as his head swirled. Always by his side, no matter what. He took a breath as tears pressed his eyes, clearing the lump to stand tall. "Aye."

"Why the change? Are you scared of me?" Bo laughed, then leered at Rav. "What if I'm loose with my words?"

"I already know," Lyra said.

"Your last visit did more than you thought." Rav glared back.

Bo blinked in shock, his intimidating façade broken. "You told the Bride?"

Rav nodded. "Aye."

"And you're still here?" He looked at Lyra.

She nodded too.

"I don't need your help," Rav repeated.

"I knew I shouldn't have believed you." Bo scowled. "Do you know why I call them Brides?" He leaned in. "Out here, where they're strong and fast, they're unified. Sisters. They're the most powerful organisation in the outer Sink. Why would they fight each other? But once you get deeper, where the mutants and the soldiers start to match their skills, where they're no longer the greatest fighters, they break apart, bickering over the World. That's their true organisation, Rav. Not Sisters from a family carrying out their purpose, but conniving harlots lusting after power, greedy like everyone else. Brides fighting over their husband. Ha'th Bey Riene looks like your friend now. She thinks you're talented, that you have the potential to be amazing. But when she sees the true geniuses of the Sink, she'll drop you and join them, spreading her legs like the whore she—"

"*Never*," Rav snarled, stamping on the floorboards as he stepped up to Bo with his hands bared like claws as though he'd become the Ghoul. "I wouldn't be here if Lyra was like the other Sisters. If Lyra ever leaves me, it'll be because *I've* let *her* down."

"When—"

"There'll be no 'when'." Rav stood firm. "Goodbye, Bo Hart."

Bo watched him a moment, then snorted. "Our deal stands. I save your life, I get information on a Heaven's Tear."

"What can you do that a Sister can't?" Rav sneered back.

Bo dropped his ferocious grin into a dead stare, his dark eyes needling. "We'll see each other again, Nameless Rav." He turned and jumped out the window.

"Rav..." Lyra started.

"Don't." Rav shut the window and ushered Lyra out his room before the growing tremble in his lip took over him. "You'll get my decision when you have to."

What are the Blood Hounds compared to my family?

Rav slipped out of bed with the thought firm in his mind. Aye, they'd fought together, saved each other, supported one another, but they weren't friends. He was only with them to raise their status. They were only helping him recover and train. He'd leave them. For Pitt. What about Lyra? Rav pinched between his eyes, chest constricted. Ha'th Bey Riene. Perhaps that's what he was about to discover. Nausea roiling at the thought, Rav got changed and headed out to his stall.

"Rav, Rav, I did all of it." Vip beamed at him when he arrived, her straw hair clean, her brown, hide clothes new. The large pan was heating above a fire, oil already starting to bubble, the board next to it covered with diced vegetables.

"Very good." Rav nodded. "Let me show you how to cook these." He grabbed a spatula and tossed a load of vegetables into the pan. *Tssss.* "Watch. You can't let any of them sit at the bottom too long, or they'll burn, but moving them too much will flick them out the pan. Turn them over like this." Rav demonstrated the technique, switching the bottom layer with the top in efficient movements. "Try." He handed the spatula to Vip.

Vip flipped the spatula over too hard and sent food onto the ground. "*Ah.*"

"Easy. Use a lighter grip."

"Rav," Samson called as he approached the stall, "how's she doing?"

"Well," Rav said. "Make one for Samson," he spoke to Vip.

Tsss, scrape, tsss. Vip seared the bun edge, burning it a little, then tentatively handed it to Samson.

He took a large bite. "Mmm. You're getting better. More meat in the next one."

Vip nodded.

"Lots of new units in Donsden after the bounty," Samson noted.

"I've seen a few around." Rav took over the cooking as the crowd grew.

"We need a big harvest this season. They've got money, but we might not have enough food to sell. You can't eat coins."

"That's true." Rav laughed.

Piyo bounced into the arena training room, stirring the dusty air. "It's come."

"An invitation?" Miels checked.

"*Yes*. Izen's called a meeting."

Miels dropped his staff and ran out the room, Piyo already gone. Rav hesitated as he watched him go, a rush of heat warming his chest and neck. So soon? Why was it all so soon? They'd worked hard. The Blood Hounds deserved it. But couldn't the coming decision just wait a little longer? He shook away his fears and chased after Piyo and Miels to the Blood Hounds' house before they'd become suspicious of his turmoil.

Amine, Mulk, Piyo, and Lyra were already waiting inside the planning room when he arrived. Rav and Miels took their seats either side of Mulk around the central table as Izen strode in, a thick piece of paper in his hand.

"The Blood Hounds have been invited to a banquet in the Keep," he announced.

"*Yes*." Mulk shook a beaming Miels and straight-faced Rav, who sat beside him.

Piyo exhaled in relief. Amine's face nearly split in two from their massive smile. Rav also grinned, hoping his eyes wouldn't betray his fear as Lyra watched him in silence.

"When?" Amine asked.

"Tonight. I hope you've still got money; my unit's going to be wearing the finest silks in Donsden."

They dashed to their rooms to find their coin pouches, then rushed out to the most lavish tailors around the market, Rav joining the frenzy while Lyra continued glancing his way. Returning late afternoon with new-cut outfits, they changed before gathering once more. Six figures stood in front of the door in blood-red robes, their sleeves and seams threaded with gold designed to look like razor-sharp teeth, complementing the bone buttons holding the lapels in place. Where their robes reached their waists was pulled across to their left, held in place by a bone buckle that had been sculpted to look like a maw biting down. Piyo, Rav, and Amine had theirs pulled tight to highlight their slim physiques, while Mulk, Miels, and Izen had more room for their thick torsos.

A line of shining fabric ran down their backs to pull the front tighter, emphasising everyone's muscles, matching the shined leather of their boots. A ruby necklace hung around Izen's neck and over his chest. Smelling sweet from crushed flower petals, Rav traced the inside of his robe, everything feeling as soft as a cloud. Sky glowing orange with the setting sun to cast long shadows down Donsden's street, Izen brought the Blood Hounds into formation.

"Is everyone ready?" he asked, standing before his unit.

Amine conducted a final check to ensure everyone's robes were crease-free. Rav stopped picking at the bone buttons at the ends of his sleeves and adjusted them so that they lined up with the rest of his outfit, the way Kayla would have done. He nodded.

"Let's go." Izen opened the door and led his unit to the Keep, the Blood Hounds marching past gawping bystanders with their heads high.

The Keep gates opened at their arrival, guards nodding their way. Ee La' Bol was waiting for them, wearing a stylised set of plate armour. She guided Izen into the Keep through the main entrance—Mulk, Miels, Piyo, and Amine fighting to keep facing forward instead of gazing around—and up the main stairs to reach the same banquet hall Rav'd met Baron Glass in. This time, mutant skeletons hung from the walls and skinned hides had been laid out as carpet and tablecloth, light flickering from the tips of candles set into bone candlesticks. A great fire blazed at the back of the room, creating shadows that brought the room to life, capturing the last moments of each creature. Fear, despair, subservience. A hall designed around victory. A show of Baron Glass' might, ruler of Blood Marsh. Rav itched under his collar, the previous weight he'd felt returning twofold.

"Welcome," Baron Glass called from his place at the table head.

Rav bowed low with the Blood Hounds, but the three gorgeous ladies in opulent gowns along the right side of the table kept catching his eye. The closest to Baron Glass had hanging glass earrings that shimmered in the light, suiting her straight black hair, dark eyes, and dainty features. Her dress was also-glass coloured, somehow opaque but tantalising, as though you could see straight through it. The woman next to her was dressed in a deep blue gown as though she were the evening sky, its cuts luring your gaze into her enthralling curves. Brunette hair wound in white thread and mischievous eyes that batted. The last had short-cut blonde hair and a powdered face with wide, glistening eyes. His lips were pursed, highlighting her cheekbones in a look that could draw empathy from a stone. Her dress was less revealing, light purple with frills. It was hard to focus on the comparatively plain man next to them.

"I'm Baron Glass."

And like that, every distraction shattered to dust.

Chapter 31

"Champion Izen Delmare greets Baron Glass." Izen maintained his bow, the Blood Hounds copying behind him.

"You fight well," Baron Glass murmured. "You need to improve your retraction speed, though; Karac almost caught you."

Izen tensed up. "I will."

"Sit," Baron Glass commanded.

The Blood Hounds took their seats down the left side of the table, Izen closest to the Baron, then Rav, Mulk, Piyo, Miels, and Amine. Lyra was seated opposite Baron Glass, beside Ee La' Bol. Aside from Baron Glass' wives, there were a few other guests. Rav recognised Niklaus, Albert Rexim, and Eman Hagrin. Seeing Eman's face, he looked to the blonde woman with glistening eyes in the frilled dress, realising she was Ilina Hagrin. Ilina's gaze lingered on him just long enough to express her curiosity without being rude. She looked away shyly, blushing. Rav's cheeks warmed.

"This is my wife, Champion Ku Suel." Baron Glass held the hand of the dark-haired woman next to him. "And my Concubines, Sarsa Payne and Ilina Hagrin."

Sarsa held her finger to her bottom lip as she perused the Blood Hounds, her gaze settling on Rav before returning to Izen, who avoided looking at her directly. Ilina gave a small nod. The Blood Hounds remained focused on Baron Glass.

"Ee La' Bol, who serves the Sisters' interests in Donsden," Baron Glass continued, "and you already know my other guests."

"It's a pleasure to be in the company of the Blood Hounds once more," Niklaus said.

"Let's have another great feast," Albert followed.

Eman pulled a toying smile. "I've seen so much of Rav these past mornings, I can't help but feel we're old friends."

Rav smiled back with a sneer in his eyes.

Baron Glass raised his hand, and servants entered with small dishes and jugs of wine. "Today, we're celebrating," he announced as the plates carrying thin strips of meat wrapped in leaves and drizzled with a cream sauce were served, the smell setting everyone's mouths watering. "I've received a request from Jinkin," Baron Glass continued. "We're seeking more units to enter Ut Sh'za and bolster our forces in Varheart. The Blood Hounds have been selected to join them."

The Blood Hounds each sucked in a sharp breath, chests swelling with pride. Rav smiled as wide as he could manage as his heart sank. The time had come. It was too early. He wasn't ready.

Baron Glass gazed at them all, eyes alight. "I've prepared one last scavenge for you. In two days, you'll go up Mount Don behind the Keep and participate in the mutant culling to clear them away from the city."

Rav flinched. Dangerous. But not that dangerous. Doable. The Blood Hounds gleamed.

"You will be working with my soldiers and Champions Guard," Baron Glass added. "In the second layer and beyond, unity is the most important quality for any organisation to function. There can be no internal conflict. Understood?"

Eman seemed to glow at the sudden pause. Izen was the first to nod, the other Blood Hounds hurrying to follow his lead. Rav gritted his teeth to hold off his scowl. How could they just forgive someone who'd tried to have Izen killed? Ilina gave Eman a glance.

Eman stood. "I know that as competing units, Champions Guard and the Blood Hounds have had a strong rivalry for the top position, but now we've both succeeded. With my strategies and your skills, we'll create a powerful unit, ready to serve and grow within Jinkin. I look forward to combining our strengths so that we can both achieve more."

Eman looked so amenable, so forgiving, so pious in her service to Jinkin. But after seeing how Ha'th Bey Riene used Lyra to hide her true self, how could Rav be fooled by her pathetic performance? No, Eman was seething behind her façade. Her precious, doted-on unit wasn't the best in Blood Marsh anymore. She'd failed again and again, and now the Blood Hounds had caught up. He glanced at Ilina, spotting the sharpness within her doe eyes, the spite she used to command Eman's behaviour. Aye, there was far more to this supposed concession.

After Eman sat, Izen stood. "The Blood Hounds are grateful for the opportunity you've given us and will do everything we can to support Jinkin. What's an old spat compared to the glory of joining those who rule this side of the Ar'za? With Champion Hagrin and Champion Trent, we'll enter Ut Sh'za with confidence, ready to carry out our tasks." He sat back down.

"Good." Baron Glass nodded. "Now, I've seen you all salivating over your plates; eat."

Mulk and Miels were ready to discard their cutlery and eat off their plates, but a glare from Amine had them eating in the daintiest bites they could manage. Only Baron Glass used his hands, and no one dared copy him.

Quiet conversation started. The Blood Hounds talked to Albert, Niklaus spoke with Ilina and Sarsa, while Eman spoke to Ee La' Bol and Lyra. Champion Suel sat quietly beside her husband.

Rav couldn't help glancing at Eman. What was she planning? There had to be something. Or was she like the Blood Hounds and willing to act nice to join Jinkin? She was a Champion; she had to have strong willpower and perseverance. Was he focusing on her to hide from the decision that he now had to face? It was easier when your enemy was someone other than yourself. One last scavenge before he had to choose. Rav downed his cup of wine. Lyra knew what he was thinking. The way she kept looking at him was drawing Ee La' Bol's attention too.

"You've come a long way, Rav," Baron Glass said to him.

This wasn't the place to worry. "The Blood Hounds have taught me a lot. Without their support, I wouldn't have recovered so fast," he replied.

"It's only been a few months since you arrived in Blood Marsh. The progress you've made is remarkable. I hear you even helped defeat a boulder-bear."

"Miels has been an excellent teacher." Rav laughed. "With his help and Izen's advice, my skills have much improved."

Baron Glass raised his eyebrow. "Does that mean you'll be joining them in Ut Sh'za with Jinkin?"

Rav froze for a moment, at last finding his words again. "I need to pursue my Calling. For now, that means working with the Blood Hounds." Sweat soaked his back as the Blood Hounds smiled at him.

Baron Glass gave an uncaring nod at his answer. "Well, I hope you've enjoyed your stay in my territory. Despite the mutants, Blood Marsh is quite beautiful, wouldn't you agree? Be glad your Calling brought you to a place like this; it's a shame most people never experience the Sink's great wonders."

Rav's lip twitched as he fought to maintain his calm. Had Baron Glass guessed that he didn't want to pursue his Calling? He looked at the Baron's head, noticing the minuscule glint on his temple as firelight met glass. He was watching.

Rav took a breath. "Aye, I have, and it is. Blood Marsh is the first place in the Sink that I've visited; I'll remember it as the beginning of everything I do."

"Good. What do you think of your Liv su Col?" Baron Glass held up one of the leaf-wrapped slices of meat.

"Delicious." Rav took another bite to make sure. The crisp crunch of the leaf, the juicy fat of the meat, the feeling of it melting in his mouth with the creamy sauce. It *was* delicious.

Baron Glass nodded. "Your companions have large appetites. We can enjoy the heart of the meal now."

Mulk, Miels, and Izen had long finished their Liv su Cols, Amine and Piyo not far behind them. Servants cleared their plates before returning with three whole roasted giant lizards on spits. All Rav could smell was that succulent, sizzling meat.

"Our raid of Cata Tryxwin's old castle uncovered her famed recipe for giant lizard. My cooks have adapted her findings, and tonight is the first time this meal will be eaten," Baron Glass announced.

A specialised knife was used to carve off the scales, releasing clear juices to dribble down the sides. Rav stared at it, guts twisted. The servants carved one slice of white meat after another, building a pile as high as a cup, then distributed them around the table. Baron Glass took the first bite, then everyone followed.

"Mmm," everyone murmured in enjoyment.

"I dined with Cata one evening and was served giant lizard," Niklaus said. "That meal cannot compare to this. Your cooks have transformed the meat from slime to a delicacy."

Servants started dishing out vegetables to complement the lizard. The hall went quiet as everyone ate.

"Rav, how's your farm work?" Champion Suel asked.

"Good," he mumbled. "It should be a good harvest."

The two spoke while Izen listened.

"The supply lines are running well," Niklaus chatted to Sarsa and Ilina. "Barons can never have enough stone for repairs. Albert, you should know better than anyone."

Albert was pulled away from his conversation with Piyo about gem cutting. "Yes, we've had to send units out to dig up the foundations of old castles to meet the orders."

"Where in Ut Sh'za have you travelled?" Eman asked Ee La' Bol.

"I visited Suelkoff on my way here," she answered.

Eman's eyes sparkled. "I've heard Suelkoff is beautiful beyond words."

"It is." Ee La' Bol nodded. "It's an excellent location to show you what the World is capable of."

"And Varheart?"

"I've never been. Few Sisters have after the treaty was implemented. Have you been there, Ha'th Bey Riene?"

Lyra shook her head. "I've only heard of it from Siere."

"I want to see it," Eman stated. "I want to know what kind of place can forge Champions."

After the giant lizard, which Baron Glass, Mulk, Miels, and Izen chewed to the bone, came a soup made from exotic fruits pressed into a paste, mixed with milk, then bronzed with fire. Rav scrunched his face as he sipped a spoonful, his tongue tingling with acidity before a burst of sweetness arrived. Izen worked hard to familiarise himself with Baron Glass and Champion Suel, the other members of the Blood Hounds doing their best to converse with Sarsa and Ilina. Rav kept eating to stay quiet, head lowered in case his expression betrayed him. He directed most of his talking points to the Blood Hounds and how they'd helped him, the knot in his soul easing somewhat as Izen and Mulk kept bumping his shoulders to show their thanks.

Baron Glass spoke when he wanted, ate when he wanted, always in control, everyone hanging off his actions. Topics changed from the important to the mundane no matter how hard the Blood Hounds worked to be interesting.

"It's been hot these last few days," Miels commented.

"I've prepared bunks for your unit in the Keep with my soldiers," Baron Glass said. "Of course, there are guest rooms for you, Sister Lyra, and you, Rav."

Izen stood and bowed. "Thank you for your generosity."

Baron Glass waved the praise away and stood from his seat. "Izen, come. I'll give you the details of your task so you can start preparing." He walked to the back of the hall and left through another door.

Izen hurried to catch up as Champion Suel, Sarsa, and Ilina bid everyone goodnight and followed, Ilina throwing Eman a last glance.

Eman gazed at the remaining Blood Hounds with a stern expression. "Think about what we can accomplish together. There's space for all of us in Ut Sh'za." She bowed around the room, then left out the main entrance.

"We'll also take our leave," Niklaus spoke for Albert, the pair heading off after Eman.

Only Ee La' Bol and the Blood Hounds remained, standing as they watched the door for Izen's return. Piyo smiled at Ee La' Bol, but her expression was flat, firm, her eye on Lyra at her side. Rav frowned. Why was she suddenly tense? Why had Lyra suddenly stopped looking his way? Before he could examine them further, Izen returned alone, a large grin on his face, and Ee La' Bol relaxed, calling servants in to guide the Blood Hounds to their rooms.

Izen laughed at their eager expressions. "It's all good. This task is difficult, but we'll complete it."

The Blood Hounds laughed too, a mix of relief and cheer, following the Keep servants out. Rav and Lyra joined them, the guest rooms close to the soldiers' barracks. Piyo couldn't stop smiling, going over the events of the banquet with Mulk, Miels, and Amine.

"Concubine Payne spoke to me," he jittered.

"How are we at the same table as Niklaus and Albert?" Mulk mumbled.

"I want to eat food like that every day," Miels added.

Amine kept shaking their head. "How have we caught up to Champions Guard so quickly?"

Izen led them all through the Keep corridors with an easy smile, his chest puffed out, his shoulders broad. Rav paused at the sight, dropping back to watch Izen walk. His posture was upright, his strides purposeful. What was wrong? Rav sucked his teeth. It was in the way Izen's hips moved, how he had to work to stop his shoulders dropping. He was unsettled. Was there more to this task than they knew? Or had Baron Glass spoken to him about something else? Rav thought back to Eman Hagrin's concession. Something to do with Champions Guard, maybe? He yawned as his mind started to tangle, too many possible explanations to consider. Maybe Izen was just nervous? Aye, Baron Glass was Ah' ke; Izen would want to do his best around him.

As the others were guided down a set of stairs, Rav and Lyra continued on at the same level. Lyra walked in silence, still avoiding looking at him, but from her terse lips and taut brow, Rav could tell she was deep in thought. She knew the problem he was facing. She so desperately wanted him to choose the World but knew that her words could push him away for sure. And she was right. Rav wiped his sweaty hands on his robes. If she'd tried to force his choice, it would've been so easy to reject her. Now... now it was like he was letting down an understanding friend. No, more than that. Much more than that. Lyra's loyalty, support, care... aye, she was like family. Two days. He had a deadline. It was a horrible silence.

What should I do?

Rav stared up at the ceiling and sighed. The question wouldn't go away, wouldn't be sated. There were no answers in the dark. *I suppose*, he realised, *the problem isn't what to do but how to do it?* How did he get to stay in Blood Marsh without letting the Blood Hounds down? How did he stay here without hurting Lyra? He wasn't ready for the second layer. That was true and that was what he'd lead with. That delayed the problem.

Dust was shaken loose and drifted down from the ceiling. Rav itched his nose. Who was moving above him? Not Ee La' Bol or Lyra, as they were down a wing adjacent to his room. Which left Baron Glass and his wives. How much influence did Ilina have over Baron Glass? Rav sifted through his memories of dinner. Ilina had been furthest from him and hadn't spoken with him much. He also remembered her large eyes and enamouring behaviour. Their relationship could be very different in private when Champion Ku Suel wasn't at Baron Glass' side.

Bo Hart's words filtered into his thoughts. Wives bickered and fought. Was that why Champion Suel had been so pleasant to him at dinner? Was she happy he had acted against Eman and, in doing so, lowered Ilina's position? Then the Blood Hounds were tarnishing her reputation too. Was that why she'd schemed to get Izen killed? What was going on?

Rav stood on the bed, getting close to the ceiling, and connected to his Heaven's Tear. Its power flowed around him in a miasma and connected him to the dream world. Rav gazed up and into the room above him, searching for any nightmares. What would they fear? His eyes widened upon seeing two nightmares above him floating next to each other. He focused, drawing more energy from the Heaven's Tear to connect his mind to the points. As he reached the closest one, he touched it and was drawn into the nightmare.

Ku stood alone outside a great collapsed tunnel, old and feeble, white, spindly hair hanging down to her feet like decaying willow leaves. Dull, blackened rock was scattered at her feet, her armour lying broken among it, the Blood Palm wiped into a smear. Staring at the once-shining rock, she cried. All her fault. Her shame and dishonour. Suelkoff had fallen because she'd failed her legacy, no heir to continue the Suel Bloodline.

Rav disconnected from her and moved to the next nightmare.

Baron Glass. He was sitting at his dining table, the head of a dozen well-dressed guests, doing his best to eat with poise while sharp, burning pain flared across his lower back. The guests laughed and feasted as the Blood Hounds had, but every now and then, Baron Glass would catch one of them looking his way with hungry eyes, sizing him up as though he were just another platter to be devoured. He met their gazes with sneering, presenting as strong a front as he could, but if anything went wrong, any wince or grimace broke through his façade, they'd pounce and rip him apart.

Feast done, he stood, the pain rising with him, up his spine and into his jaw. He leaned on the table with both hands and tried to swallow the agony back down, but it hurt even more to swallow. Sweat beaded his brow as every guest grew horns and savage teeth, all turning in his direction as saliva dripped down their chins.

Rav broke from the nightmare with a shudder, shivers jittering over him in waves. From the beginning, Baron Glass had been just like him—an actor doing his best performance in hope of survival.

Lyra had been right in Fool's March: Baron Glass was injured.

Chapter 32

Rav woke with knowledge of Baron Glass' injury still on his mind. How had he managed to act so calm with so much pain? Rav touched his napet. Because he had to. Even as a Baron, even with Jinkin's support, even with all his power, if anyone found out how hurt he was, he'd be attacked. What supposed honour was being Ah' ke meant to be? How could the abilities granted by Heaven's Tears be worth anything if everyone kept trying to kill you? The World's power was nothing but a brand.

Rav dressed and left the Keep, a little more familiar with its twisting corridors, heading to his stall. How was he going to tell the Blood Hounds he wasn't going to the second layer? Maybe he could blackmail Baron Glass into helping him. Aye, if he had Baron Glass order him to stay, neither the Blood Hounds nor Lyra could complain. But that would only make another enemy. What if Baron Glass turned his attention to Pitt in retaliation?

Then what? *Wait, is it certain that the Blood Hounds will join Jinkin?* The thought struck him hard. There was still one last task to complete. What if they failed? His guts churned the moment the idea emerged. How could he sabotage them like that after all they'd done to help him? As much as he wasn't a true part of the Blood Hounds, they were allies. How could he repay their training, advice, company, and camaraderie with betrayal? How could he ruin everything they'd worked for? That wasn't how a Carvell behaved.

As Rav neared his stall, he caught chatter ahead that drowned out most of the familiar sizzle from Vip heating fat in a pot. Peering out the alley he was exiting from, he saw his stall already bustling, Samson, Pierre, Paulo, John, Vip, and many others laughing with one another, seeming to be in celebration. Pierre was the first to spot him over Paulo's shoulder, pointing to draw everyone's attention. They turned too, smiles bright, eyes proud.

"*Congratulations, Rav,*" everyone cheered. "We knew you'd succeed."

Rav dropped his head to the cobbled street, his cheeks burning, a horrid, aching joy blooming in his heart. How kind of them all. Wasted on a fraud.

He raised his head and forced his smile, stepping out to gaze at the gathered crowd. "How did you know?"

"How could we not?" Pierre wrapped Rav up in a hug. "Piyo's been around Donsden since dawn telling everyone."

"Up late drinking?" Paulo grinned.

Rav rubbed his clammy face to wipe away his anguish, eyes bloodshot. "Up late planning." He walked through to take his place cooking, ruffling Vip's hair as he did, doing his best to keep his gait steady.

"One last task, then you can join Jinkin," Paulo said, slapping a palm on the stall counter with a thud. "When you're in the second layer, you can go after Tryxwin. With your talent, even if Jinkin catches her first, they could give you her Heaven's Tear."

"Aye. Just one more."

The pats on the back and platitudes were all noise to Rav as he cooked, each feeling like ever-burdening chains on his conscience. The meat he seared charred at the edges, the buns he folded going dry. Rav found himself rushing, soon bidding farewell to the crowd and escaping out into the fields, Pierre by his side. Rows of crops, now taller than they were, swayed golden in the breeze, hiding him away as he threw himself into work.

"Are you going to miss us?" Pierre asked, working with excited energy opposite Rav.

Rav paused, vial in hand about to tip over, another prick in his conscience. "Aye. I really am."

"Well, you don't have to miss *me* for too long; I'll join you in the second layer soon."

Rav's hand shook, and the milky liquid poured uneven over the crop base. "I feel like I'm not ready to go," he mumbled.

"Not ready? What's all your training been for, then?" Pierre laughed, coming over to pat Rav's back. "Look at yourself, Rav. You're strong, skilled; the mutants don't stand a chance. And you've been Called. With a Sister to guide you, things'll be fine."

Rav shook his head. "It's only been a few months since I came to Blood Marsh... I'm not used to the Sink." *I don't want to be used to it.*

"What did I tell you when we first met?" Pierre tapped his head. "It's all in your mind. You do want to go to the second layer, you're excited about it, you just need to learn how to be."

Seeing Pierre stand like he was dispensing gold, Rav couldn't help but smile. Was there some truth to Pierre's words? Maybe he could change how he thought about telling the others? He wasn't letting them down, they'd known he was a tagalong from the start, he was supporting himself. That's how he'd frame it. Units changed and disbanded all the time. He'd given back as much as he'd been given. They'd saved his life, treated him as one of them, joked with him, cheered with him, suffered with him. Protected him, looked after him. Cared for him. Maybe not because they were kind or because they saw him as a friend or family; they'd done it because it was their task, and Rav knew how much time and effort the Blood Hounds put into their tasks.

Rav sighed. "Thanks, Pierre. I'll try."

Rav watched the Blood Hounds prepare like never before, all the money they'd saved spent gathering smoke balls, rations, specialised equipment, as well as on repairs for their weapons and armour. A fortune disappeared. Looking over as many maps as he could, Izen noted every method they could think of to kill mutants. Rav lingered around him, waiting for an opportune moment to raise his concerns, but none ever emerged. Maybe that was for the best. Better to wait until the task was over so he didn't distract them.

Exiting the planning room, Rav caught Lyra's eye as she headed up to her room, both flinching away from each other. Just as he'd hovered around the unit, Lyra'd hovered around him. She knew the choice he'd made, and now every time he met her eyes, all he could see was her pain. She was staying with him, even as it broke her heart. How much did it hurt to watch someone reject everything you love? And how much worse was it to know there was nothing you could do to change that? So many times, Rav found himself standing outside her room, mouth open, ready to knock, to apologise, to try and soothe the damage he was doing. But there was only one way to do that, and Pitt mattered more. His mouth always closed, his hand falling to his side. The searing pressure that held his heart like a fist whenever he saw Lyra couldn't compare to the devastating hollowness when he thought of his home.

Even as he teared up every night listening to her whispering, "You are their support, you are to be at their side no matter what they do, no matter how difficult it is for you. This life is one of sacrifice. For the World, we must all do our duty."

Ee La' Bol tapped her foot against the stone floor to signal the start of the meeting, the *clack* loud in the simple lounge room. Rav looked at her, pensive, apprehensive, trying to keep his hands still but finding himself picking at the bottom of his chainmail. Why had only three of them been summoned to meet the Sister at the Keep? Why did it feel as though they were all seeking something from him? Lyra and Izen sat almost relaxed in their red-cushioned chairs, looking at Ee La' Bol as though ready to receive sour but expected news.

"I've spoken to Baron Glass and other members of Jinkin," Ee La' Bol spoke. "Ha'th Bey Riene can't come with you on this scavenge."

"Why?" Rav snapped, standing from his seat. "Lyra's always with me."

"After reading through your scavenge reports, it's clear that Ha'th Bey Riene has been assisting you in your tasks," Ee La' Bol replied calmly, pointing for Rav to sit again. "We want to see how you manage without her."

Rav stood firm. "Lyra's my guide."

"She's not the Blood Hounds' guide," Ee La' Bol tutted, turning to Izen with a raised eyebrow.

"I'm part of the Blood Hounds and Lyra is too—"

Izen raised his hand, stopping Rav. "I understand. Having a Sister accompany us has been an honour; we are lucky to have had her aid."

Rav looked at Lyra, who was also calm, accepting, his indignation sputtering. "You're agreeing to this?"

"I already have. Ee La' Bol spoke to me after the banquet. You're strong enough to head up Mount Don on your own with the Blood Hounds and Champions Guard to protect you. I think it will be an opportunity to show yourself what you're capable of without me at your side."

Rav felt her words settle in the room. Lyra *should* be at his side; she was his guide. At least... until he left the Sink. Maybe separating would be good for her. She could get used to him not being around so that when he ran, it wouldn't hurt her so much. The quiet in the room lingered as everyone waited for his decision. Rav gazed around a room of assenting faces, all looking for him to accept the decision that had already been made.

"I... Fine. If that's what you want."

Lyra shared a look with Ee La' Bol. "Baron Glass knows he'll face the Sisters' disappointment if anything happens to you. His soldiers will make sure you don't die."

Ee La' Bol smiled and nodded, but while she accepted Lyra's terms, her eyes remained hard, challenging. She broke eye contact with Lyra to face Izen. "That's all. Is there anything you need?"

"No. The Blood Hounds are grateful for your generosity. We'll continue preparing. Rav, let's go." Izen stood, bowed, then strode out, his armour clanking as he did.

Rav cast a last glare at Ee La' Bol before following Izen. The Champion stayed a few steps ahead as he led Rav through the Keep, into the courtyard, and then through the portcullis, head high, shoulders broad, seeming to be taking a strong stance against some encroaching weight. Rav watched him, breaths shallow. Was Izen actually furious too, or was it the burden of protecting a Called One that loomed over him?

Izen stopped at the end of the short passage leading out into the main city, expression hidden behind his back as he kept facing forward. "Are you sure you're alright going up Mount Don without Lyra?" What was that in Izen's tone? Something cold, hard, definitive. A certainty. Rav bit the inside of his cheek, the pressure emanating from Izen's wide back threatening to squeeze tears from his eyes. He masked his emotion and hesitancy with sternness.

"Aye, I'm just not used to it. She's been with me the entire time I've been in the Sink."

Izen turned to face him, solemn, statuesque, his green eyes boring into Rav's as though he wanted to see into his soul. "Rav, this task is too important for us. I need to know if you have any problems before we head up Mount Don. We all need to be at our best; I can't have any weaknesses in my unit."

Rav paused, heart rattling. This was the time to tell him. The opportunity had come. *I'm not going to the second layer.* He choked, holding firm to keep himself stoic. "The decision has been made. I'm fine."

"Good." Izen patted his shoulder, grabbing the muscle that had grown. "When'd you get so strong?"

"You've been feeding me well." Rav laughed, hoping it didn't sound as hollow as it felt.

"It's nice to know it's not gone to waste." Izen chuckled too, then took on a more serious tone. "Rest your arm—you're going to need it up there. We'll plan as much as we can, but something *will* go wrong, and we'll have to act or die."

Rav watched the Champion study his face as though he was committing it to memory, and in Izen's eyes, melancholy mixed in with his certainty.

"I'll be ready," Rav promised, clenching his toes in his boots as a shiver creeped up his leg.

"No, you won't." Izen gazed up at the mountain behind Rav. "None of us will be."

Rav's bed creaked as he stood from it, pacing up and down his small room with soft steps in flickering candlelight, the draft coming from the window tonight chilled. A leather map slid off his bed behind him, hitting the floor with a light thud. Rav snatched it up and placed it back with the others, studying the swirl of drawings for a moment before his eyes started stinging again. The maps had all started to blend in his head, from the marsh to the tunnel systems to the mountainside they'd be climbing. He looked away and pinched between his eyes. Even if he knew where to fight or run or hide or find water, it didn't solve the itch in his soul.

Izen was nervous. He was scared. He wasn't the bold and commanding leader he was pretending to be. Were the others the same? Were they all actually terrified of dying? Were the Blood Hounds... real people? Not Sink fanatics, but people who loved and cared and wanted to live more than they wanted power from the Sink?

Underneath the bravado, were they like the Ghoulsmen? Perhaps their greed wasn't untamed. Had they chosen a life in the Sink that they regretted yet were unable to leave? They'd committed to a decision years ago and were stuck with it, sacrificing too much to turn back now. If they didn't achieve what they initially wanted, wasn't it all pointless? What were their lives without the Sink now?

Maybe him wanting to stay in Blood Marsh wouldn't be met with the hostility he thought it would. Maybe they'd understand him. Maybe they'd even want to stay with him, finally finding the chance to break free from the life they'd forced themselves into. They needed him.

Leave everything else until we return; focus on the task ahead. Rav rubbed his eyes and went over the maps once more.

Knock, knock. "Rav?"

Lyra's voice. The itch in Rav's soul turned biting. He wet his dry lips and gathered himself, tapping his chest with a fist as though to clear the discomfort.

"Come in," he called, still flicking through the maps, although now sitting on the hard floor, his legs stretched out.

Lyra entered and sat down next to him, but instead of leaning against the back wall like he was, she sat upright, stiff, seemingly gathering her composure, like he just had.

"I've spoken to Ee La' Bol about keeping you safe. I don't think Baron Glass' soldiers will give their lives for you."

Rav frowned, looking up from his maps to see her pensive, avoiding his eyes. *Isn't that obvious?* Why had she spoken like some great secret had been revealed?

"You're in danger this time. I won't be able to help. You need to understand the risk you're taking," Lyra continued.

Rav searched her expression. Did she mean...? His hand shot to the back of his neck, feeling the smooth metal of his napet. "I'll use everything I have to survive."

"Good. Don't rely on anyone else for your safety. Take care of yourself."

"I will."

Lyra inspected him, nodding as she lingered on his muscled arms and shoulders, then focused on his ankle. “Do you need a Healer?”

Rav caught onto a sliver of her true concern, the biting in his soul pushing a new thought to his mind. Perhaps no one was quite as he thought. “No, I’m well… but, Lyra, why can’t you help?” Was this not her choice?

Lyra looked down. Rav let the silence drag. She sighed. “Bo Hart’s right: the Sisters aren’t as united as we seem. We have different approaches to being guides, and my actions have been questioned. You’ve been noticed by others further in the Sink, and they’ve acted. All you have to do is survive without me.”

Rav held her gaze. “I thought the Sisters always supported those Called.”

“They do,” Lyra hastened to respond. “This is just a test. If you do well—” She stopped, paling, eyes widening as she covered her mouth.

Too late. Rav jumped to his feet and stepped back from her, raging prickles of pain flaring through him. It was more manipulation; the Sisters were checking which method of raising him was more effective. Looking at the person before him, he felt a fool. Whenever he thought her to be human, she proved she wasn’t. All this while, she’d been making plans for him further in the Sink. *She* was manipulating him, arranging his future while she acted as his friend. She’d never let him stay here. He’d known what she wanted but believed in her kindness. A kindness that didn’t exist.

Rav swallowed his rage as the sadness set in. “How much of my life have the Sisters determined?” he whispered.

“Not me, Rav,” Lyra promised, tears building as she rose to her feet after him. “It’s not me. You met Han; you know how the others think. This wasn’t me.”

Rav stared into her eyes as her face twisted, contorted, the façade falling to reveal an ugliness he’d never noticed before. But it wasn’t the cold ugliness of an uncaring Ha’th Bey Riene. How foolish had he been to think her above the others? No, *Lyra* was horribly, *humanely* ugly.

"Why do you have to obey the other Sisters?" he whispered. "If you know how wrong this is, why are you going through with it?"

"I don't have a choice." Lyra's face scrunched up, swelling red as the tears fell. "The other Sisters have been with the World far longer than I have. I have to follow the World's will."

Unable to bear looking at her anymore, Rav lowered his head. "I'm sorry I'm not the Called One you want me to be. I'm sorry you have to suffer for that. You don't deserve it, not after all you've done."

"No." Lyra violently shook her head. "Don't say that. I believe in the World, and I believe in your Calling. My wants don't matter. You're not the person I want you to be now, but I have faith that you'll become him in the future."

In the future.

The words echoed in Rav's mind like a struck gong. Every time. Every time he thought he'd pierced the veil of Heaven, it snapped back to knock him down.

Rav steeled himself, locking down the storm of emotions threatening to rip him apart. He had a task tomorrow. He couldn't get mixed up in this now. Lyra watched him, unable to stop her horrid crying. He didn't give her the understanding look he knew she was looking for.

"I need to prepare for tomorrow." His voice was dispassionate as he stepped aside to show Lyra out his room.

"Rav…" Lyra tried once more.

"Goodnight, Lyra." He ushered her out the door and shut it behind her, falling to his knees, struggling to breathe. Why did that goodnight feel like goodbye?

Rav woke early and headed downstairs to chomp down as many of the pre-prepared goebber steaks as he could stomach. Mulk and Miels had already eaten a dozen by the time he arrived, and they focused on eating a few more, ensuring they had as much energy as they could stuff down for the day ahead. Nobody said anything; the entire house was quiet, Piyo, Amine, and Izen preparing alone in their rooms. Rav downed three cups of milk and headed to the storeroom to collect his armour. The hide had been reinforced with boulder-bear hide, which was strapped together with rabber tendon, half his fortune gone getting it done.

Back up in his room, he equipped it, thinking over every aspect of their plans. How to deal with boulder-bears. How to kill rabbers. How to position themselves on the rough terrain against greater numbers. How to press an attack to wipe out smaller groups of mutants. He pulled the straps tight until the armour felt like a third skin over his chainmail. Too tight. He adjusted the breastplate to make room for Wakeman's ashes. None of the Blood Hounds would die.

Satisfied, he moved to his alchemy room, loaded up two pouches with thirty Ant's Itch pellets, then touched the new cloth sling lying on the table before hanging it from his belt. The last items to collect were his shield, crossbow, and bag.

Back down in the storeroom, Rav went through what he would be carrying again. Instead of spare water and rations, he'd be bringing four spare quivers of bolts, two shields, and all the swords they'd found in the secret cache Cata had sent them after, ready to kill as many mutants as possible.

Izen had opted to use a rapier to pierce thicker-skinned mutants, entrusting Rav with his usual longsword. Rav made certain it was easy to retrieve. He picked up the heavy bag and moved around the room using the footwork Miels had taught him, making sure none of the dozen medicinal vials clinked, grinning as he succeeded. He was strong enough. Lastly, he loaded his belt with pouches of bandage cloth and medicinal salves to get at them as quickly as possible. Finished with his checks, Rav slung his crossbow across his chest, donned his helmet, and picked up his shield, heading into the main corridor to wait for the others, who soon joined him, each as well equipped as he was.

"Ready?" Izen stood before the door wearing his polished full-plate armour, inspecting his unit one last time.

"Yeah." Mulk grinned, standing like a metal barbarian.

"I am," Miels followed, armoured like a human fortress.

"Yes," Piyo affirmed, lithe, lethal, and gallant in his armour.

Amine nodded, their bulging bag bigger than Rav's.

Rav took a breath. "Aye."

Izen grinned, radiating the aura of a Champion. "Let's go kill some mutants." He donned his helmet and led the Blood Hounds out into the morning light.

Chapter 33

Rav couldn't help looking back at the house. Where was Lyra? He hadn't seen her since their fight. She wasn't even watching him from one of the windows. His heart stung as he realised what she was doing. Lyra knew he would be distracted if he saw her, so she'd hidden away to give him the best chance at facing Mount Don. Even without being here, she was caring for him.

As they marched through the city streets, Rav gazed at the many familiar faces of the city folk showing their quiet support for the unit as they lined the streets. Pierre grinned at him as though he was excited for the task ahead on Rav's behalf, Vip and Paulo beside him. Rav fought to think of them and not Lyra, failing. Izen led them out the city and along the wall, towards the mountain, where a path led up behind the Keep. After studying every map they could buy, the Blood Hounds knew every part of the terrain they'd be entering, from the grassy start, to the rocky region, to the woodland, and lastly, to the freezing, bleak red layer.

"Piyo, lead," Izen commanded.

Piyo was already moving to the front, Amine at his side, the pair scanning the land to guide the group forward. The first part of the task was easy. They were heading up to the rocky region, where they would meet up with Champions Guard to combine their units and enter the woodland. From there, the units would stay the night in the woodland to familiarise themselves with each other, performing their final checks before meeting with the mountain soldiers and entering the red layer. After that, it was kill or be killed. The mutants had to die. Used to the slope of Mount Don, racing up through the grassy region was quick and easy, everyone filled with nervous energy.

"Slow," Izen ordered. "Conserve your energy."

Piyo dropped his pace. Under Izen's leadership, they settled into a consistent march, stepping in unison. Rav steadied his breathing, matching it to his movements. *Step, inhale. Step, exhale.* The moment was coming. He felt it, and he was sure everyone else felt it too. A battle. A battle unlike any he'd fought before.

Lyra's crying face flashed in his mind. *Not now.* Rav maintained his rhythm. *What is she thinking?* Rav couldn't help himself. Thoughts of Lyra creeped to the front of his mind again and again. This couldn't keep happening; he needed to focus on the coming fight. A moment like this could mean him failing to support someone in time. He couldn't be the Blood Hounds' weakness. He *wouldn't* be their weakness... But the thoughts wouldn't stop no matter how hard he tried to suppress them, no matter how hard he stared at the ground. Rav relented. He had time before they reached the red layer. Let the thoughts in now and get them out the way. He relaxed. How was Lyra?

The image of her crying appeared again. Rav tried to ask more questions, but they all resulted in that same memory. Her face, red and warped, haunted him. His heart palpitated, his breath lost as his chest constricted, almost as though he were feeling the same pain she had. The pain he'd caused. The pain she deserved for trying to manipulate him.

He gritted his teeth, cheeks burning, unable to escape the dread of that sight. It was wrong, so very, very wrong. Wrong like he'd failed his home. Wrong like he'd hurt his family. Wrong like he'd broken Heaven, shattered a piece of the World that would never recover. Everything was less because of it.

Rav flinched. Had he ever thought of someone else like this? No. Nausea roiled in his stomach. Lightheaded. Disorientated. What did that mean? He thought of when he'd first met Lyra and how unattainable she had been. But now she'd been dragged into the greed and filth that mired everything in the Sink. All because of him. He'd stepped on the flower; he'd crushed the glass trinket. He'd destroyed something he loved.

...Love.

Rav shook his head. He couldn't love Lyra; she wasn't real. He *loved* Kayla. That was what love was: being understood. Kayla understood him. Lyra hurt him. But who else could cause you so much heartache yet still make you care for them but family?

Didn't his Ma and Pa still love him despite all the damage he'd done? Didn't Cyrn? Kayla? Did that mean Lyra was family to him now? And... he loved her. If this feeling wasn't love, then what else could it be? He wasn't in love. Just love. The thing that made him so reckless. He took a breath. Lyra's crying face was still imprinted in his mind, but it wasn't as tender as before. He could think of other things alongside it now. The roil of emotions dulled. Now, he could focus on the one he needed: motivation. To give everything he had for his unit.

They crossed the grass terrain and reached the rocky area. Piyo guided them to their meeting point—a small, flat space lined by a ridge to one side and a deep hole on the other that went down into the darkness to a shallow, underground river. It had been set up like a well, with a simple wooden beam and rope tied to a bucket for units to refill their waterskins. They were the first to arrive. The Blood Hounds stopped to rest, drinking from their waterskins, then refilling them. The morning ran on, but Champions Guard had yet to arrive.

"Where are they?" Mulk grumbled, scouring the path they'd climbed up for the unit.

"We've got all day to reach the woodland," Izen said. "They could be arriving in the afternoon."

"We need this time to combine our groups." Miels was pacing back and forth. "The longer we leave it, the worse our teamwork will be."

Izen maintained his calm. "They know that as well. They'll be here. Joining Jinkin is as important to them as it is to us."

More grumbles followed, but nothing more. Rav tutted. Eman was petty enough to make them wait. But if she was petty enough to do this, then she'd also be annoyed at the Blood Hounds working alongside her unit. Did she have some plan in motion? Would she take her unit alone into the red layer and claim that the Blood Hounds weren't coming or hadn't cooperated with Champions Guard to stop them joining Jinkin with them? Rav searched around the well for tracks. There weren't any. What else could she be planning? He looked at the ridge. It could be an ambush. That didn't make sense, though—Eman would become enemies with Baron Glass, Jinkin, and the Sisters if she attacked them. She was arrogant, not suicidal.

Bored by the wait, Izen called the unit into formation to practise moving through combat scenarios, first walking them through what to do against a group of rabbers. This was all about manoeuvring; you couldn't get surrounded or allow them enough space to harass and retreat as they pleased. Rough terrain slowed them, and having something to your back stopped them getting behind you. The Blood Hounds shifted as a group over to the ridge, using it to guard their backs, Mulk, Izen, and Miels taking the front line to protect Rav, while Piyo and Amine stood in a half-circle. From there, they went over weapon changes and when Piyo would strike out to turn the tide of battle.

Champions Guard still hadn't arrived. Rav wiped more sweat from his face, eyes stinging from the bright sunlight. Already too hot in his armour, he struggled to keep focus, pinching between his eyes to ease a coming headache. He wasn't the only one in discomfort; the other Blood Hounds removed their helmets as they panted. Rav pulled off his crossbow and tugged at his chainmail to cool down. Izen kept checking over them.

Midday arrived as they rested, still with no sign of Eman. Izen got them up again to keep everyone focused, this time having his unit prepare for an unorthodox defence where they defended with the well to their backs. Rav focused on his footwork, Mulk needing enough space to fight in front of him, while he couldn't get pushed back too far, or he'd fall.

"Axe," Miels called.

Amine pulled one out their bag and handed it to him.

"Smoke balls," Mulk called.

Rav handed him a pouch.

"Shield," Izen called.

Rav dropped his bag and hurried to undo the straps holding the shield in place, slick sweat worsening his grip. With a last tug, the leather came free, and he yanked the shield off, lunging over to Izen with it.

"*Ow,*" Rav yelped at a sharp sting in his chest. Hand shaking. Heart thundering. Breath quickening. *That... hurt. Really hurt.* Chest now burning. He blinked, mouth agape, staring down at where a rapier had pierced through his armour, then to the arm holding it.

Izen had turned towards him, out in a lunge of his own. A thrust. Then the Champion strode forward and kicked him into the well. Rav stared paralysed as bright sky shrank into a small circle, walls of darkness rising around him while wind rushed past his head. Weightless. Powerless. Trapped in the fall as though he were being swallowed whole by the mountain.

Ooof. His body hit mud with a wet slop, driving the air from his last gasp. Winded, choking, unable to take a full breath, he spasmed on the ground as he sank into the muck, chest searing as though a hot coal was slowly burning deeper into his flesh. The circle of light above him blurred as tears filled his eyes, then trickled down his temples. Wet and cold. Dying. Why?

"*What are you doing?*" Mulk roared above him, his voice carrying down into the black.

Three silhouettes emerged into the bright circle.

"*Rav,*" Amine shouted. "*Rav.*"

"*I can't see him,*" Piyo followed.

"*Get some rope,*" Miels bellowed, shaking the figure next to him.

"*Izen, what have you done?*" Mulk's voice shook the ground. "AAAH!"

Clang. Bash. Bang.

"Stop fighting me and calm down." Izen's voice was emotionless.

"Rope." Amine handed Miels a bundle.

Rav struggled to think, trying to thaw his frozen thoughts enough to piece them together, but the chills rattling over his body kept freezing them again. He stared gormlessly as Miels' silhouette started feeding the rope down the chasm, only for another figure to appear beside him and use a sword to strike his hand. Miels dropped the rope, and it fell, landing with a splash as it hit the water at Rav's feet. Next, Izen slammed his shield into the well contraption, splintering the wood to let that rope fall too.

"AHHHH!" Miels spun towards Izen with his axe.

The two figures left the edge of the chasm, the sound of more fighting following. Amine and Piyo stayed at the edge, but there was no more rope. Rav shivered, teeth chattering. Bleeding out. *Act or die.* Connecting to his Heaven's Tear for an instant, he tore off his breastplate with a Ghoulish hand to expose his chest with a wheezing gasp. A precise hole just to the right of his sternum kept leaking blood, feeling searing hot for an instant, then freezing cold. He fumbled at his belt, finding his emergency bandages with a shaking hand, and pressed the cloth over the wound, mouth open but unscreaming, unable to force enough air out his lungs to do more than whimper in the mud.

"*Stop fighting,*" Izen roared.

"*Why?*" Mulk shouted, voice cracking. "*You're a traitor. A murderer.*"

"Because this was our task," Izen snapped. "To join Jinkin, we had to kill Rav."

Silence followed. Rav felt his blood loss slow, a few thoughts finally melting to swirl inside his head. Amine and Piyo looked back from the chasm.

"*We?*" Miels shouted. "*Who's we?* Izen, you fool; do you understand what you've condemned us to?"

"Lyra's going to come after us. The Sisters will hate us. We'll never survive further in the Sink," Piyo raged.

"That's not true," Izen said. "This task came to Jinkin from the Sisters' headquarters. As for Lyra, Ee La' Bol is handling her for us. Lyra will be reassigned to search for a new Called One, and we'll enter Ut Sh'za with full support."

"That doesn't make any sense," Amine hissed. "Why would the Sisters want this? Rav was a good talent and he was Called. They're going against the World."

"I don't know why they want this, and I won't ask," Izen answered. "I verified the message sent to Baron Glass ordering Rav's execution myself. The task is done. The Blood Hounds are joining Jinkin."

"Izen... killing one of our own, it's not right," Mulk wailed. "Rav didn't even have a chance to fight back. We're a unit; he was one of us. This is... You've destroyed everything we stood for. How can you bear your Name?"

"How could you accept a task like that?" Amine spat. "Rav saved our lives. This is despicable; I won't be part of it. I'd rather stay here for the rest of my life than murder a friend."

Friend?

Swirling thoughts started sticking together. Why would Amine think that? Wasn't he just useful for raising the Blood Hounds' status? And yet... Amine *was* shouting on his behalf. They *had* tried to save him. Even as thoughts joined, Rav trembled, nothing making sense.

Izen sighed, uncaring, callous, dismissive. "If you want to leave the Blood Hounds, you can. But the task is done. Leaving my unit means not joining Jinkin."

Quiet followed his words as memories flitted past Rav's mind. Izen used the same tone now as he had when he'd left the meeting with Lyra and Ee La' Bol. It was the same certainty. Rav gritted his teeth, a little of his strength returning. Izen had betrayed him for his greed. Of course he had; he was from the Sink, wasn't he? And he was just a naive fool. Again. All those thoughts about how Izen had cared for him, how he had seemed humane, and all this time, the Champion had been planning to kill him. Izen would die. Rav pressed the cloth harder on his wound with a choked grunt. He'd live to kill Izen himself.

"Izen's right," Piyo muttered. Rav clenched a fistful of mud at his smarmy voice. "We can't bring Rav back to life. The decision is made. I won't let his death be wasted."

He'd die too.

"Won't let his death be wasted?" Amine fumed. "How can you think like that? How can you follow a man who'd kill the person guarding his back?"

Rav paused, stunned. *Friend*.

"Because the Sink is more important," Miels mumbled. "If this is the price to enter Jinkin, I'll pay it. But, Izen, you're not my leader anymore."

"What happened?" Mulk howled, voice filled with so much despair Rav's heart stung. "There must be more. The Izen I know would never do something like this. You know betrayal never leaves you. You know it'll consume you. You've lost all trust, and no one survives in the Sink alone. This only leads to ruin."

"Mulk," Izen started.

"*Get your hand off me*," Mulk shouted. "This was barbaric. Shameful. It's cruel of you to put this on me. We're done. I'd rather die without taking a single step further into the Sink than take joy in a friend's death."

"I'll explain—"

"No, you won't," Mulk spat. "The moment is over. You *toyed* with us making these preparations, you toyed with Rav right until the end. What was the point?"

"Rav's too smart and too paranoid. You saw him checking for tracks or an ambush when we arrived here; he knew something was up. I had to do it this way, or he might have escaped."

"No, I know why you did this. You were scared we wouldn't support you; you were scared you'd have to fight us. Scared that you'd have to face the consequences of your actions," Mulk snarled. "Is that why you kicked him down there? So we couldn't see our dead comrade and the monster that you are?"

"To get rid of the body."

"How can you be so cold?"

"I—"

Piyo shrieked.

"*Ambush*," Amine yelled. "*Champions Guard*."

Clang. The sounds of battle. *What?* Rav lifted his head from the mud, trying to sit up, struggling to make sense of what he was hearing as his thoughts swirled like water down a drain.

"*Why are you here?*" Izen bellowed.

"You had your task, and we have ours. We don't trust you to keep our secrets." Eman Hagrin cackled. "Kill them all."

More fighting. More screaming. *More betrayal*. Tears rolled down Rav's cheeks as he trembled, struggling to get to his feet. Izen, Miels, and Piyo could die—Rav grinned at the thought of ripping them apart himself—but Mulk and Amine? They'd proven who they were. They'd fought for him. Rav pushed off his knee only to fall back into the mud. More screams followed. Rav slapped the ground as he failed to stand again. Why couldn't he help them?

"*Fight me, Hagrin*," Izen roared. "You and me, to the death."

"You know you're better than me, Izen." Eman laughed. "I won't beat you one on one. But I don't have to."

Clash. AHHH. Bash. Clang.

"*Shield*," Izen called. "*Amine. Give me a shield*." More metal struck metal. "*Amine. I need— AHH*."

"*WAAH*," Rav heard Trent bellow followed by a sickening crunch.

A figure fell down the chasm, smacking into the mud next to Rav to spatter him with muck. *No*. Rav crawled to the twitching body, seeing it soon still, trying to force his hand to roll it onto its back, but the limb refused to obey. Not Amine. How could he see them like that? Not after this; not after they'd proven to be so much more than the other greedy wretches roaming the Sink. He stared towards the body's head in the dark, guts squirming. Then he realised there was no head; the figure's skull had been smashed into its armour. Such beautiful armour. Rav found himself smiling with relief, the squirming in his guts turning to hopeful fluttering. Finally flipping the body over, he felt the spindly golden hairs sticking out the mush blow in the tunnel draft to tickle his face. Piyo was dead.

Rav flinched at another scream from above, this one low and guttural. *Splash.* A body hit the water. Maybe it was Izen or Miels. But that scream hadn't belonged to either of them. How many times had he heard that voice before watching a mutant get smashed away by a hammer? Innards sinking like iron in sludge, Rav dragged himself from Piyo's body and onto the riverbank, flopping forward into the water with a loud splash as he reached out for the large, dark figure dropping beneath the surface. Holding on to the breastplate with numb fingers, Rav heaved, screaming in silence as the wound in his chest tore wider.

The body lurched off the riverbed and rose, yanked closer and closer to the riverbank one heave at a time until Rav dragged Mulk's misshapen head onto the mud and cradled it in his hands. Dead. It was obvious. No one could survive with a hole in their skull. Still, Rav held his hand over Mulk's mouth, wishing with all his heart he'd feel a breath, but how could numb hands feel anything?

Rav cried, tears wrenched from his soul—

Crunch. Another body landed half in the water a few feet from Mulk. Would this one be Amine? Too much, just too much. Rav's stomach somersaulted and he vomited into the mud until hollow, acid burning his throat, the stench of blood and sick suffocating. *Too heavy*. Rav wiped his mouth with the back of his hand, then finished heaving Mulk's torso out the water and onto the riverbank so he wouldn't drift away. *The last body had sounded too heavy to be Amine's.*

Rav felt out in the dark, touching hard plate armour filled with muscular arms, then a square head. Miels. Still hope. He pushed off Miels' corpse and managed to get to his feet this time, shaking but standing—

Shlock. Another body hit the mud behind him. Also too heavy to be Amine. Rav gathered his breath, glaring up at the well walls with his nails bared, trying to imagine just how he was going to climb up and help. A wheeze caught his ear. Rav span and almost fell.

"Ugh." Izen's voice. "Rav? Rav?"

Not dead. Yet.

Rav grabbed the knife off his belt and stumbled over to him, clenching it so hard the leather grip dug into his palm.

"You," he rasped, barely louder than the wind. "You did this. How dare you survive when Mulk didn't?" Rav loomed over him, ready to fall and plunge the knife as hard as he could into Izen's face.

"You're alive," Izen whispered, somehow sounding happy despite the gurgle in his throat. "I'm... sorry." He coughed. "I had to. It was the only way to save you..."

Rav teetered on his feet, blinking scalding tears. What? Where was the pleading? The speech about how conquering the Sink was worth any sacrifice?

"Avenge us, Rav. Kill them all. You're the Blood Hounds now. Make them suffer, make them..." His wheeze faded to choking, then nothing.

"*Stop them,*" Eman shouted, breaking Rav from his chattering.

He looked up, recognising Amine's figure jumping into the well feet first as a spear swiped over their head. Air whistled, then *splash*, they hit the river with a great shriek.

"Get down there," Eman barked. "None of them can live."

Rav hobbled from Izen's body as fast as he could manage and fell into the river, latching onto Amine.

"Who?" Amine hissed, slapping at Rav's arms.

"Me," Rav wheezed, the urge to cough growing, but it stung too much, leaving him doing a slow exhale. He found his footing on the soft riverbed and pulled, unfeeling as he focused on getting Amine ashore.

Amine gasped, hugging Rav's shoulders. "You're alive."

"Aye." Rav set them onto the riverbank and staggered out before falling.

"Drop a torch down," Eman commanded.

"Hide. We can't let them find us," Amine hissed.

Act or die.

Rav connected to his Heaven's Tear and pounced on Piyo and Miels' bodies, tearing them apart into ragged chunks. More hot blood poured down his chest at the ragged movement. Clutching his wound, he moved to Izen, then hesitated. What had Izen meant by his last words? How was this saving him? Only one part was clear: "Avenge us". Aye, he'd do that. Rav eviscerated Izen's corpse.

Last was Mulk. Rav reached the body and raised a Ghoulish claw, but as he tried to slash at it, all strength left him, resulting in a weak slap. Leaning over Mulk's body, he bawled, snot and bile dribbling down his chin. Mulk deserved to be honoured, anointed, then burned and scattered on land he loved. He deserved celebration from his family in love of the greatness he'd brought to his Name. Who was going to do that here? This was no place for someone who'd died to preserve the sanctity of their Name. Aye, Mulk was a Ghoulsmen. Rav sniffled. How could he have been too stupid to see that until now?

"Something's down there," Trent said. "Where's the torch?"

"I'm lighting it," someone replied.

Rav sniffed again, wiping away a tear to smear something wet and warm on his face. Was that mud or bits of viscera? Air thick with blood, he couldn't tell. No more time.

"I'm sorry," he whispered to Mulk's corpse as the *tch* of flint being struck echoed down the chasm. "If I can, I'll find what's left of you and honour it." Rav hardened his stomach, closed his eyes, and turned a man into mince. Now, no one would know how many bodies were down here.

He felt a hand touch his back. Amine.

"You need to scream again, like you're dying. Then come with me; I know where we can go," he whispered, the Ghoul receding as he led Amine back into the river, thinking about his maps to figure out where it would lead them.

Amine gathered their breath before unleashing a shriek so guttural Rav's teeth chattered once more. Holding on to each other, they let the current carry them away in the following silence.

CHAPTER 34

"Here," Rav rasped, recognising a sharp bend in the river.

Amine pulled him onto the underground bank, everything still pitch black.

"Tunnel... left," Rav murmured, doing his best to move the little he could while Amine crawled along the ground, dragging him. Rav reached out and touched Amine's trailing boot. "What's with... your leg?"

"Injured," Amine hissed through gritted teeth. "The river wasn't deep enough. Now, quiet."

Bit by bit, they trudged forward until they saw a circle of light ahead. The tunnel exit. Crawling onwards, they emerged out of Mount Don's base and into Blood Marsh, seeing the usually green landscape dyed orange in the setting sun. Amine stopped to catch their breath, then tended to Rav's wound. He lifted the cloth to expose the small hole to them, breathing tender but still possible.

Amine wiped the oozing blood away with a finger, Rav grimacing. "Judging by the blood, it's not that deep and nothing vital has been punctured either. You wouldn't be breathing if he'd gotten your lung. It's..." Amine's eyes widened. "Perfect. How?"

"If it's so perfect, then why does it hurt so much?" Rav gave a wheezing chuckle but thought back to Izen's last words. A strike that made him seem dead for sure yet kept him alive. A kick that had him land on soft mud and water at the chasm ground so no one could see him still breathing. Izen had planned for him to survive. If it was true that Baron Glass and the Sisters wanted him dead, then maybe this *was* Izen's way of saving him. Rav's jaw shuddered, more tears rising.

"Relax," Amine cooed, pressing back on Rav's injury while looking for something to seal the hole with.

Rav gave a terse nod, then tensed to hold himself still, trying not to think further on Izen.

Amine pulled off their belt and wrapped it around Rav's torso to squeeze a piece of cloth in place.

Rav gasped. "Tight."

"It needs to be; blood will attract mutants." Amine looked out into the marsh. "You have to change, or we won't get through the night."

Rav gazed at his red-stained body. At least the river had washed away most of the innards. He started undoing the straps of his leg armour, removing anything soaked. Amine nodded and set about helping him.

"How's your leg?" he asked.

"It'll heal."

"You need a splint, or you won't walk right."

"Do you see a splint?" Amine huffed, gesturing to the wilderness.

Rav dropped his head. "...No."

Once he was undressed, Amine scoured the marsh. "We need a place to sleep and get water."

"Not out there." Rav shook his head, then indicated the tunnel they'd come out of.

"Goebbers live underground," Amine protested.

"Aye, but I know the tunnels. We can avoid the colonies."

"The reported colonies."

"If Champions Guard thinks we're alive, they'll search the marsh. Who knows who else could be looking for us?" Rav raised his hands. "Goebbers or people?"

Amine dropped their shoulders. "Fine. But wait until it's dark; I want to enjoy the light while I can."

They took off their helmet, revealing their chalk-pale face, devoid of emotion. The pair stared out at the setting sun, watching the burning disk dip to the horizon as though it had been an ordinary day. Blood Marsh looked so normal.

"What happened by the river?" Amine asked, facing out.

"What do you mean?" Rav scratched the rocky ground with a nail, facing downward.

"Those sounds. Bodies and metal tearing apart. And you're covered in blood."

"I hacked the bodies up."

"Hmm." Amine glanced at him but said nothing more.

The sun sank below the horizon, dyeing the sky pastel pink. Amine went to drag Rav again, but he pushed them away, getting to his feet on his own, woozy and wobbly. Back aching, he moved stiffly, sure he was bruised purple.

"Here." Rav offered his arm to help Amine to their feet.

"Aren't you in pain?"

"More than I thought possible." Rav offered his arm again. "We're the last of the Blood Hounds; if we don't suffer for each other, what's the point?"

Amine looked at Rav's hand, then smiled, tears streaming down their face. They accepted Rav's arm, collected their remaining belongings, and together, they hobbled inside. Rav felt his way down the tunnel, searching for a small cavern near a stream, soon finding it, empty as the map said it would be. They collapsed to the rough and rocky ground, cold setting in. Huddled together in the dark, only the sound of their shallow breathing filled the space.

"Why are you alive?" Amine whispered, shivering.

"I-Izen," he stammered. "I think he wanted to trick everyone."

"I..." Amine choked. "Mulk died thinking his best friend was a monster."

Rav's face contorted once more as he sobbed. "Izen spoke to me before he died." He wiped the snot from his nose. "He told me to avenge them, but I don't know if I can, Amine. I don't have the strength for that; I'm, I'm... hurt. Tired. I don't want this."

Amine sniffled, hugging Rav tighter. "I'm going to help you get them all, Rav. We'll follow our leader's last command until we die."

Wakeman's ashes!

Rav snapped awake, patting his chest. "*Oww.*" He lay still until the agony faded. The bag wasn't there; he'd torn it off when he'd removed his breastplate.

"What happened?" Amine asked, checking Rav for more injuries.

"I left something in the chasm; I have to get it." He sat up, gathering his equipment.

"We can't go back," Amine hissed. "It's too dangerous."

"I don't care; I have to go." Rav got up.

"*Rav.*" Amine grabbed his arm, but Rav shook them off and headed out. "Then I'm coming with you." Amine pushed themselves up and hobbled after him, using the cavern's wall for support.

"Your leg's bad; you won't keep up," Rav called back.

"Rav, I don't know where we are." Amine's voice fell. "Don't leave me, please don't."

Rav paused. How had he forgotten something like that? Reckless. He returned for them, helping Amine lean on him. "We have to be quick," he whispered. "I'll hide you somewhere outside and come back for you."

"What's so important, Rav? Think about this. You've got no armour, no weapons. You haven't drunk or eaten. Heading up Mount Don like this is too dangerous."

"Wakeman's ashes. I have to get them." Rav rushed towards the exit of the tunnel system.

Amine's breathing was getting heavier, struggling to keep up with Rav's pace as they were practically dragged along. "I understand, but, Rav, this isn't the time. We need to rest and heal."

Rav stopped and held them. "What if it was your Zic's ashes?"

"I..." Amine's words caught in their throat as their face fell.

"Let's go." Rav continued onwards, emerging from the tunnel into post-dawn light that shined warm on his bare chest and legs. He shivered, hugging himself as he scanned the marsh for any threats, too aware of how exposed he was.

Amine limped forward to watch for him, still wearing their armour, their face possessing more colour than before. After nodding to indicate everything was clear, they donned their helmet while Rav pulled the pouches off his belt and retrieved his sling. Although the powder balls had been ruined by the river, he could use stones. Together, they had one full set of armour, a sling, three daggers, Rav's throwing knife sheath, two empty waterskins, and a few sodden bandages.

"We have the day to get back to the well," Rav said, noticing the sun was only on the other side of the mountain. "I thought I'd slept longer."

"Here." Amine loosened the belt around his chest to see the bandage black from dried blood, in need of replacing. The wound had a thin scab forming over it. "We've been underground for at least a day," they concluded, changing out the bandage before tightening the belt.

"A day? News will have reached Donsden by now." Rav grinned. Lyra. Lyra would be coming... unless Izen's other words were true and Ee La' Bol was stopping her. He snarled. What was true?

"Not necessarily. Baron Glass could suppress the news for a while. We were going on a task, and people will think we're still doing it."

Rav stuttered, catching on. "Then Baron Glass will report that we were killed fighting mutants in the red layer."

Amine nodded.

"I'm going to kill him," Rav spat.

"We don't know if what Izen said was true."

"It makes sense, though." Rav frowned in thought. "Eman wouldn't risk attacking us unless she was certain of the outcome. Glass set us up. He gave Izen the order to kill me. He deserves to die." Tears pressed the corners of his eyes. How dare he? And Ee La' Bol. She was part of this too. They had to die. They *would* die.

"Baron Glass is Ah' ke. He stays in his Keep most of the time and is guarded by a Sister and Jinkin. I want to kill him as much as you, Rav, but..." Amine lowered their head.

Ah' ke? Rav sneered. So was he. And he knew that Glass was injured. All he had to do was get inside the Keep. Lyra could help handle Ee La' Bol. "I'll make a plan later. Let's just get Wakeman's ashes for now."

Amine nodded. "We should camouflage." They pointed to a stagnant body of water at the edge of the marsh that had no signs of other animals, then led Rav down to it, limping and wincing as they moved.

Rav scrubbed himself in the shallows by its bank, dyeing the water blackish-red, then dug up some mud from the bottom and covered himself in it, Amine also disguising their armour. Once done, neither of them had a single piece of pale flesh or glinting metal showing. Strapping the rest of their equipment back on, they started the journey up to the chasm, Rav collecting suitable stones for his sling as they sneaked up the mountainside. Amine took the lead as a scout, slow but safe, taking frequent breaks to rest.

"Will Lyra help us?" Amine asked as they sat behind a boulder to catch their breaths.

Rav itched where dry mud was irritating his skin. "Aye, if she knows what happened, she will. She's not like the other Sisters. Lyra's..." Rav choked before shaking his head. "She's always there for me, even when I don't deserve it."

"What about what Izen said?"

Rav gritted his teeth. "If she thinks I'm dead, we'll have to find her ourselves."

"I hope we do. We need her, Rav."

"I know."

"And your support from further in the Sink? Could they deal with Jinkin?"

"No." Rav sighed. "Bo Hart was never a friend. We had a deal and then he left. I never had his backing."

Amine looked at their boots. "Oh."

Rav stared at the ground too. Bo would have slaughtered Champions Guard like cattle; why had he chased him away? How many mistakes had he made?

"Is there anyone else you can think of?" Amine asked.

"Not in the Sink." Rav sighed again. "All anyone cares about is that I've been Called. Without that, I have nothing."

"I care past your title," Amine whispered. "Izen and Mulk did too." They broke into a short laugh. "We really liked you. You're stubborn and rash and fit right in. You did your job, and that's rare. We respected you as Rav, not just as a Called One. Mulk said he'd miss you when you left the unit."

Rav's eyes widened. "You knew I was leaving?"

"Eventually, yes... When were you going?"

Rav traced his finger over a stone. "I wasn't going to the second layer with you. I didn't want to join Jinkin. It was such a hard decision, but I suppose it doesn't matter now." He looked up at Amine, seeing their astonishment and confusion, then sorrow.

They sat in silence a while before Amine broke it. "Why didn't you want to go?"

Rav pulled a half-smile. "Do you really want to know?"

Amine nodded.

"I hate the Sink; I don't want to be here." Rav gazed around him.

Amine frowned. "But you're Called."

"Aye. It's a problem, isn't it?"

"Your fights with Lyra..."

"How could she not know?" Rav grimaced. "I was so angry at her for forcing me towards my Calling, but I know that any other Sister would have dragged me in deeper against my will rather than have the kindness she showed me... I miss her." He sniffled. "This place feels empty without her."

"Do you love her? Lyra?"

Rav wiped his face. "Sometimes. I've not been with her long. It's... She's family." He pinched between his eyes. "The truth is, without Lyra, I'd have nothing. I'm just a Nameless vagrant. She gave me a path forward and the strength to tread it."

"That's not true. I've seen how hard you train and how much you care. You're a member of the Blood Hounds, Rav. You did that yourself."

"Lyra brought me..."

"Our task was just to protect you. Don't disrespect our acceptance of you," Amine snapped.

Rav mulled the words over, blood starting to pump like lava coursing through him. "Aye," he spat. "My brother protected me and he's in danger because of it. Lyra protected me and she's been punished for it. Wakeman protected me and he's dead because of it. The Blood Hounds..." Rav exhaled. "I don't deserve to be protected. I don't *need* to be protected. And I'll prove it. I'm going to be the danger, Amine. I swear it. I'll kill them all. Tibald, Hewett, Glass, Ee La' Bol. I'll become a monster like the Sink has never seen." He wiped away his tears and looked back at Amine, who nodded that familiar patronising nod, as though Rav were just venting.

"Let's go. I'm sick of waiting," Rav growled before getting up, then he grabbed Amine and pulled them up too, shouldering their weight as they marched on.

Afternoon had arrived. Rav breathed heavy as they entered the rocky terrain, the fresh scab on his chest threatening to tear open with his violent movements. But he'd done it. He'd half-carried Amine all the way here.

"Stop now," Amine told him.

Rav struggled on.

"Rav. You're too loud."

Rav slowed his panting but continued trudging, throat dry and stomach empty.

"You're being reckless."

Rav stopped. Was he? *Aye.* He needed to restore his energy for whatever was ahead. He lowered Amine onto the ground next to a rock and sat next to them, fighting against the urge to scratch his itching wound.

"Now what?" Amine asked.

"I need to scout the area. You can hide here until I get back," Rav said.

"I'm a better scout than you. It's better if I come with."

"But your leg—"

"But your chest," Amine countered, mimicking his concerned tone.

Rav nodded. "Fine. I can't carry you anymore, though."

"I'll crawl. It'll keep us hidden."

Amine began dragging themselves forward while Rav crawled next to them. As they got close, Amine held their hand up and cocked their head. Rav froze. Amine waited a moment, listening. Rav strained too. A breeze fluttered over them, carrying an indiscernible, faint voice. People. The well was occupied. Amine led Rav to the side, where the ridge opposite the chasm was, and they crawled onto it so they could see the open area. Rav peeked out from behind a rock to see five people in hide armour sitting near the well, sipping water and eating dried meats. A unit. Not Champions Guard. Their voices carried over to Rav's position.

"...don't want to go back down there," one of them complained.

"You said you saw more things. Look at this sword." Another held up Izen's longsword. "If there's more like this down there, we need to get it."

"You haven't seen what's at the bottom." The first one shook her head. "You can't tell what's blood and what's mud; the bodies have been shredded."

"I'm with Mika," one of the others spoke. "I don't want to stay here long enough for whatever killed this unit to come back."

"There aren't any tracks." Another shrugged. "It probably moved on."

"Look at that sword, though," Mika said. "Whoever used it had to be skilled. If this mutant got them, we'll die just as horribly."

"I'm not giving up," the leader stated. "If you don't want to go down, I will. This is the equipment we need to compete with those top-ranking units. You heard about Champions Guard and the Blood Hounds joining Jinkin. In a few years, that could be us."

His words fired up the unit. They finished lunch, tied a rope around the leader's waist, and lowered him into the chasm. A while later, he shouted to be pulled back up. When they brought him up, he was grinning, holding Mulk's shield aloft.

"There's loads of this stuff in the river. We could outfit the whole unit."

His group cheered.

"It is bad down there, Mika," he comforted her. "Work quickly."

She nodded, and the unit lowered him down again.

Amine looked at Rav. "What now? They'll kill us to protect their spoils."

Rav scowled as he continued staring at the unit. "We steal it," he concluded. "We'll follow them to their camp and ambush them at night. That should give us enough of an advantage to win, two against five."

"I can't fight, and neither can you," Amine protested.

"I can do it on my own." Hidden in the dark, the Ghoul would tear them apart.

Amine shook their head and stared back at the group.

A while later, the unit had retrieved Miels' axe, Amine's bag, one of Piyo's swords, and Izen's helmet.

"How much is left?" Mika asked.

"I saw one more thing in the mud, then we're done. This haul is plenty to see us through the next few weeks; the contents of that bag are worth a small fortune." He beamed as they lowered him back down. This time, he stayed at the bottom for a while. "*Up*," he finally shouted.

The unit heaved him out bit by bit. Reaching the top, he dumped a crossbow and some chainmail on the ground. "The crossbow's in good condition, but the mail looks like it's been ripped," he said, holding up the front half of the mud-ridden shirt where Rav had torn it off. "There was also this." He patted the small bag tied to his belt.

That's it. Rav leaned forward.

Amine put their hand on his back.

"What's in there?" Mika asked.

"Something broken," the leader said, untying it from his belt and holding it up.

"Open it."

NO. Rav scrambled to his feet, breaking free of Amine's grasp, and rushed down the ridge.

The leader opened the bag to inspect the pieces of pottery and sandlike substance inside. "It's just junk." He tipped the contents onto the ground, and Wakeman's ashes blew away in the wind.

CHAPTER 35

Rav's eyes widened, mouth open, the moment hanging in time as though it were a painting. The Last of Wakeman. But then it passed, as all moments do, and brutal reality set in.

"AHHH!" He charged at the unit as smoke poured out his skin.

"*What's that?*" one of them shouted.

"*Mutant*," the leader bellowed. "*Form up*."

The unit startled into action, dropping the spoils and readying themselves for battle. Rav drew a knife from his sheath and flung it at the leader, the blade moving like a bolt from his Ghoulish strength, striking his neck with enough force to almost decapitate him. Rav had already sent two more knives flying out by the time the man fell, and two more members of the unit died, one with a knife through their eye, the other with a knife to the chest, the blade punching through their hide armour. Five reduced to two.

One fell backwards, leaving the last defender standing alone. He raised his shield, bracing for Rav's impact. Rav darted around the shield, combining his new power with the footwork he'd learned, to attack their open flank. He punched their chest and shattered their sternum, instantly destroying their heart and lungs. Last was Mika, still on her backside, frozen. Rav threw his latest victim's corpse to the side and grabbed Mika's head. *Crack*. Her skull broke, and brain leaked out her ears. After discarding her body down the chasm, he released the Ghoul, rushing over to where the ashes had been dumped on the ground.

No. No, no, no, you stupid, reckless fool.

Rav kneeled and sifted his fingers over the ground, but he couldn't tell what was ash and what was dirt, everything dyed red. Only pieces of the urn remained distinct. He picked out a few shards and sat there a while, hands trembling.

Wakeman was gone.

If he'd attacked at the beginning, he could've prevented this from happening. His fault, his mistake. So stupid. No more tears came. He clenched his hands into fists, crushing the last remnants of the urn and cutting his hands. But he'd learn. He now better understood the power he had.

"What...?"

Rav snapped back, looking at Amine behind him. They were clumsily crawling backwards, retreating from him, shaking. Rav stood with splattered blood across his chest, red still dripping from his hands. Amine stopped. They tried to speak, but all Rav heard was shallow breathing. Amine had seen his ability; they knew he had a Heaven's Tear. Rav swallowed. He turned away and started looting the bodies, untying a waterskin from the leader's belt to throw towards Amine. "Drink. We need to get what we can, then leave before the blood attracts goebbers."

Amine made no motion to retrieve the waterskin that landed just in front of them.

"*Amine*," Rav commanded. "Get to work."

Amine ignored the waterskin and crawled over to a body, stripping it of anything valuable. Rav ate and drank as he collected the Blood Hounds' belongings. What now? Would Amine try to kill him? They had before. He glanced at them, seeing Amine pale-faced, rushing to work as fast as they could manage. Dropping his head, Rav turned away, nauseous. Killing Amine would hurt him more than their betrayal would. Besides, he'd done enough killing for today. And wasn't there even some small part of him that quite liked the idea of Amine killing him? Aye, maybe only death could stop the agony cutting through him. Before he passed on, though, he had some things to do. Some people to kill. Amine could kill him after he was done.

Amine packed their old bag and attempted to carry it, straining on their bad leg.

"Leave it," Rav ordered.

Amine tried harder, avoiding looking at Rav.

"*Drop the bag*," Rav growled.

Amine dropped it.

Rav picked it up and carried it himself. "We're going back into the tunnels."

Amine hurried to nod and trailed behind him, limping as fast as they could. Below them was a tunnel entrance that Rav recognised, leading Amine to enter it. He lit a torch from the dead unit before following his mental map to another defensible cavern and stowed his bag in it, setting the torch in the centre of the room. Amine dropped the equipment they had been carrying inside it and hovered around the exit.

Ah. The scab on Rav's chest tore open as he stood back up. Blood wet his bandage and dribbled down his torso. Sitting down, he loosened the belt, opening the cloth to see the wound red and tender but not widened. He looked at Amine. They glanced at the exit but then went to get a fresh piece of cloth from the supplies and handed it to Rav, who replaced his old one and tightened the belt until the leather bit into his skin.

"We need to take inventory," Rav said, leaning back against the wall to rest.

"Three axes, two swords, three crossbows with bolts, one hammer, six shields, five spears, two sets of hide armour, and Izen's helmet," Amine rattled off, going over every weapon they had.

"Rations?"

"Water for two days and food for five. There's enough cloth for bandages, but only one medicinal vial for cleaning wounds and two smoke balls are intact."

"What about torches?" Rav looked at the one blazing in the centre of the cavern.

"Four more."

"We need firewood, then."

Amine glanced at their leg.

"We'll gather some tomorrow. Use the spear shafts to make a splint and a walking stick." Rav picked through the hide armour pieces, finding a breastplate his size that he eased on, wrinkling his nose at the stink of blood as he warmed up. Next, he gathered the remains of his previous chest armour, now just the back piece, and set about tying it to the front of his thinner, current armour.

Amine snapped the points off two spears, broke one in half to tie either side of their leg and designated the other as a walking stick. The pair worked in silence, listening to the crackle of the torch.

"Are you going to kill me?" Amine whispered.

"No. Are you going to kill me?"

Amine flinched, then shook their head. "No. Aren't you worried that I'll tell people you have a Heaven's Tear? Why aren't you silencing me?"

"I don't want to."

Amine blinked, wide-eyed. "That's it? You're Ah' ke, Rav. You have what everyone wants and you've done so well to hide it. Doesn't this undo all that?"

Rav faced them, listless, eyes sunken, and shrugged. "We're the Blood Hounds... the last of the Blood Hounds."

Amine teared up again, wiping their face with a sniffle. "Does Lyra know?"

"Aye, her and Siere. You're the third person to find out. Except for the others that get told through their strange Callings." Rav put the hide down. "Maybe Baron Glass found out from them. Maybe that's why all this happened. It's all my fault, Amine. From the moment that 'Zet Ar arrived in Stone's Way, it's like I've been snared in a noose that only gets tighter, strangling anyone that tries to help me."

Amine frowned, then pursed their lips. "I doubt Baron Glass knows you're Ah' ke; he'd have wanted your body if that were true. As for whatever else you said, maybe that's true, but there are far too many honourless savages roaming the Sink for you to be certain. Sometimes, greedy people just do greedy things." They clenched their fist and pushed their knuckles into the ground. "Perhaps Baron Glass feared how fast you were growing and worried you'd come for his Heaven's Tear. Perhaps Jinkin worried you'd become their enemy. What I don't understand is how the Sisters could gain from this. You've been Called. Baron Glass and Jinkin might have some selfish reason to kill you, but the Sisters are different."

"Maybe they thought I hadn't been raised right," Rav muttered. "The Sisters see me as a tool for the World. If they thought I wouldn't be useful, they could decide to just kill me."

Amine pondered a moment, then sucked their teeth. "There has to be more to it."

Rav threw his arms in the air, face contorted. "Does it matter? It's done."

"Yes." Amine locked eyes with him. "I've never heard of anything like this happening before."

The torch sputtered, on the verge of burning out. Rav yawned. "I'll get my answers when I kill Baron Glass." He snuggled down, using the bag as a pillow. If he ever woke up, that was. At least if Amine did kill him in his sleep, he'd get to rest.

"Why doesn't your Heaven's Tear glow?" Amine asked.

"I don't know..." Rav yawned again. "I think... it's not... complete... yet."

Rav woke to a moment of respite, his body unfeeling as though it belonged to someone else. Then the aftereffects of fighting while injured racked him. The muscles in his back refused to work, leaving him stuck lying in an uncomfortable position, listening to Amine's deep breathing. They had huddled next to him again for warmth. Rav managed a smile. At least Amine wasn't too frightened of him. What now? So much had changed since his arrival in the Sink, yet he was just as powerless, everything he'd gained, lost.

A pang rang in his heart like a struck gong. Pitt was so far away. What would Kayla be doing now? What about Cyrn and his child? He pictured his parents, Benji, Kayla, and the Ghoulsmen all gathered around the crib, a chubby bundle wrapped in cloths giggling inside. Elder Seabrook would have announced the birth to the whole town, and everyone would have paid their respects at the child's Naming day. Reuben would have given the most expensive gift, but Kayla would have given the most meaningful. And he'd missed it. He was here, trapped underground.

The image of Tibald's face loomed in his imaginings. Almost a year had passed since he'd entered the Sink. Only two more to go before his deadline and he was worse off than when he'd started. Rav laughed at himself. Logging, mining, town politics, even guarding Stone's Way all seemed so small compared to what he was doing now. What was that simple life? How would Pitt look next to Donsden? How would Stone's Way feel under the great Mount Don? How would those skirmishes compare to the mutant bloodbaths he'd experienced? The goat herds seemed so feeble now. Rav felt Cyrn's warm palm on his shoulder, his parents' loving arms wrapping him up in a hug, and Kayla's tender kiss on his lips. He heard Lyra's lyrical voice. His imagination took him on a tour of his life, melting time into numb cotton.

"Are you awake?" Amine whispered.

"Aye," Rav answered, some feeling returning to his back.

"How long did we sleep?"

"I don't know." He rubbed his eyes and reached for a waterskin. Lyra wasn't here. "We need supplies." His rest had ended.

Amine lit another torch for them to eat, drink, and arm themselves. Ready, the pair exited the tunnels to find firewood. It was early when they arrived in Blood Marsh. Clear skies and bright sunlight; another hot day. Keeping low, Amine moving with their crutch, they approached another pool of water to clean themselves in and reapply their mud camouflage. Amine kept watch as Rav used an axe to cut down a small tree nearby, then they worked together to lug the trunk back into the cavern, where Rav chopped it up and Amine shaved the bark into kindling by torchlight.

Rav gritted his teeth as he worked. Lyra needed to know he was alive, but returning to Donsden would result in a fight. If Ee La' Bol and the other Sisters joined in trying to kill him, he'd die. He had to sneak in, and for that, he had to be fit. Lyra wouldn't set off to find a new Called One immediately, she wasn't the others, and Baron Glass would have to take some time before telling her what had happened, or she'd be suspicious. He had some time to prepare.

Rav thought through the tunnel maps for a goebber colony. "I'm going hunting. We need fresh food to recover," he told Amine.

They nodded, continuing turning the tree into firewood.

"Do you know the way out?"

"I know enough; I'll manage."

Rav collected a crossbow, shield, and his knives, then grabbed a torch and left, feeling his way along the tunnels, listening for every sound, ready to activate his Heaven's Tear in an instant. Climbing to the surface near the colony, he confirmed that the surrounding area was empty—other animals stayed out of the goebbers' territory. A cluster of rocks lay to the right of the colony exit. Rav lay between them and waited, using himself as bait. How long would it take for the goebbers to smell the lingering scent of blood on him from this close? Sure enough, he spotted an inquisitive snout poke out a burrow hole and sniff.

Rav crawled back into the tunnel entrance he'd emerged from and aimed his crossbow where the goebber would come from. One hungry goebber came scurrying over the rocks Rav had been lying between and followed his tracks towards the tunnel. Rav held his breath, straining to hear if any others were coming. Just the one. Perfect. *Twang.* Rav clicked the crossbow trigger, and it died without a whimper. After darting out to retrieve its body, Rav returned to Amine.

Amine lit the fire, and once Rav had gutted the carcass, the two enjoyed their first hot meal in days. Rav checked his wound and changed his bandages, glad to see it scabbed over again. Amine's leg was still bad, though, their knee swollen to the point that the joint wouldn't bend. At least there were no signs of a complete break in the bone.

"I'm getting grass and leaves to lie on; my back can't take the hard floor," Rav said.

"I'll come with. I need the fresh air." Amine put out the fire and followed Rav out, the sound of howling wind getting ever louder.

Rav scampered to the tunnel exit and gazed out into the marsh, the afternoon heat he'd just felt nowhere to be found. Thick, black storm clouds covered the sky, the wind so fierce it bent every tree on Mount Don, even tearing a few boulders loose to tumble down the mountainside. Hail pelted down and bounced off rock, the scent of the electric charge building in the air growing stronger, ever closer to striking out in a flash of lightning. Rav braced himself on the ground, Amine taking shelter behind him. Squinting into the wind, Rav spotted the centre of the storm swirling over Donsden, the city being torn apart in the tempest. *Flash.* A white-hot bolt streaked across the sky and struck Mount Don above the city. *GA GOME.* Thunder rumbled, shaking the mountain.

"A' HA'TH BEY RIENE GOME TSA."

Rav gasped. The storm was speaking Ca'ome. Speaking to Lyra. He crawled closer to the tunnel exit, trying to hear more, but the wind was too loud and nonsensical. Only her Name was clear. What was happening? Rav shuddered, tingles shooting up his spine and into his mind, a pressure descending onto him like it had when facing the 'Zet Ar in Stone's Way. A storm made flesh. No, this was far greater. *GA GOME.* More thunder shook the Earth, cracks forming above him.

Amine reached out to drag him into the tunnel. "*What's happening?*"

Lightning struck the side of Mount Don again, blasting huge chunks of rock into the air. *GA GOME.*

"*Something to do with Lyra,*" Rav yelled back.

Flash. GA GOME. The tunnel trembled, debris clattering over the entrance.

"*We can't stay here,*" Amine shouted. "*Move.*"

Rav nodded to Amine, then led them back into the mountain, dust and debris shaken loose over them. *Ruu.* Goebbers approaching.

"*Torch,*" Rav roared.

Amine lit one and held it as high as they could, casting flickering light over the narrow tunnel. *ARR.* The goebbers caught sight of it. Rav unleashed the Ghoul as the first mutant came scurrying around the corner. *Ru.* It reeled back, the others behind it doing the same. Rav dashed towards them and swiped out with a rotten arm, driving them into a full retreat.

"Go to the cavern," he growled.

Amine rushed down the tunnel as Rav kept the goebbers at bay. After listening until he couldn't hear the goebbers any longer, he released the Ghoul and followed Amine back, who'd started the fire again, flames blooming. *Crack.* The rock above them shook, more debris sifting down. Amine grabbed a shield and held it over their head. Rav copied, the two leaning against each other for support, sitting in a defensive huddle beside the fire.

"This storm is crazy," Amine trembled.

"It's not just a storm," Rav muttered. "It's something to do with the Sisters."

"The Sisters caused this?" Amine gasped. "How do you know?"

"I heard Lyra's Name within it." Rav hardened his eyes as the storm's pressure settled on him. "Something's happened to her; I need to get back to Donsden."

Amine's eyes widened. "Do you think the Sisters are punishing Baron Glass for killing you?"

"I don't know." Rav paused, grimacing. "It sounded more like the storm was angry with her, but I don't understand Ca'ome that well."

Clatter. Ting. More debris fell on them.

"I hope this cavern holds," Amine whispered.

"It will, but if it doesn't, I'll dig us out."

Amine nodded, squeezing closer to Rav as the mountain shook around them.

Chapter 36

"Has it stopped?" Amine whispered. It had been a while since they'd heard a rumble now.

"I think so."

Amine lowered their shield in tender motions. "We need to see if any of the tunnels have collapsed."

Rav dropped his arm as well, flexing to return some feeling to it, then lit another torch with the still-flaring fire and followed the route out, finding a few large cracks along the tunnels but only one half-cave-in. Using the Ghoul and his shield, he dug through it to reach the tunnel exit. Amine watched the Ghoul all the while, their weight on their back foot, ready to turn and run. But they didn't, standing firm behind the Ghoul.

Outside, a huge silver moon glowed in the star-glittered night sky. Amine took a deep lungful of air, stretching out into the open space. Rav gazed in the direction of Donsden and Kroom Town. Donsden was too far away to spot, but Kroom Town was easy to see in the dark as torches burned across the town. Everyone was up despite the lateness, probably repairing damage from the storm. Such a catastrophic event would mean mutants changing territory and seeking new shelter. Donsden, at the centre of the storm, would've taken the most damage and might've become vulnerable, while the surrounding Barons on the other side of Mount Don would still be well. What was going to happen now?

"Have you gotten enough air?" Rav asked.

Amine looked up at the sky, drinking in the view of open space. *Ruuu.* Mutant calls rang out across the marsh. "Let's go back." They led the way to the cavern, where they stowed away for the night.

Rav woke early, back still tender, to hunt a few yippers for breakfast. Amine was awake when he returned, inspecting their equipment for damage by torchlight.

"Breakfast." Rav held up the carcasses.

Amine got the fire blazing.

"I've been thinking about what happened," Amine said, wiping hot oil from yipper meat off their mouth. "Jinkin's well connected further in the Sink, so any message coming from them could come from the Mo'za, which is also where the Sisters are based. I think the decision came from them, not Baron Glass. He wouldn't have the ability to coordinate something like this. And while the assassination will have some far-off reason behind it, Izen's actions were different," they continued. "Why did he do what he did? If he wanted you to survive, why didn't he tell you?"

"Either he was being watched or he thought I wouldn't follow his plans. Or both." Rav sighed.

"But no note? No message that he didn't want to kill you? Izen was risking having a Called One come after him for something he hadn't done." Amine shook their head. "Izen wouldn't take that risk."

Rav frowned. "Then what?"

Amine shrugged. "That's where I'm stuck. Perhaps there was more to his plan, but Champions Guard interrupted it." They bit into a yipper leg.

Rav stared into the fire. Izen had acted with extreme secrecy, not telling any member of the Blood Hounds about the task; he'd wanted genuine reactions, which suggested he'd known he was being watched. What had Izen taught him about feints? You always hid your true actions behind a big one. Rav sat up. What had everyone been watching? Izen. Was it possible Izen had arranged for someone else to explain things to him while he held everyone's attention? Where were they, then? Scared away by the Blood Hounds getting exterminated? Caught and killed alongside them? Lost looking for him? There might be someone else out there who knew he was alive. Rav shared his thoughts with Amine.

"I can't think of anyone besides Mulk who Izen would trust that much," Amine said.

"Didn't Izen have a wife?"

"Ah, Rav..." Amine ran a hand over their shaved head. "She died a few years ago from illness."

Rav skipped a breath.

"There are stories about someone in the N'er Sh'za, the fifth layer, who has a Heaven's Tear that can heal anything. Izen wanted to bring her to them, but she died when he reached Blood Marsh." Amine stared into the fire.

"I didn't know." Rav hung his head and clutched a hand over his chest wound, pressing hard as its sting went searing. "I never asked. How could I not know something so important about the man that risked everything to save me?" The fire crackled as the quiet lingered. "Amine... tell me about your family," Rav spoke, voice soft.

Amine took a breath, then sighed. "I told you my home was a small fishing village at the edge of a large lake. On a clear day, you could see all the way across the water to the villages on the other side." They rubbed their eyes. "We spent our days in peace, fishing all day and feasting all night, with plenty to trade on the water with the other villages for things like salt and spices. Only three warriors protected the village; I'd never even held a weapon. That's the type of place my home was, even after the Sink."

Amine looked Rav in the eye. "There was a plague. Everyone died. Not just our village either, but everyone connected to the lake got sick. Me and my Zic are the only survivors I know about. The disease stops you feeling. First, you misjudge things, drop things, lose control of your fingers. Then they stop working. Next go your arms, legs, and last, your lungs. The end is tranquil, everyone so numb they can't suffer, but before that... I watched my village get locked within themselves." Amine wiped their face. "My Zic got it worse than me and lost use of their legs. I came to the Sink to find a Healer for them."

"Is that why you joined the Blood Hounds?"

Amine smiled. "That part was the secret. Izen thought he was so charismatic to have won me over, but really, I just wanted to reach the fifth layer and find that Healer with him."

Rav smiled too, imagining that moment. "What's your Zic's name?"

Amine shook their head. "No names. My Zic stays alone in my village, fishing a peaceful life. No one will find them."

"I'd like that for my family as well. I'll do what I can to make sure your Zic doesn't wait for you in vain," he promised.

Amine wiped a tear away. "Thank you, Ah' ke."

Rav checked his wound again, ensuring it continued to heal well. Once his back recovered, he'd be strong enough to fight without the Ghoul again. Only then would it be safe enough to return to Donsden. Amine needed longer, though, their knee still swollen and excruciating to bend.

Rav collected Izen's helmet and sword, along with Mulk's shield and hammer, holding them in a bundle made from his old shirt. "I need you to keep watch for me," he told Amine.

Amine stood with him. "Where are we going?"

"Somewhere with a good view," Rav answered, looking at Izen's helmet. "I want to bury these... it's what they deserve."

"And Miels and Piyo? Miels trained you and Piyo—"

"Betrayed me. They both did. I don't care why."

Seeing his fierce expression, Amine simply nodded.

"Come, I'll take us onto the mountainside."

Amine collected a crossbow and hobbled after him.

Exiting a tunnel high up the mountain, Rav gazed down at the destruction caused by the storm—trees in the marsh having been torn out and flung around, patches of rock burned black by lightning strikes, and stretches of ground turned to mud by melting hail. A multitude of mutants competed to establish new territories, lizards against goebbers, some even courageous enough to move closer to Kroom Town and the inhabited areas. Amine scanned their surroundings for anything moving on the mountain, leading them through rough, ruined places mutants were avoiding. Further along, Rav looked over the other Baron territories, seeing little movement from them, not even from scout units. They were holed up. Preparing.

"You can't keep staring, or you'll be seen," Amine whispered.

Rav ducked back from the edge and went looking for a good place to dig the grave, taking half a morning of cautious searching before settling on a flat piece of land. A rock ridge arced around it like a short wall, the front facing out over Blood Marsh. Amine climbed up the ridge to keep watch while Rav heaved up the hammer and struck the ground, breaking the rock. *T, t, t.* Back aching, he shattered the surface blow by blow, cleared what had been loosened, then swept the shards away and started on the next layer, pouring with sweat, hands rough from the hammer shaft. Amine signalled for him to pause a few times as curious yippers came nearby, then gave him the all-clear once they'd left.

Breathing heavily, Rav finished, standing over a hole smashed into the mountain barely waist deep but long enough for Izen's sword and wide enough for Mulk's shield. Seeing him done, Amine climbed down and stood by Rav. He lifted Mulk's shield out the bundle at the grave's edge like a priceless gem, then handed it to Amine.

Amine set their crossbow aside but kept their hands back from the shield, pursing their lips.

Rav shook it at Amine. "You were part of the unit far longer than I was. You knew them." He swallowed. "These are yours to bury."

"I wasn't the one they died for. I think they'd be happier knowing it was you that buried them."

Rav switched his grip to offer half the shield. "Together, then."

Amine nodded, taking the other side. They knelt either side of the grave and lowered it down to the dusty ground, placing the shield with gentle care.

"*We choose not life nor death,*" Amine sang softly.

"*Now is the time for rest,*

"*What is, is now not,*

"*Never to be forgot.*"

Rav didn't cry. He would be strong. He would be powerful. He would be who Izen and Mulk wanted him to be.

Next came Mulk's hammer, then Izen's sword, then Izen's helmet, which was set looking up into a world of possibilities. Last, he pulled out the broken piece of chainmail.

"I'm sorry I couldn't take you to your home, Wakeman," Rav whispered. "I hope the view here will suffice." He placed the mail in the grave.

The pair stood in silence, taking a last look at their comrades, then Rav started filling in the hole, leaving the grave unmarked in case other units tried to dig it up. As he walked back down Mount Don, his mind hardened with resolve, fists clenching, guts tensing. The time for grief and rest was over. He had promises to keep.

CHAPTER 37

The remainder of the day was spent preparing, Rav going hunting again to bring back enough food for Amine to heal comfortably inside the cavern over the next few days. He used the hammer to weaken the supporting rock around the entrance so Amine could collapse it quickly if mutants found them. Amine also asked him about any sections of the tunnel system that they couldn't remember, and Rav went over them in detail.

Hair cut short and face dirtied, Rav disguised himself as a common wanderer under his kettle helm, Amine helping scuff the surface of his armour to make it appear old and cheap. His knife sheath too recognisable, Rav left it behind, taking only a spear and shield from the dispatched unit along with some food and water rations, even practising a new walk to hide his training. That evening, Amine told him about how they'd once caught a crystalfish in the lake with their Zic, its scales gleaming like a hundred crescent moons, and made a pair of earrings that looked like hanging fishing lines from its bones for their Zic. Rav listened with care, committing everything to memory.

The next morning, he ate well and checked that his wound was clean, finding his back only aching when he stretched in certain positions. Amine watched him perform his stumbling walk and poor posture one more time, nodding to say it was good enough.

"I'll return in three days."

"Stay safe." Amine rose to hug him, squeezing Rav tight. "This is just to find out what happened; avoid fighting if you can."

Rav squeezed them back. "Don't worry; I've recovered enough to keep myself safe even without the Ghoul. I'll be fine."

He released them, sliding off Amine's hard leather armour. "Heal well." He strode out the cave as broad as he could, sensing Amine watching him all the way until he vanished into the blackness.

Out the tunnels, Rav emerged to see the sun past its high point, and set off jogging to Kroom Town, closing in on it by mid-afternoon.

Damaged by the storm, anything wooden in the town had been blown down, or blown away, crashing into other buildings. Stone buildings had held firm, but the downpour of hail had eroded the gutters and waterways, leaving roads flooded with mud. The sound of masons chipping away at stone carried to Rav before he entered the town, along with the squeaking of carriages and bustle of workers, though not as many as he'd expected. Rav entered the town and walked around the busy streets, watching broken buildings get torn down and their materials repurposed to repair those still functional. Most of the labour was going into Niklaus' mansion, the road near his estate already relaid for carriages to carry stone over.

All the conversations he eavesdropped on were about the storm and how much work was needed to fix Kroom Town. From the subtler bits, he gathered that most units and labourers had been called back to Donsden, leaving Kroom Town short-handed. Niklaus had hired workers for his property, but the rest of the townsfolk were on their own. Nothing was said about the Blood Hounds or Champions Guard, but a carpenter whispered something about a fight in Donsden between Sisters, and her colleague hushed her, warning her not to talk about it.

"*Hey. Scavenger*," someone shouted to Rav. "Help me lift this." He pointed to what looked like a section of roof that had fallen and was leaning against a building.

"I'm on my way to Donsden," Rav replied.

The man titled his head with a wry smile. "Can you not give me a hand on your way there?"

Rav paused. "Alright." He walked over and grabbed the other side of the wooden board. "Can you tell me what happened? I was on the other side of the mountain."

"Lucky," he muttered. "You can see how strong the winds were."

"Mm." Rav nodded, heaving the wood off the wall and laying it on the ground.

"We've been cleaning up for two days now." The man shook his head with a sigh. "And we were at the edge of it. I heard even the Keep in Donsden was damaged."

"That's also what I heard. I came over to find work, but it's more dangerous now. On my way here, I had to avoid two moving giant lizard groups," Rav said, helping the man carry the wooden board over to a woodwork table. "Do you know why the storm started?"

"How does any storm start? This is the Sink," he grumbled. "But I've not seen anything like this before, going from clear skies to thunder in a moment."

"That's why I'm curious. There're all sorts of rumours going around the marsh about a Heaven's Tear forming or the World speaking."

"Ha, a Heaven's Tear? You scavengers are always so hopeful," he said, laughing. "As for the World, that's the business of the Sisters."

Rav scratched his cheek as though embarrassed.

"Don't feel bad. Some here are even claiming that a Sister caused the storm." The man grunted as they dumped the wooden board by the carpenters and made to walk away.

"It *was* a Sister," the carpenter Rav had eavesdropped on earlier spoke up. "I saw it; two of them were fighting. All of Donsden knows."

"*Shut it*," one of the others shouted at her. "Do you want them to bring another storm?"

"Sisters fought in Donsden?" Rav asked.

A sharp glare from her tradesman kept the carpenter's mouth shut.

"I'm going to Donsden to help rebuild," Rav said, widening his eyes and shuddering as though fearful, hunching his shoulder in to appear as meek as possible. "Is it not safe?"

She huffed while turning back to sanding down the plank of wood she'd been working on, shaking her head with indecision, seeming to have been persuaded by the act. "Whatever happened, it's over now. Donsden won't pay you, but you'll get food and shelter if you work there."

Rav nodded in thanks, then faced the man he'd helped. "I need to go see if they have any spare beds, or I'll be out in the wild."

"Go. I appreciate your help." He waved Rav off.

Rav broke into a run. Two Sisters fighting? One would be Lyra and the other... Ee La' Bol. Lyra had found out they'd tried to kill him.

The surface of Mount Don above Donsden had taken a battering, rocks and mud shaken loose to cause a landslide onto the city below. The Keep had taken the brunt of the blow, protecting most of the area beneath it, but it had lost its roof in the process. Carriages worked tirelessly to carry off broken trees and chunks of stone that had caved in its roof, so masons could get to work fixing it. The courtyard wasn't so lucky and remained buried, save for a carriage access route. For the rest of the city, the Keep wall had saved them from being smashed flat, holding back the weight of the landslide.

The once-imposing outer wall was cracked and crumbling, giving Rav clear sight into the city. Although spared from being flattened, the rest of Donsden had been barraged by high winds and lightning bolts. Anything wooden was scattered around and often blackened by scorch marks, smelling as though there had been a large fire raging, soot and smoke lingering around. Still,

Donsden was alive, everyone working together to rebuild their ruined city. Merchants and guards alike formed lines in the streets to carry rubble down from the top and dump it out the city walls. Children moved stones, adults carried rocks, and horses pulled boulders.

Rav watched a team of horses drag a boulder half the size of a house out a gap in the city wall, where a guard came to scrape someone's remains off its underside and add them to a smoking pyre. A few of the elderly wept around it, but everyone able was busy working.

How were Pierre, Paulo, John, and Vip? Rav looked over to where Pierre's village was supposed to be, seeing an empty ruin. Had he and his family managed to find refuge somewhere? Rav found himself glancing at the remains being scraped off the city stone, dread in his gut. He forced himself to look away, noticing how strange the fields between the city and the villages looked... What was missing? Rav gasped. The crops. All that time spent protecting them from insects and disease had gone to waste, nothing left but waterlogged mud. How was the city going to eat?

With so many people moving around, the city gates were left open and unguarded, the soldiers tending to more pressing matters like looting. Rav walked in unquestioned with a throng of people with pale faces and confused gazes. But they were still walking. Carrying. Doing their duty. Donsden refused to collapse. Rav moved through the crowds towards the Blood Hounds' old house, finding the building smashed along with the market around it. He went to pick through the rubble, looking for what remained of his old room, acting as though he was clearing some of the snapped planks, keeping an eye out for any guards who would think he was looting. No one was paying attention to him.

It looked like the place had already been picked clean, but Rav kept searching, uncovering the remains of his room, which had collapsed onto its side, the floor broken open. He darted over. The pouches were gone, but his journal and Kayla's cloth were still there. Rav stuffed them under his breastplate, then headed back into the crowd, moving up towards the Keep.

"*Out the way*," a labourer yelled at him.

Rav saw that he'd walked into a distribution line and sidestepped out of it.

"Where are you going?" the labourer asked.

"To the Keep." Rav pointed up.

"Keep's full. Join the line." He pointed to a spot back down the street.

Rav nodded and walked back, ducking into an alley when the man wasn't watching. He tried another route up the city. This time, he made it to the Keep walls, where he spotted a garrison guarding the way forward. It wouldn't be so easy to get in.

No one was talking about the fight between Sisters and Rav didn't want to ask, as it would draw too much attention to him. He dropped back to spy on the Sisters' outpost in Donsden, finding it also ruined. Despite its importance, people were giving it a wide berth, some whispering to it as though in repentance. Failing to follow up on Baron Glass, Ee La' Bol's, or Lyra's situation, he visited Champions Guard's house. Just as ruined as the Blood Hounds'. No one was repairing it; there were no signs of the unit.

The rock in his gut remained.

Rav went looking for Pierre and Paulo, slow and cautious to hide from farmers that might recognise him even with his disguise. At last, he found the farming community on the outskirts of the city, clearing out the wreckage where Scythe's Rest had once stood, all looking miserable. Rav stayed near them a while, peeking over his shoulder as he threw pieces of wood off the streets, spotting Pierre. His friend was moving sluggishly, half-heartedly shovelling dirt to clear where the old tavern had been. Why did he look so sad? His gaze lingered too long, catching Pierre's eye. Pierre stared for a second before his eyes widened. Rav hurried to turn and walk away. Pierre dropped his shovel and chased after him.

"*Hey*," Pierre shouted.

Rav walked faster, but he could hear Pierre's footsteps quickly catching up. What if he called out his name? Scrunching his face at his own stupidity, Rav stepped into a gap in the city wall where they'd be hidden and waited between jagged stone, squeezing his spear tightly in his hand as he held his breath to abate his nerves.

"Rav?" Pierre whispered, peeking around the corner. As he examined Rav, a spark of joy flitted across his youthful face, half a smile forming while he shook his head in disbelief. "It is you. I... How? How are you alive?"

Rav blinked in surprise. "You knew I was dead? Has news of the ambush spread?"

"Everyone does. Lyra shouted it across the city..."

"You know about Lyra?" Rav dropped his spear with a clatter and grabbed Pierre's arm. "What happened?"

"What happened?" Pierre frowned, his smile dropping before it had risen. He shook off Rav's hand and gestured to the ruins surrounding them, the gloom returning to weigh down his face and bow his shoulders. "*What happened?*" he hissed, voice breaking. "This was all about you."

Dread coiled in Rav's heart. "Pierre, I've been stuck on Mount Don for the last few days."

Pierre shook his head, fierce, violent, his goofiness twisted into something savage. "Lyra said you were dead. She said all the Blood Hounds were. She accused Ee La' Bol of going against the will of the World, of killing a Called One, and fought her across the city."

Rav gasped. "Is Lyra alright?"

Pierre chuckled, dark and sickly, tilting his head to one side as tears beaded in his eyes. "*She* is. Lyra won. She beheaded Ee La' Bol on the Keep wall for the whole city to see." He took a breath. "A Sister killing a Sister, Rav. The storm started after." He gazed at Rav with a swirl of vicious despair. "Was it for nothing? Did Lyra lie? You're alive."

Rav gulped, his hands going clammy. "Lyra *killed* Ee La' Bol? Are you sure? Sisters are forbidden from killing anyone, Pierre; Lyra would never—"

"*Oh*, I'm sure. I watched the other Sisters leave their outpost and arrest her. I heard them announce how they're taking her to their headquarters to stand trial. There's no mistake."

Rav missed a breath. "No..."

"Rav, what's going on?" Pierre's voice cracked, taking on a tremble. "I need to know. I need to understand why this happened. Who was responsible?"

"Did something else happen?" Rav asked, voice just a whisper, the dread from his heart rising up his neck.

"The storm, Rav. My parents were patrolling the wall." Pierre's lip wobbled, tears rolling down his cheeks. "I can't find them. It's been two days, and I haven't seen them. No one has."

Rav grasped Pierre's shoulder, facing him straight on with serious sternness. "I'll help you look. Where were they working?"

Pierre dropped his head, a sobbing choke pulsing in his throat. "They were keeping watch over the road to Kroom Town. You saw the wall there, right? I know they're dead. I know their remains are burning on the pyre with all the others. I want to know why. Why did this happen?" He glared into Rav's eyes. "Did your guide do this? Did you kill my parents?"

"I... no." Rav released a half-wail—a horrid noise from the depths of his lungs. His words stuck in his throat like lumps of mud clogging a drain. Pierre's stare was unrelenting, the full inferno of torment consuming him imprinted in his snarl. Rav stared back, finally finding his voice. "I had nothing to do with it; I've spent the last three days healing from an assassination attempt under Mount Don." Tears ran down his cheeks, his voice fading again. "I'm so sorry, Pierre... I'm so sorry. I can't imagine... If my Ma and Pa..."

Pierre stared a moment longer, then released him, fury falling to sorrow as more of his own tears welled, his lip trembling so hard it shook his jaw. "Tell me."

Rav sniffled, wiping his nose with the back of his hand. "Izen stabbed me on the way to the red layer. I fell into a chasm and heard Champions Guard slaughter the Blood Hounds. That's all true, Pierre; Lyra didn't lie."

Pierre hardened his eyes, then his face, the veins in his neck bulging as he pressed all tears and trembling away for his ferocity to return. "Then the storm?"

"I heard it speak Ca'ome. It was talking to Lyra. I think it came from the Sisters further in the Sink. From what you've said... I think it was them calling Lyra back for punishment."

Pierre pinched hard between his eyes in thought. "Baron Glass and Sister Ee La' Bol tried to kill you. They enraged the World by going against its will, and the World punished all of us for their crimes. It's *his* fault." Pierre looked up, eyes bloodshot. "Baron Glass did this. He killed my parents. And the Sisters too." He gritted his teeth. "To think I wanted to serve him. To think I respected the Sisters."

"Ssh." Rav smothered Pierre's mouth with his hand, glancing around for any eavesdroppers.

Pierre pushed Rav off, his lips now sealed shut, but the rage didn't leave him; instead, it sank beneath his skin, where it melded with every part of his being, turning him cold. "Are you here for revenge?"

"Aye. I'm here to kill Baron Glass. But I don't have a plan yet; I'm still scouting the city."

"I want to help," Pierre stated. "When you do have a plan, don't forget me. I don't care what I have to do, I'll get it done. I want to be part of his demise. I want to tell people that *I* helped kill Baron Glass."

Rav clasped Pierre's cheek, panic rising in his chest. What would Pierre in this state? "I will." Sending him to spy on the Keep was too dangerous with him like this. Rav racked his brain for something he could focus Pierre on. Inspiration struck. "What's happening with food?"

"That's another problem. The Baron opened our food stores to units hunting Baron Tryxwin, and with the harvest destroyed, we have little left. It's enough for our people, but foreign units are still hanging around, being recruited to repair the Keep. We'll have nothing for winter. Paulo tried to speak up, but the Keep garrison and new units beat him up."

Rav grimaced as he realised what was going on. "Baron Glass needs to repair the city as soon as possible to deter other Barons, and keeping the new units working for him will help bolster Donsden's defences while preventing the other Barons from recruiting them. Even if everyone starves come winter, with his own and Jinkin's military might, keeping down a half-starved rebellion will be easy."

Pierre gritted his teeth, glaring at the Keep once more. "He's a callous monster."

"How's Paulo? Is there anything I can do?"

Pierre shook his head. "Swollen jaw and bruised ribs. He can move, but he has to hide from the new units. We'll handle it."

"What about John? Vip?"

"John's fine. His business is ruined, though. Vip's got a job cooking for the wounded. She's on the other side of the city. Can't miss it." Pierre pointed to a place beyond the city walls.

"Thanks." Rav took a breath as he readied his next words. "Pierre... killing Baron Glass will cause more chaos. The other Barons will move into Donsden with their soldiers. People will die."

"That's why we have to find a way to protect our own. It makes things harder, but I trust you, Rav. You'll find a way. You wouldn't have found me if you didn't care." Pierre forced a twisted smile. "And we're farmers in a city with little food. Any new Baron would be stupid to attack us."

"I'll find a way," Rav promised.

Pierre looked around, a few other farmers now curious about his long absence. "We'll get him, won't we, Rav?"

"Aye. We'll get him."

Pierre nodded. "Good. I've got to get back to work."

"Aye." Rav pulled his helmet down tighter. "Don't tell anyone I'm alive yet."

"Believe in me, Rav. I know about more than just crops."

Rav picked up his spear with shaking hands as Pierre walked back to the farmers.

Chapter 38

On the other side of Donsden, Rav found large canvas tents filled with patchwork beds. Bits of wood had been hastily nailed together for the wounded to lie on and few had any bedding. Most beds were filled with patients, ranging from almost recovered to living their last moments. Healers walked between them, answering questions, checking on wounds, and chatting to pass the time. Rav walked in and wrinkled his nose at the smell of festering, the scents of medicine and soup swamped by the putridity.

Those on the mend had small cuts and bad bruising, sitting up to converse. Long-term care had bandages wrapping up entire limbs from bad breaks or internal damage. The others lay quiet, wheezing. Rav paled at the sight of one of them. Her legs had been crushed to paste but were still attached, slowly leaking blood and pus. How was she still alive? How could she ever hope to recover? Glancing around, medicinal vials were scarce, Healers only providing care for those who would recover. Walking to the back of the canvas, he searched around the kitchen area, where several large pots of soup were warming on hot coals.

Vip walked behind one, carrying a small wooden stool that she then set down and stood on to look into the pot. She grabbed hold of the ladle handle sticking out and stirred. Rav stepped past a long table stacked with empty bowls to reach her, waving to catch her attention.

Vip turned to look at him and stared a while before her mouth dropped open. "Ra—"

Rav put a finger to his lips. "Call me Wakeman. You remember the chainmail I used to wear, right?"

Vip nodded, then hopped down from her stool and came close enough to whisper. "Wakeman. You're alive."

"Aye. No one can know that I am yet, though."

"The Sister said—"

"I know. I'm here to check on you." Rav held her shoulders and smiled at her full cheeks. "I'm glad you survived the storm."

"Me too. I hid in a well. But, Rav." Her joy fell and brought down her grin with it. "Pierre..."

"I know. I saw him before I came to you."

Vip lowered her head. "And your stall's gone. I couldn't find any of it."

"That doesn't matter. It's enough that you're safe." Rav winked, glad to see the gloom darkening her face brighten a little. "And cooking."

"They needed people to help the wounded, so Paulo sent me over." Vip puffed out her chest. "I'm making game soup for everyone. The head chef is Cetch, and she's got a face like this." Vip lowered her cheeks as though she had jowls.

Rav chuckled at the display. "Good cooks are always welcome."

Vip leaned closer. "She's not as good as you, though, but you can't tell her I said that."

"I never will."

"Good." Vip checked on the coals under the pot she'd been stirring, using a poker to even them out and disperse some heat.

"Vip, things will get dangerous in Donsden soon. You should stick close to Paulo and Pierre."

"Like another storm? Or is it the other Barons?" she whispered.

"The Barons." Rav matched her volume as he leaned in. "How do you know?"

"It's obvious. Information like that reaches the streets first. A few of my friends said people have offered them things if they tell them about Donsden, things like money and positions under them in exchange for stuff like how many soldiers are in the city and where the wall is broken. One even said he was asked to cause mischief in the repair lines, but the Donsden guards are too vicious to risk that. They said I could get lots of stuff by reporting the wounded, but I don't want to do it."

"Good, don't get involved. Can you tell me who met with them, or where?"

Vip near-mouthed the details to him, eyes darting to ensure no one was listening.

"*Vip*," a rotund woman with tied, greasy-grey hair and sagging jowls called out, walking over to the soup pots from the flapping tent entrance. "Why aren't you cooking?"

Vip jumped like a startled cat, while Rav straightened his posture and stepped back, watching Cetch storm towards him with balled fists and bluster.

"Out," she barked, jabbing a finger at Rav. "Now."

"Stay safe," Rav whispered to Vip with a last smile before hurrying out in a wide berth around Cetch.

"Don't talk to strange men," he heard Cetch scold Vip.

Rav dropped his shoulders. Vip was in good care.

Rav returned to Donsden and pottered around, filling time before the evening. The citizens now slouched around, weary, the little that he could eavesdrop consisting of grumblings. It seemed speaking about Sisters had become taboo. Finally, the sun began to set. Rav climbed onto the remains of a caved-in roof on a ruined stone building at the outskirts of the city where he'd have a good view of the Keep and stay hidden from those below him.

Atop the Keep wall, an enormous bonfire flared to life, its fiery light visible far beyond Donsden's limits to signal the end of the workday, labourers putting down their tools to look up towards it. Baron Glass stood tall beside the bonfire, his figure clear despite being so far away. He stripped off his armour, gazing out across his city, making each inhabitant feel as though he was watching over them, and after his armour came his clothes until he was naked. Exposed. Vulnerable. Then he stepped into the flames.

Rav gasped, but Baron Glass didn't burn; instead, his entire body had turned to glass, his skin now see-through to show his light pink organs and crystal bones. As the fire blazed around him, it lit him up like a stained-glass statue, multicoloured lights glittering across the city. Rav gawked at its beauty. Baron Glass sparkled as Donsden's star.

"*Ah' ke*," people cried out. The city hailed their leader.

Rav tore his eyes from the spectacle and watched the alley below him. While everyone was distracted, a young boy and a cloaked figure were meeting, the boy handing over some papers. The figure flicked through the notes and handed the boy a pouch, then the two split up, the boy joining the crowd in the street while the figure disappeared through a hole in the wall. Rav climbed down from his position and gave pursuit outside the city.

The figure was cautious, constantly glancing over their shoulder and sticking to the shadows cast by the setting sun. Rav was patient, keeping a large distance between them, also hiding in the poor light. He followed the figure along the base of Mount Don until the figure climbed up the side, heading for a rocky area. Rav increased his pace, but as he entered the boulder-lain area, he couldn't see anyone ahead. Scouring the ground for tracks, he soon found a fresh print still leading up—

Crunch.

Rav dived behind an outcrop and readied for a fight, but the footsteps passed by him, continuing down the mountainside. He emerged from his hiding spot and used the last of the light to follow the brand-new marks up to a small cave. No one was inside, but tracks indicated that this was a meeting point.

Rav rushed down the mountain and back to Donsden.

Rav squinted as the dawn sun peeked over the city wall and caught his eye. Hand over his face, he trudged uphill after the line of labourers ahead of him. Their shadows stretched far across the streets and over broken structures that used to be homes. Few guards watched over them as they climbed towards the Keep, most yawning. Close to the Keep, though, dozens of Baron Glass' soldiers still stood in makeshift shelters either side of the street, watching vigilantly as everyone climbed. Rounding the corner, Rav saw the portcullis sitting open but with even more guards inside the courtyard and outside, six also standing atop the parapets ten feet above with crossbows. None of these men yawned or stretched or picked their teeth. Any labourers who sought to enter the courtyard were stopped, searched, and questioned.

Rav slowed, shifting to the deep shadows by the eastern wall, then turned and hurried back down the city while climbing labourers grumbled at him. He counted twenty-eight guards. More would be manning the wall out of sight. Maybe fifty in total. And that didn't include those inside the Keep. If he couldn't get out the Keep the way he'd get in, that's what he'd face. The Ghoul could only do so much.

Looking down the city, more problems presented themselves. With most tall structures humbled, there were few places for him to escape the sight of the Keep to hide even if he did get out.

After slipping back out the city wall, Rav retraced his path from the night before to the meeting cave and found a large, leaning boulder to hide beneath. As he sipped water from his waterskin to quiet the grumbling from his stomach, lying on his back to watch the sun rise, then fall into evening, he focused, finding himself gritting his teeth the more he imagined the coming fight.

Glass was injured, but he was also more experienced than he was, had better techniques, and would have better control of his Heaven's Tear. Imaginings of their fight rarely had him winning. Even if he won, there was still Champion Suel and the other Keep soldiers to contend with. Narrow corridors would help him, but they could just as easily trap him. He had to sneak in and kill Baron Glass in his sleep, then use the chaos to escape, but how could you sneak up on someone who was always watching?

Bright light lit up the mountainside around him as Baron Glass shimmered across the land once more. Rav hopped to his feet and wiggled his toes, as they tingled from staying still for so long, listening.

Crunch.

The spies were coming up to the cave. Rav counted twenty breaths before following, stopping a dozen feet from the cave entrance.

"Many...mountain...wall...grain...guard..." A male voice. "...report...Barons..."

The response was inaudible, then came more footsteps, this time leaving.

Rav darted back to his hiding place as the hooded figures left, mulling over the little he'd heard. These people were after grain, and he'd said "Barons". More than one army was heading for Donsden. Would they start a war? Would the Barons be willing to divide Donsden? While that might work at the beginning, a partnership like that wouldn't last. Barons wouldn't go to war for a competitor's benefit, so without a guarantee that they would get Donsden, they wouldn't move. Then what?

Grains. Food. Donsden was the primary provider for Blood Marsh, and they were struggling to feed themselves. Other Barons couldn't live off the marsh alone and needed to buy food from Donsden to feed their soldiers. Summer would end and winter would come. Barons would be worried about starving in the dark months. They were organising a raid on Donsden's food stores. Guaranteed benefits, little risk. Rav rubbed his temples, easing his headache. The raid would be a good distraction for the Keep's guards. Now, he needed to know more about it.

Three days after arriving, Rav left Donsden, careful as he travelled back to Amine, changing direction and covering his tracks to prevent himself being followed. It was hard, necessary work that turned the journey from an afternoon to most of a day. He'd visited Vip to ask if she could find out what the Barons were planning, and he'd visited Pierre to tell him to be careful spying on the granaries, as others were also after them.

Once he reached the tunnel system, he went hunting for yippers to replenish the food Amine must've eaten. Stocked up, he returned to the cavern. Rav creeped down the dark tunnel, unable to even see his nose, waving his spear in front of himself to search for any obstacles while sticking close to the wall to maintain his direction.

Closer to the cavern, Rav caught the scent of woodsmoke and excrement over damp stone. He licked his lips to wet them, listening beyond the echoing wind but failing to hear anything else. Shouldn't the glow from Amine's fire be visible by now? Stepping closer, Rav sensed the space before him open further into the cavern, the air shifting to fill the larger space.

Heart palpitating, he called out, "Amine?"

A torch bloomed to life inside the cavern, revealing Amine, filthy but smiling. Rav broke into a smile too, hurrying towards them with outstretched arms, his spear and shield cast aside.

"You're back." They stumbled over to him, their leg still splinted, and gave him a hug.

"Lyra killed Ee La' Bol?" Amine gasped, the fire crackling next to them as yipper meat spits sizzled over it. "And she's been taken away by the Sisters? Are you going to do something to help her?"

"I... it doesn't seem real. Lyra would never kill... she's sworn not to, and she loves the World too much to ever betray it." He wiped his face, a building sob starting to choke him. "No, *Ha'th Bey Riene* would never kill. She was the Sister, the World's servant. Lyra was my friend, the person always by my side, always helping. I spent so much time trying to figure out which was which, so many nights certain that Lyra was only a façade, a trick designed to lure me deeper into the Sink."

He looked up at Amine. "Ha'th Bey Riene was the illusion. That's what this means, right? Lyra proved who she was. A real person. How did I not see it, Amine? I saw her kindness, her compassion. I saw her bleed for me. Even after she thought I was dead, she never stopped fighting for me. She *killed* for me, Amine. Me, a Nameless wretch too blinded by selfishness to see her for who she was. I don't deserve her. I never did." He shook his head. "And now I have a chance to prove who I am. Who I want to be, who I *should* be. So, why am I so scared? Why can't I do what she did and sacrifice to do what's right?"

"Easy, Rav." Amine rubbed his shoulder. "A lot has happened in the past few days; there's time to think. I will say this, though. You're Ah' ke. You *will* succeed in whatever you choose to do."

Rav wiped his nose and dried his eyes. *Focus on the now.* "You're right. First, I'm going after Baron Glass. There should be more information on what happened in the Keep."

Amine raised an eyebrow. "Like why they wanted you dead?"

"Aye." Rav turned the spits.

"Baron Glass might've burned the letter he showed Izen."

"I know. I'll find out when I go looking for it."

Amine nodded as they poked the fire with a charred stick. "I thought of another point that supports the Barons just raiding food: Jinkin. Baron Glass might be vulnerable, but he's still a representative of Jinkin. Attacking him could anger them."

"Wouldn't getting his Heaven's Tear make it worthwhile?"

"But Baron Glass is Ah' ke. Killing him won't be easy. If he wanted to escape, it would be hard for any Baron to stop him."

Clear, hot fat dripped off the spits to sizzle in the fire with a succulent aroma, signalling they were ready. Rav pulled one out and handed it to Amine, then grabbed one for himself.

"Smells good," a voice rumbled behind them.

Rav jumped up, holding his spit like a dagger, heart thundering. Amine stood beside him, wielding their crutch like a staff at the intruder.

A large figure in hide armour strode into the firelight with a malicious grin on his scarred face. Bo Hart. "Give me one." He reached out with a huge palm.

How long had he been listening? Rav acted calm, sighing with relief before handing Bo his spit like he was an old friend. "Amine, this is Bo."

Amine stared in awe. "The man from Mo'za."

"I like that expression." Bo pointed at Amine's face. "That's how I should be treated everywhere. But your lips are pale. Gives away your fear. You should learn from Rav here. If I didn't know he had no support and no leverage over me, I might've fallen for his act, heh heh." He took a bite out of the yipper meat. "Not bad."

"Why are you here?" Rav asked.

"For information on a Heaven's Tear. That's our deal, isn't it?" Bo bit down on the yipper meat and slid it off the spit, swallowing it in one gulp.

"You have to save my life first." Rav kept his voice as even as he could, hoping Bo didn't notice the wobble tickling his throat. At least it seemed he hadn't heard him speak about Lyra.

"But I have." Bo chuckled. "Every moment I spend here with you is time I don't spend telling Haymitch Glass that you're alive. And if you think I can't threaten you"—he leaned closer, Rav smelling his foul breath—"I'll remind you that your Bride is far away, locked in chains."

Rav held Bo's stare, mind whirring, then nodded. "Aye. Information on a Heaven's Tear, as we agreed. But this information is more complex than the first."

"Oh? It better be worth more than what Haymitch will pay me." He looked at Amine. "Do you think I'll get more for bringing him Rav alive or dead?"

Amine stayed silent.

"If we use my information right, you'll get a Heaven's Tear," Rav stated. "And this time, you'll get to it first."

Bo's eyes lit up. "Where is it?"

"The Heaven's Tear I'm offering is inside Baron Glass' neck."

CHAPTER 39

Bo burst out laughing. He saw Rav's steadfast expression and laughed even harder. "Instead of…" Bo took a breath to calm himself. "Instead of getting easy resources and a favour from an Ah' ke, you want me to try and kill him?" He laughed again. "You're bold, Rav. Or just simple."

"I'm neither." Rav stood firm. "I was planning on killing Baron Glass myself; this is me letting you reap the spoils as thanks for keeping my secret."

"There'll be no secret, Rav; you'll be dead." Bo scowled at him.

"Has your failure in Harton made you cowardly? It's no wonder you've been in the Sink so long and failed to get a Heaven's Tear."

Bo cracked his knuckles. "Shut your mouth, or I'll break it."

Rav had to flatten his smile. Bo was still listening. "This is a unique opportunity for you. I've got a way inside the Keep and a few armies for distraction."

"But those things don't matter. Haymitch is Ah' ke trained by Jinkin."

Rav grinned. "That's why my last piece of information is so important. I know… that Baron Glass is injured."

Bo paused. "How do you know?"

"That's a secret." Rav smirked.

"So, it's not been tested, then. I'll not die for someone's musings."

"Tested, no, but it is true. I'm putting *my* life at risk for it."

"From who?"

Rav pursed his lips as he gathered his composure, feigning being distressed to cover signs of his deceit. "Lyra."

Bo frowned. "Why would a Bride tell you that?"

"Have you been to Donsden recently?"

"Where d'you think I spotted you?"

"Then you know about the storm."

"With such a huge event nearby, I had to check it out. I knew a Called One and a Bride that would be involved."

Rav narrowed his eyes, holding Bo's gaze. "Lyra was suspicious of Baron Glass and Ee La' Bol for a while. She told me she'd found his weakness in case I needed it. I'll be going into the Keep. If you want to come along, contact me tomorrow. Think about it, Bo. If I'm wrong, which I'm not, can't you just escape? Not much risk, and the reward..."

Rav watched Bo's expression, spotting the greed coiling in his eyes.

"Tomorrow?" He smirked. "I could wait a day before turning you in, heh heh. I'll do some scouting, Rav. If your plans look good, maybe we can sort something out. If not, I'll be rich." Bo laughed again.

"Good." Rav nodded, confirming the agreement. "I need to go to Donsden to sort out a few things, then I need to check my way inside the Keep. Once those things are complete, I'll be going in." He turned back to the fire. "Want more?" Rav offered another spit.

"I'll take one." Bo grabbed it. "See you tomorrow, Rav. I hope you make us both happy."

"I will."

Bo sauntered back into the darkness.

Amine released an exhale like their entire body was deflating. "How did he find us?"

"It's Bo." Rav shrugged, continuing to act in control in case Bo was still watching them from the dark.

"That's it?" Amine dropped their spit and hobbled over to get a crossbow.

"Amine, that won't do anything. If Bo wants us dead, there's nothing we can do."

"We can fight back," Amine declared, loading it. "Even if we die anyway, I won't let it be easy."

"Please," Rav whispered. "We can't antagonise him."

Amine stopped, then continued arming themselves. "He can't sneak up on us like that." They shook their head. "We can't let him."

Rav gave up, picking up a spit.

"Rav." Amine stared at him. "I won't be ambushed again."

Rav looked at his spit and put it back down. He went to Amine's side and helped load the other crossbow.

Rav returned to Donsden the next day. Pierre was waiting outside the wall, scanning the crowds. Rav hurried over. Spotting him, Pierre pointed to a secluded area by the wall and walked over to it. Rav waited a while to watch the crowd, making sure Pierre wasn't being followed and no one was waiting in ambush. To be certain, he entered the city and came out a hole in the wall, then sneaked over to his friend.

"What took you so long?" Pierre hissed.

"I was being careful," Rav whispered. "Has something happened to the granaries?"

"I've got a message from Vip. She said you had to get it as soon as possible." Pierre pinched between his eyes. "'When you heat the pan, the thieves will come.' Argh, it was something like that. The 'thieves' part is right, but I can't remember the exact wording of the rest."

Rav remembered teaching Vip to heat the pan at his stall at dawn each morning and nodded. "I know what she's talking about. Pierre, we need to prepare. The Barons are coming."

"What's the plan?"

Rav hurried to explain before racing back to Mount Don. Would Bo Hart meet him in time? Hopefully, he'd been watching. Rav found Amine sitting by the fire, guarding the entrance to the cavern, crossbow at their side.

"It's happening," Rav panted. "Tomorrow at dawn, the Barons are going to raid Donsden for food. We need to get moving."

Rav held out his torch, lighting as much of the tunnel ahead of him as he could. Looking back the way he'd come, he noted the side tunnel and curve, matching them to his memory of the tunnel maps. This was it, the path towards the supposed dead end he'd seen. What lay ahead? What if he got lost or trapped or swarmed and killed by packs of mutants? He took a deep breath. He had the last smoke ball, his knives, a spear, shield, crossbow, and, if all that failed, he had the Ghoul. The Keep would need an escape route, and the tunnels under Mount Don were perfect. Somewhere down here, there was a way in.

Rav set off as fast as he dared, only having until dawn to find the way in, or... He shook his head. It wouldn't matter. He *would* find the entrance and he *would* kill Baron Glass. The tunnel extended further than the maps showed... until Rav saw the light hit a wall. *No.* He dashed to it, hitting the rock with his fist. Solid. This should've been it. He continued hitting various sections of the rock, but there were no hollow points, no signs of a way through. Even hacking at the stone with the edge of his shield, nothing gave. The tunnel had come to an end. Rav suppressed his panic. He just had to keep looking.

Up and down the tunnel he searched until he slumped to the ground, panting, torch sputtering. Was he in the right area? What if the escape point was away from any known maps? Pierre and Amine would be in place, but everything else was up to him. Rav closed his eyes and sipped from his waterskin as he tried to figure out what he'd missed.

"You look tired," Bo noted.

Rav flinched but kept his eyes closed. "Aye, I need to rest."

"You've not covered much ground. Aren't you worried you won't find the way in?" Bo jeered. "What happens to your friends then? Good thing you brought me along."

Rav opened his eyes and paled. Bo was standing over him, the flickering torchlight dancing across the serrated-bone armour that lined his body with hundreds of vicious teeth-like spikes. They shifted in the shadows as though alive. Hungry. A full helm covered his face, Bo peering out through two small slits at Rav, looking like a beast mid-bite, ready to tear into his victim and shred them apart. A war hammer was slung across his back. He held out his hand to Rav, who clasped it and was lifted to his feet.

"We've got some time before dawn." Bo leaned on Rav's shoulder. "Let's hear about this injury."

Rav sipped some water, but his throat remained dry. Bo's grasp clamped down on him. His breath started racing as the sensation of being trapped set in. "I…" Rav focused. "The blow struck him on his right midriff, here." Rav pointed to the spot on himself.

Bo released him to demonstrate.

Rav took a quick step to leave his reach. "Here, just under the rib, but some of the force travelled towards Glass' spine." Rav ran his finger along the damage path. "He was hit while turned to glass, so he cracked. The muscles split and haven't joined together again properly. He has pain sitting down, standing up, twisting." Rav showed the positions. "His ability to generate force from that side should also be weaker."

Bo nodded, unreadable behind his helmet. "Take off your breastplate and show me again."

Rav obeyed, Bo having him go over every aspect of the injury again and again, hunting for greater detail and better understanding. Rav's torso was bare, pointing to each specific point of weakness that he could remember. The more Bo asked, the more he recalled, the specificity of the questions guiding his mind.

Bo poked Rav's midriff. "Here?"

"Slightly lower."

Bo lowered his finger slightly and looked at Rav for confirmation.

"Aye, there. The angle's a bit higher, like this." Rav showed Bo.

Bo nodded and moved on to the next part, never laughing once throughout. Rav gulped. Was this the preparation you needed further in the Sink? The precision required to take advantage of such tiny aspects was far beyond what he was capable of. Was this how skilled Bo was? It took a long time before Bo was satisfied, and finally, Rav strapped his breastplate back on as Bo thought over what he'd learned.

"You said the Bride told you this?"

"Aye, she did."

"The Bride knew how it felt for Glass to sit down?" Bo stared at Rav.

"Th-that's what Lyra told me," Rav stammered, his heart thrumming as he stared at the bone-clad titan.

"She told you all that detail? Every aspect and sensation Glass is feeling?"

"Aye." Rav heard the hollowness in his own lie. "After telling you so much, do you still doubt that it's true?"

"I'll see." Bo began walking off down the tunnel where Rav had checked.

"Where are you going?" Rav rushed to collect his equipment.

"The Keep."

"That's a dead end." Rav hurried after Bo.

He caught up and trailed behind him until they reached the end wall. Rav stood back; was Bo going to smash through it? But Bo's war hammer stayed on his back; instead, he grabbed hold of the wall with one hand and pulled himself up to punch the ceiling. The rock shattered, shards bouncing off his armour, to reveal an open space above them. Bo climbed up and reached down to pull a dumbfounded Rav up after him.

"Come on. I need a distraction if this goes wrong," Bo muttered, leading Rav into a small section of tunnels where they had to crawl, squeezing through some areas. Rav's torch kept dimming, then flaring as they moved through pockets of air, occasional sparks scattering over him.

Crack. Bo jabbed out with his war hammer to break through another blockage.

Relentless crawling into unending darkness. Rav shuddered, mind on the cusp of panic every time his back scraped against the ceiling. He sucked in a breath, hoping for a fresh breeze, only tasting stagnant, dirt-ridden air as he followed Bo Hart. *Just crawl.* That's all he had to do. That's how he'd make it. That's how he'd kill Baron Glass. Rav gritted his teeth and dragged himself onwards.

"Torch," Bo hissed.

Rav stubbed it in the dirt, smothering the flame. Black. *Tack, tack, tack,* the echoes of something scuttling ahead of them. Rav held his breath.

"Stay," Bo whispered.

Rav obeyed, dragging his crossbow in front of him as quietly as he could while listening to Bo continue crawling, swatting at the space before him, feeling like there could be something right in front of him, waiting to pounce. At least anything trying to reach him would have to get past Bo first. *Depending on how big it is.* What if it was small enough to scuttle over Bo and jump at his face, striking through his visor with a barbed tail? What if it wasn't just one small thing? What if a swarm of them poured over him, scurrying under his armour to burrow into his skin? Rav strained to catch any noise he could. The sound of Bo crawling softened, then vanished. Silence. *Tack, tack.* It moved again. Bigger than before. Closer. *Tack.* This time, it wasn't an echo. *Tack, tack, tack,* it raced down the tunnel towards him. Rav readied his crossbow. *Smash.*

"Light," Bo called.

Rav lifted the torch with shaking hands and relit it. Bo nodded at him, then carried on moving. He strapped his crossbow back on and followed. When he reached the place where Bo had been waiting, he saw the smashed black carapace of something the size of his head with a wicked, sharp stinger, leaking clear fluid. Twitching. Rav drew a knife and stabbed it twice more, watching it go still. He wiped the fluid off his blade and worked to catch up to Bo.

Four more of those mutants scuttled along the tunnel. Bo handled them all. For the last two, he didn't call for Rav to extinguish the torch, facing them head-on. Finally, they emerged into a cavern they could stand in. Rav stretched his arms out wide, relieving the discomfort in his body. Gauging his surroundings, he searched for where they would go next. Bo found the way forward, an even smaller tunnel midway in the wall to their left. Rav dropped his shoulders. Bo noticed.

"We're at the Keep," he whispered. "This should be the last tunnel. We need to find out which part of the building it leads to. Stay here." Bo rolled his shoulders, then tucked them in and climbed inside, squirming along to avoid his armour scraping the walls.

Rav sat and gulped water, sweat soaking his armour from the journey, soon draining his waterskin. Now the hard part began. It wasn't long before Bo returned.

"The tunnel's short, leading to a stone wall. I didn't hear anything on the other side," he informed Rav.

"What time is it?"

"The stone's cold, so it should be night. We'll have to listen and guess when it's dawn."

Rav thought over his plans. They could afford to err; as long as most of the soldiers were busy holding off the Barons, the Keep would be empty enough for them to reach Baron Glass. Once that was done, he could meet up with Pierre and then Amine.

Rav nodded to Bo, who checked over his bone armour for any damage, noting a few blunted points, and inspected his war hammer. Rav had performed his checks during his rest and stood by the tunnel.

Finished, Bo approached the tunnel and lifted his visor to give Rav a ferocious grin. “Let’s hunt a Baron.”

Chapter 40

Ba, ba, ba, someone was running. Bo thrust his war hammer forward to punch through the stone wall, then dived into the gap, entering a corridor with a cloud of dust. He completed his roll and swung his war hammer as he stood up. *Crunch. Clatter.* The guard running by had his breastplate caved in, dead in an instant. Bo pulled his weapon out the corpse and ran down to the right.

Crunch. Clatter. "AH!" *Crunch. Clatter.*

Rav fell out the hole, hurrying to his feet with his spear and shield raised. Where was he? The corridor was short, with a large door to his left and a corner to the right where Bo's heavy steps echoed from, the brute already out of sight. Rav recognised the door and crouched to its keyhole to make sure, peering into the empty banquet room at the back of the Keep. He looked back at where Bo had run off to, hesitating before chasing after him. Charging around the corner, he almost slipped on the pool of blood forming from two smashed bodies crumpled on the floor. Rav jumped over them and followed Bo's red footprints up a set of stairs at the end of the hall.

Crunch. Crunch. "AHHHH!" *Crunch.*

Rav saw body after body as he ran up the stairs and across another corridor, trying to visualise where he was going. He should now be heading towards the guest area, just up a floor, towards where he'd seen Baron Glass' nightmare. The dying screams of the guards would attract attention. Rav listened for reinforcements, trying to anticipate where they would come from as he hurried to catch up to Bo, finally seeing the titan at the end of another corridor. Bo wielded his war hammer like a meteor to decimate two more guards before turning back and signalling for Rav to hurry up. Rav moved as fast as he could, and once he'd reached Bo, Bo slammed his war hammer into the ceiling to collapse it, barring the path they'd come down.

"Glass is through here." Bo opened the door the soldiers had been guarding and pointed to a large set of double doors at the end of a hall.

Rav adjusted his grip.

"You lead," Bo ordered.

Rav strode forward, flaring the fury writhing inside of him until it consumed him, eyes growing hot as they turned bloodshot, muscles eager to act. To kill. "Avenge us," he heard Izen's last words, coursing with the pain of betrayal and sorrow of their deaths. Of Wakeman's death.

"I guard my home with all I am,"
"To honour those who gave me life,
"We march far to conquer our foes,
"A Bloodline to keep out all strife.
"Go forth and fight 'til your last light,
"Gifting land and lineage to our flesh made young,
"We'll love and marry for our blood to carry,
"Into the future bright."

Rav reached the doors and kicked them open, entering a large, empty bedroom, only a double bed, desk, and empty armour rack for furniture. No windows, just a blazing fire burning at the rear wall. Baron Glass stood in front of the fire, equipped in a strange luminescent armour made from translucent scales, with two thin swords, already drawn, and a grin on his face, seen through his translucent helm.

"AHHH!" Rav darted at him, jabbing out with his spear, aiming for Glass' throat.

Glass flicked his sword and parried the attack away before retreating to the side. Rav lunged again, using the footwork Miels had taught him to its fullest extent. Baron Glass parried again and thrust with his other sword, the blade driving at the gap in Rav's armour at his waist. Rav moved his shield to block the strike and was forced to halt his momentum, mindful of overreaching.

They retreated from each other. Rav stared at him, working on building as much power as he could for his next blow. Glass looked calm. Perhaps even puzzled. Rav raged harder, launching a new barrage of attacks, this time maintaining his distance, using the advantage of a spear. Glass continued to parry with ease, shifting around his room, looking as if he was focusing more on his problem than the fight. Rav tried predicting where Glass would move, tried boxing him into a corner, tried throwing more weight behind his blows so the Baron couldn't parry them. Glass moved faster than Rav could predict, danced around the room as though he were at a ball, and deflected Rav's heavy blows just the same as the light ones.

Rav thrust out again, causing Glass to retreat again, but then he dived back into a roll before using the new space to grab a knife and throw it at Glass' shoulder. Glass closed the gap between his breastplate and pauldron, causing the knife to bounce off the armour. Rav followed up with his true attack. *Pa.* The last Ant's Itch ball struck the centre of Glass' breastplate and burst into powder, glittering in the air. Rav grabbed his spear again and readied himself in a defensive position, watching to see the effect. Glass raised an eyebrow before stepping back and flourishing his swords, blowing the powder away, the little that still lingered around not affecting him. Then his eyes gleamed as he finally solved his problem. He lowered his swords.

"I was assured that you were dead."

"*Why?*" Rav shouted, a slight tremble in his voice as he saw how useless his attacks had been.

"I don't know." Baron Glass shrugged. "Sometimes I get orders like that. I'm not told why, and I don't ask."

"*Ah,*" Rav charged in again.

Baron Glass defended with nonchalance. "The order came from Zera, and where she got it, I also don't know. Though, whoever gives them must have complete control over the Sisters, or maybe it is the Sisters? Well." Glass repelled another one of Rav's thrusts and went through the motions of countering, letting Rav block in time. "Not all the Sisters. Ha'th Bey Riene must've believed in you. Maybe she even thought you were the avatar of the World... But that doesn't matter now. Sisters are forbidden from killing each other due to the scarcity of their members, so Ha'th Bey Riene will live, but what she did is unforgivable. knowing those fanatics, her punishment will be unimaginably brutal."

Rav tried so hard to be stronger, to be cleverer. He soaked in Glass' gloating words to force himself to burn hotter, but nothing worked. At his best, Rav wasn't worth Glass trying.

"Know that I did try to avoid this mess; I did try to be clever." Glass sighed. "Had Izen died in his Challenge, you could've joined Champions Guard and suffered an unfortunate accident, dying alone without Ha'th Bey Riene ever knowing of the kill order. I presume he and the others are actually dead, yes? That's why you're here alone, isn't it? Your plan was decent." Glass rewarded Rav with an opportunity to strike, which, of course, he parried. "There are some things I'm curious about, though. It's good to learn from your mistakes, and it seems I've made a few."

He launched into his own sequence of attacks, driving Rav into a retreat to give himself time to think. "You being alive isn't my fault, though next time I should send a professional to oversee things so this doesn't happen again. How did Izen fail to kill you? I heard he ran you through with a rapier."

Rav panted before throwing more knives. *Clang, clang*. They bounced away, harmless.

"I suppose Izen purposely kept you alive, then. Now I'm curious about why. He must have had some confidence to go against me. Do you know where it came from?" Glass asked, standing still.

Rav moved to the other side of the room, drew his crossbow, and shot a bolt at Glass.

Glass dodged it. "How did you get into the Keep? Did you sneak in? Wear a disguise? Bribe someone?"

"*Ahhh.*"

Glass frowned at the rude behaviour. "Fine, I'll track your path here and find out that way." He pursed his lips in thought. "I will admit, the timing of your trespassing was well thought out. You knew Champion Suel and most of my soldiers would be at the city walls, deterring those foolish Barons; in fact, I was just getting ready to lead my army myself, so here's the last of my questions. How did you get past my guards so quickly? And why did you think you could kill me? Rav, you're not even as good as a Champion."

Rav panted. Where was Bo? Had he just sent him in here to tire Glass out a little? Would he have to use the Ghoul already? Was this what Bo was planning? Did he also want to see his secrets?

"Not going to talk? That's fine, I'll figure it out myself." Glass manoeuvred over to the fire, standing before it as he had when the fight started. "If you have some secret weapon, I'd use it now. Seeing as you're Called, I'll give you a death befitting the World." Baron Glass repositioned his swords, casting aside his playfulness for deadly intent. "Know what it means to face an Ah' ke."

He turned to glass.

Firelight gleamed through his skin and armour, casting flecks of light over Rav and the room in a dazzling display. Baron Glass became hard to see as he shimmered, and by the time Rav realised he was no longer by the fire, Haymitch Glass was already slashing a sword at his throat. No time to block, use the Ghoul, or even breathe, trapped in an inescapable instant, leading only to dea—

The blade shining at his throat suddenly vanished. Glass shot backwards, guard raised.

"You were right." Bo was standing at Rav's side, war hammer at the end of its sweep. "He is injured, heh heh."

Glass shifted ever so slightly to protect his right side.

"Go guard the room," Bo ordered. "They're digging through to us. Let me handle Baron Sparkle."

Rav drew an ecstatic breath. "You wanted to know my secret?" He glared at the Baron. "This is Bo. He's going to smash in your head." Rav laughed as he walked out the room and shut the doors behind him.

Crack. He heard glass break.

Out in the corridor, Rav could hear people scrabbling on the other side of the blockage Bo had caused. He closed the other set of doors as well, ensuring Bo couldn't see him, looking forward to the coming bloodbath. Now was the time he could attack without reserve. Now was the time he would claim his revenge. Now was the time for the Ghoul.

As the first soldier broke through the rubble, smoke poured out Rav's skin. Rot and festering. Death and terror. Rav became the nightmare of Donsden Keep.

"*Ahhh,*" the soldier screamed as Rav stabbed his spear through her head.

The first scout died. Then the second. And the third. The soldiers started to widen the path through to their Baron, seeking to get a group through to face whatever was on the other side. Rav didn't wait. He drew two daggers, then dived through the opening, rolling up the other side to see twenty soldiers crammed into the narrow corridor. The front line had nowhere to run. Rav's daggers flashed, throats slit, ribs shattered, hearts crushed. A breath later, the front line was no more. Within the nightmarish smoke, the Ghoul cackled.

"*Form up,*" someone at the back called.

The second line tried to raise their shields to protect themselves, but Rav dived at the front man and shoved him back, breaking the line while knocking down a group behind him. From his position, the soldiers either side of him had their flanks wide open. Trapped. Rav stabbed one through the armpit and the next through their chin. Someone lunged at him with a spear, stepping over the chaos of knocked-down bodies in the way. Rav saw it coming and parried the strike away with enough force to break the weapon out of the soldier's grasp, then followed up by throwing a dagger at them, the blade cutting across their neck. Blood sprayed across the corridor, spattering over those trying to get off the floor.

Rav grabbed a shield from a dead soldier and smashed it down on the soldier lying closest to him, breaking through his helmet to crush his head, then he grabbed the body to fling it at those who'd just gotten to their feet, knocking them down again. He threw his other knife to stop others from getting in formation at the back and grabbed a sword off the floor, hacking away at everyone in front of him, soon turning the corridor into a swamp of limbs, blood, and viscera. The few soldiers at the back were able to compose themselves better, but the terror of the Ghoul had their hands shaking. The attacks they made were either dodged or blocked by Rav's armour. Then they were open for the monster to tear into.

All Rav saw was red. All he smelled was iron. All he felt was satisfaction. Soldier after soldier stood before him, and soldier after soldier was slain. He swiped at the next enemy and failed to connect, realising he'd reached the stairs. There were no enemies left. Looking back down the corridor, no part of the floor wasn't stained red.

Rav dropped his now-blunt, cracked sword and took a moment to breathe. Was this what it meant to be Ah' ke? He shook his hands, flicking scarlet droplets off them. More. *More.* Rav steadied his breathing. More would come.

He released the Ghoul as he poked through the bodies, collecting a spear, shield, more knives, and two daggers, then sat at the top of the stairs, resting and waiting to see who else wanted to die, soon catching the sound of footsteps. *Ba, ba, ba.* Rav sat up and connected to his Heaven's Tear. Someone was coming. Someone in heavy armour. Someone important? He stared down the stairs as a person wearing gilded full-plate armour with a Blood Palm in the centre of their breastplate, carrying a shield and axe, arrived.

She stuttered in her run as she looked at him. "Ah' ke."

Rav recognised Champion Ku Suel's voice and stepped back from guarding the steps, inviting her to come up to him, shield raised, spear poised. "Better hurry," he called, the Ghoul turning his voice guttural. "With no one to lead the defence, Donsden will fall."

"I am Champion Ku Suel, daughter of Suelkoff," Champion Suel spoke the words like they were a threat.

"I don't care," Rav spat.

Suel tensed. "It is my duty to be Haymitch Glass' wife. If you interfere, I will kill you."

Rav paused. She knew he was Ah' ke and still thought she could win? Was there more to her than he knew? Did he care? "Glass will die."

"Then so will you."

Rav laughed as Suel climbed the stairs with her guard raised. She peered over the top step to see the massacre in the corridor. Rav bristled with pride.

"It's shameful for Ah' ke to butcher soldiers like them," Suel hissed.

"Shameful?" Rav laughed harder, the Ghoul's sinewy mouth clacking open. "What do you care about shame? All that matters to you is power."

"It is the duty of Ah' ke to serve the World, to help its people."

"What World? Even the Sisters are slaves to their greed," Rav roared.

"The Sisters are honourable," Suel retorted. "They carry out their duty until death."

Rav shook his head. "The Sisters plot and lie and murder, just like everyone else. You had a Called One murdered just outside your city."

She trembled at the accusation. "*Ha'th Bey Riene lied*," Suel shouted. "She murdered her own Sister. She's the enemy to us all. I serve the World, as my family has for—"

"I don't care," Rav growled. "I know the truth. You've had enough time." He advanced to the stairs, towering above her.

Champion Suel moved into a defensive position, peeking at the Ghoul from behind her shield. Rav jabbed down at her with his full strength, aiming to knock her down the stairs, but Suel angled her shield to deflect the spear tip to the side and stepped up to swing her axe at his leg. Rav blocked the axe with his shield and made another jab aimed at her head, yet Suel shifted her head to the side, dodging the strike. She slammed her shield upwards, knocking Rav's spear up so he couldn't make another quick jab, and moved into an uppercut with her axe.

Rav roared. Why wasn't he battering her around like he'd battered those soldiers? He smacked his shield down on Suel's axe, hoping the force would disarm her, but her uppercut was a feint, and her axe curved around his shield to swipe at his head. Rav had to lean backwards to avoid it, and his poor footing from the failed shield bash meant he stumbled as he did. Suel darted up the stairs, using her axe as a hook to pull herself up off Rav's shield. Rav kept hold of his shield and whipped his spear across, cracking it into Suel's shoulder. She smacked into the wall but kept her momentum moving forward, falling to the top of the stairs. Rav backed away, letting her reach the top step. Had he injured her?

He launched another sequence of attacks, trying to force Suel back onto the stairs. With no space to retreat into, Suel weathered the blows, relying on the precision of her movements to disperse as much of Rav's power as she could. Rav gritted his teeth. Suel kept feinting, deflecting, tricking him. *Clang.* He hit her again, but it was with the shaft of the spear and did little damage. Why wasn't Suel hurt? How was she still fighting as well as before after taking so many blows? No. Better than before. She was starting to read his movements.

Rav used his footwork to strike from another angle; however, Suel predicted the shift. Rav was caught off balance as she lunged inside his guard, axe slashing down at his shoulder. He twisted as hard as he could, watching the axe head bite down through the image of the Ghoul and into his breastplate underneath, *crunch,* just about failing to break through completely. He hurried to manoeuvre his shield to swat the axe head away, but Suel halted her attack before positioning herself again. Rav caught his breath, too aware of the large gash in his armour. He studied Suel and realised she was now two steps further from the stairs than before. This was just her gaining more space to move in; she hadn't truly started trying to kill him yet.

How was she so good? How could she keep up with him? There was nothing mysterious about her movements, which meant... she was just better than him. Much better.

Rav dropped into a defensive stance, blocking the path to Baron Glass. Suel sneered as she gave chase, her entire body jolting, the air shifting. She Squeezed, getting past his spear in an instant. Rav braced his shield arm. The axe chopped deep into his shield but didn't break through. Arm shuddering from the force, he held. The Ghoul held. But Champion Suel wasn't Contender Karac. She followed up with a bash from her shield, also using the Squeeze. Rav bellowed, driving his feet into the floor as her shield connected with his, juddering every bone in his body as she worked to drive him further back.

But she overreached. Rav released his spear to grab her shoulder, rotten nails sinking into the gap, Ghoulish strength holding her in place. She hissed, trying to pry her axe from his shield while wriggling to escape his grasp. Rav continued crushing her arm and punched with his shield, sending her backwards, his nails scraping down to her bone from the sharp movement; however, the impact also helped free her axe.

Suel chopped down at Rav's outstretched arm, the angle ensuring he couldn't move his shield across to block in time. He had to let go. He shoved her, sending her stumbling back to the top of the stairs, where she regained her poise before raising her shield. But Rav could see her arm shaking with the effort. Blood flowed down from her shoulder to her gauntlet, dripping on the floor. Rav backed up and threw a knife at her. Suel moved her shield to block it before attacking again, Squeezing, air shimmering. Shield damaged, Rav backed away again, using the long corridor behind him, watching as blood continued to pour down her arm. How long would it take before—

CRACK. SHATTER.

They both paused to glance at where Bo and Glass were fighting.

Bo's laughter rumbled down the corridor.

Chapter 41

Champion Suel fled, Squeezing to escape down the stairs as fast as she could. Rav threw a few knives after her, but he didn't pursue. The Ghoul receded as he raced back to Baron Glass' room, Rav bursting through the doors with a manic grin. There, lying on the floor at the back of the room, was the half-shattered statue of Baron Haymitch Glass. He stopped, the storm of emotions flooding through him too much to bear. All that mattered was... he'd succeeded. His plan had worked.

Bo was slumped against the wall next to the body, panting, bone armour riddled with cuts, blood oozing out at his elbow and waist. Visor open, Rav could see shards of glass freckling his face, causing dozens of tiny scratches.

"*You did it.*" Rav rushed over to wrap Bo up in a hug.

"Stay there," Bo growled, raising his war hammer between them. "I'm not too weak to kill you."

Rav obeyed. "Aye, I know." He looked around the room. Gashes covered every surface, the bed and desk shredded, the armour rack shattered. One of Glass' swords was stuck in the ceiling in a corner of the room, while the other lay next to his body. As he glanced over the remains of the desk, he spotted some paper. Rav grabbed every scrap he could find and stuffed them in a pouch on his belt. Bo was still sitting.

"I've got a way out that you can follow. Rest once we leave,"

Bo smirked. "Do you know how long I've waited for this?"

"No, so let's get the Heaven's Tear and go. Get back to Mo'za and hunt some mutants," Rav encouraged him. *Wait*, encouraged? Why did he feel he had to do that? Looking further at Bo, he seemed... sad. Despondent. What was wrong?

"This thing?" Bo held up his fist and opened it, revealing a golden-glowing cube.

Rav gasped at the sight, his very being palpitating. If his Heaven's Tear was a space of nothing, then this cube was a space of everything, impossible to explain, like looking at a shard of life itself. Incomprehensible but vital and infinite. It was as though Bo were holding someone's soul in his hand.

Bo pressed it to his forehead. The cube remained solid, unmoving. "The World." Bo laughed at himself. "As if I could hate it any more."

Oh.

"I wish you'd seen me fight, Rav," Bo whispered, staring into the Heaven's Tear. "I was at my best. Every move, every technique, all perfectly calculated, all perfectly angled. I worked so hard. I killed an Ah' ke with my own strength. I did it." He closed his fist, shutting off the golden glow. "But the World is cruel. Do you understand what it is to be Called now? Do you know what it means to drink three drops of King's Blood? People like me sacrifice everything for the Sink, but it's not for us. It's for you, Rav." He pulled a pained smile. "And you don't want it. It's not fair." His expression twisted with bitterness.

Rav took a breath. "There's more to life than power. Whatever you've sacrificed to get here, it can be rebuilt. You can create something new. Nothing is over until you give up. That's the hard part, Bo." Rav thought back to Wakeman. "Fixing your mistakes."

As Bo sat, his eyes lost focus, staring at Rav but seeing nothing.

"Bo, I have to go. People are waiting for me. Come with me."

Bo shook his head. "You go. I'm going to sit here a while."

Rav nodded. Pierre and Amine needed him. He turned to leave.

"Rav," Bo called.

Rav faced him.

"Thanks for honouring our deal. You're the only person I know who's done that."

Rav smiled. "Thank you, Bo Hart. For saving my life and for helping me keep my promises."

Bo nodded, falling silent. Rav closed the doors and dashed off to meet Pierre.

Sprinting through empty corridor after empty corridor, Rav saw no one, not even servants. As he moved out the back of the Keep, he heard noises from outside.

"WAAAH!" War cries rumbled through Donsden, but there was no metal clashing. The fighting hadn't started yet. Rav pushed himself harder. The Barons couldn't reach the Keep before he'd let Pierre inside.

"What are you doing? Get out," Rav heard from a room ahead of him. "Champion Suel has ordered everyone to abandon the Keep."

"I'm saving Baron Glass' tapestries," another voice argued.

"Leave them. There's a monster in here with us."

Rav stopped running. Who else had Suel warned about him? Why'd he let her go? Another mistake; she could be leading an ambush in the courtyard, waiting for him to emerge. Rav turned around and ran to the top of the Keep, and as he climbed another set of stairs, fatigue dulled his speed, his armour hanging heavy. The adrenaline wore off, leaving him cold and panting. He took a moment to rest and fidgeted. What was happening in the city? No more time to waste, he pressed on, clambering to the Keep's roof to climb out through a hole caused by the landslide, from which he had a clear view of the city in the overcast light.

Donsden's walls were lined with soldiers and units alike, standing behind wooden barricades, wielding bows and crossbows. A multitude of different colours and armours, they were in high spirits, shouting and jeering over the wall. Beyond the wall marched four arriving armies, each a few hundred strong, set up to charge through different holes in the wall. These soldiers were well disciplined, standing in locked formations with consistent colours and banners, ready to advance when the order was given. Anyone too old, injured, or sick to participate had evacuated the city to the remaining nearby villages.

Looking just beyond the Keep wall, Rav spotted the building Pierre and the farmers were supposed to be hiding in. No soldiers were near it. He sighed with relief, then turned his attention below him, where the courtyard was filled with the Keep's servants and the last of its guards, who'd formed a defensive arc around the door, protecting the others behind them. The guards on the Keep walls were facing inward, crossbows ready and loaded. He didn't see Champion Suel.

Rav climbed onto the roof and down the side of the Keep, using the masons' scaffolding. He moved quickly and quietly, heading for the battlements where he could get access to the gate. Whatever Champion Suel had told the guards kept their focus firmly on the Keep doors with white-knuckle grips and wide eyes, the servants shaking behind them as though they could all be slaughtered in an instant. Rav lowered himself down a layer and ducked behind the corner of the Keep. After this layer, he'd be out in the open. Time to bring out the Ghoul again. Rav sweated and struggled to breathe as the power flowed out his skin, the burden wearing him down, recognising that he didn't have much time left. *Get it done.*

He sprinted off the scaffolding and jumped down, landing with a roll on the wall. The guards flinched as they paled, those closest whipping their crossbows around to shoot at Rav, but the quick turns made most of the bolts fly wide, the few that were aimed true sinking into Rav's shield. Rav threw a knife, taking out the guard closest to him, and dashed to the gate. The next guard in his way was thrown off the wall, followed by another. Rav glanced around the courtyard, wary of the other guards shooting at him, but they were all cowering, postures low, weapons lowered.

"Ah' ke," they whispered.

Rav continued to the gatehouse, the soldiers on the wall fleeing out his way. Inside, he found the chain mechanism that opened the gates and heaved it, *ee, ee,* the gates slowly opening before, *jrr,* they locked into place. He emerged from the gatehouse and faced the trembling soldiers, Ghoul about to slip away and leave him paralysed.

"Baron Glass is dead," he shouted, and shock rolled through the soldiers. "Donsden will fall. Take what you can and leave. Go home to protect your families."

The soldiers and servants stayed still, hesitant.

"*Go,*" Rav heard Pierre shout behind him.

A large group of farmers with a few guards came rushing out the building and charged through the gate, many staring up at him before being shoved forward. The Keep guards just watched, standing by as the farmers entered the Keep basement and began carrying out sacks of grains, fruit, and dried meat. Servants were the first to join them, then the guards gave in, pushing in to get what they could before it was all gone. Rav looked back to the outskirts of the city, where small skirmishes preceding the battle had just started, occupying everyone's attention.

"Take only what you can carry," Pierre shouted to the group. "Hide the rest. Come, we have places to store it."

He led a line out of the Keep to various parts of the city where the farmers had prepared hiding places for the food. Rav climbed down from the wall and ran into the city, finding a secluded alley to release the Ghoul with a relieved gasp, his skin tingling, on the verge of splitting. From there, he headed to the west of the city, finding the small gap hidden in the wall where it met Mount Don. The unit guarding the section ignored him, Pierre's bribe working. Rav passed through the wall without issue, arriving at the starting slope of the mountainside. The path ahead was open, a clear run to the tunnel systems.

He ran up the mountain and waited behind a tor, keeping watch as farmers began to come through the hole, escaping onto the mountain to avoid the clashing armies. Pierre was the last through, pushing everyone forward. Rav stayed longer in case anyone pursued them, but the army closest to them stayed in formation, now sending in their main forces to breach the city. Rav watched bolts rain down on them, sticking in their shields and armour to make them look like metal porcupines, then turned and left.

As he walked, he noticed just how much blood he was covered in. Going near the marsh like this would be worse than barbequing fresh meat. He found a small stream and washed his hands, face, armour, anything red and sticky. From there, it was a long walk back to the cavern.

Amine was standing outside the tunnel entrance when he returned, explaining the underground system to Pierre and Paulo. Paulo's face was bruised and swollen, a crutch under his arm.

"*Rav.*" Amine spotted him and came hobbling over to hug him. "You did it."

"Baron Glass is dead?" Pierre came over to confirm the news, Paulo behind him.

"Aye." Rav leaned on Amine. "Bo killed Baron Glass. I saw it myself."

Pierre nodded before emotion overwhelmed him. He turned away to wipe his face.

"Did you get the food?" Rav asked.

"All of it. We carried what we could and hid the rest. The Barons will get nothing," Paulo answered, patting Pierre's back.

"It's good to see you."

"You don't mind me knowing you're alive?" Paulo grinned.

"Life is for friends and family. You look pretty beat."

"You don't look too good yourself." Paulo chuckled.

Amine examined the gash through Rav's breastplate.

"It was close." Rav sighed. "There were a lot of guards. Without Bo, I wouldn't have survived."

"Is that the Ah' ke?" Paulo asked.

"Aye," Rav lied. He faced Amine. "Help me out of this." Rav tugged the straps of his armour.

Amine sat Rav on the ground and began loosening his breastplate.

A guard came out the tunnel. "We've searched the tunnels and blocked off the route leading to the goebbers," he said to Paulo. "We should be safe to stay here for a few days."

"Good." Paulo nodded. "Store the food in the cavern and organise a watch; I won't have any thieves."

"I'll see to it." The guard looked at Rav. "Who's this?"

"Wakeman." Rav bowed. "I was keeping watch from Mount Don."

"Ah, one of Pierre's helpers." The guard smiled. "We can use good scouts."

Pierre stifled a laugh as he turned back, his tears drying. "Yes, Wakeman's one of my scouts. Good work, scout." He patted Rav's back.

The guard bowed to Paulo and left, glancing over his shoulder before he entered the tunnel again.

"Stop that." Rav swatted Pierre away. "I'm too tired."

He tasted salt, touching wet on his cheeks. How foolish he looked. He pulled off the last piece of his armour, looking at his pale torso as though it belonged to someone else. Where was that familiar glint of chainmail? Why did the taut muscle look so much weaker? It was almost like he was thinner than when he'd arrived. Finally, he plucked off his napet, exposing the warped skin of his neck, and stretched, ensuring everyone watching noticed. Amine collected his armour, remaining quiet.

"What's going to happen to Lyra?" Paulo whispered.

Rav lay awake in the dark, listening to Amine also trying to sleep beside him, thinking. He was dead. Nameless Rav, the Called One, had died on Mount Don, and no one was using him anymore. He was free. He could go home. He could leave this horrible place behind. In less than a year, he'd forgotten Kayla's smell and lost Wakeman's ashes, failing every objective he'd set himself. He didn't belong here; he *couldn't* belong here. How many times had he nearly died? His efforts were futile. He was Bo Hart lusting over a Heaven's Tear. This wasn't the place to obtain what he wanted. The longer he spent fighting here, the more of everything he loved faded, worn away by endless bloodshed.

Lyra's crying face flashed in his mind.

He'd lost her too. The best thing about the Sink was ruined because she'd fought for him. Because she'd *believed* in him. That was undeniable. He'd experienced Lyra's faith, and its power bloomed through every part of him. How was it that a girl he'd met a little over a year ago could stand next to his home of nineteen years? She was special. If he loved Pitt for its caring people, he had to love Lyra just the same. They'd do anything for him no matter how self-destructive. And he'd do anything for them. That was the deal. That was the Ghoulsmen. *I'll die for you, and you'll die for me.*

"What now?" Amine whispered in the dark.

Two years. Power. An army. A Name. Lyra. Rav lifted the note he'd taken from Baron Glass' desk papers from where it lay beside him, recognising it in the dark by the way it sat delicately in his fingers as though it possessed the same weightlessness as Sisters.

Only this one note among all of Baron Glass' papers had mentioned him. A simple message without a seal. "Kill Nameless Rav."

Revenge. Jinkin and the Sisters. He was coming for them. But he was too weak. Baron Glass and Champion Suel had shown him how great the disparity was between him and his enemies. He thought back to Siere's words. *A place where I can find myself.* Varheart.

Rav faced Amine. "We're going to the second layer."

Chapter 42

"I'll miss you," Vip said, hovering around Rav as he packed in a cavern. "Will you come back?"

Rav ruffled her hair. "I'll miss you too." He reached past her to grab a blanket, then folded it into his backpack. "And aye, I'll be back."

"You promise?"

Rav looked her in the eyes. "I promise." He carried on packing. "You have to promise me something as well."

"What?"

"Keep cooking." Rav smiled. "I want a hot meal when I see you again."

"I will, I'll keep cooking," Vip swore. "Cetch is still teaching me, but when you come back, I'll be a proper cook by myself. You'll see, I'll have my very own tavern in Donsden and no one will go hungry."

Rav stayed smiling, eyes glistening. "Come here." He pushed his bag to the side and hugged Vip.

Amine walked into the cavern, still with a slight limp when they flexed their knee. "Are you ready?"

Rav released Vip and faced Amine. "Nearly. I'm going over everything again."

"You've unpacked and repacked your bag four times already."

"Aye, I know. I just..." *Without Lyra...*

"You'll be fine, Rav. I'll be with you. I've redone my bag six times. Don't worry about packing when you've got the best porter in Blood Marsh."

"Aye." Rav stuffed everything else into his bag. "I'll do the killing, you do the rest."

"You'll never fall with me at your back," Amine promised.

"Rav?" Pierre entered the cavern, running his hands over each other before holding them still. "Can we talk?" He looked at Vip and Amine.

"Come." Amine led Vip out the space, understanding Pierre's silent request.

Pierre moved to the back of the cavern, acting covert. Rav followed. "I've been thinking," he whispered, "about a lot. I... I haven't done my parents justice. I don't feel better. It's not enough."

"Pierre..."

"I have a plan." He looked stern. "I want to come with you. You're going after Lyra, right? That means you're fighting against the Sisters. I want to help; I want to do *something*, Rav. That storm destroyed everything I had. How can I let that go? What's the point in training so hard if I can't fight back?" He gritted his teeth. "I have to do it."

"Pierre, I'm going to try and help Lyra, not attack Sisters. I'm too weak for that. It's too dangerous."

"I know you're looking out for me, Rav." Pierre leaned even closer. "I told you, I'm clever. I don't know how you hid it, but the moment I saw that monster attack the gatehouse, I knew it was you. You're Ah' ke. You're going to fight Jinkin and the Sisters, just like you fought Baron Glass. Let me join you. I helped before, didn't I? I can help again."

Rav touched his napet. Seeing the look in Pierre's eyes, he knew he couldn't lie.

"I don't want your Heaven's Tear," Pierre continued. "I'll get my own one day, and together, we'll go to war against the Brides."

Pierre was angry, spiteful, vengeful.

"Have you packed?" Rav asked.

Pierre's face softened at the acceptance. "Yeah."

"We'll be leaving for Afil Forest at midday. Eat and drink as much as you can before we leave."

"Thank you, Rav. Thank you. I won't let you down." Pierre rushed away.

Rav rubbed his hands down his cheeks. How could he argue against someone driven by the same desires he had?

Amine strode into the room with an eyebrow raised. "What did he want?"

"To come with us. I said yes."

Amine sucked their teeth. "Pierre's got potential, but..."

"He won't let us down."

Amine grimaced, then sighed. "If he's ready, then let's leave earlier. Paulo says a few people are starting to question who I am."

Rav picked up his bag. Staying unknown was essential if they were going to catch Jinkin off guard. Rav stood outside the tunnels, looking over Blood Marsh. It all still looked so big. Even after so much, he hardly knew the place. How had he ever thought he'd find hope and purpose here? The marsh only held one thing for him. The clue was in the name.

"Wakeman." Paulo exited the tunnel and came to stand next to Rav. "You wanted to know about Champions Guard?"

"Aye. Have you found anything?"

"Some people saw Champion Eman Hagrin leave Donsden a day before the storm, heading towards the second layer. I think Champions Guard are gone from here."

"I'll find them." Amine stomped determined out the tunnel behind him. "They'll die for what they did."

"Be careful," Paulo warned. "Jinkin doesn't have its reputation for nothing. If Champions Guard has joined them, you'll have a hard time getting to them."

"It doesn't matter where they are," Amine bristled.

Paulo dropped his head. "I have some other news, though, I don't know if I should tell you." He clicked his tongue. "I'll have to trust in you. Don't be cruel. Whatever you do is on me as well; don't make me part of something I'll regret."

Early afternoon, Rav led Pierre and Amine across Mount Don, towards Donsden. A city on the mend now looked a city broken. Four armies occupied four sections of the city, tension sparking as they eyed each other's territory and the empty Keep. Another battle was about to break out. Instead of heading down, the trio hiked up the mountain, trekking a path through the landslide's destruction, past the chasm, and up towards the woodland. They arrived at dusk, the trees casting long shadows.

"Ready?" Rav checked.

Pierre and Amine nodded, weapons drawn. They set off on their hunt.

The small fort in the depths of the woodland was easy to spot as torches burned inside its walls, marking a square structure made of stone, with a watchtower on its roof, able to house a dozen guards. Two guards kept watch over the woods, armed with bows. Rav hid in the shadows of the trees, stalking his prey, Pierre and Amine flanking him. He creeped closer, shield and spear out, until he arrived within charging range. Smoke poured out his skin as the Ghoul dashed out from cover, bounding towards the doors. Rav kicked out, splintering the wood, and searched for his first opponent in the wide corridor. The guards who saw him ran, hiding further in the fort.

"*What's going on?*" someone bellowed.

"*The monster's here,*" another guard cried out.

Rav went defensive, advancing slowly. Two guards came into the main corridor, one taller than the other, weapons lowered.

"Ah' ke." The tall one bowed. "She's in the back."

Seeing his submissive behaviour, Rav growled, "Tell your men to gather in the dining hall. My companions will keep watch."

The tall one nodded. "Go," he commanded the shorter man, who ran off, yelling for everyone to group up.

"Have mercy, Ah' ke," the leader pleaded. "Protecting her was our duty given by Baron Glass. With his death, we are no longer bound."

"I understand." Rav flexed his Ghoulish body. "After I deal with her, I'll leave. But if even one of you attacks me, I'll tear you all apart, heh heh," he mimicked Bo Hart.

The leader hurried to nod.

"Did you hear that?" Rav called over his shoulder.

"Yeah," Amine shouted back, deepening their voice. They came out the woods to stand by Rav's side, bow loaded. "Joude's keeping watch," they informed him.

Rav grinned. "Then let's go see Ms Hagrin."

He led Amine past the tall guard as the man pointed straight down the corridor. They followed his direction, not seeing anyone else. Every door was shut. Torchlight blazed, and wisps of smoke drifted along the ceiling, hanging over them as they walked. At the corridor's end stood an iron-rimmed door with an ornate handle. Rav reached it, clasped the cold metal, and twisted. *Click*, the latch opened, and the door swung open. Rav grinned with Ghoulish savagery as he stepped inside the cozy bedroom.

Ilina Hagrin sipped a cup of wine, wearing a modest light-blue dress, sitting at a small table next to her bed. Amine closed the door behind Rav, the pair glaring at her. Ilina put down her cup and bowed low to Rav, loose hair falling to frame her cleavage.

"Ah' ke. It's a pleasure to be in your company."

"You weren't so welcoming when we last met," Rav commented, scanning her for any hidden weapons or any traps in the room. It looked clear.

"We've met?" Ilina rose and placed her hand over her chest. She blinked her big eyes, the wine reddening her cheeks.

Rav saw through it all to the calculating thoughts racing in her mind. "Aye. I look different, but my companion is much the same." He looked at Amine.

"How can I expect Concubine Hagrin to recognise me?" Spite dripping, Amine stepped closer. "I was at the bottom of the table, after all."

Focusing on Amine, some recollection returned to Ilina. "Are you from Donsden?"

"Not originally, but I lived there for the last six years. Surely you must have some idea of who I am; after all, I was quite the nuisance to your niece." Amine stared at her, and Ilina stared back, big eyes searching.

Amine looked back at Rav. "I guess people really do believe we're dead."

Ilina jolted in her chair, shaking her head, turning so pale with fright she almost glowed. "Y-you can't be."

"Can't I?" Amine mused.

"Eman searched the chasm herself. She said there was some mutant that..." She looked at the Ghoul.

"Tore the bodies to pieces so nothing could be identified?" Rav finished.

"You're Amine Son from the Blood Hounds," Ilina said, "but you... None of the Blood Hounds had a Heaven's Tear." She shivered, shaking her head. "Champions Guard made sure their attacks were lethal before pushing the bodies down; you can't be one of them."

"Did Champions Guard deliver all the killing blows?" Rav asked Amine.

"And who in the Blood Hounds could become Ah' ke?" Amine asked Rav.

"No, it's impossible for someone like that to be Ah' ke," Ilina whispered, gripping her chair.

"Oh, but I am." Rav released the Ghoul, smoke dissipating to reveal himself underneath.

"Nameless Rav..." Ilina trembled.

"You already know that I killed Baron Glass. I'm here to tell you I'm going to kill Eman too." Smoke poured out his skin again. "I'll carve a line through Jinkin and tear out her heart.

Hagrins won't exist in the Sink or anywhere else in the world. I'll make sure of it."

"N-no, d-don't," Ilina stammered, frozen in place, all confidence gone as her eyes went wild.

"That's the look I wanted to see." Rav grinned. "Are you satisfied?" he asked Amine.

"I am." Amine knocked their bow, taking aim at Ilina.

"*Wait*. I can make it right. I'll do anything. I can tell you all about Jinkin," Ilina pleaded.

Amine drew back the string.

"Sarsa Payne and Ku Suel," Ilina shouted. "I can find them for you. You want revenge, right? Sarsa's gone to Fermuch, and Ku's boarding a ship to Suelkoff. She's injured; you can get her too."

Rav remained unmoved. Amine released the arrow straight into Ilina's chest, pinning her to her chair. Her head lolled forward, still amid her last pleas.

"Do you want the body?" Rav asked Amine.

"No. Let the guards feed her to the mutants."

The three spent the night in the woods, Rav and Amine finally able to use some of the planning from their last task. At dawn the next day, they set off. Pierre wasn't as dextrous as Rav over the marsh, but he worked hard to keep pace, treading wherever Rav did as they moved in silence, not just meant to avoid mutants and units. Leaving Blood Marsh. What if speaking about it sucked them back in?

Pierre might hesitate, second-guessing the life he'd chosen for himself. Perhaps he should stay in Donsden and rebuild his home; after all, who was mad enough to try fighting against the Sisters?

Amine might think of their Zic and how lonely they must be in their empty village. Perhaps it was better to return home now. Was a cure worth more than the time they could spend together?

Rav might give in to his terror, abandoning Lyra to flee back home. His parents were worrying about him, Kayla was lonely, and Cyrn was having to face Baron Hewett without his help. How could Rav help them if he was so far away?

Plod, plod, plod until the marsh ended.

They stared out across that magnificent grassland. Rav took a breath, drinking in the beauty of the bright sunlight on the deep green land that stretched to the horizon. Far in the distance, he could just about make out the hazy outline of Afil Forest. Amine stood to his left, Pierre to his right, also enjoying the feeling of breaking out the mire.

"Please don't protect me," Rav broke the silence, gazing out. "I don't need it, I don't want it, and you'll only suffer for it."

Pierre snorted. "I think you're mistaken, Rav. I'm not here to protect you; I'm here to kill some Brides. I'll be causing danger, not hiding you from it. This is revenge. For my parents and my home."

"What Ah' ke needs protecting?" Amine laughed. "We need you to protect us. Afil Forest is filled with 'Zet Ar. I'll have your back, not your front. Protect *me* until Jinkin's gone and I have a cure for my Zic."

Rav grabbed their shoulders and pulled them both in. "Good. Believe in me." He sniffed. "Now, let's get going; it's a long way to walk."

The trio set off down the escarpment.

"How about a song?" Rav suggested.

"*I guard my home with all I am,*
"*To honour those who gave me life,*
"*We march far to conquer our foes,*
"*A Bloodline to keep out all strife,*
"*Go forth and fight 'til your last light,*
"*Gifting land and lineage to our flesh made young,*
"*We'll love and marry for our blood to carry,*
"*Into the future bright.*"